The Old South...

It was a world of vast sugar plantations—and of cotton—of dueling and slavery and death. It was soon to become a world of smoldering rebellion and incipient war. But in the city of New Orleans the sophisticated salons still sparkled, and out on the bayou the voodoo people still chanted.

At Mandragore, a stranger had arrived from the North. He came in peace, with boundless energy and farsighted dreams. His ways were different, his manner rough, but his love for the land was as great as Odile's, and his passion was greater . . .

Odile

by

R. F. Joseph

Odile

by

R. F. Joseph

BALLANTINE BOOKS · NEW YORK

Library of Congress Catalog Card Number: 77-6939

ISBN 0-345-25953-X

Manufactured in the United States of America

First Edition: December 1977

*Dedicated to my
mother and father,*
Irene and Frank Joseph

Part One
1835

1

The moment he shoved off from shore and urged the cumbersome flatboat into the swift Ohio current, Jim MacKay knew he would never return to the lush green valleys dotted with sheafs of golden wheat, the gently rolling hills, the blue-tinged mountains beyond. Not that he didn't love his native Ohio—he did —but the memory was too bitter, the pain too acute.

Tall, lean, and sinewy, Jim had labored at his father's side carving a home out of the wilderness, a farm which had prospered and grown and supported the expanding MacKay family. Then, just a few short months ago the Bloody Flux had swept like a cyclone across the state, sparing very few in its wake. Among its victims were Jim's entire family: mother, father, two sisters and younger brother. Jim, at twenty-four the eldest of the four children, had also contracted the dread disease, probably brought to the Ohio valley by boatmen who plied the Mississippi and its tributaries and were in frequent contact with the cities of the South, where it was endemic. By some miracle Jim, alone in the family, survived the soaring fever, pain, and ultimate debilitation. He had somehow managed to rise from his bed and dig the graves for his family beneath the comforting branches of the enormous chestnut tree on a hill behind their log home. All five now lay side by side in the rich Ohio soil: his mother, Ellen, a shy, wiry woman from Glasgow whose clear blue eyes and shiny blond hair he had inherited; his father, Charles, a blustering giant of a Scotsman who spoke in a burr so thick that many had difficulty understanding him; his sisters, the demure Elizabeth and the fiery Margaret; and his brother, Andrew, who at

3

eighteen was still looked upon as the baby of the family.

On the first day of spring Jim sold the farm to a newly arrived immigrant who signed his name with an X. The new owner's first move had been to set the house ablaze, fearful that it might yet harbor the dread pestilence. At times Jim still heard the crackling of the flames and saw the billowing black smoke curling softly against the clear blue sky.

Jim began work on a warm morning in early April. He felled giant timbers which grew along the river bank and lashed them together into a flatboat, or broadhorn, as such a craft was frequently called. The boat measured approximately fifteen by forty, had a crude shed as protection from the rain, a curved bow, and a great oar, or sweep, projecting from either side —from which the name "broadhorn" derived, after the breed of cattle. Sometimes the oars were used to increase the speed of the boat, but their main purpose was to shove the unwieldy craft off mud banks and sand bars. Constructed of massive timbers and thick planks, the flatboat, Jim estimated, could carry about thirty tons of cargo.

With money from the sale of the farm, he went up and down the Kentucky side of the river and across into Indiana, buying up flour, hams, bacon, hides, hemp, tobacco, and kegs of whiskey and stowing them aboard. The staples, he knew, would always be in demand, but the whiskey was the real prize, and he expected it to bring a nice profit in New Orleans. The previous season the western grain crops had failed miserably, and as a result, liquor would be scarce. With the kegs of the amber-colored, gently sloshing spirits, Jim intended to seek his fortune in the fabled port city at the mouth of the mighty Mississippi.

The trip down the Ohio was relatively uneventful as the boat moved slowly and precariously along the wooded shores, powered only by the natural current of the river. By manning the oars when necessary, Jim managed to keep the craft in the center of the current, successfully negotiating the rapids, sliding free of sand bars, and avoiding the snags, sawyers, and rocks which might have ensnared it or, worse, ripped great holes in the bottom. At night he put in along the shore, moored the boat to sturdy trees along the river bank, and slept aboard wrapped in a fur blanket. En route his diet consisted of the various smoked meats on board washed down by swallows of whiskey. Occasionally he shot wild game to vary his diet.

The trip was lonely, as Jim had known it would be. Most flatboats the size of his were manned by a crew of five or six men, but Jim had known from the beginning that he would have to make the trip alone. Most of the flatboatmen in Kentucky and Ohio were a rowdy, brawling, drunken, ferocious, sometimes murderous bunch, each of whom had but two ambitions in life: to wear the red turkey-feather which proclaimed him the undisputed champion brawler of the river and to drink himself into a stupor and wallow in the various fleshpots for which New Orleans was famous. It was not unheard of for these raucous brutes to murder the owner of the boat on which they served and steal his cargo at the end of the voyage. After surviving an epidemic of the Bloody Flux and twenty-four years in the Indian-infested Ohio wilderness, Jim had no desire to be done in by drunken boatmen he had hired. In addition, he would have had to split the proceeds from the sale of his cargo with the crew, something he had no desire to do. It would take every cent he could lay his hands on to fulfill his ambition of buying land and starting a farm in the South, where the soil was purported to be incredibly fertile and the growing season nine months a year. Besides, Jim was used to being lonely now. He had been lonely since the disease had felled his family.

Near the growing towns of Louisville, Madison, and Evansville there had been concentrations of other vessels, but it wasn't until he reached Cairo, Illinois, situated at the junction of the Ohio and Mississippi Rivers, that he suddenly found himself amid a profusion of river traffic, an infinite variety of crafts ranging from canoes and rafts to flatboats like his, keelboats, ferryboats, scows propelled by horses and cattle in treadmills, and, of course, the true royalty of the river: majestic steam-driven paddle-wheelers.

At Cairo Jim had a chance to witness firsthand the legend which had been perpetuated for years by riverboatmen, who swore that the waters of the two great rivers, the Ohio and the Mississippi, were totally incompatible. From the mouth of the Ohio to some hundred or so miles down the Mississippi, Jim observed that the clear, swift waters of the former seemed to persist stubbornly, independent and unsullied by the brown, seemingly sluggish, silt-laden waters of the latter.

As he drifted south Jim not only concluded that the Mississippi was the muddiest river he had ever seen but also that it was the crookedest as well, often meandering several hundred miles between two points separated on land by only a fraction of that distance. In addition, these crooked miles seemed inordinately full of logs, sawyers, shoals, sand bars, tricky currents, and dangerous rapids, all of which presented considerable hazards to a flatboat of limited maneuverability manned by a single, inexperienced individual.

The Lord protects the ignorant, Jim said philosophically to himself as he draped a cowhide across two poles to shield his fair, freckled skin from the burning late-spring sun, wishing that he knew even less about river pirates, hostile Indians, collisions, logjams, storms, and other risks of the undertaking.

At New Madrid, Missouri, and even more so at Memphis, Jim began to notice that the lofty paddle-wheelers dominated the mighty river, truly magnificent with their twin stacks spewing clouds of dark smoke, brightly illustrated paddleboxes, names in huge gold letters and flags flying proudly from the jackstaffs. The upper decks of the steamboats were often crowded with passengers, some of whom were boatmen heading north on their way home. Since the advent of the powerboats, few men who could afford otherwise undertook the arduous and hazardous overland route known as the Natchez Trace, a journey which frequently took as long as nine months.

As he drifted south, the weather grew steadily

warmer, and Jim realized from counting the notches he had carved in the flatboat that it was June, two months since he had left Ohio. If all went well, he would reach New Orleans in another month, or perhaps less. Having discarded his fur blanket long ago, Jim now wore only a pair of heavy brogans and trousers of linsey-woolsey, a coarse cloth made from linen and wool.

One day a huge paddle-wheeler skirted dangerously close to Jim's flatboat, nearly overturning it and forcing the clumsy, poorly maneuverable craft onto a sand bar. In spite of his strenuous efforts, Jim realized he would not be able to free the craft from the sandy shoal before dark, and he decided to spend the night there, hoping that with a shift in tides and renewed strength after a night's rest he might be able to get his boat into the mainstream again.

Just as the last glimmer of twilight illuminated the sky, Jim, who was finishing a meal, heard a call from the river. Coming toward him was a small canoe bearing a lone figure.

As the small boat drew near Jim studied the appearance of the man paddling. Although kneeling on the bottom of the hollowed-out log, he appeared to be of medium height, slender, and dressed not in buckskin but in black wool trousers, a frock coat, and a battered black derby hat. Jim observed that the traveler sported a luxuriant handlebar moustache, thick muttonchop sideburns, and unruly dark brown curls protruding from beneath the brim of his derby.

"So . . . ?" the stranger said, docking his canoe alongside Jim's raft. "What have we here?" His speech was peculiarly accented, and Jim thought at first he might be a German. "Maybe you need help?" The frock-coated stranger appeared to be in his late thirties, with a dark, swarthy complexion and alert brown eyes which gazed curiously at Jim from beneath the brim of the derby.

Inviting the man aboard, Jim offered his hand to the stranger. "My name's MacKay, Jim MacKay."

Accepting his handshake, the other man replied,

"DaCosta, Isaac DaCosta. Pleased to make your acquaintance."

"Are you Spanish?" Jim asked.

"My antecedents were Portuguese," Isaac replied. "I myself was born in Holland, but my family came to Curaçao when I was very young. That's an island in the Caribbean, in case you don't know. I left Curaçao for the United States when I was sixteen." Gazing at Jim proudly, he announced, "By religion I am a Jew."

The only Jews Jim had ever heard of were in the Bible, and it seemed incomprehensible to him that a descendant of Moses and Abraham and all the other Hebrew patriarchs of that holy book should suddenly appear in the middle of a Mississippi wilderness paddling an Indian dugout in a frock coat and derby. "If I might ask, Mr. DaCosta, what brings you to these parts?"

"I am a merchant, a peddler," he replied, and Jim noted for the first time his peddler's pack in the canoe. "The boat I purchased from a tribe near Natchez. The French call it a *pirogue*. It's not a bad way to travel the river. I had a horse and wagon, but I was ambushed and the horse stolen. What good is a wagon without a horse?" Isaac said with a philosophic shrug. "What do you say we try to free your flatboat.

"Go stand on that side," the merchant directed, indicating the edge of the boat closer to the water. "That'll make it easier."

Jim's weight was just sufficient to tilt the craft, and while it was so inclined Isaac slipped the stout oar under the beached side and, using it as a lever, nudged the flatboat off the sand bar and into the water once again.

"You see how easy?" Isaac grinned as he hopped aboard, winded and puffing from the exertion.

Jim smiled back, and the two new friends drifted on in their journey.

❧ 2

After months of trudging alone through the wilderness bringing buttons, needles, combs, scissors, knives, mirrors, thread, and patent medicines to the settlers attempting to forge farms from the American frontier, Isaac was glad for company and offered to secure his pirogue to the flatboat and accompany Jim downriver. Naturally he was delighted when the young Ohioan accepted his offer.

Normally Isaac would have booked passage aboard one of the steamboats returning to New Orleans, where he made his headquarters, at Memphis or Vicksburg or Natchez, but Jim's flatboat seemed somehow a more interesting prospect than a lonely trip aboard a paddle-wheeler. Besides, Isaac liked the strapping youth with his open, friendly manner, adventurous spirit, and air of independence. Despite their vastly different backgrounds, he intuitively felt they were somehow kindred spirits. Since emigrating to the United States from Curaçao he had made few friends. His trade kept him on the move and away from the city most of the time, and besides, the French-and-Spanish-descended Creoles were too snobbish to admit a foreigner—especially a Jewish peddler—to their midst, and the Americans—the English and the Scotch-Irish who poured into the region in droves when in 1803 the Louisiana Purchase made the vast French territory part of the United States—were too absorbed in establishing themselves. As for his fellow Jews, there were scarcely enough in the city to establish a temple, and the Sephardics like Isaac had to join with the German Ashkenazim to organize a synagogue. Because the Germans outnumbered the Sephardics, their rite predominated in the temple, and Isaac missed the Portuguese manner of worship in which he had been raised.

In spite of the hot sun bearing relentlessly down on the flatboat, the mosquitoes which attacked in droves at night, the diet of moldy, nonkosher smoked meats and whiskey, and the muddy water which sloshed up through the rents in the bottom of the craft, Isaac was glad to be aboard, firmly convinced that in this day and age no man should travel alone if he could help it.

After a week or more of drifting down the river, the flatboat eventually reached the city of Baton Rouge, which, Isaac pointed out, was only about a hundred miles or so from New Orleans. The city abounded in greenery and tropical blooms, and the sweet, heady scent of the huge snowball-like magnolias growing in wild profusion wafted out over the muddy water of the river. When Jim saw the vast green plantations with their smoking sugar mills and clusters of slave cabins, he knew that at last he was in the fabled Deep South, where the burning sun and moist, heavy air united to produce a tropical swelter.

At this point the river changed suddenly, free of the usual sand bars, snags, and debris, now a clean, deep, rapidly flowing channel.

Near New Orleans, the water level was high from the heavy spring rains, almost reaching the top of the earthen dikes which, Isaac pointed out, were called "levees" in this part of the country. Over the tops of these sloping ramparts Jim observed a steady succession of plantations, most of which his companion could readily identify by name. Some were relatively small in acreage and the homes modest, while others seemed vast, graced by magnificent residences on a scale Jim had never seen before. One in particular caught his eye, located as it was amid fields of waving green cane which were bordered by acres of dense marshland full of willows, cypresses, sycamores, and graceful white egrets. The great house stood majestically on a slight rise several hundred yards from the river landing, or batture, and was fronted by a long, sweeping alley of moss-laden live oaks. Faced with six slender white columns characteristic of the popular Greek-revival style, it was surrounded on both upper and lower floors by verandahs, or galleries. Three dormer windows symmetrically punctuated the gently sloping slate roof which was capped by a cupola, or widow's walk. It was a truly impressive sight, and Jim gazed in awe.

"You like it, eh?" Isaac asked with a contemptuous half sneer which surprised Jim.

"What's wrong with it?"

"What's wrong?" Isaac repeated. "Nothing's wrong with the house. I admit it's beautiful. Mandragore is the most magnificent plantation along the river."

"Who lives there?"

"Rotten people," Isaac snapped. "The Martinons. Now there are just two of them, a brother and sister."

"Why do you call them rotten?" Jim persisted.

"If you want to know, I'll tell you," Isaac replied. "Once when I still had my horse and wagon I called at Mandragore. At that time I carried in the wagon miniature models of furniture—chairs, divans, daybeds, and so forth—so that my customers could select the styles they liked and have them made to order. The 'lady' of the house at the time was a girl of about sixteen—Martinon's younger sister—very pretty. With her Negro mammy she selected a set of chairs she wanted made for the dining room. All well and good. She took so long making up her mind about the fabric to cover the chairs and the wood for the frames that by the time I was ready to leave, it was almost dark and a storm was coming up. So I asked Placide Martinon, the master of the plantation, if I might spend the night in his *garçonnière*—that's a little house separate from the main house. Mandragore has two *garçonnières,* and at that time both were empty. Martinon refused, abruptly ordered me off his property, and canceled his sister's order in return for what he said was my cheekiness. He had two of his biggest slaves escort me down the carriageway to the river road. That very same night as I was attempting to return to the city, I was ambushed by the thieves who stole my horse and merchandise, leaving me alone with an empty wagon in the rain. I will never forgive those Martinons for that. It's an unwritten code along the river to give a stranger hospitality and shelter, especially among the Creoles. Placide Martinon violated that code," he said bitterly, and drew on a corncob pipe. "I vowed that somehow, someday I would come back to Mandragore, not as a humble peddler but as an equal, and Monsieur Martinon himself would be forced to welcome me."

The flatboat reached the outskirts of New Orleans late in the afternoon, and Jim was seized by a sudden burst of excitement. Had he really reached the end of his long journey? Isaac, too, was affected by the sight of the city, lying as it did below the levees as though nestled in the bottom of a deep saucer. The itinerant merchant doffed his battered bowler and rubbed his thinning head of curly brown hair flecked with gray. "Home," he sighed, and muttered a short prayer of thanks in Hebrew.

Jim was amazed to learn that the city, like the upriver plantations, also lay below the level of the water and depended on the levees to protect it from inundation.

"The one thing everyone fears is a crevasse," Isaac explained. "That means a crack in the levee. They have to be constantly on guard against any leaks so that small ones don't get bigger from the pressure of the water and flood the city."

At Isaac's direction, Jim headed for the flatboat anchorage in front of Tchoupitoulas Street and, carefully maneuvering his boat among the other vessels, moored it to a post driven into the mud. Much to his surprise, he discovered that his was only one of a myriad of flatboats anchored at Tchoupitoulas Street. In fact, there were so many that it appeared possible to walk almost a mile by merely stepping from the deck of one boat to another.

"Well," Jim said, "I've arrived right side up and with all my cargo intact."

"Consider yourself lucky," Isaac replied, taking his pack from the dugout and hoisting it onto his back, preparing to disembark.

The first night in port Jim refused to leave his boat

and cargo in the care of a powerfully built stevedore armed with a shotgun who offered to guard it until morning for a modest fee. The stevedore was well known to Isaac, who heartily endorsed his services.

"Let Ambroise take care of your boat and come to my boardinghouse and get a good night's rest on a real mattress," Isaac urged.

Although the prospect of sleeping in a bed again sounded enticing, Jim refused to relinquish his boat and cargo to the care of the stevedore and stubbornly insisted on sleeping aboard.

Realizing that Jim would not be swayed, Isaac ceased his entreaties and left, promising to return again early the following day.

At sunrise the next morning, Jim, who had slept only fitfully because of the heat, mosquitoes, and a desire to protect his valuable cargo from the thieves and marauders who prowled the waterfront at night, was awakened by the clamor of activity all about him. Noisy crews were unloading the flatboats, yelling and brawling among themselves. Merchants, agents, and factors were dickering over commodity prices. Foreign sailors strolled the wharves, frequently accosted by prostitutes and vendors, while brawny stevedores unloaded the big oceangoing vessels bringing spices, furniture, glassware, perfumes, silk, laces, china, building materials, and other imported goods for the affluent citizens of this burgeoning city, prospering on its cotton and sugar economy. One particular ship flying a Dutch flag caught Jim's attention because of its cargo: human beings. Nearly all his life Jim had been aware of slavery, which originally had existed throughout the nation both North and South, having only lately disappeared by attrition in the North. Recently this "peculiar institution," as it was frequently called, had become an increasingly controversial issue inspiring considerable agitation, especially in the New England states, to outlaw it throughout the entire United States. Naturally, such a view was hotly resented in the South. Slavery was an issue from which Jim felt remote. It did not touch his life, and thus held little interest for him.

Jim watched a seemingly endless line of shackled Africans emerge from out of the hull of the Dutch ship, human beings like himself in spite of their strange and exotic features. Most were naked or almost naked, many ill or lame from the long and arduous sea voyage; all were chained together to prevent their escape, prodded along like cattle by harsh-voiced slave traders who cursed them and lashed at them with whips.

True to his word, Isaac appeared shortly after sun-up, freshly bathed and shaved and in clean clothes similar to those he had worn on the trip down the Mississippi. With the energetic merchant was a Negro, whom Isaac identified as a slave belonging to the proprietress of the Seamen's Rest Hotel, a woman of rather notorious reputation known as Mother Easter.

"Mother Easter wants your entire cargo," Isaac announced. "And she's willing to pay a good price for that Kentucky whiskey," he added with a wink as he pressed a sack of gold coins into Jim's hand. "I made a deal with her last night."

Jim was astonished. "So fast?"

"Why not?" Isaac shrugged. "When you got something everybody wants, it sells."

The merchant directed the slave to Jim's flatboat, where he easily hoisted kegs of whiskey onto his shoulders.

"Let's go eat," Isaac suggested, taking Jim by the arm.

Together they strolled through the muddy streets to the public square, or Place d'Armes, as it was called, filled with people. Along the iron fence surrounding the square were booths where hawkers sold oranges, bananas, ices, ginger cakes called "Mulatto Stomach," and oysters which were opened fresh and eaten directly from the shell. Inside the square a Greek vendor in a red fez sold fruit-flavored sherbets to quadroon girls who were ogled by swaggering guards in trim uniforms. Old Creole men in knee breeches sniffed snuff from tiny gold boxes, and young dandies in suits of gray or green and starched cream-colored shirts full of ruffles and frills strolled by. Amid the bustling throng a pair of nuns passed with downcast eyes.

Beyond the Place d'Armes was the French Market, where Spaniards, Frenchmen, Italians, Greeks, and even a few Chinese sold fresh fish, shrimp, fruits, vegetables, and flowers. Indians offered brightly colored baskets and pottery for sale.

Taking Jim's arm, Isaac steered him to his favorite café opposite the Market, where under the orange trees patrons sipped coffee and sweet drinks and passed the time of day.

Breakfast in New Orleans, Jim soon learned, was not of the hearty Ohio variety. Instead, residents of the Crescent City preferred lighter fare: little square doughnuts called "beignets" and pungent, chicory-laced coffee.

After breakfast they returned to the flatboat, and Jim saw that in a relatively short time the slave had totally transferred the cargo. The deck looked disconcertingly bare, and Jim felt a momentary twinge of sadness, which was quickly assuaged by the thought of the sack of gold coins in his pocket.

"I can get you a good price for these timbers," Isaac declared, tapping the empty deck with his booted heel. "Good heavy lumber is scarce here."

"They're not for sale," Jim replied.

Isaac stared at him in amazement. "What do you mean?"

"I mean I'm not going to break up my boat just to sell the wood."

"What are you going to do, pole your way back up the river to Ohio?" Isaac scoffed.

"No. I'm going to stay here."

"Then what good is it?" Isaac argued. "What else can you do with a flatboat?"

"I don't know yet," Jim admitted. "These timbers are all I have left of home. I want to hang on to them awhile."

Isaac shrugged. "Whatever you say."

Although he did not succeed in persuading Jim to break up his boat and sell the lumber, Isaac did persuade him to give up sleeping aboard the craft now that the cargo was gone and join the merchant at the boardinghouse.

Once again they strolled through the narrow streets of the French Quarter, or "Vieux Carré," as it was called by the Creoles, where the sidewalks were wooden walkways termed "banquettes." Jim was amazed by the houses, which were several stories high, massed together in blocks, plastered outside, and adorned with the fanciest decorative ironwork he had ever seen. Whether cast iron or wrought iron, the designs were intricate, often incorporating motifs, initials, and symbols.

The boardinghouse where Isaac maintained a room was on the eastern edge of the Vieux Carré, and for the most part housed recent immigrants: Irish, Swedes, Germans, Italians. It was run by an attractive mulatto named Alphonsine, who was given to wearing brightly colored silk scarves around her head and huge loop earrings dangling to her shoulders. She had come to New Orleans from the West Indies, which accounted for the unique, lilting manner of her speech. Officially a Free Woman of Color, Alphonsine owned several slaves, who helped her around the large boardinghouse, bestowed on her by a wealthy lover as a parting gift. Sympathetic with their condition, she generally granted her slaves their freedom when they had earned their purchase price in service, and many remained with her even after they were freed. A woman of great charm and personableness, she smiled graciously as Isaac introduced Jim and clasped his hand in hers, addressing him as "Monsieur."

Alphonsine personally conducted Jim to his room on the third floor and threw open the jalousied shutters which extended from floor to ceiling, as windows did in this tropical climate, where the inhabitants wished to capture every possible breeze.

"This is one of my most pleasant rooms," she said. "I hope you will like it."

While she was fussing about the room, Jim stepped out onto the gallery, which overlooked a small central court, or patio, where a fountain trickled and cape jasmine, tuberoses, oleander, camellias, crepe myrtle, and purple bougainvillea grew in jumbled profusion. In the corners of the patio were orange, lemon, and banana trees, among whose shiny green leaves hummingbirds and brilliantly colored parakeets flitted.

"If anything is lacking, you will tell me, won't you, Monsieur?" Alphonsine said.

"I'm sure everything's fine," Jim replied.

"What of your clothes?" she asked, pointing to his mud-caked trousers and grimy muslin shirt. "Shall I have them washed for you?"

"Yes. That would be nice. Thank you."

"Then take them off and I will have them laundered right away," she directed. "Don't be embarrassed. I have only men in my house. I am quite accustomed to male nakedness. I do not faint at the sight of a naked man, as I am told our more delicate Creole beauties do."

More concerned about having his clothes washed than about his modesty, Jim stripped and handed her the dirty garments, noting that Alphonsine discreetly appraised his physique with her soft brown eyes and, smiling, nodded her approval.

When she was gone, he tested the mattress and discovered that, rather than goose down, it was filled with dried Spanish moss. Lying down, he listened to the clamor of street noises beyond the walls of the garden: the clatter of horses and carriages, shuffling washerwomen with snowy bundles on their heads, chimney sweeps and coalmen, berry-sellers hawking their produce with cries of *"Fraises!"* and *"Framboises!"*

As he lay on the clean sheets of the soft bed—his first bed in nearly three months—he inhaled the heady floral scents wafting upward from the patio below and tried to contemplate what his next step would be now that he had finally arrived at his destination. It was difficult to think clearly, he was assailed with so much that was new, different, and exciting. He fingered the sack bulging with the proceeds from the sale of his cargo, sure that his future lay in these gold coins as well as in this great city at the mouth of the mighty Mississippi.

❧ 3

At the public bathhouse, only a few blocks from Alphonsine's, rowdy sailors, shy foreigners, and brawling western frontiersmen soaked in rows of wooden and metal tubs, while a giant of a black man made steady trips to and from the cookhouse in the patio with pails of steaming water. Slave girls kept the noisy bathers supplied with soap, towels, and shaving equipment, and for an extra fee a girl could be hired to scrub a back or scrape calloused feet and palms with a pumice stone. It seemed to Jim that the bath girls were the ugliest women he had seen in New Orleans, but it didn't seem to discourage the lusty patrons from pinching their behinds or attempting to grab them with soapy hands as they passed.

The girl attending Jim kept her eyes decorously downcast as she scrubbed him from head to toe, but her apparent modesty didn't prevent her presence from evoking a response in Jim which caused him considerable embarrassment when she directed him to stand in the tub to be rinsed with buckets of clean water.

"Hey, how long's it been since you had a good piece?" the grizzled frontiersman in the next tub said to him. "I think you ought to get yourself over to Mother Easter's right quick. She's got the best girls—not a one over seventeen. There's a mother-and-daughter combination you can have for fifty cents."

Shaved, bathed, and dressed in his freshly laundered clothes, Jim left the bathhouse feeling cheerful and invigorated. Thrusting his hands in his pockets, he whistled and contemplated taking the frontiersman's advice and paying a call on Mother Easter's Seamen's Rest Hotel.

Preoccupied by the excitement of being in a lively and exotic city like New Orleans after twenty-four years in the Ohio wilderness, Jim paid little attention to the carriage heading down the street at a good clip. As it sped past him its wheels dipped into the gutter beside the banquette, splashing his clean clothes with mud.

"Damn!" he swore at the black coachman perched up in front. Angry, he picked up a rock and threw it at the carriage, striking the crest—a florid letter M—in the center of the door with a loud thud.

At once the coachman brought the carriage to a halt and the crested door flew open. Out stepped an elegantly dressed young woman about seventeen or eighteen.

"Please, Miss Odile," the maid who accompanied her pleaded, "you get back in here. I don't want for you to get into no trouble, hear?"

"Verbena's right, miss," the coachman echoed. "You better get back inside."

Ignoring their entreaties, she delicately raised the hem of her black silk hoopskirt to avoid the mud and headed straight for Jim.

"How dare you throw a rock at my carriage!" she said, her dark eyes blazing with anger.

Jim stared at her in astonishment. He had never seen a woman with eyes like hers; the irises were nearly as black as the pupils. Her mouth formed a perfect red bow, and long, silky blue-black curls swirled about her dazzlingly white neck. He had heard that the women of New Orleans were renowned for their beauty, but this one, shaking her small hand, gloved in the finest kid, in his face, exceeded all his expectations. Unquestionably she was the most beautiful woman Jim had ever seen.

"Your carriage splashed me, ma'am," he replied, indicating the mud stains on his trousers.

"Then you shouldn't walk so close to the gutter," she retorted. "In any event, you have no right to throw rocks at my carriage. I shall report this matter to my brother, Monsieur Martinon."

Martinon . . . Martinon . . . Where had he heard that name before? Then Jim remembered: This was the family that, according to Isaac, owned the upriver plantation—Mandragore—he had admired so much.

"If your coachman promises not to splash me again, I won't throw any more rocks at your carriage," Jim said.

The maid lumbered after her mistress. "Get back inside, Miss Odile," she urged. "You ain't got no business talking to no strange man this way. Your brother will whip my hide if he finds out."

"Come on, miss," the coachman said. "Father Daubigny's waiting on us."

Without further comment, the young woman capitulated to the urging of her servants, turned her back abruptly on Jim, and flounced back to her carriage. The coachman smacked the reins across the horse's back and they were off.

As Jim stood looking after her, rubbing his freshly shaved chin, he could have sworn that the young woman turned and gave him a furtive smile as the carriage rounded the corner and disappeared.

The carriage passed St. Louis Cathedral, with its three lofty towers facing the Place d'Armes, and stopped in front of the Presbytère, a residence for priests which incorporated the most attractive aspects of eighteenth-century French architecture.

The black coachman climbed down from his seat, opened the door, and helped Odile out.

"Thank you, Cecil," she said, and proceeded through the arched portico to the main entrance. Her maid, Verbena, followed closely behind.

A young seminarian politely received the two women. "Father Daubigny is expecting you, Mademoiselle Martinon," he announced as he led them down a long hall to a study where Daubigny, a plump, jovial priest, was sharing a bunch of purple grapes with a mockingbird perched on the windowsill. The moment Odile entered, he left the bird and hurried across the room to greet her, kissing both her cheeks.

"Ah, my child, how good it is to see you!" he exclaimed. "What brings you to town? A fancy-dress ball? A party? Shopping? It's not the season for the opera . . ."

"I am here to see you, Father," she replied, and her tone indicated to the priest that she wished to speak to him in private. "A spiritual matter." Her late mother had always placed great emphasis on seeking the counsel of the clergy in all matters and insisted that her daughter do likewise. In her own way Odile tried very hard to emulate the almost fanatic devotion of Maristela Martinon, but she felt she had been only moderately successful, distressingly convinced that faith, like musical talent or ability with figures, was divinely bestowed and reserved only for a select few. Nevertheless, Odile believed that if she strove very hard and did not let her impatience and frustration interfere, the gift might someday be hers.

"Would you excuse us?" he said, and indicated to the seminarian that he was to leave and escort the maid outside. Father Daubigny was one of the few men with whom Verbena would leave Odile unchaperoned. Her primary responsibility was to see that her mistress's reputation remained above reproach.

When they were gone, Daubigny closed the heavy oak doors to assure Odile privacy and confidentiality.

"Now then, my child, what did you wish to discuss?" he asked, seating himself in a large armchair and motioning to her to do likewise.

"A most difficult matter, Father," she replied, dabbing lightly at her temples with a lace handkerchief scented with French perfume, which filled the austere room at once with a discordant fragrance. Odile had a special passion for scents and was forever ordering them from Paris, hoping to acquire one which would be distinctly hers and hers alone.

Daubigny had known the Martinon family for many years. Odile's mother, Maristela, had been a great beauty herself and the daughter of Don Andrés Valdéz, a wealthy, powerful, and aristocratic Spaniard. Sadly, Maristela died when Odile, youngest of her three children, was still very small. Having been raised in New Orleans, Maristela had frequently sought spiritual guidance from Daubigny, and continued to do so after her marriage and residence at Mandragore. The priest had also counseled Odile's elder sister, Eugénie, guiding the girl through a turbulent period of her life some years previously, and had been instrumental in her decision to join the order of Ursuline nuns. As influential as Daubigny was with the females in the Martinon family, he had had little or no effect on the males. The old man, Antoine Martinon, father of Odile, had been a rake who simultaneously kept not one but two octoroon mistresses and rarely attended mass. One thing which could be said in the old patriarch's favor, however, was that he was generous in his financial support of the church—one of many who mistakenly thought they could buy their way to heaven. His son, Placide, who had assumed the stewardship of the plantation upon the death of old Antoine a year ago—a loss which affected Odile greatly—was a thorn in Daubigny's side. Even as a child young Martinon had been given to both heresy and blasphemy, displaying undisguised contempt for the clergy which caused his poor mother no end of grief. Almost at puberty he had engaged in all manner of debauchery with the slave girls on the plantation and the loose women in town as well as gambling and drinking heavily, all of which caused Maristela great anguish, which the priest firmly believed hastened the poor woman's death. Daubigny had great difficulty tolerating the rude and arrogant profligate who now controlled the vast holdings of his father as well as the life of his beautiful young sister.

"Has this difficult matter of which you speak, my child, anything to do with your brother?" he asked.

"Partly," she replied. "But it pertains more to myself. And my cousin . . ."

Cousin? Daubigny wondered which one it could be. The Martinons had many relatives up and down the river, legions of cousins.

Odile volunteered the answer. "My cousin Narciso. Narciso Valdéz."

This Valdéz youth of whom she spoke was the son of Efrén Valdéz, Maristela's brother, who owned an enormous cotton plantation a considerable distance from Mandragore. He recalled that Efrén and his wife, Adela, had a frail, thin lad with a bad heart who all the doctors in the South agreed would never live to adolescence. If indeed this boy was the Narciso Valdéz of whom she spoke, he would now be in his early twenties and a living refutation of the physicians' prognostication. Daubigny recalled having seen this son of Efrén and Adela at a wedding a few years ago and noted at the time that he had a sickly pallor and a feverish look in his dark eyes.

"What of this Valdéz youth?" he asked.

Odile sighed, twisting her handkerchief in her gloved hands. "I am hopelessly infatuated with him. I think of him day and night. I am like one possessed."

Daubigny shook his head. "That is no way to talk, my girl."

"But it's true, Father."

"Is your brother aware of these feelings?"

"Only insofar as he discovered a letter from Narciso in which he expressed his affection and esteem for me. Placide was furious and accused me of the most serious indiscretions."

"Untrue, of course?"

"Of course," she affirmed. "When we are together Narciso and I spend our time engaged in music. He plays the harpsichord and I my harp. Sometimes I sit at his feet while he reads the poetry of Garcilaso de la Vega and Luis de Góngora in the original sixteenth-century Spanish—lovely works that my dear mother loved so much."

"Your mother was a woman of great culture, my child," the priest said. "But tell me, what was your brother's reaction to the letter?"

"He has forbidden me to see my cousin."

"What is his objection?" Intermarriage between cousins was quite prevalent, often used to prevent the breakup of plantations and keep the large fortunes intact. Although the practice really didn't produce the large number of defective offspring claimed by some, it did result in many loveless marriages, rivalries, and blood intrigues.

"Like everyone else, he is afraid Narciso is going to die at any moment. If I were to marry him, Placide is sure, within a short time I would be a widow and his responsibility once again," she replied.

"He has a point," Daubigny conceded, although he hated himself for supporting Placide Martinon in anything. He was sure that the planter would have no scruples about using his sister to further his personal ambitions. Undoubtedly he had bigger things in mind for her than Narciso Valdéz.

"My aunt Adela, Narciso's mother, is planning a ball for his birthday. I am so anxious to attend, but I am certain my brother will never permit it."

"You are your brother's charge, my child. If he forbids you to go, you must obey him. As a priest, I cannot advise disobedience to your guardian," Daubigny said, adding hastily, "no matter how I may personally feel."

"But if I don't go it will break poor Narciso's heart," Odile said, her voice full of anguish.

"Is it pity or love you feel for your cousin?"

"Love," she replied at once. "I think of him night and day. I long to be with him. I am completely devoted."

"Such strong passions should be reserved for Our Lord and not squandered on mere mortals," he said solemnly.

Odile sighed and rose as if to leave. "I must be going now," she announced, looking disappointed that the priest had not been more sympathetic to her cause.

Plucking a plump grape, Daubigny plopped it into his mouth and escorted her to the door. "Pray, my child. We must all pray. If we take all things to God in prayer, He will guide us and show us the way," he advised. "Never forget this."

"Thank you, Father," she murmured, and left to rejoin Verbena, who was waiting impatiently in the hall.

From the Presbytère Odile had Cecil drive her to the Ursuline convent a few blocks away, where a novitiate admitted her and Verbena, ushering them into a small herb garden fragrant with sage, thyme, rosemary, and oregano. While the young fledgling nun went to summon her sister, Eugénie, Odile waited patiently on a delicate wrought-iron bench while Verbena fretted.

"Marse Placide's not going to like you coming here to see your sister one little bit," the maid scolded, shaking her kerchiefed head.

"He's not going to know unless you or Cecil tell him," Odile replied, wrapping her hands gracefully around the handle of her parasol and tilting it so that it shaded her porcelain-like complexion from the burning rays of the sun.

"We don't have to tell him nothing. Marse Placide always knows when you done something you ain't supposed to," Verbena declared.

The maid's fretting was cut short by the appearance of Eugénie. Ten years older than Odile, Eugénie bore a resemblance to her sister, although few would have considered her strikingly beautiful. Her delicate-featured face beneath the stiffly starched nun's wimple broke into a joyous smile when she saw Odile.

"What a marvelous surprise!" she exclaimed, warmly embracing her sister and then Verbena. "How happy I am to see both of you! How is everything at home? I have been so busy lately with my pupils— fifteen girls from some of the finest families in the state —that I've scarcely had time to think of anything else. They are such sweet girls—so dear." She stroked Odile's cheek affectionately. "Some of them remind me so much of you, baby sister."

Gathering the folds of her voluminous habit around her, Eugénie squeezed between Odile and Verbena on the bench, clasping their hands in hers. "What brings you to town?"

"I had a number of things to do—the dressmaker, the milliner, the bookstore—I wanted to get a present for Narciso's birthday—the china shop . . ." Odile enumerated. "I also called on Father Daubigny."

"The dear man," Eugénie said. "Tell me, does Placide know you have come to see me?" She knew that their brother disapproved of any contact between them. Some years earlier Eugénie had become embroiled in a scandal, which Placide alleged had brought permanent disgrace on the family, and he feared she might be a bad influence on the impressionable young Odile. He also resented the fact that the scandal forced her into the convent and prevented her from making an advantageous marriage, one which might have helped further his own ambitions.

"I won't lie if he should ask me," Odile replied.

"And you ain't going to tell him unless he asks," the maid said.

"What were you seeing Daubigny about?" Eugénie inquired.

"Narciso. Placide has forbidden me to see him or go to his birthday ball. You know how much it would hurt Narciso if I didn't attend, but Daubigny says I must obey my brother," Odile said.

"We all know how fond you and Narciso have been of one another ever since childhood. The rest of us used to taunt him because he was not permitted to run and play as we were. We used to laugh at his spells when he became blue and gasped for air. How cruel we all were—except for you, Odile. You were never cruel to him. It was as though he had some secret fascination for you. You held him in awe and treated him as though his handicaps were of no importance and made him special in some mystical way," Eugénie mused.

It was true that the physical defects which set Narciso apart from others as a child had fascinated her. His gaunt, frail body and pale face reminded her of paintings of the tormented and afflicted saints so graphically depicted in her mother's beloved *Lives of the Saints*.

A slight blush colored Odile's cheeks as she admitted, "Well, I have always admired our cousin."

"More than admire," Verbena interjected.

"In any event," Odile went on, ignoring the maid's comment—no one except Father Daubigny and perhaps Narciso himself would ever know the true extent of her feelings—"Placide has no right to forbid me to go to his birthday celebration. Everyone up and down both sides of the river will be there. Even the Valdéz from Cuba are coming."

Eugénie seemed startled by this bit of news. "You mean Aunt Carlota?" she asked.

"Yes," Odile confirmed. "She's coming for a visit with the two oldest boys, Ernesto and Luis."

"What about Beatriz?" Eugénie asked anxiously, referring to their Cuban aunt's youngest child.

"Aunt Carlota made no mention of Beatriz in the letter Aunt Adela received," Odile replied.

Eugénie looked at her sister imploringly. "You *must* go to that ball," she said. "You simply must."

Odile was quite surprised to hear her sister encouraging her to disobey both Placide and Father Daubigny.

Verbena, too, was shocked. "Now what you telling this child to do, Miss Eugénie?"

Eugénie ignored the maid and kept her gaze fixed on Odile. "You must go to the ball and tell Aunt Carlota to come and call on me. I must see her about a matter of the utmost importance. I have sent her letters repeatedly, which she refuses to answer. I must see her. Do you understand?"

"I'm not sure I do, Eugénie." Odile was puzzled by the urgency in her sister's voice.

"I know that as far as the family is concerned I am an outcast," Eugénie continued. "Nevertheless, even an outcast is entitled to certain consideration."

Verbena put her arm maternally around the nun as though soothing a forlorn child. She had nursed both girls from birth, raised them, and thought of them almost as daughters. "Now you hush, Miss Eugénie, hear? Don't you go getting yourself all stirred up."

"What is the important matter?" Odile persisted, with the typical curiosity of an adolescent.

Verbena turned to her and snapped, "And you hush, too, Miss Odile!"

Once more Odile was mystified, as she had been for the last few years—ever since Eugénie's so-called predicament. When she was about nine and Eugénie was in her late teens, her sister had mysteriously become pregnant. The family was scandalized, and it was decided to pack her off to Cuba until after the baby's birth, but matters intervened which kept her from going, and she was confined instead to her room at Mandragore. The whole situation was rigorously hushed up, and her father sternly ordered everyone to protect Odile's young ears from the sordid details of the scandal. Fortunately, the baby was stillborn, and it was interred immediately in the plantation cemetery behind the chapel, but the situation had had a devastating effect on the family.

A few weeks following the birth of the child, after many lengthy conferences with Father Daubigny, Eugénie entered the Ursuline convent, where she had remained ever since.

As to the identity of the child's father, little was known. To the best of Odile's knowledge, no one had learned her sister's secret.

In the convent chapel a bell began tolling, calling the nuns to prayer. Eugénie rose, kissed both Odile and Verbena again and said, *"Au revoir.* I must be off now." Crossing her arms and inserting them in the sleeves of her habit, she added softly, "Odile, don't forget—the ball—Aunt Carlota . . . I'm counting on you." She smiled imploringly a final time before she disappeared behind a pair of dark, heavy doors.

4

Dignified in his black livery edged with silver piping, Romulus shuffled across the bedroom, through the floor-to-ceiling, triple-hung window onto the second-floor gallery, and emptied the porcelain shaving bowl over the balustrade onto the lawn below while his master, Placide, his neck swathed in towels, waited impatiently. The slave, who served in the multiple capacities of houseman, butler, valet, and majordomo, gently dried his master's freshly shaven face before applying fragrant pats of bay rum, completing the ritual with a dusting of talcum, which filled the room with a flurry of fine white powder. Placide fanned the air in front of his face and held out his hand for the mirror, which Romulus promptly furnished. Moving his head slowly from side to side, Placide carefully inspected the slave's handiwork: the evenness of the black sideburns, the edge of the slender dark moustache, the smoothness of neck and chin. Satisfied, he whipped off the towels, tossed them carelessly on the floor, and stood up, indicating to Romulus that he was now ready to dress.

The slave helped him into a creamy white silk shirt ruffled at the cuffs and down the front, gray sharkskin trousers of the latest Parisian cut, and a trim waistcoat richly embroidered in gold thread. Placide crossed to the mirror and studied the fit of the trousers in the long glass. A fine layer of glittering dust lay on the floor at the base of the mirror, silvery flecks which had flaked off the backing and was called "diamond dust" by children, who believed it was valuable. Frowning, he poked his thumbs into the waistband of the trousers to indicate the looseness of their fit.

"Remind me that I must see the tailor again," he remarked.

"Yes, Marse Placide," Romulus agreed.

At twenty-nine Placide Martinon was still lean, and secretly proud that his clothing never had to be let out to accommodate increased girth, as in the case of so many of his friends. Both Valentin Chardonnier and Jules Seguin, with whom he had shared the same Harvard-educated tutor during his teens, had put on considerable weight since their recent marriages.

While Valentin and Jules have run to fat with Louise and Anais, Denise keeps me thin, he mused, thinking of his mistress.

From the huge armoire in the corner—there was not a single closet in the house—Romulus selected a

well-cut frock coat and held it for his master to slip
into. Just as the first arm slid into the silk-lined sleeve,
they heard the sound of a horse and carriage below.

"Miss Odile, no doubt," Placide said, and calcu-
lated his descent down the narrow spiral stairway to
coincide with Odile's entrance. She was followed by
Verbena, whose arms were loaded with her young
mistress's purchases.

"Bonjour," Odile said, smiling at her brother as she
snapped her parasol shut.

"Been shopping, eh?" Placide said, glancing at the
packages in the maid's arms.

"Yes." Odile nodded, hoping she could brush past
him to her room without further questions. "I had to
get a few things."

"And what is this?" he asked, taking one of the
packages from Verbena. It was a book of Spanish poetry she had bought as a birthday gift for Narciso;
she had hoped her brother wouldn't see it. "Looks
like a book." He opened it and flipped some of the
pages. "And so it is—Spanish poetry."

"It's for Narciso," she said.

"Speaking of our dear cousin," Placide said, returning the book to the maid and hooking his thumbs
in the tiny pockets of his waistcoat, "there is something
I must discuss with you regarding him."

"Please, Placide, not now," Odile said. "It's very
hot, and the trip from town was grueling. I have a
headache and must retire to my room. Will you excuse me?"

"No," he answered flatly. "I want a word with
you."

"After supper—"

"Now," he said emphatically, and took her firmly
by the arm, steering her toward the study. Turning
to Verbena, he said, "You may take those purchases
to your mistress's room."

"Yes, Marse Placide," the slave replied, and started
up the twisting stairs.

Since the death of their father, Placide had assumed
not only the stewardship of the plantation but the
guardianship of his young sister as well, and he had

no qualms about asserting his authority over either. When the senior Martinon was alive he would never have permitted his son to treat Odile in such a fashion, but now that he was gone Placide enjoyed flaunting his newly acquired power, as though to remind her that she no longer had anyone to whom she could turn for intervention or support.

Once in the study, Placide closed the doors and seated himself behind the huge desk—because the rooms at Mandragore were large and high-ceilinged for maximum air circulation, the furniture was necessarily oversized as well—and indicated to Odile that she was to sit opposite him in the stiff, horsehair-covered *fauteuil* that had been their late father's favorite chair.

"I hope you are not planning to deliver Narciso's birthday gift in person," he began.

"That would be my wish," she replied.

"At the ball?"

"If possible."

"But I have said you may not attend that ball."

"I was hoping that perhaps you might be prevailed upon to change your mind."

"I'm afraid not—not as long as that silly wretch continues to write you those ridiculous love letters."

"He wrote me a single letter."

"From a hopeless invalid, a single love letter is enough."

"It wasn't a love letter," Odile disagreed. "It was merely an expression of his esteem. That's all."

"You forget, dear sister, that I read it," he countered. "I read about the 'passion burning in my bosom,' the 'longing in my loins . . .'"

Angry and embarrassed, Odile jumped to her feet. "You had no right to read that letter. It was intended only for me."

"You forget, my dear, that until you marry I am your guardian, and, as such, you are under my exclusive protection. Thus, I must protect not only you but the good name of our family as well. We cannot afford to be besmirched by another scandal such as that our sister, Eugénie, brought upon us," he reminded her.

"You have nothing to fear from Narciso," she assured him. "He is a dear friend, a cousin, a beloved companion, a poor invalid who intends no harm to anyone."

"Invalid or not, he has the same desires as any man —and, I might add, the ability to carry them out, as several of the young slave girls at Florestal will attest," Placide asserted with a sly grin.

"Narciso has never touched any of the slaves at Florestal," she said indignantly.

Placide chuckled. "I marvel at your innocence."

"Have you finished with me? My temples are throbbing. I must go and have Verbena prepare some cool compresses for me," she said, rising to leave.

Placide got up from behind the desk and stood between her and the door, blocking her exit. Rocking back on the heels of his highly polished boots, he said, "First you are going to write a letter."

"To whom?" she demanded.

"I shall dictate it."

"To whom?" she repeated.

"To Narciso."

Taking her firmly by the arm, he led her to the desk and sat her in the chair. Picking up a pen, he pressed it into her hand and got a sheet of paper from the drawer.

" 'Dear Cousin Narciso,' " he began aloud. " 'It is with the deepest regret that I decline the kind invitation to attend your birthday ball—' "

Odile slammed the pen down. "I won't write *that!*" she said.

Standing behind her, Placide suddenly seized a lock of her lustrous hair and began twisting. "You will do exactly as I say," he ordered.

Odile squealed, and her cries brought Verbena downstairs.

"What's the matter, honey?" she called through the closed doors. "What you doing to that poor child, Marse Placide? If your mama was alive, she wouldn't like you hurting your baby sister, and you know it."

Ignoring the maid, Placide said to Odile, "You will write what I tell you or I shall pull your hair out by the roots."

Knowing from several frightening past experiences that her brother was capable of carrying out his harshest threat, Odile, weeping, once more picked up the pen.

"That's better." He smiled, relaxing his grip on her dark locks, but it wasn't until she had actually written the salutation, "Dear Cousin Narciso," that he completely released the tresses clutched between his strong, slender fingers.

Placide was extremely proud that Denise Couronneau was his mistress, and after the trying scene with his sister earlier in the day he looked forward with more pleasure than usual to an evening in Denise's company.

At thirty-five, Madame Couronneau was considered one of the Crescent City's most glamorous and charming hostesses, and invitations to the town house she shared with her aged husband, Victor, on Rue Royal, where the cream of Creole society resided, were eagerly sought. Tall and statuesque, the auburn-haired Denise was admired for her beauty and her wit by a society which prided itself on the attractiveness and allure of its women. To the world at large, Monsieur and Madame Couronneau, whose marriage had been arranged by her family when she was only fourteen and he forty years her senior, were a harmonious and even affectionate couple, but it was common knowledge that privately Denise detested Victor and treated him with disdain and contempt, caring only for his wealth, which provided her with the lifestyle she felt she deserved, frequently and indiscriminately violating their marriage vows.

The Couronneau town house, while not large and sprawling in the manner of many of the plantation homes, such as Mandragore, was elegantly furnished with the finest French and Italian antiques. Typical of the better homes in the Vieux Carré, it rose three stories from the street, the upper two with galleries wrapped in exquisitely designed wrought iron. Also typical of these homes were the drab wooden slave quarters attached by an ell to the rear of the main house. Although not out of the ordinary in appearance, the Couronneau slave quarters caused a certain stir in the neighborhood from time to time when neighbors and various passers-by mentioned hearing cries, shrieks, moans and groans from within, usually in the dead of night. Investigations by city authorities who sought to uphold the *"Code Noir,"* a body of laws intended to protect slaves from cruel and inhuman treatment, were quickly dispatched by Denise's charming assurances that the strange sounds were attributable to the wind and other natural phenomena or the slaves' being overly emotional after attending the Sunday-afternoon dances in Congo Square. Her explanations were corroborated by her butler, a handsome mulatto by the name of Valcour, who swore that Madame Couronneau was the kindest of mistresses, adored by all her slaves. When confronted with Denise's gracious manner and striking good looks, it was difficult for anyone to believe that nefarious activities could possibly be taking place under her roof.

The soirée for which Placide had so carefully groomed and dressed was a small, intimate one, which would become even more intimate after the departure of the other guests, when he and Denise would be alone. Dismounting, he tossed his horse's reins to a waiting groom and approached the ornate front door of the elegant town house in the company of a torch-bearing slave.

The butler, Valcour, admitted him, greeting him coolly but politely, and ushered him into the salon. The room, decorated with hand-painted wallpaper from Paris, carpets shipped from Italy in seventeen-inch strips and later sewn together by the Couronneau slaves, satin damask drapes framing French windows covered by curtains of the finest Belgium lace, was filled with guests. The moment Denise laid eyes on Placide she left the adoring circle of friends around her and rushed to greet him, allowing him to kiss both her cheeks.

"How good of you to come, Placide," she said, fluttering her lacy black Spanish fan coquettishly.

"My pleasure, madame." He smiled, taking her hand and raising it to his lips.

At the conclusion of the magnificent seven-course meal served with an assortment of the finest French wines, the guests returned to the salon, where they amused themselves at euchre, charades, poker, gossiping, and drinking until well into the early morning hours. Summer nights in New Orleans were hot and muggy, encouraging the populace to keep late hours, relegating sleep to the early morning, when it was somewhat cooler. In his easy chair Victor Couronneau persistently dozed after the big meal, and Denise ordered Valcour to put him to bed. Thus, when her guests began to depart, Denise alone bid them good night, offering apologies for her elderly spouse. "Poor Victor," she said. "He becomes so weary. You must excuse him."

When everyone had gone, Valcour strolled quietly about the house, extinguishing candles and locking up for the night.

At last alone with his mistress, Placide gathered Denise into his arms, slipping his hand into the bodice of her silk gown. Cupping her full breast, he squeezed the firm nipple until she winced. Chuckling, he nuzzled her ear and inhaled the exquisite scent of her perfume.

"Why do I love all your perversities so?" she asked, stroking the back of his hands.

"Because I love all of yours," he replied.

Her eyes bright with excitement, she announced, "Tonight, *mon petit chou,* I have a marvelous surprise for you." Taking him by the hand, she led him toward the attic stairs.

"New toys?" he asked with eager anticipation.

"You'll see," she teased.

"Tell me about them," he coaxed as he followed her up the winding staircase.

"They just arrived from Paris. Some are ingenious —truly the most imaginative. You will not believe!

Ah, what pleasures we shall enjoy! What pleasures indeed!"

Grabbing playfully at her buttocks, he persisted, "And new playmates?"

"Perhaps." She chuckled.

"Tell me, are they young?"

"Ah, so many questions!"

At the top of the stairs, as she was about to unlock the door of the secret attic chamber, he seized her and kissed her hard, pressing her lips against her teeth until she whimpered. Her talk of new toys and games they would play, perhaps with new companions, never failed to arouse him, and tonight, her exploring hand discovered as it slid upward along the inside of his thigh, was no exception.

"Tonight, *mon chéri,* will be most amusing," she promised. "So very amusing."

✤ 5

Crawling out from under the mosquito netting, Jim padded naked—it had been far too hot to sleep in any kind of garment—across the room to the basin on the night stand and splashed the tepid water on his face. Today, he remembered, drying his face, was the day he was going upriver to look at some land which Isaac thought might be a good investment. Jim was anxious to see this property about which Isaac was so enthusiastic. After a couple of weeks in New Orleans, he was confident that city life wasn't for him. His heart was still in the soil, and the sooner he could establish himself on a farm, the better.

"I was born with dirt under my nails," he told Isaac. "Farming's all I've ever known."

Naturally, he realized, farming in Louisiana would

be very different from Ohio. For one thing, the growing season was about twice as long. That, combined with warmer temperatures and more rainfall, dictated a whole new spectrum of crops which could be raised in the rich soil, heavy with Mississippi silt. Granted, he knew little about raising sugar cane, cotton, indigo, or rice, but he consoled himself with the thought that so did the Creoles when they first settled in the region, and the later-arriving Americans, who had thriving plantations up and down the Red River as well as the Mississippi. If they could do it, so could he. Jim looked forward to both the challenge and the change.

From what he gathered, sugar cane seemed to be the most profitable crop, although there were those who championed cotton. Most, however, said the rainfall was too heavy and the soil too rich for cotton, which, since the invention of the cotton gin, was sweeping the entire South and supplanting all other crops. One of the young men at the café Jim and Isaac frequented insisted that sugar would eventually be replaced by cotton as Louisiana's major crop. "I can see the change coming," the youthful Creole said, sipping his bitter-tasting, deep-green absinthe. "Soon we will not be able to compete with Cuban sugar. Cotton will take over. I can see the signs already. Cotton will be king of the whole South. A smart man will go with cotton."

Isaac was already wolfing down breakfast when Jim arrived at the table, where Alphonsine's boarders aggressively competed for mounds of corn bread, flapjacks, bacon, pork chops, grits, and ham. Jim never ceased to be amazed at the enormous quantities of food that Isaac, who was by far the slenderest man at the table, consumed without any perceptible change in his weight.

Following breakfast, the two men headed for a nearby livery stable, hired a pair of horses, and headed out of the city along the River Road. At first Jim had wanted to make the trip in his flatboat, which was still anchored, though empty, at Tchoupitoulas Street and guarded by a Negro lad whom Jim paid a few picayunes a day, but Isaac quickly dispelled any notion of that, since the only two methods of taking a flatboat upstream against the current were bushwacking—keeping the boat close to shore and moving it along by pulling on the bushes which grew on the bank—and poling, both of which were far too strenuous and required a much larger crew.

"The boat is out of the question," Isaac said. "We go by horse."

Although Isaac mounted clumsily and sat uneasily in the saddle, Jim observed that in actuality he handled the horse with adequate skill, if not with great style.

As they rode along, Jim noticed that there was an abrupt transition from city to country. The vast green fields of cane grew right up to the city limits. As they rode along the River Road, they passed the various plantations. Each had its individual name, and Isaac could tick them off from memory.

"That's Riverdale over there," he pointed out. "We just passed Rock Hill, and Blackhawk is coming up next. After that it's Union Point, L'Espérance, Carthage, Vidalia, then Forest Home. I've sold goods to nearly every one of them and spent the night at most, too—all but Mandragore."

Generally the plantations included a large main house for the master and his family, clusters of slave cabins, a barn, miscellaneous other buildings, and— usually somewhere between the planter's residence and the edge of a bayou or swamp—the sugarhouse. The latter was usually a massive pile of bricks with a towering square chimney. Since the grinding, or sugar-making, season didn't begin until fall, the sugarhouses were idle.

To Jim these huge plantations represented farming on a scale he could scarcely imagine, although he kept telling himself not to be intimidated. *I'm going to do it too. Someday I'll have a plantation the equal of any of them.*

"We sure didn't have farms like those back home," he remarked as they passed a particularly grand plantation about an hour by horseback out of the city.

"And you didn't have the number of slaves they have, either," Isaac reminded him.

The whole idea that slaves were critical to a farming operation was new to Jim and as yet had no reality for him. The memory of the slave ship with its shackled human cargo he had seen in the harbor his first day in the city made him vaguely uncomfortable, but he had no strong feelings against slavery as an institution, and was certainly not in agreement with agitating abolitionists.

Eventually they came to the most majestic plantation along the river, and Jim recognized it instantly as Mandragore. Jim recalled Isaac's story of the inhospitality to which he had been subjected there, and the arrogant but stunning girl whose carriage had splattered him with mud.

Ironically, the land which Isaac had in mind adjoined the Martinon plantation, but it couldn't have been less like it. A severe disappointment to Jim, instead of being endless green fields the property was a dismal swamp, choked with water hyacinths and abundant with elephant ears, rozo cane, willows, and moss-draped cypresses. At Isaac's insistence, they departed from the River Road and skirted the land, the horses' hooves sinking deep into the black mud. Graceful white egrets glided across their path and joined marsh wrens, laughing gulls, hawks, wild ducks, and geese overhead. At the sound of horses and human voices, white-tailed deer scampered off to denser cover and muskrats and otters scurried into their burrows.

Unimpressed with the potential of this swamp as farmland, Jim was hardly interested when Isaac assured him that it was approximately three hundred and twenty arpents, an arpent being slightly less than an acre.

"More than enough for one man," Isaac said.

"And most of it is underwater," Jim reminded him.

"So what?" Isaac countered. "You drain it, that's all. Then you got good land—the best around." He dismounted and scooped up a handful of the black, silty mud. "Beautiful, isn't it?" he said in his most persuasive tone. "First you drain it—it's not such a job. Every one of the plantations we passed was the same at the start—some even worse. Once you drain it with ditches, canals, and locks, you build levees to keep the water out. After that you plant and get rich. Simple."

As they sat astride their mounts contemplating the marshland, the baying of hounds was heard, followed by a sudden crackling and snapping of branches and sloshing of water from within the dense cypress thicket which separated this marshland from the lush green acres of Mandragore. The horses pricked their ears and whinnied softly. Simultaneously, Jim and Isaac tightened the grip on their reins and gazed expectantly in the direction of the noise. Eventually a rider on a bay horse, armed with a whip and a pistol, emerged through a clump of willows, followed by a black boy in his early teens astride a mule, both surrounded by a pack of yelping bloodhounds. Isaac was certain that he was Martinon's overseer.

"What right you all got on this land?" the supposed overseer demanded, spitting a mouthful of tobacco juice through the considerable gap in his front teeth. A wide-brimmed hat pulled down low on his forehead shaded his round, ruddy face. One eye appeared sightless, gray and glazed over by a cataract. "This here is private property—Martinon land—and you all ain't got no right to trespass."

Unperturbed, Isaac swept off his black bowler. "I beg your pardon, mister," he said. "I was not aware to whom this land belonged."

"Well, you know now," he said, fingering the trigger of the pistol. "You got no business here, so get moving before I fill you full of lead."

Ignoring the threat, Isaac smiled genially. "Ah, but, mister, you don't understand, my friend and I *do* have business here. In fact, it's with Monsieur Martinon himself."

The overseer cocked his head skeptically. "Now is that a fact?"

"My companion here is interested in purchasing this piece of land," Isaac said, indicating Jim.

"What fool would want to buy this no-good piece

of swamp?" the overseer asked, eyeing Jim contemptuously.

"Mr. MacKay is no fool," Isaac replied.

The overseer rode forward until his horse was parallel with Jim's and the two men face to face. "You must be touched in the head, man," he said. "This land is worthless."

"He doesn't happen to think so," Isaac put in.

The overseer turned and glowered at the merchant. "What's the matter, can't he talk for himself?"

"Tell him, Jim," Isaac urged.

The overseer addressed himself once more to Jim. "Are you serious?"

"Yes," Jim replied, almost without realizing what he was saying. Moments before, he had had no intention of buying such land.

"He'd like to talk to Monsieur Martinon," Isaac said. "Today, if possible."

"You'll talk to Monsieur Martinon only if he feels like talking to you!" the overseer snapped. "I'll have to go ask him. In the meantime, you all wait here."

"Much obliged," Isaac said, tipping his hat.

Without another word, the one-eyed overseer turned his horse around and signaled to the black boy on the mule, and together they rode off through the cypress thicket from which they had emerged.

✺ 6

As she began to write, Odile's hand trembled slightly.

Dearest Cousin,

I am writing to advise you to dismiss the previous letter, in which I stated that I shan't be able to attend your birthday ball. I shall indeed attend! And with the greatest pleasure. As you may have guessed, that letter was written under great duress. I know there is no need for me to say from whom. We both .know the culprit. Impatiently I count the hours until we see one another again.

Your Affectionate Cousin,
Odile.

Tipping the lighted candle slightly, she allowed a drop of wax to fall onto the envelope, sealing it.

When Verbena came in to turn down the daybed and help her undress for her afternoon nap, Odile presented her with the letter.

"I want this delivered to my cousin Narciso at Florestal," she said. "Naturally, my brother must know nothing about it."

Verbena shook her head. "You trying to make trouble for both of us, ain't you," she said.

"There will be no trouble if Placide doesn't find out," she assured the maid.

"Sooner or later, some way or other, Marse Placide finds out everything around here. He's got his spies all over this plantation. Ain't nothing going on he don't find out. You can't trust nobody nohow. That white trash Davis is just itching to lay that bullwhip of his across my black hide," the slave declared. "I don't mess with that brother of yours. You get somebody else to deliver that letter for you."

"Please, Verbena," she coaxed, batting her long black lashes the way she did as a child to beg favors from others.

"How can I do that, child? How can I get myself all the way up the river to Florestal?" she protested.

"You go shopping at the French Market every Thursday, don't you?"

"So what?"

"Take the letter with you."

"What am I going to do with it at the French Market?"

"Give it to Kitty. She'll be there buying provisions

for Florestal, just as she does every Thursday. She can be trusted to see that Narciso gets it," Odile assured her. Kitty occupied roughly the same position in the Valdéz household that Verbena did at Mandragore. Both black women ran their respective masters' homes and supervised the other house slaves. Kitty was especially devoted to the semi-invalid Narciso, and because of this Odile knew she could be trusted.

"I ain't getting Kitty in no trouble," Verbena said.

Realizing that the maid was going to be stubborn, Odile said, "All right, then I shall take the letter myself."

"I think you'd best burn it before Marse Placide finds it," Verbena advised. "Then you in real big trouble."

"I'm not scared of him," Odile replied, her dark eyes flashing defiantly as she slipped the letter back under the pillow. She wasn't sure how she would accomplish it, but somehow she was determined to get the letter to Narciso.

Later, unable to sleep because of the heat, Odile rose from the daybed, dressed without Verbena's assistance, dabbed at her neck and shoulders with cologne, and went downstairs, intending to practice her harp in the music room. Passing the study, she noticed that the door was slightly ajar, and inside she heard Placide conversing with Hiram Davis, the plantation overseer.

Lavinia, one of the younger house slaves, was sweeping black mud from the straw mats which replaced the carpets in summer. "Sticks like glue, it do," the sweaty black girl complained. "Don't have enough sense to wipe his feet before he comes in here. Lives like white trash, he do. That's all that Davis is—white trash. Ain't no nigger as trashy as him. He's mean, and mighty peculiar besides." The slaves repeatedly referred to Davis as "peculiar," although Odile hadn't the faintest idea what they were talking about. She found him repellent and had little contact with him, regarding him as merely an employee and nothing more. Unlike other planters and their families, the Martinons did not mingle socially with whites in their employ, considering them social inferiors. Her involvement with the everyday workings of the plantation was minimal. All that was expected of an unmarried seventeen-year-old girl was that she sit on the gallery and entertain beaux who came to call, attend dances and parties, and spend time in New Orleans at the French Opera, soirées, and the newly organized Mardi Gras balls. It was a life she found exceedingly dull and trying at times, and she was grateful for the temporary respite her father's death had given her.

Hearing Odile in the hall, Placide summoned her into the study. She noticed that he looked tired and drawn from his night at the Couronneaus'.

Hiram Davis, who rarely came into the main house except on urgent business, was standing by the desk. He removed his hat when Odile entered and greeted her civilly, although she sensed, as always, a mutual antipathy between them. She acknowledged his presence by a cool nod and then directed her attention exclusively at her brother.

"Davis tells me that a certain MacKay, a *Kaintock*," Placide began, using the Creole pejorative for all non-Creoles, whether or not they actually originated in Kentucky, "wishes to purchase some land from us."

"Really?" she replied, wondering why he was conveying this information to her. Granted, according to her father's will she had technically inherited half the plantation, but the actual control of it was still in the hands of her brother, who had the authority to do whatever he pleased without consulting her, being required only to support her from the income and divide half the proceeds with her in the event of a sale. In essence, her fortunes were completely at his mercy.

"I feel it is to our advantage to sell this worthless swamp to Mr. MacKay if he is able to meet our terms," he proposed.

Odile wondered why her brother would sell land to a Yankee outsider. Were Mandragore's troubles deeper than she suspected?

"Those damned Yankees are pouring in here like

a plague of locusts," Davis said, pushing his plug of tobacco into his cheek. "Only a Yankee would be fool-hardy enough to buy land that's nothing but muck."

Addressing himself to his sister, Placide said, "Mr. MacKay will be coming here later to discuss the possible purchase. I should like you to be present when he arrives and receive him with the same graciousness we extend to any visitor."

"He's got that damned Jew peddler with him," Davis said.

"The one selling furniture with the horse and wagon?" Placide inquired.

Davis grinned. "He ain't got no horse and wagon no more."

"When you go back to them, Davis, tell MacKay that he is welcome but his friend must wait out at the gate," Placide said. "I recall very well his last visit here. His behavior was outrageous when I informed him he could not indeed stay in our *garçonnière* for the night. He swore that one day he would return and force us to welcome him to our midst."

Odile threw her head back and laughed. Though not inherently cruel, Odile considered her family aristocracy. Certainly far above heathen peddlers.

"Cheeky devil," Placide said.

"If you insist, I shall greet Mr. MacKay in the same civil manner I would any other Christian gentleman," Odile agreed. "But the afternoon is rather close and I haven't had my nap. Really, I would prefer to remain in my room . . ."

"I insist," Placide affirmed.

"In that case, I must go and find Verbena and freshen up," Odile said, starting for the door. "You will excuse me, won't you?"

Twirling the end of his narrow moustache, Placide said, "I understand from Davis that Mr. MacKay is a young and rather attractive gentleman."

"For a Yankee," Davis added with a sneer.

"I have no interest in Yankees," she said, and left the room.

❧ 7

Reluctantly Jim left Isaac at the gate, as the surly overseer insisted, and followed the great circular carriageway around the stately house to the rear portico, able to observe at close range the finer details of its construction: the hand-carved capitals atop the slender columns, the special cornices and moldings, the well-turned balustrades in the railings around the upper and lower galleries. Such details were not evident when the house was viewed through the alley of oaks from the River Road, and although one got a sense of its grandeur and size, the more subtle touches were lost.

At the porte cochère he was greeted by a black groom, a boy of ten or twelve, who helped him dismount, watered his horse, and tied it to a hitching post.

The door was opened by a dignified butler, who ushered him directly to a study, saying, "Monsieur Martinon is expecting you, sir."

The study walls were lined with all sorts of antique firearms as well as a few half-empty bookshelves. Straw mats covered the wide-plank floor, and between two French windows a fireplace with a mantelpiece of black-and-gold Carrara marble interposed itself. Behind an enomous desk sat the master of the plantation, Placide Martinon, impeccably dressed in the latest mode. He rose casually and greeted Jim as he entered. "Good day, monsieur—Monsieur MacKay, is it not?" he said, extending his hand.

After inviting him to sit in a very large armchair upholstered in horsehair, Martinon instructed the butler to serve them cool drinks. "I find mint juleps most refreshing any time of the day in summer," he said. "Even before breakfast."

Resuming his seat behind the desk, Placide offered Jim a humidor of cigars. "These are made of special perique tobacco grown on our own land," he said.

Jim accepted a cigar and instantly realized that it was by far the strongest tobacco he had ever experienced. "Thank you," he said, trying very hard not to choke.

"I understand from Davis, my overseer, that you are interested in some land I own," Placide said. "Is that correct?"

"Possibly," Jim replied.

"I assume then that you intend to settle in Louisiana?"

"I'm considering it, yes."

"And you are from Ohio?"

"That's correct," Jim affirmed.

"You know," Placide mused, "I often wonder why so many of you Americans come down here." The Creoles habitually referred to their fellow countrymen as "Americans" when not using more derogative terms. "The climate is ghastly—nine months of suffocating heat, mosquitoes, and pestilence followed by three months of miserable cold and rain. If I may ask, MacKay, what is your reason for wanting to settle here?"

"I can't think of any way to sail my flatboat upstream," Jim answered, rather facetiously.

"Then you arrived in a flatboat?" the Creole planter said, a disdainful note in his voice. "I am surprised you have any money remaining to buy land. Usually you American flatboatmen are parted from your money a few days after you arrive and sell your cargo, victims of the thieves and various vices along the riverfront."

"I'm different," Jim replied. "I hung on to mine."

"So you did," Placide acknowledged. "You are interested in the marshland directly upriver from here, is that correct?"

"Correct," Jim assured him.

"There are three hundred and twenty arpents there,

most of it unusable. My price for that land—in case you are interested—is one hundred dollars an arpent, making the total price thirty-two thousand," Placide said.

"I had in mind more like twenty dollars an acre—excuse me, arpent," Jim offered, following guidelines set up earlier by Isaac.

The Creole planter rocked back in his chair, emitted a great cloud of highly aromatic smoke, and laughed, rolling his dark eyes upward. *"Mon Dieu!* You don't think I would sell for *that,* do you? First of all, eight arpents of that land lie directly on the river. Land on the river is now very scarce. It is prime land, often bringing far more than one hundred dollars an arpent. Naturally I am aware that land in the interior seldom sells for more than twelve to twenty dollars an arpent, but one must consider the advantages. If you plan to raise sugar on land thirty to fifty miles from the river, you will have to pay from four to six dollars for every hogshead you send to a shipping port. On the river you avoid that expense. Most of the sugarhouses are close enough to the river so that our slaves can roll the hogsheads of sugar on board the steamboats which transport them to New Orleans. Therefore, there is no other cost except the shipping tariff charged by the boat company itself, which is currently one dollar a hogshead. So, Monsieur MacKay, you see why I ask the price I do."

"Twenty-five dollars an arpent, then," Jim said.

Placide looked at him indignantly. "I could never consider such a ridiculous offer," he said.

"As it stands, the land is worthless to you," Jim said.

"Because it is presently a swamp does not lower its potential value," Placide countered. "No, I cannot accept less than one hundred dollars an arpent."

"Thirty," Jim offered.

"One hundred is my price," the planter said adamantly. "I refuse to bargain."

"All right," Jim conceded. "In view of the fact that the land in question is not only directly on the river, but also adjacent to one of the finest plantations in the state, I raise my offer to fifty dollars an arpent, and I will go no higher."

"Really, Monsieur, such a price is insulting," Placide said, mounting irritation in his voice.

The increasing tension in the atmosphere was relieved by the reappearance of the butler with a silver tray of frosty mint juleps, which he offered first to Jim.

"*A votre santé,* Monsieur MacKay," Placide toasted.

"Cheers," Jim replied.

Instead of returning to the bargaining in which they had been engaged before the entrance of the butler, Placide began making small talk: the weather, sights in the city, the current year's cane crop.

Eventually Odile swept into the room, radiant in a dress of black silk which revealed her high, youthful breasts above its low neckline. Jim immediately rose to acknowledge her presence, and she stared at him in amazement.

"I believe we've met before, monsieur, have we not?" she asked.

"Yes," Jim replied, while Placide, puzzled, listened to the exchange.

"My carriage splashed you with mud," she said sweetly, a hint of amusement in her dark eyes.

"Unfortunately," he replied.

Circling Jim, she inspected his pants. "Aren't they the same trousers?"

Blushing slightly, Jim wondered whether she had correctly guessed that they were the only pair he had. "Yes, ma'am," he replied.

"I'm glad you chose not to discard them," she said. "They suit you very well. If you don't mind my saying so, monsieur, you have excellent legs and those trousers display them nicely. They are the legs of an excellent horseman. Do you do much jumping?"

"Not much, ma'am."

"Shall I ask Romulus to bring you something to drink?" Placide interrupted, hoping to steer his sister's conversation in another direction.

"No thank you," she replied, and returned her attention immediately to Jim. "I understand you may be our neighbor?"

"If your brother and I can agree on a price for the land upriver," Jim said.

"Sometimes my brother can be so greedy," Odile said. "Shame on you, Placide," she said reproachfully, playfully rapping his knuckles with her folded fan.

Placide was fast losing his patience with her, but in spite of his efforts to silence her, she continued her provocative banter. "You must convince my brother to be reasonable. It would be so nice to have such a handsome neighbor just across the cyprière," she said, using the Creole word for a cypress swamp.

Struggling to control his temper, Placide closed his hand around the handle of an ivory letter-opener until his knuckles were nearly as pale as it was. "I believe you were just about to go pay a call on Victorine Pilette, were you not?" he said.

Odile laughed. "Why, Placide, you know perfectly well that Victorine and the children are in Saratoga for the summer."

"Then it was Louise Chardonnier," he corrected himself. "In any case, we will excuse you."

"Louise is in Natchez visiting her mama," Odile reminded him.

"Then you were going for a drive."

"It's much too warm," she complained.

"On the contrary, I think you will find the air in a moving carriage most refreshing," Placide pressed.

Gazing at Jim with her limpid dark eyes, she asked, "What do you think, monsieur?"

"Monsieur MacKay thinks you are impeding a serious business discussion," Placide responded, irritation in his voice.

"Is that true, sir?" she asked, turning to Jim.

"Not exactly, ma'am," he said, thoroughly enjoying the presence of the stunning, mischievous girl.

Fearing the later consequences of her brother's temper if she persisted, Odile decided she had done enough mischief for the time being. "Perhaps I shall have Cecil drive me along the river," she mused.

"A delightful idea," Placide encouraged.

Offering her outstretched hand to Jim, she giggled behind her fan as he kissed it awkwardly, attempting to imitate the European style of hand-kissing prevalent in the city.

"*Au revoir,* monsieur," she said, starting for the door. Then, pausing on the threshold, she added, "You must come and call again, monsieur—whether or not you find my brother's conditions attractive."

When she was gone, Placide forced a seemingly indulgent smile and said, "My sister is still very young and fond of jokes. You must not mind if sometimes she is too bold."

"She's delightful," Jim said, his eyes still fixed on the door through which she had just departed.

It was Placide who suggested they return to business. "We were discussing the price of the land . . ." he began.

"And I offered you fifty dollars an arpent," Jim reiterated.

"One hundred," Placide insisted, "is the price."

"Seventy-five," Jim countered, his mind still on Odile.

"A deal, monsieur," Placide agreed, startling Jim, and leaped up from the desk to shake his hand vigorously.

During the long ride back to the city, Isaac continuously berated Jim for agreeing to the price of seventy-five dollars an arpent.

"You were a fool," he charged as they guided the horses down the levee toward the river to drink. "You agreed to pay far too much for that land—twenty-four thousand dollars. You forgot the whole strategy we planned. You should have gotten it for sixteen thousand, maximum." Isaac looked at him suspiciously. "I guess when that sister of his came in you lost your head?"

"How did you know she was there?" Jim asked.

"How did I know?" Isaac repeated. "Am I such a fool that I don't know Martinon will use every trick he's got to turn things to his advantage? He knew the moment his sister walked in you'd lose your head."

"She *is* beautiful," Jim admitted. "The most beautiful lady I think I ever saw."

"Fool," Isaac said, shaking his head in disgust. "Fool."

When they got to the boardinghouse Isaac conveyed his sentiments about Jim to Alphonsine when she brought the cold supper she had prepared to his room.

"Many a man's brains have gone soft over a pretty face, Isaac," she said in her musical West Indian way. "You can't hold that against him. You've probably done a few foolish things in your day, too."

"Never," Isaac declared. "At least, not like that."

The next morning Jim asked Isaac to accompany him to the bank to see about obtaining a mortgage loan on the property.

Much to Jim's amazement the bank readily agreed to grant him a twenty-thousand-dollar loan on the property. Jim decided that Isaac's presence and his endorsement might well have been a factor in the easy acquiescence. The bank was well acquainted with the peddler and considered him an excellent risk, having financed him many times in the past.

That night Jim was so excited over the prospect of owning his own farm that he could scarcely sleep. Now all that was required was Placide Martinon's signature on the papers and the land was his. No more harsh winters of ice, snow and sleet, and frozen earth. No more worrying about feeding the livestock through the long, cold months. No more isolation amid howling winds, endless forests, and troublesome Indians. He had traded Ohio's winter chill and bitter memories of a family decimated by disease for the balmy subtropics, where the growing season was practically year-round and the land so fertile almost anything would grow. At harvest time no one had to worry about shipping produce hundreds of miles to market. The market was right at hand in the thriving port city, with its population of well over one hundred thousand. Not only was New Orleans thriving, it was a highly civilized and sophisticated city, alive, vital, and exciting, full of interesting places and beautiful women. One of the most beautiful would be residing on the adjoining plantation—not that such an uppity, arrogant creature as Odile Martinon was even going to look at an unpolished, uncultured dirt farmer like Jim MacKay . . . at least not for the present. Perhaps, though, if he were a successful planter, a patrician beauty like Odile might just consider him something more than an uncouth Yankee newcomer. It might take a while for him to accomplish all the things he wanted, but he knew that if luck was on his side he could do it. Drive and determination surged restlessly within him whenever he thought of her.

8

Martinon wasted no time in signing the papers, and the day after the deal was closed Jim rose at the crack of dawn, went to the livery stable, purchased the best horse he could afford, packed up his recently acquired equipment—ax, shovel, pick, and wheelbarrow—and headed for his new land. Standing in ankle-deep black mud, swatting mosquitoes, he had to admit that it wasn't much to look at, but for a man of vision it was more than a mournful morass— it was a beautiful sight.

Throughout the day he worked, shirtless in the blazing sun, swatting flies, mosquitoes, and other insect pests buzzing about his sweat-streaked body, digging the planned network of intersecting drainage canals, dislodging rocks with a pick and carefully saving them for the projected levee which would prevent the spring floods from inundating his land once it was drained.

Late in the afternoon, when the heat was a little less intense, Isaac appeared on the scene, much to Jim's surprise, with a shovel strapped to his saddle.

"You think I would miss the first day?" he asked rhetorically as he got off his horse with the same lack of grace with which he mounted. Removing his black bowler, he wiped his sweaty brow with the back of his hand. "Where do I start?"

After an hour or so of steady digging and hauling dirt to the site of the levee, Isaac finally removed his shirt, exposing his pale torso to the sun. Although he worked with the same determination and drive as Jim, he did not have the sheer physical power to accomplish as much. His shovelfuls were smaller, his wheelbarrow loads lighter. Everything he did was accompanied by huffing and puffing, grunts and groans.

"Let's stop and take a rest," Jim suggested, and as they sat on the bank in the shade of a clump of willows, Jim asked Isaac the question that had been nagging him.

"Martinon didn't bother to drain this swamp because these landed Creoles have grown lazy and fat," Isaac answered. "What was enough for their fathers is enough for them. They no longer have ambition. They also have no memories of hunger. Their bellies have been full too long."

"Not like us," Jim said.

"Not like us," Isaac agreed. "You know, Jim, I have been thinking since you bought this land about making a change in my own life. Perhaps I should give up peddling and open a store in the city. There's a good location not far from the French Market. I think I'll look into it. You want a farm. Me, I'm no farmer— I'm a merchant. A good merchant doesn't go around with his pack on his back forever. Right?" He turned to Jim for affirmation.

"Right," Jim nodded.

"He gets a store," Isaac continued. "Eventually maybe he owns two, three, four, a block—who knows? He's really got something—not only for himself, but something he can pass on to his sons."

"You don't have any sons," Jim reminded him.

"Someday I will," he replied. "You can't have everything at once. One thing at a time. Yesterday I had a pack on my back. Today I'm thinking about opening a store. Tomorrow maybe I get married. And you—look at you. Yesterday you had nothing. Today you've got this swamp. But tomorrow . . . tomorrow who knows what you'll have?"

Rain or shine, Jim spent every day, including Sundays, on his land, toiling from dawn until dusk, much to the consternation of his boardinghouse owner, Alphonsine, who felt he owed it to himself, if not to the Lord, to rest one day a week.

"You going to kill yourself, Jimmy," she warned. "And you much too young and good-looking to die yet."

As a rule, Jim saw little of either the Martinons or their personnel. Once or twice Placide had ridden over to check on Jim's progress and exchanged a few pleasantries with him. At times Jim got the feeling that the Creole planter was envious of the transformation he had almost single-handedly wrought from the formerly worthless swampland. Occasionally Davis and his inevitable black companion would wander through the small cypress-and-sycamore thicket which separated the two properties, ostensibly hunting for possible runaway slaves. Even though discovery would mean a sound whipping, the Martinon slaves, who numbered about three hundred, frequently did sneak away from their backbreaking labor in the cane fields and lie along the river below Jim's new levee, where they knew it would be difficult for Davis to track them down. The slaves seemed fascinated and amused to see a white man working hard in the hot sun at the sort of labor disdained by the white men with whom they were familiar.

"You works like a nigger, Mister Jim," one of the slaves chuckled as Jim came upon him fishing along the river, a gleaming machete at his side. Jim often wondered how Davis had the audacity to assail these powerfully built black men with a whip when they were armed with such potentially lethal weapons.

"None would dare raise a finger," Isaac said. "The retaliation would be more horrible than you could imagine. Slaves have been dismembered alive for leading rebellions against their masters."

One especially hot, muggy September day Jim went

to the river, stripped off his clothes, and plunged into the muddy but refreshingly cool water. As he was floating, hands under his head, willow branches brushing his face, he vaguely heard the sound of a horse along the top of the levee. Assuming that it was either Placide or Davis, he paid little attention until he discovered that Odile Martinon was galloping down the side of the levee toward him on a sleek chestnut mare. From the manner in which she rode he could see that she was an expert horsewoman. Strangely, she appeared to be alone. Whenever he had seen her in the past, invariably she had been accompanied by a female slave. Embarrassed, Jim contemplated his clothes lying on the bank under the willows and realized that they were out of reach.

"Good afternoon," Odile called out.

"Hello," Jim replied, hoping the waist-deep muddy water served his modesty well.

"It looks very refreshing," she said.

"Come join me." He grinned.

"I would if I weren't swathed in corsets and petticoats," she answered.

"Don't let a few garments stop you."

She smiled at his cajolery, displaying white, even teeth behind the perfect red bow of her mouth. "When I want to do something badly enough, Mr. MacKay, nothing stops me," she said boldly.

Riding unhesitantly to the edge of the bank, she suddenly dropped her jovial manner and took on a serious tone. "There's a grave matter about which I wish to speak, Mr. MacKay."

Surprised, Jim repeated, "Grave matter?"

"You are working much too hard for a white man," she said critically. "As you know, my brother has many slaves. I am going to ask him to send some to help you."

"I have no interest in having slaves do work that is rightfully mine," he replied.

"If you will allow me to say so, Mr. MacKay, such pride is most foolish."

He frowned. "Foolish?"

"Not only that, but it's downright arrogant as well —to say nothing of inconsiderate."

"I don't understand?"

"It's difficult enough to get ignorant Negroes to respect us, and when they see a white man working as you do every day, they lose respect for the rest of us. It's as important for a white man to know his place as it is for a Negro."

Jim was perplexed. "I'm sorry, ma'am, but—"

"Sorry won't do, Mr. MacKay," she interrupted. "You will have to stop. It is simply not fitting for a white man to work this hard at manual labor. I don't know what folks did in Ohio, but it isn't done here."

"If I may ask, ma'am, why have you taken it upon yourself to tell me this?"

"My brother and the other planters up and down the river are disturbed by the situation. You are the talk of all their Negroes. When my brother sold you this land, he didn't expect you to work it yourself."

"How did he expect me to work it?"

"He thought you'd at least have the pride and decency any self-respecting white man would have and get yourself a couple of slaves," she snapped.

At that moment unseen, by Jim or Odile, a dark cottonmouth slithered through the tall grass toward the river bank, spooking her horse, which, panicking, let out a loud neigh and reared. Caught off guard, Odile struggled to control the frightened mount. Fearing that she might be thrown, Jim forgot his modesty and dashed from the water. Grabbing the reins, he held them fast, and eventually succeeded in calming the frightened animal.

"Thank you," she gasped, adjusting her riding hat, now askew.

Realizing for the first time that he was naked, she averted her gaze while he reached for his clothing and dressed.

As he was buttoning his breeches, Jim suddenly became aware that they were being observed. On the levee, astride his Arabian, was Placide Martinon.

Odile's hand trembled slightly as she parted the sliding doors of the study. Since earliest childhood she had resented her older brother's authority, his right to impose his will on her. Even when her father was alive to protect her, she had sensed and resented Placide's authoritarian nature. Perhaps the fact that he was twelve years her senior added to his power, but he had exercised the same sort of control over Eugénie before she entered the convent, and she was only two years younger than he. More likely, it was because he was the oldest son and oldest sons in this male-dominated society were expected to act as surrogate fathers in the absence of the real father. In any event, it angered Odile that she had to account to Placide for anything she had done which displeased him.

Seated behind the enormous rosewood desk, Placide was going through a stack of papers—mostly accounts of his large gambling debts. The suave Creole planter thought nothing of losing vast sums in the luxurious gambling casinos on Carondelet Street, where the croupiers and dealers wore evening dress and complimentary liquor and sumptuous buffets were served.

"Close the doors behind you," he ordered, scarcely looking up as she entered.

Laying his pen down and shoving the papers aside, he rose and strolled around to the front of the desk. Carefully arranging the folds of his well-tailored coat so that it would remain unwrinkled, he lounged casually on the corner. "I want to know what you were doing with MacKay this afternoon," he demanded.

"Just chatting with him," she replied.

"What about?"

"His work."

"What about his work?"

"How it was coming along, that's all."

"And why did you pick a time when he was naked to talk to him?"

"I didn't know he was naked. The water is very muddy."

"But you saw his clothes lying there, didn't you?" Placide persisted.

"I didn't pay attention to them. A cottonmouth

frightened Comet and I lost control of her. Mr. Mac-Kay ran out of the water to help. That's the first time I knew for certain he was naked."

"But you suspected?"

"I thought perhaps there was a possibility," she admitted.

His suspicions somewhat abated, Placide rose from the corner of the desk and began pacing the room. "As you may have realized, Mr. MacKay is a Yankee interloper. He is rude, vulgar, uncouth, and ignorant, and therefore has nothing in common with us. There is no reason why you should speak to him. Ever. About anything. Especially unchaperoned when he is naked. Do you realize that you could have easily precipitated a scandal today? Suppose someone else had come along instead of me and witnessed that scene? Someone like Jules Seguin or Henri Pilette? What do you think they would have thought? We would have been disgraced. It would have created a scandal equaled only by our sister Eugénie's, because of which you, as her younger sister, though innocent, are already in jeopardy. In the future, if there are any exchanges necessary with MacKay they will be carried out by me, and only me. Is that clear?"

"You seemed anxious enough for me to carry out an exchange with him the day he came to see about buying the land," she reminded him.

"That was an entirely different situation."

"In what way?"

"He had not as yet purchased the land. Now he has. The transaction has been completed."

"Tell me, if you find Mr. MacKay so odious, why were you so anxious to sell him the land in the first place, knowing perfectly well he would be our neighbor?"

"There are many things from which I have tried to shield you because of your tender age and because they are of no concern to a woman," he replied. "However, since you have asked, I feel obliged to tell you. Despite our seeming prosperity, Mandragore has been in fiscal difficulties for some time now. Before Papa died, he incurred several large debts."

To say nothing of your own, dear brother, she wanted to add, but, not wishing to risk his anger, she restrained herself.

"In addition," he continued, "for the last couple of years the crops have fallen below expectations. These two factors have placed the plantation in rather difficult straits. In order to restore our credit and preserve our good name it was necessary that I come up with a substantial amount of money to pay some of our debts. MacKay was able to provide that cash when it was desperately needed." He paused a moment. "In any event, all that is merely background to enable you to understand our present situation better."

The cash, Odile decided, was needed for a pressing gambling debt and had nothing to do with the plantation's credit or their good name. Preferring to pursue another tack, she said, "I think Mr. MacKay is a gentleman in his own way—which, to be sure, is different from ours—but a gentleman nonetheless. If Comet had thrown me today, I might have been seriously hurt. I think he did a very admirable thing by dashing out of the river and quieting a frightened horse—naked or clothed," she asserted.

"Still, my decision is firm. You are not to speak to him again," Placide insisted, obviously irked by her opposition.

"First you forbid me my poor cousin Narciso's companionship and now you tell me I must no longer speak to a neighbor who may very well have saved my life," she complained. "What will be next? Perhaps it is this proscription against seeing my cousin which forces me to seek out the company of men like Mr. MacKay."

"You could have all the male companionship you desire, dear sister. In fact, nothing would please me more than to see you make a suitable marriage. It is you who have chosen to remain in mourning for our father more than the customary year," he reminded her. "Should you doff your black garments and announce your return to society, I am sure Mandragore would be deluged with the finest gentlemen in the parish, all seeking your company."

"I am thinking of ending my mourning period," she said.

"Perhaps Narciso's birthday ball would be a good occasion," he suggested slyly.

Odile could scarcely believe her ears. Was he really giving her permission to attend?

Continuing, Placide said, "Aunt Adela has persuaded me to attend the dreary affair. I capitulated in a moment of profound weakness. So, should you decide to go, I shall be there to keep an eye on you."

"Of course I shall go!" she said.

"By the way, I had the second letter you sent Narciso intercepted," he casually remarked. "Thus, your presence at the ball will be a complete and total surprise to him. I hope his heart can take it."

❧ 9

One evening, when Jim returned to the boarding-house, weary from the day's work and the long ride back to the city, he was greeted by Isaac, who was in an unusually excited state.

"I signed it!" he said. "Today I signed the lease for my store. Now, I'm going to be a shopkeeper—a respectable merchant. No more a peddler with a pack on his back. Come on, let's go celebrate!"

Instead of ending up at Xenia's where they usually drank, as Jim assumed they would, Isaac instead conducted him to the Orleans Ballroom where one of the famous Bals du Cordon Bleu, better known as the Quadroon Balls, was in progress.

On the outside the Orleans Ballroom was unimpressive, with its wide, low façade devoid of any adorning graces of architecture. Inside, however, was quite another story. Crystal chandeliers, paintings, statuary, and fine wood paneling adorned the walls and ceiling. The actual ballroom itself was on the second floor, the ground floor being divided into private card and reception rooms of varying sizes.

A strict policy decreed that, for the fee of two dollars, white men only were admitted, and some effort was made to try to restrict the guest list to men of means and social standing. All weapons had to be checked at the door because of the high incidence of attendant violence when volatile tempers flared over rival attentions to a dusky beauty or some imagined slight.

Notorious for their uninhibited gaiety as well as outbreaks of violence, the balls actually served the function of providing philandering white men the opportunity to look over the current crop of available mistresses. Mothers, aunts, cousins, and other sponsors of the quadroon girls—most of whom were teenagers —dressed their charges in the best finery available and paraded them for the pleasure and inspection of the men, hoping to attract the attention of an affluent gentleman who would eventually establish the girl as his mistress.

At first Jim and Isaac's entrance was barred by the huge Irish bouncer at the door, and it was only through the intervention of one of the older mulatto women that they were admitted.

"Isaac!" she cried, throwing her arms around him like a long-lost friend.

"Iris," he replied, somewhat taken aback by the effusiveness of her greeting. "Good to see you. What are you doing here?"

"I might ask you the same question," she said. Then, indicating on the patio, where wines and cordials were served, a slim, pretty girl of about fifteen conversing with an older man who was gazing at her with a mixture of lust and paternalism, Iris replied, "I am here with my niece, Aurélie."

Obviously Iris's aspiration was to get her niece "placed," as they called it. If a girl was lucky enough to capture the fancy of the right man, he would eventually approach her sponsor and a suitable financial arrangement would ensue. Sometimes such liaisons were as permanent as marriages and the quadroon women and their subsequent offsprings well provided for. Such had been the case for Iris and her son, Roger. Often they proved to be short-lived and the girls derived little if any benefits, soon finding themselves back at the balls, beginning the cycle over again. Although a source of popular amusement for the white male population of the city, the balls were serious business—a means of survival—for the women of mixed blood.

"It would be such a comfort to know that my little niece was in the care of a gentleman—preferably one with a generous nature," Iris said, linking her arms through Isaac's and Jim's and leading them past the Irish bouncer to the ballroom upstairs.

Jim was struck by the large number of attractive women present; he had never before seen so many in a single place. Most were dressed in bright-colored silks and satins, adorned with plumes and glittering jewelry, making the city's Creole women seem drab by contrast. Many had complexions as fair as white women's, Jim observed, and conducted themselves in an elegant and generally proper fashion. He also noted that some of the women, whose prime was rapidly fading without their apparently having secured a patron, dressed with a certain boldness: necklines plunging, arms, shoulders, and backs often bare. Occasionally even nipples were partially exposed. Isaac's friend Iris seemed just such a woman.

At the top of the grandly sweeping divided staircase, Jim was startled by a dusky beauty who stood chatting in an animated fashion with a group of admirers. She was the most striking woman Jim had seen since Odile Martinon. As Iris passed with the two men in tow, the quadroon's attention wandered from her companions to Jim, and she smiled, displaying white, even teeth behind a generous, full-lipped mouth.

"Lovely, isn't she?" Iris said, sensing Jim's interest.

"Who is she?" Isaac asked.

"Delphine Desforges," Iris replied, waving to the woman in question. "The mistress of Étienne Bourrier."

"If she has a protector, why is she here tonight?" Isaac inquired.

"She is chaperoning her young cousin," Iris answered. "Half the men in New Orleans are crazy for Delphine, but Bourrier would kill anyone who pressed his attentions. He is so jealous! Fortunately for Delphine, he is away in Martinique, looking after his interests there. Probably he would be very angry with her if he knew she were here tonight."

Later, in the ballroom, a long chamber gaudily decorated with subtly erotic murals depicting nymphs, satyrs, and fauns, with a lofty ceiling, balconies overlooking the gardens of St. Louis Cathedral, and a dance floor of three thicknesses of cypress overlaid by highly polished oak—said to be the finest in the United States, Jim, Isaac, and Iris watched Aurélie whirl about the floor in the arms of a prospective protector.

"Ah, if my niece would just find a man half as good as my late Hippolyte, I would be very happy," Iris declared, going on to explain at length that Hippolyte had been a wealthy cotton factor who fathered her only child, who was currently finishing up his education in Paris. "He is a genius, my Roger. He will be returning home soon. You must meet him," she said, turning to Jim.

"A fine boy," Isaac said.

"Hippolyte provided very generously for Roger in his will, although the majority of his estate was bequeathed to his wife and legal children, in spite of the fact that they barely spoke for many years prior to his death. I was the only woman he truly loved. He told me so many times. Ah, if only I could find another man as fine as Hippolyte." She sighed, gazing at Isaac.

Later in the evening, fortune smiled on Jim as Delphine Desforges joined them, greeting Iris like a long-lost friend, kissing both her cheeks. No sooner had Iris presented Isaac and Jim to Delphine than she hastily whisked the merchant off to the dance floor, leaving Jim alone with the quadroon beauty.

"Well," he said. "shall we also dance?"

"I'm sorry, monsieur, but I can't," she replied regretfully. He noted that her eyes beneath their thick, dark lashes were a luminous gray-green. "You see, I am here only with my little cousin, not for my own amusement."

"Please, just one dance," Jim persisted.

"Really, I must refuse," she said. "You see, I have a protector. If he should learn that I was dancing with another man, he would be displeased."

Ignoring her protests, Jim took her by the hand and pulled her to the center of the floor.

Enveloped quickly by the captivating music of an orchestra composed entirely of black musicians—the only black men permitted anywhere near the ballroom —Jim felt the accumulated fatigue of the past week disappear. With Delphine in his arms, he wanted to dance forever. It was a marvelous feeling—one he had almost forgotten—and he pulled her as close as she would permit. In addition to being exceptionally attractive, Delphine was light on her feet, her body soft and supple. As they spun about the floor, she smiled at him, gazing into his eyes with more interest than her initial reluctance to dance would have indicated possible.

"I want to see you again," he said.

"I'm sorry, I can't," she replied, a note of regret in her voice.

"I must see you," he insisted.

"It's impossible."

"Nothing's impossible," he said, and pulled her still closer. The whirling dance and the alcohol Jim had drunk made him bold. Before Delphine could prevent him, he stole a kiss, and then another, slipping his tongue deep into her mouth.

Delphine felt as if she were going to faint, as if she were flying, not dancing, across the ballroom floor, locked in the strong arms of this tall, fair man, so unlike the Creole men in her past. One part of her mind shrilled a warning: To accept another man's advances here, in public, was madness; Bourrier was sure to find out! But the other part, the womanly part, forced the lovely quadroon to return Jim's kiss, his masculine scent weakening her as no other man's aura ever had.

Jim steered Delphine across the dance floor to a corner dimly lit for just such a tête-à-tête. Around them other couples were beginning those relationships which would allow plantation masters release and secure advancement for their dark, lusty ladies.

"I don't care who you belonged to in the past," Jim whispered. "It doesn't matter—"

"You don't understand," Delphine interrupted. "It is no longer my choice. I belong to Étienne Bourrier. He has schooled me, supported me, made me the person you see here before you. He would kill before allowing another man to steal my love."

"As I shall," Jim said, kissing her again. Gently he caressed her breasts, feeling her nipples rise to his touch beneath the taut, thin fabric of her bodice.

"As you *have, chéri* . . ." And with that she tore away, leaving Jim with a depth of passion previously unexperienced in his young life. Left him with her perfume in the air, and his throbbing blood coursing through his brain and between his thighs.

❧ 10

At the last moment Placide decided that they would take the steamboat upriver to Florestal and ordered Cecil to return the barouche to the carriage house. In addition to Verbena and Romulus, who would be traveling with them as always, several other house slaves, carrying torches of kerosene-soaked rags both for illumination and to keep away the swarming mosquitoes, escorted the four of them to the bateau.

Aboard the paddle-wheeler, Placide headed immediately for the saloon, hoping to assuage his annoyance at having to attend what he considered a boring affair with liquor and a lively game of craps. The

thought of spending the evening with the Valdéz—
Uncle Efrén with his gout and old-fashioned ideas,
silly Aunt Adela with her endless chatter and visions
of a brilliant marriage for her son, and sickly Narciso
with his moldy tomes of ancient Spanish poetry and
harpsichord—was insufferable. He cursed himself for
having allowed Adela to coax him into attending the
ball by hinting that it might well be the last birthday
poor Narciso would ever celebrate.

*What a fool I am to have agreed to go—especially
when there is a quadroon ball in town tonight,* he
thought as he vigorously shook the dice and gazed out
the window at the stern-wheel churning the dark water
and leaving in its path a trace of white foam.

In another part of the boat, Odile was avoiding her
fellow passengers, most of whom were also going to
the Valdéz plantation, and sulking about the restric-
tions her brother had placed upon her: She was not
to dance more than two dances with any one man—
including Narciso—champagne was forbidden except
for toasts, and before leaving Mandragore he had ordered that the décolletage of her mauve gown be severely reduced by the insertion of lace.

"You are going from mourner to tart in a single
step," he had said.

At the earliest opportunity, Odile vowed, she would
rip out the lace which Verbena had been commanded
to sew into the neck of the gown. She realized that
her enjoyment of the evening was dependent on
Placide's becoming bored and leaving early, which,
knowing his inclinations, she felt certain he would do.

When the boat stopped at the Florestal landing the
sounds of a lively slave orchestra echoed through the
warm night from the great house, which stood several
hundred yards from the river. Slaves with lanterns met
the guests and escorted them to the mansion.

Adela Valdéz, a slender, fluttery, birdlike woman,
greeted them at the door and hugged and kissed Odile
and Placide effusively. "My very favorite niece and
nephew!" she exclaimed, adding in a whisper, "But
don't tell the others. How delightful you all could
come."

Her husband, Efrén, plump, short, and square-shouldered with a florid complexion dotted with yellowish lumps clustered around his eyes and the lobes of his ears, scarcely resembled his late sister, Maristela, Odile and Placide's mother. He chose to receive the guests from a velvet chair in the parlor, where he sat resting his foot, swathed in linen bandages, on a wooden gout stool.

"This damned gout," he cursed as he shook hands with Placide. "I hope you never get it, my boy. They say it runs in families, you know."

Later, Adela took Odile aside and confided that Narciso would have been heartbroken if she hadn't come. "I'm so glad your brother changed his mind."

"So am I," Odile agreed, anxiously looking into the crowded ballroom just beyond the parlor for Narciso, who was nowhere in sight.

"Aunt Carlota is here all the way from Havana with your cousins Ernesto and Luis," Adela chattered on. "My, how those boys have grown! And so handsome, too!"

"What about little Beatriz?" Odile asked, referring to her Cuban aunt's youngest daughter, who, although ten years of age, was still referred to as "little" and probably always would be.

"She remained behind in Cuba."

"And Narciso?" Odile finally asked. "Where is he? I don't see him."

Adela's face took on a serious, concerned expression. "He's in his room," she answered quietly. "The anticipation of the ball proved a bit of a strain for him. Dr. Zehner ordered him to bed after he took a spell this afternoon."

"How is he now?" Odile asked.

"The doctor is with him upstairs."

Odile glanced behind her to see if Verbena still had the birthday gifts she had brought for Narciso.

"I got them right here, Miss Odile," the maid assured her, holding up the fancifully wrapped packages. In addition to the volume of poetry, she had discovered a Swiss music box which played "J'ai perdu mon Euridice" from Gluck's *Orphée et Euridice,*

Narciso's favorite opera. Last season they had shared a box and heard it at the French Opera House, and Narciso had reached out in the darkness and laid his hand on her thigh during this particular aria. Thinking of it even now brought on a strange tingling within her. Narciso's dark sexuality excited her in strange, perplexing ways that other men did not.

Seeing the packages, Adela said, "Why don't you take them to him?"

Upstairs, a strong medicinal odor pervaded the dank air of Narciso's gloomy room, with its book-lined walls and harpsichord in the corner.

Narciso sat propped against a mound of pillows beneath the high tester of the ornately carved rosewood bed, looking pale and weak. His slight frame seemed overwhelmed by the vastness of the room and its massive furniture.

Dr. Maurice Zehner, the family physician, a German from Alsace-Lorraine, sat on the edge of the bed, taking Narciso's pulse and looking grave. He had treated both the Valdéz and the Martinon families for many years.

The moment the youth's eyes, with their extravagantly long, dark lashes, caught sight of Odile, his face brightened and a pinkish color suffused his sunken, pallid cheeks.

"Odile!" he cried. "Dearest cousin—"

"Please," Zehner cautioned. "You must not become excited."

Snatching his wrist out of the doctor's hand, Narciso threw aside the covers, swung his scrawny legs over the side of the bed, and ran to greet her in his ruffled nightshirt.

Verbena was scandalized. "Please, Mr. Narciso!" she said, attempting to interpose herself between the two young people. "That is no way for a gentleman to greet a young lady."

With surprising vigor, Narciso shoved the maid aside and threw his arms around Odile, squeezing her in an ardent embrace.

"This is not good for your condition, my boy," the doctor sniffed. "Not good at all."

Seemingly improved by Odile's appearance, Narciso insisted on dressing and going downstairs despite the warnings of the doctor and the admonitions of his mother, who had been called in to mediate.

When the orchestra, composed of the musically talented slaves at Florestal, struck up the grand march, Narciso pranced around the ballroom with Odile on his arm while Adela and Efrén looked on in delight and Placide shook his head in disgust.

Resplendent in his blue velvet frock coat and cream-colored trousers, Narciso danced until well past midnight, seeking Odile for his partner at every possible opportunity in spite of her halfhearted protests that he was neglecting the other female guests.

"Remember what your brother done told you," Verbena warned Odile, referring to Placide's edict that she not dance more than two dances with any one man.

Knowing that Placide had retired to the taproom over the warming kitchens in the rear of the house to continue the game he had begun on the boat, Odile ignored the slave's warning. "Who cares what he says?" she answered flippantly.

"Don't you go getting yourself too tired," Verbena cautioned, trying another tack when Narciso came to ask her mistress to dance a lively quadrille with him.

"I could dance all night," Odile declared as she dashed off, hand in hand with Narciso, to join the three other couples making up the quadrille.

Later in the evening, Odile, remembering her promise to Eugénie, sought out her Aunt Carlota, a rather imperious lady with a distinctly Latin look, whose English was thickly accented and imitated the staccato rhythms of her native Cuban Spanish.

"My sister, Eugénie, says she must speak to you while you are here," Odile said, urgency in her voice.

"Really?" Carlota said coldly, fluttering her lacy fan. "And what is the reason for this request?"

"I don't know," Odile admitted. "I am only relating her message."

With a trace of annoyance in her voice, the Latin woman said, "The Ursuline convent is very far."

"Only a couple of hours by river boat," Odile reminded her.

"I know what she wants to find out. That's why I refused to answer her letters," Carlota said, snapping her fan closed and turning away from Odile. "It's better for everyone if she hears nothing."

11

For the remainder of the quadroon ball Jim trailed Delphine wherever she went, imploring her to see him again, scarcely able to tear himself away from her. For the moment Odile Martinon had been obliterated from his mind. Eventually, when his attentions became too obvious, Iris, worried about her friend's safety, took it upon herself to steer him toward other, more available girls.

"Come," she said, grasping him firmly by the arm. "You must meet the daughter of my good friend Cecile. Such a sweet child with the voice of an angel. She was at school with my Aurélie and took all the prizes in music."

While Jim danced an obligatory dance with the angelic-voiced girl of fifteen or sixteen, Iris reproached Delphine for her part in the flirtation.

"If Bourrier were to hear how you've been carrying on with that Yankee tonight, both of you would be in a lot of trouble," she warned.

"I've only been dancing." Delphine shrugged indifferently. "There's no harm in that."

"Everybody can see by the looks he's been giving you that in his mind he's already bedded down with you," Iris went on.

Delphine smiled slyly. "Then I hope it was a pleasant experience for him," she retorted.

When the dance concluded, Jim immediately went in search of Delphine, who had been led off to a powder-room by Iris, and encountered Isaac instead.

"I can understand your interest in Delphine," he said, tapping Jim on the chest with his finger. "I find her attractive myself. But I don't dance with her, and I'll tell you why. I don't dance with her because she belongs to Étienne Bourrier."

Impatiently Jim said, "I've heard that several times before, tonight. Bourrier doesn't scare me."

"Let me tell you, there are at least a dozen men in early graves because of Bourrier. He's a champion swordsman. He hasn't lost a duel yet. Once a man like that challenges you, you're as good as dead."

"If he wants to challenge me, I welcome it," Jim said.

Sometime after midnight there was a flurry of excitement throughout the ballroom, and at first Jim merely shrugged it off, assuming that yet another fist-fight had broken out. There had been several brawls during the evening, and the participants had been quickly escorted to the door by the burly Irish bouncer.

"Every quadroon ball ends up in at least two or three duels. It never fails," Isaac assured Jim.

The commotion now, however, was over not a fight but over the entrance of Placide Martinon, accompanied by his body servant, Romulus. Since the start of his affair with Denise Couronneau, Placide's attendance at the balls had been infrequent. Several of the chaperones assumed that his presence meant that he was once more on the prowl for a young mistress and felt encouraged. There were very few bachelors as eligible as this debonair young planter, and every fading quadroon dreamed of him as the protector of her daughter or niece.

"So," Iris said, hands on hips, "another gentleman-of-means has deserted the white trivets to gather black grapes. Placide Martinon! What a catch for a girl." With that, she scurried off to find her niece and try to finagle some way for her path to cross the Creole planter's.

With Iris gone and Isaac trailing after her, Jim once again sought out Delphine, and found her among another group of her friends. When he interrupted and, raising several eyebrows, asked her to dance, she readily accepted.

"Tell me when and where I can see you again," he insisted as they whirled about the floor. "I won't take no for an answer."

Delphine surveyed the ballroom anxiously, as though to be certain no one was listening or watching them.

"I have a little cottage near the ramparts—close to St. Philip Street. It's white, and in the window you will see a vase with roses. Red roses mean that Bourrier is in town and I can see no one. White roses mean he is away," she said.

"Red for danger. White for safety," he said.

"Yes." She nodded.

"Then when I see white roses I can come to you?"

"And we shall have our time." She smiled.

Overcome with excitement at her promise, Jim drew the beautiful quadroon close in an embrace.

"You must never touch me again in public!" she gasped. "Someone may see us and tell Étienne. Please, we must be discreet for both our sakes."

During the course of the ball, which lasted until dawn, it was inevitable that Jim and Placide should cross paths, although it was obvious that the prominent planter didn't relish Jim's presence at the same affair.

"Ah, my neighbor," he said coolly, keeping his hand closed over the handle of his riding crop instead of extending it to Jim.

Jim nodded, equally coolly.

"I am gratified to see that you don't spend all your time groveling in the mud," Placide said. "And that you have a taste for our beauties of mixed blood. The one you were dancing with, Delphine, is especially lovely. It's too bad that my friend Étienne Bourrier has made her unavailable. Too bad indeed."

❦ 12

O dile had not been in the least surprised when
Placide confided to her that he was bored with
Narciso's birthday celebration and was taking the next
steamboat into New Orleans, especially since she had
overheard Romulus tell Verbena that one of the notorious quadroon balls was simultaneously in progress.
Before leaving, he arranged with Adela, who was none
too pleased at the prospect of his departure, for Odile
to spend the night at Florestal, promising to send Cecil
with a coach for her the following day. Seeking out
Verbena, who had been assigned to assist Kitty in the
cookhouse, preparing the midnight supper, Placide
instructed her to see that Odile behaved in a manner
of which he would approve.

"I'll do my best, Marse Placide," the slave promised
as she stirred the enormous copper kettle full of her
own special gumbo. "But you know Miss Odile. That
child's done got a mind of her own."

The moment Placide was gone, Odile went straight
to Narciso and informed him that they were now free
to dance together as much as they pleased. "Until
dawn, if we wish." She laughed.

"Until dawn it is," he said, and took her in his arms
for a waltz.

At dawn, the remaining guests gathered under the
huge oaks on the front lawn for a hearty breakfast of
ham, eggs, sausages, grits, corn bread, relishes, jams,
jellies, boiled peanuts, and coffee. They sat about on
cushions, afghans, quilts, and blankets, weary but
happy, and cheered as the sun rose over the east bank
of the river. A group of slaves gathered around Narciso, making impromptu music with instruments fash-

ioned from whatever was at hand—goatskin drums, bamboo flutes, gourds—accompanying a young black girl who did an impromptu dance, her bare feet scarcely touching the ground.

Taking Odile's hand in his, Narciso pressed it to his lips. "Your being here like this is the finest birthday gift anyone could ask for," he murmured.

After breakfast the revelers departed, and Odile went to a guest room on the second floor, where a weary Verbena helped her undress.

"My feets is aching," the slave complained.

"Mine feel wonderful," Odile said as she kicked off her satin dancing slippers. "I could still be dancing."

As she was donning her nightgown, Adela came in.

"How can I ever thank you, child?" she said, clasping Odile's cheeks between her hands and kissing her squarely on the mouth. "You alone worked a miracle tonight. Before you arrived Narciso took a terrible spell. Dr. Zehner was very pessimistic about his prognosis. But when you arrived he was well in a flash. And did you see him? He danced with every woman present. And it's a good thing, too, with some of the men like your brother, deserting our young ladies and running off to those low activities in the city. I could scarcely get him to rest. My, he did have a wonderful time."

Odile had to agree that she had never seen Narciso in such good spirits. At times during the evening he had appeared almost frenzied, his normally pallid face flushed, his eyes gleaming, beads of perspiration trickling down his forehead, and she worried that the exertion might produce another of his spells.

"Oh, the ball was such a success!" Adela went on. "I do believe everyone had a marvelous time, don't you? Well, if I've done nothing else for my son, at least I've given him this ball to remember." Embracing Odile a second time, she said, "How much happiness you have given my son!"

Embarrassed, Odile said, "I did nothing special."

"Such modesty," Adela chided.

"Hah!" Verbena grunted as she folded one of Odile's many petticoats.

Changing to a quiet, almost supplicating tone, Adela asked, "Odile, dearest, would you do your aunt one last little favor?"

"What's that?" Odile asked, noticing that Verbena was eyeing the small, birdlike woman suspiciously.

"This child needs her rest," the maid put in.

Ignoring her, Adela continued to address herself to Odile. "Would you tiptoe into Narciso's room and say good night to him before you retire?"

"Now you know, Miss Adela, that it ain't fitting for a young lady to go to no gentleman's bedchamber," Verbena protested.

"In this case I can assure you it will be perfectly all right," Adela said.

"Stop being a silly goose, Verbena," Odile chided. "What can be the harm in slipping into my cousin's room for a moment and saying good night to him?"

"You know your brother would never allow it," the maid reminded her.

"Why should she mind a brother who is rude enough to leave our lovely ball to go off to other more base entertainments, leaving the lovely daughters of some of this state's finest families without dancing partners?" Adela argued. "Placide is the one who should be ashamed."

"Aunt Adela is right," Odile agreed, reaching for a wrapper to throw over her nightgown. "I shall go and say good night to Narciso."

Verbena shook her head. "Your brother's going to whip us both if he finds out," she warned. "Don't say I ain't warned you."

"Verbena, I want you to go downstairs right away and help Kitty put the silver away," Adela said.

"I ain't leaving here until I knows Miss Odile is safe in her bed," the slave said adamantly.

Struggling to control her anger, Adela said, "You will go downstairs this instant or I shall call Samples." Munro Samples was the overseer at Florestal. He had a reputation for sadism, and the mere mention of his name was enough to frighten any slave into obedience.

"Yes, ma'am," Verbena acquiesced, and reluctantly she left the room, pouting.

At the doorway of her son's room, Adela kissed Odile good night and disappeared into her own room, closing the door behind her. Odile could hear Efrén's loud snoring from within, and Carlota talking in Spanish to her maid next door. Her sons, Luis and Ernesto, were housed out in the *garçonnière*.

On tiptoes she approached Narciso's bed in the darkened room, its shutters closed against the brilliant early-morning sunshine. Snuggled down among the covers, wearing a lace-trimmed ivory nightshirt, Narciso smiled as she drew near and reached out his hand to her.

"Dearest Odile," he whispered, pulling her close with wiry strength. "I'm so glad you've come. Thank you."

He took her hand and pressed it to his lips, as he had done earlier on the lawn, and when she made no attempt to draw it away, he began slowly and sensuously to kiss her fingers individually, drawing each into his mouth and running his tongue over the tips in tiny circles. Little shivers of excitement ran down Odile's spine, and she lost her balance, tumbling onto the bed beside him.

As she tried to get up, he put his arms around her and restrained her. "Stay," he whispered.

"I can't," she protested. "Oh, please, Narciso, I mustn't."

He rolled over on her, partially pinning her to the bed. Odile marveled at the sinewy hardness of the invalid's slender body. Though ill, Narciso's lifelong convalescent diet and special exercises had left him trim and fit in terms of musculature.

"Narciso, you're too heavy, you're hurting me," she whimpered. "Please let me go."

Instead of complying, he increased his weight on her, and at the same time pressed his mouth against hers, poking his tongue between her soft lips. Then, taking her hand, he forced it between his legs. She tried to pull it away.

"Don't be afraid to touch me, dearest Odile."

"I don't want to," she protested.

"But I want you to. Please . . . it feels good."

Obligingly she allowed him to press her fingers around his turgid hardness, enclosing it in her trembling hand. She was surprised that the fierce pounding of his heart was transmitted below as steady pulsations.

Overcome by the surge of conflicting emotions she was feeling, Odile gasped, "Please stop, Narciso! Someone will come in. Your mother—"

"My mother is asleep."

"Kitty—"

"She's occupied in the kitchens."

"Verbena—"

"She's with Kitty."

"Aunt Carlota—"

"No one will come in," he assured her as he slipped her wrapper off and her nightgown over her head with practiced hands.

Shivering with excitement, Narciso tossed away his nightshirt and stretched his body above Odile's nude, vulnerable form. Supporting himself on his arms, he licked first one and then the other of Odile's nipples, watching as they rose to meet the flicking tip of his tongue. Slowly he licked and caressed each part of her body, watching her protestations turn to writhing gasps of pleasure.

To Odile it seemed as if Narciso's tongue was painting her with liquid fire. All thoughts of spurning his affections were lost as the dark lover of her childhood dreams enveloped her in unimagined sensuality.

Narciso lowered himself and slowly rubbed his body the length of Odile's outstretched form, savoring the velvety softness of her creamy skin. He slid his hardness into her open, wet center, and Odile found that she had no mind left with which to protest or question how this had come to pass. Odile, aristocrat, princess of Mandragore, lost her identity as she and her Narciso rocked and clasped and moaned their way to sweet oblivion.

Odile awoke in a panic. From the position of the sun—high in the sky—she realized that it was already late afternoon. Beside her, Narciso lay on his stomach, his face buried in the pillow, breathing in long sighs, his naked body bathed in a thin film of perspiration, one arm flung across Odile's chest.

Oh, dear God! she gasped to herself. Sliding deftly from beneath his arm, she got out of bed and looked about for her nightgown and wrapper. Where had Narciso tossed them? Anxious to cover her nakedness, she crawled about the floor on her hands and knees, her heart pounding wildly, while her cousin slept blissfully in the afternoon heat.

Finally recovering her nightclothes from under the bed, she put them on quickly and fretted about what kind of alibi she could possibly concoct to save herself from ruin. How on earth could she possibly explain these hours alone with Narciso in his bedroom to her aunt—and, worse, to Verbena? She shuddered in dread at the thought of facing the maid who had been her personal guardian since infancy, when she suckled at the black woman's breast. Casting a final glance at the man with whom she had made love in the early hours of the morning, his exposed buttocks reflecting a thin ribbon of sunlight that pierced the slats in the jalousied shutters, she crossed herself and murmured a prayer for luck and headed for the door. Opening it a crack, she peered out into the hall.

No one seemed to be stirring. She could probably return to her room undetected, but she would still have to account for the hours spent in Narciso's arms. The prospect of Verbena's inevitable questioning filled her with fear and anguish. When the story was related to Placide, would he force her into the convent, too? There was no bribe short of granting Verbena her freedom that would prevent the maid from telling him. For a moment she wondered why Verbena hadn't come looking for her—that was very strange. Why, when she had returned from helping Kitty with the silver and failed to find Odile in her bed, hadn't she tried to locate her? Certainly her concern about preserving Odile's good name was foremost in her mind. There seemed to be no ready explanation for Verbena's lapse of vigilance, and Odile was puzzled by it.

Silently she slipped out of the bedroom and tiptoed down the hall.

"Odile, is that you?" Adela's voice called out.

Feeling her knees grow weak and wobbly beneath her, Odile grabbed the doorknob of the guest room for support as her aunt dashed out of her own room across the hall.

"So you're finally awake?" Adela said. "What about my son?"

"Your son?" Odile repeated automatically.

"You were just in his room, weren't you?"

"Well, yes, I . . ." Odile hesitated.

"Is he awake or not?" Adela persisted.

"I don't know."

"Then I'll just have to see for myself."

"No. Don't wake him," Odile said, the image of the naked Narciso fresh in her mind.

Adela looked at her with a puzzled frown. "Then he *is* asleep?"

"I think so," Odile said. She entered her own room filled with apprehension.

Whenever she stayed overnight at Florestal, Verbena always slept in the guest room with her on Efrén's folding campaign bed, a relic of his days in the military under Andrew Jackson. As a child Odile had been subject to nightmares and insisted that the maid not leave her, and thus the practice had started. Quickly scanning the room, Odile saw with surprise that the campaign bed was untouched. Verbena had apparently slept elsewhere. Odile breathed a sigh of relief. *Thank God!* she said to herself as she headed straight for the big canopied bed, attempting to rumple the linens so that it would appear slept in.

Just as she was pummeling a pillow to make it look as though her head had lain on it all night, Adela entered, and Odile started at the sound of her voice.

"I suppose you're wondering where Verbena is," she said. "The poor soul slept on a bench in the warming kitchen all night. I guess she had too much brandy."

"Brandy?" Odile repeated, knowing that Verbena's tolerance for liquor was extremely low.

"Yes. You see, she and Kitty did such a fine job

with the silver, I decided to give them a special treat —since it was my son's birthday and all. Personally, I don't believe in giving Negroes spirits, but this was a special occasion. To tell you the truth, dear," she said, patting Odile's trembling hand, "Verbena refused at first, and I had to practically force it on her. But once she had one drink, she kept coming back for more. Negroes are so weak where spirits are concerned. Naturally I didn't approve of her and Kitty drinking so much, but since I decided last night was special, I let them enjoy themselves more than is fitting or proper. Your Uncle Efrén will probably kill me when he finds out. While she was drinking glass after glass, Verbena kept fretting about you and how she'd better get upstairs to look after you, but I told her there was nothing to worry about. And I was right, wasn't I, honey?" Adela said, putting her arm around Odile and giving her a delighted hug.

Late in the afternoon, Odile bade farewell to the house slaves and Adela and Efrén, and to Carlota and her two sons, and climbed into the carriage, preparing to leave Florestal. When he got wind of her departure, Narciso, who had been sleeping, ran to the railing of the second-story gallery in his nightshirt and called to Odile that she had forgotten something. Instead of sending one of the slaves to fetch whatever it was, as Efrén suggested, Odile got out of the carriage and announced that she would go herself, since she had not had the opportunity to say good-bye to Narciso. As she hurried toward the house, Verbena called after her, "Don't you run up no stairs! A lady don't never run up stairs."

In his room, Narciso gathered her in a last fervent embrace. "I don't want you to go," he declared.

"But I must," she insisted, tenderly kissing his drawn, pale face, the lips tinged once again with blue.

"But when will I see you again?"

"I don't know. It will be difficult to come back soon. Placide is already too suspicious. You know how he disapproves."

"Listen, there will be a special mass celebrated here

for the safe return to Cuba of Aunt Carlota and our cousins. Surely he will permit you to attend," he said.

"I don't know," Odile replied. "He's so unpredictable."

Squeezing her very tight with a kind of desperation, he implored, "You must try to come. Promise me."

"I promise," she agreed, kissing him tenderly.

As she was descending the stairs, he leaned over the banister and called after her, "When you do come back I shall have every poem in the volume memorized and recite them all to you."

As the barouche clattered down the carriageway toward the River Road, Narciso was still standing on the gallery, waving and shouting promises to her.

During the trip from Florestal to Mandragore, while the barouche lurched and bounced over the badly rutted River Road, Verbena moaned and groaned and clutched her stomach, going so far as to ask Cecil to stop several times.

"Oh, mercy," she complained, rolling her eyes skyward. "I've never stayed so sick."

While Verbena suffered, Odile reviewed the events of the previous twenty-four hours. Just as in everything Narciso undertook, his lovemaking seemed propelled by a kind of inner frenzy, as though it might be the last thing he would ever do. For her, it had been the first time, although she had long contemplated what it might be like to make love, and her avid curiosity about the act had more or less prepared her for the awesomeness of her reaction. Certainly Narciso was an ardent lover with ferocious energy, but then, she had no one with whom to compare him.

As the carriage lumbered and swayed along, the horses raising great clouds of dust, Odile's thoughts wandered inexplicably from her thin, sickly cousin to the strapping Jim MacKay, and she found herself wondering what sort of lover he might be. Certainly, physically and in many other ways he was the direct antithesis of the frail, sensitive Narciso. True, this rugged, uncouth Yankee with the sun-streaked hair could never recite that marvelously sensuous, ironic, and slightly acerbic Spanish poetry, or play the harpsichord with such skill, but he possessed a kind of vigor and drive she found somehow appealing, although she wished he had a greater sense of dignity and responsibility as a white man and would stop his degrading nigger work. The contrast between the two men could not have been greater, and she wondered how she could feel drawn to two such diverse types at the same time.

Since childhood she had loved Narciso and felt a great, though perhaps unnecessary, need to protect him, fascinated by the aura of sickness that seemed to hover around him and made him unique and different from other children. It was his physical disability —never clearly defined but vaguely associated with his heart—that had dictated a childhood apart from his contemporaries. Months on end in bed had made him a voracious reader. Forbidden participation in all sports and vigorous activities, he gravitated to music and became a near virtuoso on the harpsichord. Yet underneath the apparent delicacy and sensitivity lurked a certain masculine spirit yearning to break free, to disregard the defective body in which it was imprisoned and express itself in vigorous ways. Last night, Odile believed, that spirit had finally burst forth, and she was proud to have played a part in its liberation.

When her father was alive, she thought, there might have been some possibility of marrying Narciso, a dream they had both cherished since childhood, but under Placide's guardianship such a union seemed unlikely. She was certain her brother was saving her for much bigger stakes.

As they approached Mandragore Verbena made a desperate attempt to pull herself together, fearing Placide's wrath if he learned that she had been drinking and, as a result, remiss in her duties toward her charge. Odile was certain the slave had no idea she had spent the night in any bed except the one intended for her.

As the barouche continued down the winding River Road, they passed Jim's land. Odile spotted him splitting logs in front of the cabin he was erecting and waved to him. Resting on the handle of his ax, he wiped the sweat from his forehead and waved back.

"Who you waving to, child?" Verbena asked.

"Mr. MacKay," she replied.

"You got no business waving to that Yankee trash. Look at him out there, working hisself like a field nigger. Now you stop that waving, hear?"

"There are worse things than waving," she retorted with a mysterious smile.

❧ 13

Isaac's newly opened store appeared to be a success, with the number of customers increasing every day. A shrewd, experienced trader, he sensed what the needs of the people were and how much they were willing to pay, and he knew where to obtain quality goods. As any new endeavor will, the store made increasing demands on his time and energy, and when living quarters in the two floors above the store became vacant, he decided to leave his room at Alphonsine's and move there.

Jim had serious doubts that he would continue to live at the boardinghouse once the merchant was gone. The ride back and forth to his land every day was a long one, exhausting after a hard day in the fields. Off and on for the last month he had been building a cabin on the newly reclaimed land as temporary housing, and now, with Isaac gone, it seemed like a good time to contemplate living there permanently. Aside from Isaac and Alphonsine, Jim had little more than a polite, nodding acquaintance with the other boarders at the house, except for a German immigrant named Hans Oberdorfer, who spoke broken, guttural English and worked on the docks. In the evening Hans and Jim frequently played dominoes together in the parlor.

When Alphonsine was gone, Isaac asked Jim, "Have you seen Delphine since the ball?"

"No," Jim replied.

"In one way it's too bad, but in another it's good," Isaac said, checking the bureau drawer to be sure he hadn't forgotten to pack any of his belongings. "You start seeing her and pretty soon you get into trouble with Bourrier."

Recently, unbeknown to anyone, Jim had taken to riding past the white cottage near the ramparts, where the graceful vase in the window remained discouragingly filled with red roses.

One day as he was passing, he ran into Iris, herself en route to Delphine's. "Better stay away from her," the older quadroon warned. "Bourrier's in town. God only knows how long he'll stay this time. Poor Delphine is so skittish. He watches her like a hawk. I think he got wind that she went to the ball and flirted all night with a blond Yankee. It was probably that maid of hers. I don't trust that Darcie any more than I would a cottonmouth."

Isaac decided to move his belongings to the new residence on a Sunday, and he and Jim loaded everything in a small cart, which they hitched to the back of Jim's horse. Alphonsine wept as they headed down the street toward the French Market.

"I wonder if Alphonsine will cry when I tell her I'm moving, too," Jim said musingly.

Isaac stared at him in amazement. "Moving? Where?"

"To my own land."

"I think you're crazy. There's nothing there. Well, anyway, I'd like your opinion on something." The merchant removed a folded sheet of paper from his pocket, smoothed out the creases, and handed it to Jim. "Read this."

Jim read the letter and passed it back to Isaac with a puzzled frown. "I don't understand. 'Pleasing, prosperous merchant, good appearance, thirty-five years of age, good health, good provider, devout Jew, no bad smoking or drinking habits . . .' " he quoted.

"It's for the *shadchen*," Isaac said, using the Yiddish word for a matchmaker. "He's in New York. I'm writing to ask him to find me a nice girl. I wrote this because I want the girl to know exactly what she's getting. I don't want her to be disappointed. You should get married, too. It's no good for a man to be alone. Take it from me, I should have married ten years ago, when I was your age."

"I'll get married someday," Jim said.

"And in the meantime you're going to live in a cabin in the middle of the swamps?"

"For a while."

"Well, you don't have to worry. When you bring in your first crop and have money, you'll have plenty of girls chasing after you," Isaac assured him.

Jim wanted to respond that he didn't want "plenty of girls"—he wanted Delphine—but he remained silent. Since the night of the quadroon ball he had thought of little else. True, she had not totally erased from his mind Odile Martinon, with her patrician bearing and striking beauty, but Delphine was warmer, less arrogant, and—most important—more available. In spite of repeated warnings about Bourrier's volatile temper and his reputation as an expert dueler, Jim was willing to take the risk in order to be with Delphine again, and longed to see white roses in her window.

One hot afternoon, after what seemed like hours and hours of splitting logs, Jim finally laid his ax aside and decided to quit for the day.

After bathing in the river, he hopped onto his horse and headed back to town and the cottage near the ramparts. He had become so accustomed to seeing red roses in the window that the change to white blooms didn't register at first.

Jubilant, he jumped off his horse, tied it to the hitching post outside, and ran to the door and knocked.

In a few minutes a haughty black maid, her head tied up in a red kerchief, opened the door a crack. "What you want?" she demanded.

"I'm here to see Miss Delphine, please," he answered politely, hat in hand.

"Miss Delphine don't see nobody," she snapped, and tried to close the door in his face. Getting a whiff of familiar perfume, Jim slammed his foot against the doorjamb, preventing her from shutting it.

"If you ain't got your foot out of there by the time I count three, I'm going to scream," she threatened.

From inside, he heard Delphine's husky voice. "What's the trouble, Darcie?" she called.

"Some riffraff trying to force his way in here," the maid replied.

"Delphine, it's me—Jim," he called out.

In seconds Delphine, in a brilliant green silk dressing gown, appeared at the door, looking surprised to see him. "What are you doing here?" she asked coldly.

Her demeanor astonished him. Hadn't she arranged the signal in the window? "The white roses—" he said.

"You have no right to come here," she reproached him. "You'd better go."

"I don't understand—"

Cutting him off again, she snapped, "You heard me! You'd better go."

Hurt and puzzled at first, Jim suddenly realized that she was unable to talk freely in front of the maid.

"I've come about those bolts of silk you ordered from Mr. DaCosta's store," he said, deciding on a ruse to test his supposition.

Her face brightened instantly, and Jim knew he had made the correct assumption. "Why didn't you say so in the first place instead of trying to force your way in here and frightening my maid half to death," she said reproachfully, opening the door to admit him. "Where is that silk? Why hasn't it been delivered?"

"That's what I'm here to explain, ma'am," he said.

"Let's go in the parlor," she suggested.

The maid followed them and hovered about, pretending to be occupied with a potted fern.

"Darcie, would you bring us something cool to drink?" Delphine said. "It's frightfully hot today, don't you think, sir?"

"Quite," Jim agreed.

"We ain't got no ice," the maid retorted.

"Then go to the icehouse and get some," Delphine directed.

"That's all the way down by the river," the girl whined.

"The walk will do you good. You may carry my new parasol if you like," Delphine replied. "Now hurry and run along."

Reluctantly the maid shuffled off, grumbling under her breath. When she was gone, Delphine breathed a sigh of relief. "That girl," she said, shaking her head.

Excited to see her once again, Jim reached out to embrace her, but Delphine resisted until she had closed the sliding doors leading to the hall and the jalousied shutters over the French windows overlooking the street. Assured that they were safe from prying eyes, Delphine threw herself into Jim's arms with unexpected abandon, covering his face with fervent kisses.

"I've wanted to see you so," she breathed. "I've been thinking of you constantly since the ball. I thought Bourrier would never leave. It seemed like an eternity. Once I glimpsed you passing the house on your horse. I wanted to run out into the street and call to you. I was so afraid you would tire of finding red roses day after day and stop coming back."

"I was beginning to think it was hopeless," he said, caressing her neck and shoulders.

"Every day with Bourrier grew more insufferable. I longed to see you, to have you hold me in your arms like this."

"Why do you stay with Bourrier?"

She smiled a twisted, ironic smile. "What choice do I have?"

"You could leave him."

"And then what would I do? Besides, I fear the revenge he would carry out if I did. His wrath knows no bounds. He can be diabolical if he wants to be. Besides, I owe all I am and all I have to him. He's the only man I've ever known. He took me from my mother at thirteen and sent me to France to be educated. When I returned I automatically became his mistress. I had no other choice."

"You couldn't run away? Leave him?"

"And then what would become of me? I have no talents. I could not become a dressmaker or a milliner. I would probably end up at Mother Easter's over in 'The Swamps' behind a red curtain, like so many other girls with no means or family," she said. "Besides, I am weak and spoiled. Since girlhood I have only known a life of ease and luxury—nothing else. The price is, of course, being at the disposal of a man who possesses me body and soul, who has usurped my freedom. Fortunately, since the death of his uncle Étienne has had to spend a great deal of his time in Martinique, so I have been able to breathe a bit. But when he is here I simply endure. If there is one thing I have learned, it is to endure."

Touched by her plight, Jim caressed her hair and kissed both eyelids. Beneath them, her gray-green eyes were brimming with tears. "Delphine . . . Delphine . . . I can't believe you are really in my arms at last."

"I'm so happy . . . so happy," she murmured, slipping one hand inside his shirt and the other along the inside of his thigh. "I want you, Jim. I want you so badly."

"And the maid?" he asked, apprehensively glancing at the doors.

"She won't be back for a while," Delphine assured him, adding, "I know Bourrier has her spying on me. Probably he's promised her her freedom if she catches me in some grand infidelity. I am the slave of a slave," she said, laughing ironically. "Sometimes I am tired of it all and no longer care about anything." Placing her hand over his and pressing it to her full breast inside the dressing gown, she whispered, "I care only for you."

Jim removed his clothes, grinning at Delphine's approving stare as she visually devoured his tall, hard body. They made love slowly, intensely, their kisses turning to sighs as their bodies locked and sped to a swift mutual climax.

Jim covered his beloved Delphine with kisses, and the skilled mistress brought Jim to heights of incredible ecstasy.

It was only when the sounds of Delphine's maid returning penetrated their joy that Jim gathered his clothes and slipped away. He chuckled to himself as he made his way home. At last he understood Bourrier's determination to kill anyone who would steal away the precious Delphine.

❧ 14

Isaac rode out to Jim's place one Sunday, bringing him as a housewarming gift a plow, which shared the seat of a rented carriage with the merchant.

Greatly pleased by such a useful gift, Jim said, "Now all I need is a decent team of horses to pull it. I guess I'll have to go into the city and hire a pair when I get ready to plow in January."

"The city?" Isaac echoed, raising his eyebrows. "What about the next plantation?"

Assuming that Isaac was referring to Mandragore and not to the Pilette plantation, Palmetto Place, which lay upriver to the north, Jim said, "I haven't spoken to Placide Martinon since the night of the quadroon ball."

"Then speak to him."

"I hesitate to ask him," Jim admitted. "I don't exactly know why."

"Ask him," Isaac directed. "The worst he can say is no."

Encouraged by Isaac's advice, Jim decided to go to Martinon, bypassing Davis. For some unexplained reason, the overseer displayed such great animosity

toward Jim that Jim knew it would be a waste of time
to ask him for any kind of favor.

As he rode up the carriageway toward Mandragore,
Jim saw Placide on his horse, returning from the fields
with a huge sack. The Creole planter tossed the sack
to a young Negro groom who had run to help him with
the horse.

"You got yourself a whole mess of them blackbirds,
didn't you, Marse Placide," the boy said, smiling glee-
fully as he peeked into the bag.

"Take them on around back to the cookhouse and
give them to Verbena," Placide instructed the boy as
he dismounted. "Tell her I want them prepared for
dinner."

Romulus met his master on the gallery, relieved him
of his shotgun, and helped him off with his hunting
coat. As Placide shoved the heel of his boot into the
bootjack, he noticed Jim approaching.

"Good morning," Jim said, tipping his hat.

Eyeing him warily a moment, Placide asked, rather
coolly, "What can we do for you today, MacKay?"

"I'd like to talk to you a moment if I may," Jim
replied.

Indicating a wicker chair on the back gallery beneath an awning of cotton ticking, the planter motioned for him to have a seat.

"And what is it you wish to talk about?" he said,
handing the butler his mud-caked boots for cleaning.

"Well, you see, I'm hoping to plant in January—"
Jim began.

"How many arpents do you have ready?" Placide
interrupted.

"Approximately forty," Jim responded.

"I see." Placide nodded. "And what do you intend
to plant?"

"Cane," Jim answered. "I was wondering if I could
arrange to borrow a team of horses from you for the
plowing."

"That would depend upon whether or not we could
spare them at the time."

"Naturally I'm willing to pay whatever reasonable
fee you ask for the use of the horses," Jim added.

Amused, Placide grinned, perhaps remembering the

original sale of the land. "When have my fees not been reasonable?" Then, with a more serious expression, he added, "As far as I'm concerned, you may use them without payment. You will have to arrange it with Davis. He knows when we can most easily spare the horses."

"I didn't want to go to your overseer without taking up the matter with you first," Jim said.

"That was wise," Placide replied, reaching in his pocket for a cigar. "Not only can you borrow my horses, MacKay, you may borrow my slaves as well."

"I don't need slaves. I plan to do the work myself," Jim answered, remembering his father on the family farm in Ohio. He certainly had required no slaves.

Lighting the cigar, Placide raised his eyebrows incredulously. "Plow and plant forty arpents *yourself?*"

"That's my hope."

"As you probably know, MacKay, Mandragore is one of the largest and finest plantations in the state—perhaps the entire South. I have approximately three hundred slaves. With a number that large, it is important that they have absolute respect for white authority. If they lose this respect they are liable to become restless and rebellious. We have never had a slave uprising here, and I would not want to see one. It's not that we don't have the means to put down an uprising—we do. It's just that I don't want to see a lot of valuable property destroyed—and the slaves *are* property. Fortunately, I have an excellent overseer in Hiram Davis. He has his little idiosyncrasies, but I choose to overlook them as long as he does his job the way I want it done. He has methods for keeping even the most unruly black buck in line. From time to time he has been forced to make an example of a rebellious nigger, and I can assure you that when Hiram Davis is finished, the man—if he's still alive—is no longer rebellious." Placide paused and took a long drag on his cigar. "But I am getting away from my point," he said. "You are here because you need horses to plow your fields. I am willing to lend you my horses, but only if you agree to allow my slaves to do the plowing. You cannot work in the fields."

"The only way I'll let a slave work for me is for pay," Jim declared, regarding the Creole's terms as a kind of extortion.

"That won't be necessary," Placide answered. "I can assure you that the slaves at Mandragore are well taken care of. They are much too valuable to be ill-treated. A sick slave or an undernourished slave is a useless slave."

"Still, I would insist on paying them wages," Jim persisted stubbornly.

"Very well." Placide sighed impatiently. "If paying my slaves a wage will keep you from behind a plow, I will agree to a dollar a day per slave."

"A dollar a day it is." Jim nodded.

"Shall we drink to that?" Placide said, seizing on any excuse to imbibe, and signaled to Romulus to bring a bottle of brandy.

On the day Jim requested, about a dozen Martinon slaves, together with plows and teams of horses, appeared ready for work under the supervision of a powerful black driver named Dratt. Working steadily, they prepared the newly reclaimed ground, and Jim observed that for cane the ground had to be more deeply plowed than for other crops. When the furrows had been made, Dratt divided the slaves into three groups. One group cut off the top and side leaves of the seed cane, leaving only the part of the stalk to be planted. Each joint of a cane stalk had the capacity to sprout when buried in the soil. The second group of slaves laid the cane in the furrow, placing a pair of stalks side by side in such a way that joints— and thus future cane stalks—occurred approximately every four or five inches. The third group followed with hoes and covered the stalks with earth to the depth of three inches. In addition to supplying the slaves, horses, and equipment, Placide also agreed to supply the seedling cane. His unexpected generosity surprised Jim and made him wonder what sort of remuneration the Creole planter expected in addition to a dollar a day per slave.

In a ledger he got from Isaac Jim kept an accurate

account of each slave's name and the days worked, intending to pay them individually at the end of each week, but Placide was rigidly opposed to such a plan.

"You will not give money directly to my slaves," he said sternly. "A nigger with money in his pocket can be very difficult. We must keep them beholden to us for everything. A slave must depend completely on his master for his most basic needs. If you allow them the merest shred of independence, you are cutting your own throat. Therefore, MacKay, you will give all their wages to Davis. He will see that they receive what they need."

"But I want to be sure each is paid fairly for his work," Jim insisted.

"Davis will see that it is fair," the planter assured him. "I have complete confidence in him. I entrust the management of my slaves entirely to him. If I trust Davis with such responsibility, you must also trust him."

As they spoke they were riding along what would eventually be Jim's main canebreak.

"I'm not at all sure I have the same confidence in him you have," Jim said.

Annoyed by this remark, Placide jerked his horse's reins. "In any event," he said, preparing to depart, "if you wish to continue to use my slaves, you will allow Davis to handle all the monies. Is that understood?"

Knowing he could not risk Placide's withdrawing his slaves at such a crucial time, he was forced to nod his assent, although he hated the idea of turning the slaves' wages over to Davis, knowing full well it would probably never reach the hands of those who had earned it.

One evening, after a particularly strenuous day working the land, Jim rode into town and stopped at Isaac's store en route to Delphine's.

"Let me make some coffee," Isaac said, scooping a handful of coffee beans from a sack and transferring them to his grinder. He and Jim were in the stockroom at the rear of the store.

"What do you hear from the marriage broker?" Jim asked.

Isaac's face broke into a wide smile. "He thinks he's found me somebody—a girl from Amsterdam named Silvia. The trouble is, she's only eighteen."

"What's wrong with that?" Jim asked, perching on a barrel of flour.

"For you maybe eighteen is all right, but for me it's perhaps too young. Still, I'm going to write her. After some letters between us, I'll decide." Dumping the ground coffee into a pot, Isaac asked, "So how's the farming coming?"

"All right," Jim said. "It's a lot of hard work. I get pretty tired."

"What about lonesome? You don't get lonesome way out there?" Isaac inquired.

"That's why I came into town tonight."

Isaac squinted at him suspiciously. "But not to see me?"

"I came to see you too," Jim assured him.

"And who else?"

Hesitating a moment, Jim admitted, "Delphine."

Isaac shook his head sorrowfully. "So you're still seeing her?"

"Whenever I can."

"I don't want to tell you what to do," Isaac advised, "but maybe you should stop."

"Stop?" Jim questioned. "I look forward to my visits with Delphine."

"As a friend, I'm telling you to stay away from that girl. Iris told me people are already starting to gossip."

"I couldn't stay away from her."

"Don't you see how crazy it is?" Isaac said. "She belongs to Bourrier. He's a dangerous man."

"She doesn't love him."

"So what difference does that make?" Isaac sighed wearily. "I'm sorry I ever took you to that ball. I never thought this would happen. Poor Iris! She feels bad she introduced you to Delphine."

"It's my worry," Jim reminded him. "If it comes to a showdown with Bourrier over Delphine, I'm ready."

"Hah! Big talk," Isaac scoffed, searching in a cabinet for some coffee cups. "By the way," he continued, in a more amicable tone, "Iris's son has returned from the university in Paris. Such a clever boy! He has this idea—a way to extract sugar from cane that he says is five times faster than the way they do it now. Five times! Can you imagine what it will do for sugar if what he says is true? It'll be bigger than the cotton gin. He's looking for somebody to sponsor his idea. Maybe you should talk to him. What can it hurt? At least talk. I promised Iris."

"Just what is this sensational method of his?" Jim questioned.

"What do I know about things like that? All I can tell you is he has the plans for this new method of his all drawn up. You should see him."

Jim mulled over the proposal. Isaac was right— what harm could it do to talk to a boy with ideas, fresh from the French university? "When does he want to talk?" Jim asked.

"Any time," Isaac said. "I could send for him now if you want . . ." He started toward the door.

"I don't have time now," Jim said, getting up off the barrel.

"What about coffee?"

"I'll stop by later."

"Later it won't be fresh," Isaac said, looking disappointed but resigned to the fact that Jim was anxious to move on.

❧ 15

J im lay in bed with his head on Delphine's gently swelling bosom as she hummed contentedly, her smooth brown fingers sifting through his thick, sunstreaked hair. When he was with her his cares and worries seemed trivial and unimportant, and his body, numbed from hours of backbreaking toil working shoulder to shoulder with the slaves from Mandragore —much to the chagrin of the Martinons, he was sure —was thoroughly relaxed. At moments like this he could scarcely be concerned about the bank loan, the repayment of which depended on the success of his first sugar crop, or with the ill-concealed animosity of the one-eyed, tobacco-chewing overseer, Davis, who Jim was certain was pocketing the money paid to the slaves.

Although aware that Delphine, too, must have her own share of troubles, Jim rarely got any inkling as to what they might be. In his presence she seemed content, smiled serenely, laughed frequently, and seldom mentioned any difficulties, choosing instead to pamper him, humor him, caress him, and cater to his comfort and pleasure. Whenever he dropped by her tiny, one-story white cottage near the ramparts of the city, decorated with handsome wall hangings, gold candlesticks, fine furniture imported from Europe, and glittering girandoles aflame, she inevitably welcomed him with warmth and affection. Naturally, neither of them could avoid the awareness that Étienne Bourrier was a looming and significant specter in her life. She never attempted to deny that she owed her entire present life to him, although his name was rarely mentioned. It was as though neither of them wanted to acknowledge his existence.

Despite her reluctance to discuss her benefactor, Jim forced Delphine to talk about her feelings for the Martinique-born planter.

"Do you love him?" Jim asked.

"Love him?" She mused. "I love him the way a child loves a father or a generous uncle. But not the way a woman loves a man. Not the way I love you, my darling."

"If only I could be sure," he said.

"What more can I do to prove my love?" she asked. "I risk my life when I see you like this."

"And if he finds out about us?"

Delphine shrugged indifferently. "I suppose it's inevitable that he will find out one day."

"And?"

"Who knows?" She smiled wistfully, and kissed the tip of his nose.

Almost miraculously, the white blooms had remained in the window day after day. Despite the work at the farm, Jim managed to see Delphine several times a week, and their love blossomed, the only impediment to perfect bliss being the maid, Darcie. So far Delphine had successfully managed to dream up complicated and time-consuming errands on which to send her whenever Jim was expected, although the lovely quadroon did not fool herself for an instant into believing that the wily servant was deceived about the true nature of their relationship. Somehow —Jim could never figure it out—Delphine always managed to keep Darcie from returning at an inopportune moment and never seemed stressed or conveyed a sense of anxiety about the girl's sudden or unexpected intrusion.

Overcome with feelings of love and gratitude, Jim raised himself on one elbow and lightly kissed her smooth neck. Feeling his mouth against her skin, Delphine, her eyes closed, smiled happily.

"Do you know what I'm thinking at this moment?" he asked, running his fingers down her belly, wondering how his rough, callused hand must feel to her silky skin.

"What?" Delphine murmured.

Gently teasing her deep mahogany nipple between his parted lips, he said, "I'm thinking I love you."

Unexpectedly, her smile faded. "Love?" she repeated. "For us love is very foolish."

"Why do you say that?"

"Worse than foolish," she said, her voice taking on a slightly resentful edge. "Impossible. I am a *'femme du coleur'*—a 'colored woman'—in addition to being the mistress of another man. Even if I were free, the laws of Louisiana forbid us to marry. Love between us is illegal. Such hypocrisy! Decent, sanctified marriage forbidden by law while sinful cohabitation and the proliferation of poor pathetic half-breed bastards—like me—are rife." She grabbed the covers in her fists and began to twist them. "Many white men regard their colored mistresses more highly than their legal, church-sanctioned wives, and yet these women are condemned to a status lower than a man's dogs in the eyes of the law," she said bitterly.

"Maybe some day those laws will change," he suggested.

"Not in my lifetime or yours," she said, sliding away from him and sitting up against the pillow. "No, my dearest, you will marry a white wife and have your white children and I will endure as black people have endured for so long. Perhaps I will go on being the mistress of Étienne Bourrier for five or ten more years, until he tires of me and seeks a younger, fresher woman. He will turn me out, and if I am lucky he will settle a house or shop on me and I will be like your friend Alphonsine or Olympe, the modiste. They are the fortunate survivors. 'The Swamp' is full of others less fortunate—and the cemeteries, also. No, my love, you are one race and I am another. It is our fate, and we have no choice but to accept it."

Jim wasn't receptive to her fatalistic outlook. "There are other ways than just giving in and accepting what you are opposed to," he said.

"Not when you are powerless." She sighed.

"We could leave Louisiana," he said.

"The laws are the same throughout the United States—North and South," she informed him. "One must flee to Europe to be really free. On the Continent people are truly civilized. In France we could marry if we chose. Race and color are of no matter to Europeans. Oh, Jim, wouldn't it be wonderful if we could go to Paris at this moment—you and I?"

"What would I do in France?" he asked. "How would we live?"

"I don't know," she confessed, kissing his brow. "Still, you must admit, it's a very nice dream—you and I together in Paris."

The slamming of a door in another part of the house interrupted their speculation. Startled, Delphine bolted upright, hopped out of bed, and dashed for her robe. Jim reached for his own clothes.

"That's probably Darcie back sooner than I expected," Delphine said.

Pulling on his breeches, Jim hoped she was right.

Tying the sash of her robe, Delphine opened the door and nearly collided with Darcie in the hall. Hands on hips, a sneer on her face, the maid gazed at Jim as he struggled with the buttons on his shirt.

"Don't you all be fretting about me," Darcie said. "I ain't going to say nothing to nobody. I knew what's been going on between you all for a long time. I ain't stupid."

Indignant at the maid's bold attitude, Delphine reproached her. "You have no right to speak to me like that."

Unfazed by the reprimand, the maid went on. "I just wanted to tell you so's you all didn't have to be sneaking around no more and sending me on all those damned fool errands."

"You'll do what I tell you to do," Delphine said.

Raising his hand, Jim silenced Delphine and then, dipping into his pocket, produced a gold coin, which he gave to the girl. Darcie stuck it between her teeth and bit down. Convinced it was good, she smiled and tucked it in the pocket of her apron.

"As for Marse Étienne," she said. "You all don't have to worry none about him finding out neither—least, not from me. I ain't going to say nothing to nobody as long as you all treats me right."

At first not happy with Darcie's knowledge of their affair, Jim eventually realized that it held certain advantages. For one thing, he and Delphine were now able to see each other more frequently than before, and under less trying circumstances.

"I wish we could do away with the roses-in-the-window signal," Jim said one day as they lay in bed.

"We can't." Delphine sighed.

"Why not?"

"Because I can't take a chance on your coming here and running into Étienne."

"Sometimes I think I'd like to meet him and confront him with our situation," Jim asserted. "And see what he has to say about it."

"It's not that simple. You don't understand. Étienne regards me as his personal property—like his land, his house, his livestock, his slaves. He would consider you a thief," she replied.

"I'd still like to tell him about us and see what happens," Jim persisted.

"Well, don't," she said.

"Sometimes, Delphine, I think you actually *want* to remain his mistress," he accused her. "I think you like him."

"My feelings for Étienne are very confused," she admitted. "I owe so much to him."

"You owe him nothing," Jim insisted.

"He's been like a father to me in many ways—a harsh and demanding father, but a father nonetheless. The feelings I have for him are those of a dutiful daughter."

Jim merely shook his head helplessly, as he had done so often whenever Bourrier was discussed.

At the farm there was little to do throughout the winter months. Four weeks after planting, the cane began to sprout, and it grew with great rapidity, requiring little more than hoeing. Thus, Jim had more free time than a few months earlier and was able to see more of Delphine. He also saw more of Isaac, stopping off at his store on his way to or from the cottage near the ramparts. Isaac had been helpful in directing him to a goldsmith, who fashioned a medallion for Delphine engraved with the words *"More than yesterday, less than tomorrow."* When he presented it to her she was delighted with the gift and had him fasten it around her neck.

"The only good thing about this affair of yours," Isaac said, "is that I get to see more of you."

One day Jim arrived at the shop opposite the bustling French Market at closing time and found the merchant sharing coffee and beignets with a slightly plump, scholarly-looking youth with a caramel complexion and an unruly mop of densely curled hair.

"Jim," Isaac said, "I'd like you to meet Iris's son,

Roger Guillon, recently arrived from Paris. Roger, this is Jim MacKay."

The two men shook hands, and Isaac poured Jim a cup of the highly aromatic coffee he customarily brewed.

"A very smart boy, Roger," Isaac declared, tapping his long bony finger to his temple. "And he's got something that's very interesting—very interesting indeed."

"I'm afraid that the last gentleman to whom I presented my ideas didn't find them so interesting," Roger said, blushing slightly at Isaac's buildup. Jim could see that he was rather shy and modest, quite unlike his mother.

With a knowing glance at Jim, Isaac said, "The last gentleman Roger's talking about was Placide Martinon."

Interested in hearing what Roger had to say, Jim asked, "What are your ideas?"

The youth immediately started on a lengthy discourse generously sprinkled with a myriad of technical and scientific terms which Isaac, realizing that Jim was not comprehending them, felt compelled to interpret. "It's a new way to make sugar," he simplified. "At one fifth the cost. And I can tell you that if it works as Roger says, it's very good—very, very good."

Once again embarrassed by Isaac's enthusiasm, Roger said, "My method is a way of extracting sugar five times faster than any presently existing mill is able to do."

Jim frowned. "What you're saying is that your method makes five times as much sugar as the mills currently can in the same period of time?" he asked.

Roger nodded.

"I've known Roger for a long time," Isaac said. "The boy is a genius. If he says this method will work, it will work."

"It hasn't been subjected to an actual test run yet," Roger explained. "It's all on paper."

Isaac laid his pale, bony hand on Jim's shoulder. "This is what you need," he said, referring to Roger's plan. "Listen to him."

"I'm trying to convince one of the sugar planters

along the river to construct a new mill incorporating my ideas and the equipment I've designed."

"Go ahead, do it, Jim," Isaac encouraged.

"Me?" Jim said.

"So why not you?" Isaac replied. "If you build a new modern, efficient mill which produces five times the sugar at the same cost to the grower, you know what will happen? They'll all bring their sugar cane to your mill for grinding, because your way will be a fifth the cost and more efficient. They'll close their own mills down for good."

"But what's to stop them from converting their own mills to the same method?" Jim posed.

"My patent, for one thing," Roger said.

"What do you think of this boy?" Isaac said. "He went to Washington and got himself a patent on this process."

"But couldn't they get around the patent some way?" Jim asked. "Or just outright steal it?"

"To convert their old mills would be too expensive," Isaac answered. "It wouldn't be worth it to them, especially when they consider the price you'd be offering to them to grind their cane. It would be cheaper to bring it to you and let you do it. They'd still make more money. I tell you, Jim, Roger can make you rich. You wouldn't have competition for years. I wish I could say that about my business."

"What do I know about running a sugar mill?" Jim protested.

"You can learn, can't you?" Isaac replied. "Roger will teach you. He will supervise the construction of the mill and the whole operation."

"And how is the construction of this mill going to be financed?" Jim asked, still unable to share his friend's enthusiasm so completely.

"By the bank," Isaac replied. "I can tell you, you won't have any trouble getting money for the construction. Those greedy Gentile bankers know a good thing when they see it." The merchant winked good-naturedly. "Have I ever given you bad advice? Tomorrow we go to the bank—you with your credit and your land, Roger with his plans, and me with nothing."

❧ 16

Because of the hardships and inconveniences of travel, visits from one neighboring plantation to another were frequently overnight, often stretching into several days, so when Carlota Valdéz de Alicante and her two sons, who had journeyed all the way from Cuba, remained at Florestal for several months, it was hardly considered unusual. In fact, if it hadn't been for a cold spell in late January which proved too much for the Caribbean visitors, accustomed to a more gentle climate, Carlota and the boys might have stayed until spring.

In honor of their departure a special mass was arranged in the plantation chapel at Florestal, and Odile and Placide were invited to join the Valdéz family and their friends in the service. Odile elected to make the trip by carriage, accompanied by Verbena and Cecil, with Placide declining to attend. No one was surprised, since it was a well-known fact that he hadn't been to mass in years.

"Sometimes those who need the benefits of the mass most attend the least," Adela remarked when Odile arrived without her brother.

"You must forgive Placide, Auntie," Odile said. "He's terribly busy these days."

"He's busy all right," Verbena mumbled. "With the cards and the liquor and the ladies."

Entering the receiving hall, breathless with excitement, Narciso greeted her with a fervent embrace, his lips tinged with blue, his cheeks pale. "Dearest cousin." He sighed. "I've missed you so."

Aware of Verbena's disapproving gaze, Odile gently tried to push him away, fearing the maid might report the zealousness of his greeting to Placide. She was relieved when he released her without protest. "I've missed you also, Narciso," she said, hoping her eyes would convey what the coolness of her words did not.

Narciso gazed at her relentlessly throughout the service, although Odile kept her eyes fixed on her missal, hoping that Verbena, seated in the rear of the chapel with Kitty and some of the more privileged house slaves, wouldn't observe his persistent attention.

Following mass, a sumptuous meal was served, and afterward Narciso invited Odile for a walk along the river.

"No, sir, Mr. Narciso," Verbena protested. "This child ain't going out in that damp and cold. She'll catch her death."

At that point Adela intervened and ordered Verbena to help Kitty and the other slaves in the kitchens.

"Marse Placide sent me here to look after Miss Odile, Miss Adela," Verbena asserted.

"You'll do what I order you to do!" Adela snapped. "Now get in that kitchen and help Kitty or I'll have Munro Samples lay a whip on your black hide. You heard me, march!"

Pouting, Verbena muttered, "Yes, ma'am," and shuffled off sullenly to the kitchen.

Clutching her long woolen cape around her as protection against the January chill, Odile took Narciso's arm and strolled with him on the levee. Below them the river, dotted with chunks of ice, looked gray and cold, and in the branches of the sycamores lining the bank the Spanish moss hung stiff and frozen.

Pausing beside a pile of charred logs which had probably burned brightly on New Year's Day, remnants of one of many traditional bonfires dotting the levees up and down the river, Narciso clasped Odile's face between his gloved hands and gently pressed his mouth to hers.

"Oh, God, how I've missed you!" he declared. "Have you missed me too? Please say that you have."

"Of course I have," she said, smiling.

"Later, will you come to my room?" he asked.

"I can't do that again. The last time we must have been mad to dare such a thing. I was quite giddy from all the champagne and the dancing and the whirling about. My God, Narciso, if we had been caught . . ."

"So what?"

"I dread to think of the consequences."

"Please, come."

"No. Not unless we are married," she said adamantly.

"You know that I would marry you tomorrow if your brother would give his permission."

"But he won't."

Narciso gave an ironic laugh. "He's afraid that I shall die and leave you a widow. The precarious state of my health prevents him from giving his blessing to our union—at least so he claims."

"Sometimes I am afraid he may force me to marry someone I loathe," she fretted.

"If he does, I swear I'll kill him," Narciso declared dramatically.

Odile placed her hand, gloved in the finest Italian kid, over his mouth. "Please, dearest, don't talk that way," she cautioned. "It's very foolish."

Afraid he might have offended her by his talk of killing her brother, Narciso decided to pursue another course. In quite a different tone he said, "I have recently come across a marvelous poet, Luis de Góngora. I should like to read you his works—if you will come to my room."

"I told you, Narciso. I can't."

"I promise you that nothing disagreeable will transpire—on my oath as a gentleman."

In her heart Odile would have liked nothing more than to retire to his room, away from the other guests whom she found so tiresome, and listen to his expressive voice reading that marvelous verse she loved so much, but she was forced to decline. "Verbena is watching me like a hawk," she said. "I think she's suspicious of us."

"Mother will help get her out of the way," he replied. "You saw what she did a little while ago."

Hearing that, Odile considered a moment and decided that her aunt had purposely gotten the maid inebriated on her previous visit.

Looking into his bright, almost febrile-looking eyes, she found the invitation difficult to resist. Remembering that only the grace of God had enabled her to escape total disgrace the last time at Florestal, she was reluctant to tempt fate again.

"I'm getting a little chilly. Let's return to the house," she suggested. "Besides, I must chat a little with Aunt Carlota and our cousins."

Returning to the house, Odile found her Cuban aunt in the parlor in front of the fireplace, holding an embroidered firescreen in front of her face to prevent her delicate complexion from becoming flushed and reddened from the heat of the flames. Settling beside her on the horsehair settee, Odile asked, "Did you get to see Eugénie?"

"It was impossible," Carlota answered, looking slightly annoyed that she had asked such a question.

"Poor Eugénie," Odile said. "She will be so disappointed. She was so anxious to talk with you while you were here."

Carlota sighed impatiently. "I shall write her from Cuba. My letter shall contain the information she is seeking, although it's a matter which would be better forgotten. I hoped that once she took the veil she would put it out of her mind. It doesn't seem possible that she should want to cause herself such anguish after all these years."

Later, bedded down in a guest room with the other female guests, Odile was unable to nap, puzzled by Carlota's attitude and the ambiguousness of her words. Restless, anxious to get up and seek some diversion, Odile slipped out of the room when she was certain the other women were asleep and Verbena was still occupied in the kitchens, and tiptoed down the hall to Narciso's room. The door was open just enough for her to peer in.

Instantly aware of her presence, Narciso ran to greet her, throwing his arms around her. "I was so afraid you wouldn't come."

Gracefully extricating herself from his eager embrace, she reminded him that he had promised to behave and read to her.

Resignedly he honored his promise, selected a leather-bound volume from the many on the shelves, and began reading aloud. Odile sat on the floor in front of the fireplace, snuggled against his bony knees and listened with rapt attention.

> *Mientras por competir con tu cabello*
> *Oro bruñido el sol relumbra en vano,*
> *Mientras con menos precio en medio el llano*
> *Mira tu blanca frente el lilio bello . . .*

He paused and asked, "Did you understand that?"

"Not all," she answered honestly, a slight frown creasing her exquisite features.

"It says, 'While in competition with your hair, the sun like burnished gold gleams in vain, while your white face despises the lovely lily in the middle of the plain,' " he translated.

"Oh, it's lovely," she murmured.

Bending forward, he kissed her and whispered, "Like you, my love."

Odile encircled his slim thigh with her arms and begged him to continue, pressing her cheek against his leg.

Narciso tried very hard to concentrate on what he was reading, but the excitement of her presence made his attention wander from the printed page, and his voice grow husky and hesitant. Finally he stopped reading and closed the book.

"Go on," she urged. "Please."

"I can't," he said.

In spite of his earlier promises, he seized her by the nape of the neck and, unable to restrain himself, planted his eager mouth on hers, so hard it was painful and she was forced to protest. "Please, Narciso . . ."

Then, without any significant resistance, she allowed him to lead her by the hand to the bed, where they lay entwined. The excitement of the situation gave Narciso temporary distress, but he recovered quickly and began fumbling with the buttons on the bodice of her dress. Odile observed that his hands were shaking badly.

"I'll do it," she offered shyly, and slipped her agile, slender hand around the button. The bodice fell away, revealing Odile's ravishing breasts to her lover, who caressed each creamy globe in turn.

Once again Narciso began his slow, tantalizing seduction of his reluctant bed partner. Odile fast found her initial reluctance turning to passion as the skilled young man's fingers glided softly over her entire body. Narciso seemed to take special delight in her bottom, lightly stroking and squeezing each firm, rounded cheek and then sliding his fingers across the moist, warm area between her thighs.

Odile giggled with delight as Narciso's hardness danced at the mere touch of her finger. The outside world faded from her troubled mind as the dreamy-eyed young woman took delight in her new toy.

Soon Narciso lay over her, writhing and moaning, thrusting and withdrawing with remarkable vigor while Odile's throaty cries were muffled by the ornate depths of a cushiony pillow. She wrapped her long, shapely legs tightly around his slender back, riding Narciso to some far, far place where the world was reduced to the magnificent sensation of their flesh joined together in orgasm.

❧ 17

With Isaac touting Roger Guillon's new method as sure to revolutionize the sugar industry, Jim obtained a second loan from the bank to finance the construction of the new sugar mill with little difficulty, once more reminded of how much easier loans were to obtain in burgeoning, bustling New Orleans than in other parts of the country.

Both Jim and Roger were anxious for the building of the mill to begin as quickly as possible—Jim because he hoped to have it completed in time for the fall grinding season and Roger because he was eager to test his new process. Once the financing was obtained, the next step would be to find capable artisans —bricklayers, ironmongers, masons, carpenters, and mechanics—to undertake the construction.

Mandragore, like most large plantations, had a full staff of such artisans among its slaves. In the off season slaves were required to repair old buildings and erect new ones, fix chimneys, make posts and rails, put up fences, reshingle roofs, and repair machinery and equipment, as well as perform many other maintenance duties about the huge estate, which was virtually a self-sufficient town in itself. Jim was well aware that the slaves who had helped with the cane planting were too unskilled to work on the proposed mill. As distasteful as he found the prospect of going to Placide Martinon with a request to borrow his craftsmen, Jim saw no other alternative.

Halting his pacing back and forth in front of the fire burning brightly in the study, Placide opened the decorative coal shuttle and threw some fresh lumps on the hearth. "These are not ordinary field hands you're asking for," he said. "If you want skilled artisans— and that's what you've got to have to build a sugar mill—you're going to have to pay more than a dollar a day for them. Frankly, MacKay, I don't see how you're going to afford it—or even need a mill, for that matter."

"You supply me with the men. I'll worry about paying them, and everything else," Jim answered.

"Yes, of course."

Extensive negotiations ensued between the two men. Placide required that Jim carefully estimate the number of artisans he needed and for what length of time. Fortunately, estimates of this kind had already been carefully worked out by Roger, and Jim merely presented his figures. Placide was amazed by the exactness of the estimates.

"If you are going to use my slaves, MacKay, there is one condition on which I must insist," the Creole said, allowing the smoke from one of his perique cigars to filter through his thin lips. "That condition is that you function solely as supervisor. These craftsmen are my most intelligent and independent slaves. I do not want you or any other white man laboring in their presence. Is that understood?"

"I suppose." Jim nodded reluctantly.

When all the conditions were agreeable to both parties, Placide ordered Davis to escort the requisite slaves to Jim each day.

On the first day, the overseer lined up the dozen or so slaves and, astride his horse, gave them their instructions while the ever-present black boy, whose name Jim had learned was Willie, waited patiently in the background on his mule.

"I want every one of you niggers to give Mr. MacKay the same day's work you would give me or Mr. Placide, hear?" he bellowed out, spitting tobacco through the gap in his front teeth. "If I hear tell of any laziness, you'll feel the sting of leather across your black hides, understand?"

When he finished his haranguing, the slaves sullenly nodded their assent and looked to Jim for their assignments.

Later that day Jim noticed that an elderly, emaciated-looking carpenter—Martinon had definitely not lent his best slaves, in spite of his claims and the wages he demanded—had a wracking cough and periodically spat blood-tinged sputum. Assuming that the man was suffering from a bad chest catarrh, Jim ordered him to rest for the day. When Davis heard about it, his single eye flared with anger.

"He ain't sick," the overseer declared, fingering the whip on his belt.

"I happen to think he is," Jim disagreed.

"Listen, mister, you got to pay that nigger whether he works or not, hear?"

Unperturbed, Jim nodded. "I know," he said.

Angry, Davis goaded his horse in the old man's direction, forcing him to scurry out of the path or be trampled.

"Move your black ass!" he yelled. Then turning to Jim, he said, "I told you he ain't sick. When a nigger can get up and run, he's all right."

When the construction started, Roger Guillon was on the job every day at dawn and communicated his ideas to the workmen extremely well. They seemed able to follow his instructions without difficulty, even though the mill he was proposing to build was quite different—far more innovative and complex—from any to which they had been previously exposed.

The progress of the new mill was avidly reported at Mandragore, where Placide listened attentively to Davis's daily reports.

"That MacKay's crazier than a bedbug," Davis declared as they stood talking at the end of a canebreak. "He's got that half-nigger Guillon running the whole thing. Anybody knows that when a nigger has his hand in something it ain't never going to amount to nothing." He spat a mouthful of brown tobacco juice at an insect crawling along the ground, killing it instantly.

Placide rubbed his closeshaven chin thoughtfully. "We'll just have to wait and see," he said.

When Odile returned from Florestal, she came down with a fever and cough, which in the damp, cold of winter persisted several weeks, causing all considerable concern. Dr. Zehner diagnosed her illness as a catarrh, the result of bad weather and too much excitement, and ordered her confined to bed until her symptoms abated.

When Placide heard the diagnosis he eyed her with great suspicion. "I can't understand what could possibly be exciting about attending mass," he commented wryly.

"You had no business going out walking with Mr. Narciso down along the river in that cold. A lady don't go out like that in winter. It ain't fitting," Verbena fretted later when they were alone. "You just lucky you ain't done gone and come down with a case of pneumonia."

Confined to her room, Odile had time to contemplate her fledgling affair with Narciso and wonder where it might eventually lead. Marriage should have been her inevitable goal—to preserve her honor, if nothing else—but she wondered if she loved her cousin sufficiently to make so serious a commitment. Until recently she had had no misgivings about the depth of her feelings, but since Jim MacKay had come on the scene and taken up residence nearby, she had been beset by doubts and strange stirrings which, previous to her illness, she was reluctant to admit to, even to herself. She found herself making comparisons between her cousin and Jim MacKay, certain there could not be two men more dissimilar. As much as she was excited by Narciso's impulsive, insistent ardor, she felt it arose from a kind of frenzied, desperate desire to reaffirm life and rebuke the ever-present specter of death which hovered about his day-to-day existence. Despite the vigor with which Narciso attempted to live, an inevitable aura of morbidity seemed to dog him, imparting a sense of frailty and transience. Momentarily, she wondered if it had anything to do with her attraction to him, but she preferred to try to convince herself that it was his sensitivity and love of poetry and music instead. At times she feared her fascination sprang from darker roots, but such an admission would have disturbed and frightened her, and she quickly brushed it aside by turning to thoughts of MacKay, who in his sheer physical stamina, straightforwardness, and sincerity contrasted markedly with most of the other men she had known. By the Creole standards in which she had been raised, he was considered boorish, uncultured, and undesirable. In addition, he was an upstart who refused to conform to acceptable standards, a newcomer to the land her ancestors had occupied for more than a century, a man beneath her consideration. Placide's feelings about MacKay were far less complicated. She was sure her brother despised him, although expediency and an ingrained sense of courtesy forced him to be somewhat tolerant. Try as she might, Odile could not deny that she was attracted to this stalwart, determined Yankee, perhaps for no other reason than a deep-seated desire to defy her brother.

Odile stared at the delicate veilleuse flickering on the night stand beside her bed, its china pot boiling away with the tisane Verbena had prepared from magical herbs gathered by the first rays of the new moon, insisting it would be good for her cough.

With many of her contemporaries already married —some had been wed as young as thirteen—Odile knew that any day her brother might present her with a prospective spouse. Jules Seguin, her former beau, had unexpectedly married his cousin Anais Pons from Mobile when she came for a visit to Forest Point, the Seguin plantation, last year. Their marriage had been a blow to Placide, who had hoped for the union of his sister and his best friend. Her brother knew many eligible men and undoubtedly would soon come up with a replacement for the lost Jules. At times she wondered how opposed he really might be to her marrying Narciso, suspecting that his objections might not be as strong as they seemed.

Because of her illness, Odile asked Father Daubigny to come to the house to hear her confession. With yellow fever, cholera, dysentery, malaria, and tuberculosis rife, she felt it was important to be in a state of grace. The priest was glad to oblige, even though it meant a rather arduous trip from the city. As always, Verbena saw that his favorite foods were prepared by the kitchen slaves, which, together with the opportunity to gaze on Odile's stunning beauty, was more than ample compensation for the cleric.

As he sat patiently at her bedside, Odile, in a whisper, confessed her indiscretions to the shocked priest, who, when he had recovered his composure, recommended a quick wedding as the only possible course.

"Tell me, my daughter," he inquired hesitantly, "was he . . . that is, was your cousin completely . . . capable?"

"Yes. Completely," she answered, bringing up her lace handkerchief to hide her smile.

When Daubigny left for the kitchen, smacking his lips in anticipation at the aroma of crab gumbo emanating from a huge copper pot, Odile got out of bed and went to the window, gazing across the endless fields of burgeoning cane. She wondered if Father Daubigny's advice would have been the same if she had confessed to having had relations with Jim MacKay.

ᘓ 18

Winter warmed into spring and spring into summer, and in early August Placide rode through his endless fields of thick green cane while long rows of slaves working in gangs completed the final hoeing. Cane required three extensive hoeings during its growing period, and this was the last. About the middle of September whatever cane was needed for seed would be cut and stacked in ricks, and sometime in October the general cutting would begin. It was important that cane be cut at precisely the right time. If it was cut late, after it had grown too tall, much of the sugar content would have been lost.

Davis, bullwhip in hand, pistol and Bowie knife stuck in his belt, rode at his employer's side at the rear of the slave gang. As always, the overseer, trailed by Willie and the yelping bloodhounds, kept a sharp lookout for idlers, not hesitating to lay a couple of lashes across the back of any slave he suspected of laziness.

The summer air was hot and humid, and although it seemed to cause Placide no great discomfort, Davis was sweating profusely.

"When we start cutting this cane, we're going to need every nigger we got," Davis said. "Are you fixing to let MacKay keep on using our niggers for that damned mill of his?"

"I suppose we'll have to ask for them back," Placide answered.

"Can't be too soon for me," Davis said. "That Yankee's been putting a lot of bad ideas into the heads of our niggers. Some of them's been getting pretty damned sassy with me."

Placide stared at him. "Really?" he asked, eyebrows raised. Davis rarely had any trouble with the slaves; that was the main reason he was kept on as overseer.

"But you don't have to worry none," Davis assured him, lovingly fingering the coiled whip in his hand. "I know how to put an ornery nigger in his place when he gets sassy."

"That's why I hired you," Placide said, secretly relieved. With three hundred slaves, he dreaded anything which might signify the possibility of an impending rebellion or uprising.

At the end of the canebreak they came to the levee. Placide urged his horse up the steeply sloping side to the top, followed by the overseer, Willie, and the bloodhounds. They rode upriver along the top until they came to a point from which they could view MacKay's land.

"Well, it looks as if it won't be long until our friend has his mill completed," Placide remarked.

"The niggers say he swears it'll be ready for this year's grinding season," Davis said.

"And where is all the cane going to come from that he's planning to grind—that little bitty forty arpents of his?" Placide asked skeptically.

Davis glanced at his employer with his good eye and at the same time spat a mouthful of tobacco juice at a dragonfly that hovered before his face, hitting it squarely and sending the delicate insect plummeting to earth. "I heard from Abram that Seguin is making arrangements for MacKay to grind his cane," he revealed.

Placide was astonished. "What?! Jules sending his cane to MacKay?"

Davis nodded. "That's what I heard," he affirmed.

"I don't believe it," Placide scoffed. "That's impossible."

"That's what the niggers are all saying," Davis persisted. "Abram is a nigger you can trust. He's one of my best boys."

"It's a lie," the Creole declared stubbornly, his dark eyes blazing. "Why should Jules Seguin deal with an upstart outsider after all these years of bringing his cane to me?"

Placide felt agitated and confused, angry with Davis for being the bearer of such distressing news. Had he really been betrayed by Jules, one of his oldest and closest friends?

"I can't believe it," he said. "I can't believe Jules would do such a thing."

"They say MacKay's been going up and down the river contacting all the planters and offering to grind their cane at a real good price," Davis related. "So cheap that it don't pay for them to start up their own mills."

"The audacity!" Placide muttered, his fists clenched.

"That half-breed Guillon he's got working for him claims that MacKay's new mill can grind cane for one fifth what it costs us."

"That's impossible!" Placide snapped.

Davis shook his head. "You can't be so sure," he said.

The planter glared at him. "I can," he declared.

"A man will always go for the best price, friendship or not," the overseer reminded him, exchanging a quick, furtive smile with Willie, who seemed amused by his master's distress. Almost gloating, Davis added, "You know what they say—money talks louder and better than almost anything else you can name."

On the long-awaited day when the mill was to begin its operation, Jim and Roger shared a mutual excitement. At dawn the young engineer pounded on the fledgling planter's cabin door, anxious to get things started. For days he had been going over the mechanical apparatus, checking and rechecking every belt, gear, wheel, motor, axle, lever, valve, and drive shaft in minute detail, making certain all parts were in working order. For Roger, the successful operation of the mill represented not only possible financial rewards—he owned a hefty percentage—but the materialization of dreams and ideas which theretofore had only been lifeless drawings and diagrams on paper.

"Come on, let's go," he urged as Jim crawled sleepily out of bed.

The first cane carts from Forest Place, the Seguin plantation, were due at approximately eight o'clock. Jim had arranged special rates for Jules Seguin because of his expressed willingness to be the first to submit his cane to the new extraction process, fully aware that no one could guarantee its success. As part of the agreement Seguin had consented to provide a sufficient number of slaves not only to unload the carts but to remain at the mill throughout the day and feed the cane to the conveyor belt. The remainder of the personnel operating the mill had been recruited from among the Mandragore slaves who had been trained by Roger in the operation of the various aspects of the plant. Although he had not guaranteed the availability of these slaves, Placide implied that Jim could depend on them so long as he continued to pay the prescribed wages. Fortunately, because of the many innovations Roger had incorporated into the design of the mill, far fewer key personnel were required to operate it than in the older mills, but a minimum of eight to ten men were absolutely vital.

Turning to Roger, who was far more preoccupied by the machinery than by the fact that the operators had not yet arrived, Jim fretted, "Where the hell is the work crew? Davis is hardly ever late bringing them over."

"They'll be here," Roger said confidently, and Jim wished he could feel as certain.

A short while later, as the Forest Place carts were

lining up along the conveyor belt in the shed, Davis appeared on the scene, alone except for the half dozen or so bloodhounds and Willie.

"Where the hell are my workers?" Jim asked, confronting him anxiously. "We're all ready to go."

"Mr. Martinon is real sorry, MacKay," Davis began quietly, feigning an expression of mock compassion, "but he sent me to tell you that his slaves are no longer able to work for you. You see, we need every hand we can get out there in the cane fields. It's the cutting season."

"What!" Jim exploded. "He can't do this to me. I've got cane coming in here all day for grinding. We talked about this and he assured me that he could spare the eight or ten men I need to run my mill."

"Mr. Martinon knows how hard this is going to be on you and he sends his regrets," Davis said. Behind him, Willie covered his mouth with his hand to suppress a snicker.

"Regrets! What the hell good are his regrets?" Jim retorted.

"There ain't nothing he can do," Davis said with a shrug, his good eye blinking nervously and betraying his tension. "You see, MacKay, you got to cut cane when it's just right, and now's the time. We got every nigger on the place out there cutting—man, woman, and child. There ain't a one of them we can spare."

"He's got to let me have at least a half dozen men," Jim insisted.

"I don't rightly see how we could do that," the overseer replied.

Furious, Jim shook his fist in Davis's face and shouted, "I'll tell you what you can do, you and your boss both can go to hell. Now you take that baboon behind you and get out of here. Go on, get!"

"I don't like you calling Willie a baboon," Davis said angrily, completely dropping his former sympathetic air.

"Get out of here, I said!" Jim yelled, kicking Davis's horse in the flank. The animal whinnied and reared.

"You'll be sorry for this," Davis threatened, and

spat a mouthful of tobacco juice in Jim's direction before he and Willie galloped off.

During Jim's heated exchange with the Mandragore overseer, Roger, unaware of what was transpiring, was inside the mill, checking the steam generators. As Jim approached he said, "You can start up the conveyor belt now. We can begin running the cane through. Everything seems to be working fine."

"There won't be anybody to run the mill," Jim informed him. "Martinon isn't letting us use his slaves any longer."

Stunned, Roger dropped the wrench he was holding. "What? He can't do that to us—not *today*."

"Well, he's done it," Jim assured him. "I should have expected something like this. Martinon knows we've got a good thing here. In spite of what he said, he's worried we're going to put his mill out of business. Even if he doesn't need to grind outside cane, he knows he won't be able to compete on the open market with the other planters who bring their cane here. His sugar will be too dear. Right now we only have Seguin and a couple of other small planters, but if this operation is successful—as I think it will be—we'll be grinding all the cane up and down the river for miles."

"No matter how good my process is, this mill is useless without help to run it. I spent weeks teaching those slaves the various operations," Roger lamented. "One thing is certain—the two of us can't run it by ourselves, no matter how much we want to or how hard we try."

"We could ask Seguin for some of his slaves," Jim said, "but, frankly, I want to get away from depending on somebody's slaves. This morning taught me a good lesson."

"Where are you going to find free men to do this kind of work?" Roger asked.

"I don't know," Jim said, scratching his chin. "There must be somebody we can ask."

Roger's face brightened. "Let's ask Isaac," he suggested.

As always, Isaac did have a solution to the dilemma. "Alphonsine," he said. "She's got a lot of new boarders—European immigrants fresh off the boat. Her house is full of them, and all without jobs and hungry for any kind of work. Most of them don't know much English, but so what? How much English do you need to run a sugar mill? When I first came here as a kid I was selling and I didn't know English."

Without wasting a moment, Jim and Roger headed straight to the boardinghouse and located Alphonsine in the patio, feeding her parrot pumpkin seeds from her own lips. The minute she saw Jim, she threw her arms around him.

"Jimmy! I'm so happy to see you!" she cried in her melodious West Indian accent. "You bad boy, you forgot Alphonsine. Why didn't you come to see me? Let me look at you. My goodness, how skinny you've gotten."

Turning to Roger, she greeted him almost as effusively. "I adore your mama," she said. "Iris is one of my closest friends."

Eventually, over coffee, they got down to business and Jim explained his predicament to her.

"I have a house full of men eager for work," she declared, and immediately sent one of her girls to round up those she felt might be suitable. When the six she recommended appeared, they represented a whole spectrum of nations: German, Irish, Norwegian, Italian, Greek, and a free Negro. The free Negro, whose name was Roarke, was a particularly valuable find. A strapping six-footer with a gold earring dangling from the lobe of his left ear, he had been a sugar-maker as a slave, but since gaining his freedom upon the death of his master he had been working at various odd jobs around the city.

"I sure will be happy to get back to making sugar again," he said with a happy smile.

At the nearby livery stable Jim made arrangements for a team and wagon to transport the six men to the farm every day.

"How many slaves you got?" Roarke asked as the wagon bumped along the River Road.

"None," Jim answered.

Astounded by his answer, Roarke said, "How you expect to run a sugarhouse without slaves?"

"I don't know, but we're going to try," Jim replied with determination.

❧ 19

The glass-enclosed cupola atop the house had been originally constructed by the early Martinons so that they might monitor boat traffic on the Mississippi, but this November day Placide had his spyglass trained in a different direction. Across the acres of green cane and cypress swamps, he watched the thick clouds of black smoke billowing from the brick chimney into the gray fall sky while a steady stream of carts and slaves rolled into the sugarhouse shed. Through the powerful lens he was able to recognize several of the drivers as slaves owned by Jules Seguin, Peter Anspacher and Valentin Chardonnier, smaller planters all of whom in the past had brought their cane to Mandragore for grinding.

"Damn!" he swore, lowering the glass from his eye. Never had he dreamt that his friends would betray him by taking their cane to the Yankee upstart. His only hope was that the half-breed bastard's plans would be the failure he had believed them to be when Guillon first presented them to him.

Still smoldering with anger and outrage, he descended the narrow spiral staircase from the cupola to the attic nursery and then down to the second floor, where he encountered Odile, dressed to go out.

"Where are you going?" he asked.

Although quite accustomed to his inquiries into her

comings and goings, Odile was taken aback by the harshness of his tone.

Clutching her bag of needlepoint, she replied, "I am on my way to Louise Chardonnier's for my weekly sewing circle."

"You are *not* going to the Chardonniers' today," he declared sternly.

"What?" she said, surprised.

"You heard me, I forbid you to set foot on Chardonnier property."

"Have you gone mad?"

"You heard what I said."

"Really, Placide, you are being ridiculous. Louise is one of my dearest friends."

"Ridiculous, am I?" he said. "Then come with me. I want to show you something." Taking her by the arm, he dragged her up the stairs to the cupola and thrust the spyglass in her hands. "Look over there," he commanded, directing the lens toward Jim's farm.

Resignedly, she peered through the glass as he ordered. "Well, what am I supposed to see?" she asked impatiently.

"Take a look at those cane carts in the shed."

"I have no interest in cane carts—"

"Look at the drivers."

"I have no interest in the drivers either," she protested.

"Those carts belong to Valentin Chardonnier. They are full of cane from Laureldale," he pointed out.

"Well, I still don't see—"

"You don't see! You don't see!" he repeated angrily. "Are you an even bigger fool than I think you are? Don't you understand that Chardonnier, as well as Seguin and Anspacher and God knows who else, is bringing his cane to MacKay to be ground? For as long as I can remember they have brought their cane to us."

"Well, we still have plenty of our own cane, don't we?" she retorted. "Why do we need to grind theirs?"

"We cannot afford to lose any of our outside business. Mandragore is mortgaged to the hilt. This house, the slaves, the equipment—everything is mortgaged," he said. "That Yankee is stealing the very bread from our mouths, so to speak. What's more, I cannot believe that our friends—Chardonnier, Seguin, Anspacher, and the others—have betrayed us this way. That is even more difficult to accept. I cannot imagine how he managed to persuade them to switch their loyalties this way."

"Perhaps he learned some secrets from that friend of his—the Jew. He's a very clever fellow," Odile said. "When he used to call here, I always ended up buying something for which I had no need, merely because he was so persistent."

"A wily swine. I'm glad I threw him off the property that time," Placide said.

Returning the spyglass to its tripod, Odile started for the stairs.

"Now where are you going?" he asked.

"To Louise's," she replied. Just because Valentin Chardonnier had elected to have his cane ground elsewhere was no reason—so far as she could see—why she should sever her friendship with Louise.

"After what I've just said?" he asked, scowling.

"But she's expecting me."

"You will not attend her sewing circle," he said emphatically. "And you need not send word to tell her so."

"Really, Placide, I think you are carrying things to extremes."

"It won't seem extreme if we should lose Mandragore," he informed her. "I tried to shield you from these matters because of your age and sex, but perhaps that was a mistake. As I just said, we are deeply in debt. Not only do we depend on our own sugar crop, but on processing the sugar of others as well. Our credit is nearly exhausted. We cannot depend on this year's cane crop alone to see us through. If we do not meet our obligations, we—you and I, dear sister—are finished. If we default on our debts, Mandragore will belong to the banks and our other creditors."

Despite his effort to keep her uninformed about the business affairs of the plantation, Odile was not totally ignorant of the situation, having picked up bits and pieces of information from many sources.

"Most of our debts are *your* gambling debts," she reminded him.

"I gamble in an effort to extricate us from our present financial predicament," he replied.

"Don't make me laugh," she sneered.

"We were in serious trouble long before that upstart built his mill," he said, ignoring her skepticism. "If MacKay's mill is a success—which, fortunately, I don't believe it will be, since Guillon's plans were preposterous—he could bring us to the brink of disaster."

"If that's the case," she replied, "it would seem to me that we must then think of some way to stop him and regain the business we are losing."

"How can we possibly stop him when he is charging only one fifth of what I must charge to grind their cane? And all of this without slaves, I might add," he said.

"Is there no way to beat MacKay at this game?" she said, secretly admiring the Yankee for his enterprising spirit and willingness to take a risk on Guillon's method when no one else would, even if it did spell possible disaster for Mandragore.

"If we don't beat him," he replied, "we may have to join him." Making a disagreeable face, he added, "A loathsome thought . . ."

Placide lay beneath the canopy of Denise's carved rosewood bed, puffing nervously on a cheroot while she paced the room in a black negligee from Paris. In the adjoining room her aged husband, Victor, was snoring blissfully. Above them in the attic noises resembling muffled cries of pain emanated from time to time, causing Denise to stare at the ceiling and wonder aloud, "What on earth is Valcour doing?"

"The usual, I would assume," Placide replied, releasing a thin stream of smoke from between his lips.

"I told him you were in no mood for games tonight."

"That's right," he affirmed.

"You know, sometimes you can become quite boring," she said with a sneer.

"I'm sorry if my mood keeps you from your pleasures," he said.

"Tonight Valcour had prepared a special entertain-

ment for you: 'Beauty and the Beast.' I have never
seen him so excited. He could hardly contain himself.
He swears this is the best he has ever prepared," she
said, her dark eyes bright with excitement.

"Which are you, 'Beauty' or 'the Beast'?"

"I don't mind that you are solemn and gloomy as if
you were at a funeral, but I don't like your sarcasm.
You know very well that I don't participate in Valcour's
entertainments," she declared.

"I have heard otherwise," he said. "I have heard that
you have entertained Valcour rousingly on occasion."

Denise's eyes blazed with anger. "Who told you
that?"

"It's common gossip."

"It's not true. Valcour is nothing more than a slave
in this house. Any other assertion is a lie," she said.
"You don't believe that, do you?"

Placide sighed. "I don't know what I believe."

Denise stopped her pacing and plopped down on the
bed beside him. Running her fingers through his dark
hair, she asked, "What is wrong, my darling? I have
never seen you in such a dark mood."

"I told you," he replied impatiently. "I have many
things on my mind."

Poking her finger inside his ruffled silk shirt, she
coaxed, "I really don't understand why you don't
want to go upstairs tonight. Valcour will be so disappointed. He has provided a spectacle of which Paris,
with all its decadence, has never seen the equal. It will
make you forget all your cares."

"I told you before that I'm not interested, and I
mean it," he said, angrily yanking the cheroot out of
his mouth and snuffing it out in a chamber pot concealed in a drawer of the night stand.

Extruding her lower lip in a sullen pout, Denise
complained, "Sometimes I think you are growing tired
of me."

He sighed wearily and took hold of her hand, giving it a reassuring squeeze. "I'm not tired of you at
all. I am simply concerned about the plantation."

"I wish you would forget about the plantation when
you are with me. Our time together is precious, and I

want it spent in exquisite pleasure. I want you to cast all serious thoughts from your mind," she said.

"Something has happened which may endanger Mandragore. That Yankee I sold the swamp to and his nigger-designed mill are about to ruin me," he told her.

"You mean MacKay?"

Placide was surprised to hear her mention Jim by name. "How do you know of him?"

"The entire Vieux Carré knows of him by now," she replied. "He has set all the tongues wagging."

His interest whetted, Placide sat forward and stared at her curiously. "What are you talking about?"

"I am talking about Mr. MacKay and the affair in which he is currently embroiled."

Placide was incredulous. Jim MacKay embroiled in an affair? "Impossible. He spends all day in his cane fields or in the new mill. The man knows of nothing except work from dawn until dusk. How could he possibly be part of a scandal?"

"He doesn't work all the time," Denise revealed. "Sometimes he can be found in a quadroon's little cottage near the ramparts."

"Cottage? With a quadroon? What cottage?" he asked impatiently. "MacKay has no money to support a mistress."

"This mistress is supported by another."

"What mistress?"

"Delphine Desforges."

Placide could scarcely believe his ears. So the casual flirtation he observed at the quadroon ball had actually blossomed into an affair! "Delphine Desforges? You mean the mistress of Étienne Bourrier?"

"The same." She nodded with a sly smile. "All of New Orleans knows of the affair—all except you."

He seized her by the shoulders. "How do you know?" he asked anxiously. "Are you sure?"

"The slaves gossip with one another at the French Market about the personal lives of their masters. Both Valcour and Lili have told me about it on separate occasions," she replied.

"Then Bourrier must know?"

"No. He is in Martinique," she answered. Then, casting a glance in the direction of the room where her husband was sleeping, Denise added, "The cuckold husband or wronged lover is always the last to know." Denise felt pleased with herself at having succeeded in distracting him from his former preoccupations. It bored her to listen to men ventilating anxieties about their business affairs. She much preferred other pursuits. "I feel very sorry for MacKay when Bourrier does find out—and he will," she said. "Very sorry indeed."

Étienne Bourrier, in his middle forties, loved nothing more when in New Orleans than to promenade through the French Quarter with Delphine, dressed in the finest and latest fashions, on his arm. He was proud to be seen with such a beauty, half his age; he knew his rivals would give almost anything to possess such a mistress. A realistic man, Bourrier had no illusions about her love for him. He knew full well that she had none, although she respected him and was grateful for the many luxuries he provided. Nevertheless, he made it clear that he expected fidelity from her at all times and was prepared to deal harshly and severely with her for any infraction or violation of his honor and trust.

"I regard you the same as my wife," he told her many times.

"But you are *married* to her," Delphine reminded him. "I am merely an accessory to your life."

"You *are* my life, dearest," he declared, kissing her smooth, tawny neck.

On his first day back in the city he was startled to find Delphine looking peaked, but nevertheless insisted that she accompany him to his favorite restaurant, on Rue Royal.

Delphine had been feeling ill for several days and had no desire to sit in a restaurant sipping sazerac, eating rich foods, and exchanging small talk with those who passed by their table, but because he insisted, she agreed to accompany him.

As the headwaiter was conducting them to Bourrier's favorite table, Delphine, feeling dizzy, reached out for a nearby potted palm for support and promptly collapsed in a faint, pulling the palm down with her.

Alarmed, Bourrier hailed a passing carriage and took her home immediately, sending Darcie for the doctor.

"Go right away," he ordered the maid, and when she dawdled, he planted a kick squarely on her behind. "Get a move on, I tell you! Can't you see that your mistress is ill?"

"I'm going. I'm going," the maid grumbled.

The doctor came, examined Delphine, and ascribed her present condition to peculiar vapors which rose from the river in November, causing many ladies to swoon. He prescribed a tonic of tincture of opium, chloroform, camphor, and alcohol, and bed rest until she was feeling better.

That night Delphine pleaded with Bourrier to allow her to sleep alone and he grudgingly consented, ordering Darcie to make up the daybed for him in the same room.

In the dead of night while the veilleuse flickered at Delphine's bedside, they were aroused from sleep by a loud knock on the front door. Instantly Bourrier was out of bed and into his trousers. Pistol in hand, he dashed to the hall.

"Who's out there?" he shouted.

Too weak to follow him, Delphine called out from the bedroom, "Be careful, Étienne."

Cautiously he opened the door, which gave immediately on the street—Delphine's cottage lacked the usual galleries of the homes in other parts of the city —and stepped outside. The street was empty. He shrugged, and was about to return to bed when he noticed affixed to the door a large drawing of a fist with the index and fifth fingers extended: the unmistakable symbol of cuckoldry.

Grasping its significance at once, he tore the drawing from the door and stormed into Delphine's room with it, holding it before the veilleuse for her inspection.

"What is it?" she asked, puzzled.

"Look at it and tell me."

Recognizing the symbol by the flickering light of the small flame, she gasped and instinctively clutched the bedclothes protectively about her.

Throwing the drawing to the floor, Bourrier grabbed her by the shoulders and forced her to look at him. "What is the meaning of this?" he demanded.

Knowing his terrible temper, Delphine feared he might well kill her on the spot. "I swear, Étienne, I know nothing about this," she protested, tears in her eyes. "You must believe me."

"You lying bitch!" he shouted, shaking her violently. "You tell me the truth, or so help me God, I'll kill you!"

"I am telling you the truth. I swear—"

Not satisfied by her repeated avowals of innocence, Bourrier stormed to the slave quarters and dragged Darcie, who was hiding in fear under her bed, to Delphine's room. There, he began grilling her in front of her frightened mistress.

"If you lie to me, wench, I'll sell you upriver," he threatened. "You'll pick cotton like all the other field niggers. You won't be a lady's maid any more."

"Oh, please, Marse Étienne, don't do nothing like that." Darcie pleaded on her knees before him.

Huddled against the headboard in one corner of the bed, Delphine clutched her rosary and prayed fervently that the maid would not break down and betray her in the face of such threats.

"I swear, Marse Étienne, I don't know nothing about this here drawing," she vowed, trembling. "They done put it on the wrong door. Lots of the ladies around here is loose, but not Miss Delphine. She ain't like the others."

"Don't lie to me, you black wench, or I'll take this pistol and blow your brains out right here and now!" he shouted.

"I ain't lying, Marse Étienne," she cried. "I swear I ain't. I ain't never lied to nobody in my whole life."

While he continued to harangue the maid, Delphine glanced into the parlor through the open door and in the light of the moon filtering through the cracks in the jalousied shutters noticed that the roses in the vase in the window were still white. She gasped silently, suddenly remembering that she had forgotten to instruct Darcie to change them.

Following the night of the accusing drawing, Bourrier scarcely left Delphine's cottage except to attend to urgent matters, giving up his favorite diversions: fishing, gambling, drinking in the cafés with his friends, attending cockfights, boxing matches, and circuses.

Because Delphine's weakness and lassitude continued, Bourrier summoned several prominent physicians to examine her, but they could find nothing seriously wrong and unanimously recommended that she remain in bed until she had regained her strength. In addition to her earlier symptoms, Delphine had developed persistent nausea and was revolted by the mere mention of food. The physicians treated this aversion to food by suggesting that Darcie prepare a variety of appetizing dishes each day and coax her mistress to eat a tiny bit of each. Bourrier, too, took a hand in trying to persuade Delphine to eat with a dish of fragrant crab gumbo from a particular restaurant she favored, but his attempts were met with failure when a single spoonful of the soup brought on a violent attack of vomiting.

"It's her liver," a specialist from Boston diagnosed, promptly prescribing a tonic of asafetida, sulphur, and belladonna.

One day, looking harried and anxious, Bourrier announced that he was forced to return to Martinique because of an unexpected emergency. Delphine tried to disguise her joy at such news with a proper display of regret, but the anticipation of seeing Jim once again obliterated all else. During Bourrier's stay in New Orleans the only contact she had had with the Yankee planter was through Darcie, who secretly exchanged messages at Isaac DaCosta's store. In spite of Jim's repeated desire to meet with Bourrier face to face and openly discuss the present situation between Delphine and himself, the maid managed to convince him that such a move would be ill-advised and would put her mistress in great danger. Reluctantly he agreed to abide by her wishes, having no other course to follow for the present time.

Leaving Delphine in the care of Darcie and her doctors, Bourrier regretfully departed for Martinique.

"Good-bye, my darling," he whispered, tenderly kissing the lovely quadroon.

The day following his departure, Delphine immediately felt better, got out of bed, managed to eat a hearty breakfast without vomiting, and ordered Darcie to go out and get some fresh white roses for the vase in the window.

"The best you can find," she said.

That very evening Jim called at the cottage, aghast at Delphine's pallor and loss of weight. Taking her in his arms, he asked her repeatedly what was wrong.

"Nothing," she insisted, fingering the gold medallion engraved with the words *"More than yesterday, less than tomorrow,"* which she had once again placed around her neck; she had not dared to wear it in Bourrier's presence.

"Something's wrong," he insisted.

"No, nothing, *mon amour,*" she said, burying her face against his neck and weeping, so overcome was she at seeing him again.

Later, they retired to the bedroom, where Jim held her quivering body in his arms and tried to comfort her, kissing the tears that rolled down her dusky cheeks.

"Oh, Delphine, I've missed you so much," he murmured.

"I've missed you, too."

"Lying here with you like this makes everything else seem unimportant. I wish there were some way—any way—we could be together without having to sneak around and hide our feelings for each other."

"The only way is for us to elope to France," she said.

"That is running away. I don't want to run away. Why won't you let me confront Bourrier? What is the point in his trying to hold you a prisoner if you no longer love him?"

"I never did."

"Then let me talk to him," Jim insisted.

"There is no talking to Étienne," she said. "He is not a reasonable man. He cannot be dispassionate. It is impossible with his temperament and upbringing. He would simply feel compelled to kill both of us for the sake of his honor."

Clenching his fists, Jim said, "I hate everything that keeps the two of us apart."

Casually, Delphine remarked, "There may soon be three of us."

Stunned, Jim wondered if he had heard correctly. "Three?" he repeated.

"I believe I'm pregnant," she revealed. "In fact, I know I am. The child I am carrying is yours. I haven't slept with Étienne for months."

"Pregnant?" he repeated. "My child?"

"Yes," she assured him. "Some of the doctors Étienne had examine me suspected as much, but I lied to them and told them the monthly curse had descended as usual, so they pressed no further in their questioning and dismissed the possibility."

Gently Jim touched her still-flat belly with his finger tips and then pressed his face to it, kissing the dark, silky skin. "A baby," he said, his voice full of awe and surprise. "Our baby."

During the night, they slept peacefully in each other's arms, grateful to be together again, happy that a child had been conceived regardless of what future problems such a situation might engender. At this moment both felt confident that eventually everything could be solved, being young enough to have a certain measure of optimism about the future.

Suddenly, in the middle of the night, the dark silence engulfing the little white cottage was broken by a terrible racket as the bedroom window came crashing in, glass and bits of wood from the shutters flying in all directions. Delphine bolted up and screamed. Before Jim could reach for his pistol on the night stand, Étienne Bourrier burst into the room through the demolished window and seized him by the throat. In the darkness the two men fought savagely, rolling over and over on the floor, upsetting the night stand, toppling chairs and a washstand.

The noise summoned Darcie from the slave quarters, and she rushed to her mistress's side.

"Marse Étienne!" she cried, shocked to see him. "You's supposed to be on your way to Martinique!"

"Étienne! Jim! Please stop!" Delphine pleaded.

Eventually Bourrier, the element of surprise on his side, got the upper hand and pinned Jim beneath him.

"Please, Étienne, don't harm him," Delphine begged, tugging at his coat.

Ignoring her, Bourrier directed his words to Jim. "So you are the one who's been giving me the horns?" he said, referring to the drawing of the cuckold symbol. Then, calmly reaching into the pocket of his waistcoat, he withdrew an engraved white card signed in red ink and threw it in Jim's face.

Knowing the implication of such a card, Delphine gasped. "No, Étienne, I won't let you—"

Shoving her away roughly, Bourrier snapped, "You, my dear, have nothing to say about it."

"No duels, Étienne, please," she begged.

Addressing Jim once again, he said, "Will you accept the challenge of my card, monsieur, or do I have also to slap your face?"

Detesting fisticuffs as much as his fellow Creoles did, Bourrier released his hold on Jim, rose from the floor, and attempted to straighten his elegantly tailored clothing, which had been ripped and badly disheveled in the fracas.

Delphine threw herself protectively across Jim, who still lay on the floor.

"I won't let you engage him in a duel!" Delphine cried. "You'll kill him! Kill me if you must kill somebody. I'm the guilty one. Kill me and free me from my misery!"

"You have only begun to know misery, my dear," Bourrier predicted.

Jim sat up, reached for Delphine, and attempted to comfort the distraught quadroon.

"What is your answer, monsieur?" Bourrier said, referring to the duel challenge.

"I accept," Jim replied, and with that Delphine let out a shriek and fainted.

❧ 20

Thoughts of the upcoming duel between Jim Mac-Kay and Étienne Bourrier swirled about in Odile's head and distracted her from the harp lesson elderly, genteel, and impoverished Mademoiselle LeDoux was trying to impart.

"You aren't listening to a word I'm saying, are you, Odile," the white-haired Frenchwoman said, lifting her thin, bony fingers from the strings. She had been demonstrating the correct arpeggio technique. "Are you in love?"

"No," Odile replied. "I don't think so."

"Your cousin Narciso is a genius on the harpsichord."

"Why do you mention Narciso in connection with love?" Odile asked.

"That's who you were thinking of, wasn't it?"

"I was thinking of no one in particular," Odile lied, rising from her seat behind the harp. "I think that's enough for today, Mademoiselle LeDoux. I'm feeling rather tired. You know I've been ill recently."

Looking a little miffed, Mademoiselle LeDoux said, "Very well, my dear," and prepared to leave.

Odile waited with her on the gallery while Cecil readied the carriage and horses to take the harp teacher back to her tiny living quarters on the edge of the French Quarter.

"Ah, your sister was the one," Mademoiselle LeDoux declared. "Eugénie could have played with the angels in heaven. That girl was born with music in her soul. Thank God, you were gifted instead with a lovely face. That will save you."

"Save me from what?" Odile asked, indignant at

such a remark, but forced to endure it out of respect
for the other woman's age.

"From the burdens of this world," she replied cryp-
tically.

Just then the carriage appeared in front of the gallery and Cecil stopped and helped the elderly woman
inside. With threadbare gloves, she waved good-bye
to Odile. As the carriage pulled away she remarked,
"Poor Eugénie. Music was her undoing."

For the remainder of the day Odile ignored the
harp teacher's comments and continued to concern
herself with the duel that was pending. She was anxious to advise the brash Ohioan that Bourrier was
equally adept with both sword and pistol, and since
the choice of weapons was his, Jim should choose rifles or shotguns, but she wondered how he would take
such advice coming from a woman. If she did warn
him and Placide found out, all hell would descend on
her. Why then, she wondered, did she feel so compelled to do so? She tried to convince herself that it
was from her sense of fair play, but was nagged by
the thought that perhaps she cared more for Jim Mac-
Kay than she was willing to admit, especially after she
had heard about his daring affair with a quadroon
mistress.

After years of single-minded longing for her cousin
Narciso, they had at last become lovers at his birthday ball and even marriage was conceivable in spite
of Placide's often-voiced opposition. Yet, she was
forced to admit that, try as she might to suppress it,
the husky, blond Ohioan held an increasing and inexplicable fascination for her. Doubts about the depth
of her feelings for Narciso had lately begun to plague
her.

After dinner, instead of napping as she usually did,
Odile ordered one of the grooms to saddle her horse,
and she rode along the top of the levee to Jim's place.

The sugar mill was still going full blast, its steam
boilers chugging away. The conveyor belt, piled with
cane, clattered along, and the iron rollers crushed the
sugar-laden stalks, squeezing out the sweet syrup, with
a loud rumble. The air was heavy with the black

smoke of burning stalks and the sweet-sour smell of ground cane. It was a scene familiar to Odile since childhood.

In the shed she recognized several of the Seguin, Chardonnier, Anspacher, and Pilette slaves, who removed their hats in respectful greeting as she rode past.

"Afternoon, Miss Odile."

"How are you feeling, Miss Odile?"

"How are things at Mandragore, Miss Odile?"

Out of the central door of the sugarhouse came a red-faced, round-bellied man with a thick shock of white-blond hair. He stopped in his tracks and stared at her curiously, as though a woman were the last thing he had expected to see.

"I'm looking for Mr. MacKay," she said, straining desperately to be heard above the din of the mill.

The man looked puzzled and shouted something to her in what sounded like German.

"Mr. MacKay," she repeated in a near shout. "I would like to see Mr. MacKay, please."

"Ja, ja." He nodded and went inside again.

Fully expecting Jim to appear, Odile was disconcerted to have to face a huge strapping Negro with a single gold earring and a battered straw hat.

"You want to see Mr. MacKay?" he asked. There was nothing of a slave's obsequious manner in the way he addressed her and failed to remove his hat.

Her dark eyes blazing with anger, Odile demanded, "You will address me as 'ma'am' when you are talking to me, boy."

The Negro glanced at her contemptuously. "I ain't no 'boy,' *ma'am,*" he said, giving the term of address a sarcastic emphasis. "I happen to be a free man."

"Free or not, you will address me properly and remove your hat when you speak to me," she snapped. With her riding crop, she knocked his straw hat to the ground. "There's nothing I hate more than an uppity free nigger."

About to retort, the Negro held himself in check when he saw Jim MacKay coming toward them.

"Well, Miss Martinon," Jim said in surprise, wiping

the sweat from his forehead and attempting to make himself presentable. "What can I do for you?"

"The first thing you can do," she said, indicating the Negro with the earring, "is teach your niggers some manners."

"Roarke is not 'my nigger,'" Jim answered. "He's a free man. But I'm sure that's not why you're here."

"I'd like to talk to you," she said. "If I may."

"Fine." He nodded. Although surprised and pleased by her call, he was also wary. Recently he had wondered if the Martinons had had anything to do with Bourrier's learning of his affair with Delphine. He was aware that Placide and Bourrier were friends, who often played cards together, and also that Placide had seen him with Delphine at the quadroon ball. Delphine had disappeared immediately following the night the planter from Martinique caught them together and challenged Jim to duel, and Jim had been unable to locate her. Through Darcie he had received a brief note from her saying she was going away with Bourrier and never wanted to see him again, but Jim discounted it, certain that Bourrier had forced her to write it.

"It's too noisy here," she said. "Could we go somewhere else?"

"My cabin?" he suggested.

"No, not there."

"Down along the river?"

"All right," she agreed.

He led her horse to a clump of willows, helped her dismount, and spread his jacket out on the grass for her to sit on.

Resting against the trunk of a willow, Jim folded his arms across his chest and said, "Well, what did you want to talk about?"

"I've come with a warning," she began solemnly.

"What about?" He grinned. "To tell me to stop working like a nigger or I'll be treated like one by my neighbors?"

"No, Mr. MacKay," she replied indignantly. "This is more serious."

"To tell me my employees are rude and have no manners?" he joked.

"That's true," she pointed out, "although it's not why I'm here."

"If you're referring to Roarke—that's the black man with the earring—he's what you Southerners classify as a 'Free Man of Color'—he's a damned good sugar-maker. So good, in fact, I've made him boss."

"But you have white men working there," Odile protested. "I saw one of them."

"That was Hans Oberdorfer," Jim said. "He's from Germany. We used to live in the same boardinghouse. He's indentured to the captain who brought him over and is working to try to pay off his passage. Roarke is his boss. There's no trouble, because Hans doesn't speak much English. Actually, I've had more trouble with Roarke accepting the fact that these Europeans are in his charge and supposed to take orders from him than from them. Once everybody saw what a good sugar-maker he was, they forgot the color of his skin, and so did he. He's been doing a real fine job."

"Good," Odile said, anxious to dismiss the topic of Roarke.

"But that's not what you came to talk about, is it?"

"I came to warn you that Étienne Bourrier fully intends to kill you," she blurted.

Jim took the revelation in stride. "I assumed he did. But I don't intend to let that happen."

"Don't be fooled by his reputation as a swordsman, he's equally adept with a pistol," she said.

Impressed by the genuine concern expressed in her eyes, Jim said, "I thought he would be."

"That's why when you choose the weapons it's got to be rifles or shotguns," she continued, a note of urgency in her voice.

"Why have you taken it upon yourself to advise me this way?" he asked, still suspicious of her motives despite the apparently genuine concern for his welfare.

Odile lowered her eyes. "I don't know," she admitted. "Perhaps it's because I don't want to see you or anyone else needlessly slaughtered in these silly duels. It's such a ridiculous custom you men insist on perpetuating."

Reaching out and taking her hand, he said, "Well, Miss Martinon, I thank you for your concern."

"If you have any regard for me at all, Mr. MacKay, you will say nothing about my coming here like this to my brother," she requested, rising from the grass with his assistance.

"My lips are sealed," he said with a sly smile, giving her hand a conspiratorial squeeze.

When Jim first approached Isaac with news of the impending duel, it sent him ranting and raving about his store.

"A duel with Étienne Bourrier?" Isaac cried, slapping the side of his head. "My God, have you lost your mind? You'll be killed for sure. Leave town . . . hide . . . do anything to avoid such a confrontation. A duel, for God's sake!"

"Then I guess there's no use in asking you to be my second?" Jim said.

Isaac was aghast. "Me? A second in a duel? Now I know you're crazy for certain."

Unfazed by the merchant's tirade, Jim said, "I assume your answer is no."

Isaac stared at him soberly a moment. "So what are the weapons?"

"Double-barreled shotguns," Jim answered.

"Double-barreled shotguns." Isaac considered a moment. "Better than pistols or swords."

"That's what I decided after talking to Odile Martinon," Jim said.

Isaac looked at him with surprise. "You listened to her about weapons?" he asked incredulously.

"Yes, I did," Jim replied confidently, ignoring Isaac's skeptical grunt. "I felt her advice was sincere. And correct."

Returning to the particulars of the duel, Isaac asked, "How many paces?"

"Forty," Jim replied.

Isaac frowned and shook his head. "You should have made it more."

"You haven't given me your answer yet," Jim reminded him.

With a big grin accompanied by a helpless shrug, Isaac said, "My answer is that I must be crazy, too."

Assuming his reply to be an acceptance, Jim leaped up off the cracker barrel on which he was sitting. "I knew I could count on you," he said, embracing his friend.

The morning of the duel dawned gray and chilly, blanketed in a thick fog. When he emerged from the cabin to feed his horse, Jim could scarcely see ten feet in front of him.

How the hell am I going to see at forty paces? he asked himself as he dumped a bucket of oats in the animal's trough.

When he was dressed, he rode into town and picked up Isaac at his store. Together they rode through the fog to the agreed site, a desolate spot on the Metarie Road called Les Trois Capelines, so designated because of three huge oaks growing there, so heavily draped with Spanish moss that they resembled capes.

"This fog is very bad," Isaac remarked.

"Be glad you don't have to try to shoot somebody at forty paces in it," Jim replied.

Because they had arrived a few minutes before their opponents, Isaac had time to poke around among the foliage, trying to uncover a booby trap or other treachery, but he was unable to discover anything irregular.

"I don't trust these frogs," he confided to Jim.

Soon Bourrier arrived in a carriage with two other men. Looking relaxed and dapper, he exchanged cool but courteous greetings with Jim, introduced his companions as his second and a surgeon, and apologized for his tardiness.

"It was the fog, you know," the red-haired planter said.

"We came the same route," Jim reminded him, and proceeded to introduce Isaac.

Bourrier and his companions seemed amused that Jim had selected the merchant as his second. What they didn't know was that in spite of his lack of physical grace and total ignorance of the intricate dueling code, Isaac was a good shot, especially with a shotgun.

Without much ado, the two parties reviewed the conditions of the duel—double-barreled shotguns loaded with ball, forty paces, and Isaac to give the order to fire—and inspected the respective weapons. Isaac was to say: "Fire—one, two, three, four, five!" and the opponents were to fire both barrels between the words "fire" and "five."

"The duel will end with the first blood drawn, will it not?" the surgeon suggested, hoping he would not have to attend another fatality, as he had had to already three times that month.

"No," Bourrier refuted. "Death."

The surgeon looked expectantly at Jim.

"As Mr. Bourrier wishes," Jim agreed.

The surgeon nervously cleared his throat. "Then death it is, gentlemen," he said resignedly.

When all seemed to be in accord, Bourrier's second said impatiently, "Shall we get on with it?"

The two combatants counted off the paces and at the signal fired simultaneously during the agreed period. Bourrier's bullets missed Jim completely, but one of the slugs from Jim's gun knocked off the planter's high silk hat.

The ritual was repeated, but a second exchange of shots produced no injuries.

"Enough!" Isaac cried.

"Perhaps the distance should be shortened to thirty paces," Bourrier's second suggested.

"No," Bourrier insisted, "I will kill or be killed. Give the signal once again, Monsieur DaCosta."

The third time shots were exchanged, Jim once again escaped injury but Bourrier, now hatless, received a scalp wound. Blood streamed down over his face and into his eyes, causing him to blink.

The surgeon ran to his aid and suggested that the duel be discontinued because of his injury. "Enough, gentlemen, enough."

"Feel my pulse," Bourrier directed. "If it's weak or irregular I will retire from the field. If not, the duel will continue."

The surgeon took the planter's wrist and counted silently to himself. "The pulse is regular," he declared, "but it is my opinion that the duel should cease."

"Nonsense," Bourrier said, snatching his wrist from the surgeon's hand. "It will go on. Once more, please, Monsieur DaCosta."

Reluctantly Jim loaded his gun for the fourth and what he hoped would be the final time.

As Isaac once more gave the signal, Bourrier immediately discharged both barrels. Jim ducked, heard the shot whiz by his ear, and then, raising his gun, fired once, his seventh shot of the duel. Through the dense fog he observed his opponent drop his shotgun, reel forward, and, after a few steps, fall to the ground. Jim withheld the second shot.

Immediately the surgeon and his second ran to where the planter lay among the leaves and acorns, the front of his smartly cut frock coat soaked with blood. As the doctor checked his pulse once again, Bourrier's chest heaved with labored respirations.

"We've got to get him to my surgery," the doctor said.

"No," Bourrier protested in a gasp. "I prefer to die here than to live in disgrace."

Ignoring his protests, all four men—his second and the surgeon as well as Jim and Isaac—carried him to the waiting carriage.

In his hotel suite Bourrier lay in serious condition, attended by the surgeon and several nurses. Jim's shot had landed near the junction of the neck and left shoulder, causing a considerable loss of skin and underlying muscle but sparing serious injury to vital organs. During the recuperative period the wound developed an infection, and despite the best efforts of those attending Bourrier, it healed with a severe stricture that caused his head to tilt to one side and his shoulders to assume unequal levels. Not only disfiguring, Bourrier's wound restricted the movements of his neck, shoulder, and left arm as well. While in the suite he remained shirtless, forcing Delphine, who was a prisoner in the quarters, and who he felt was responsible for what had befallen him, to view his scarred and twisted flesh.

As soon as he was well enough to travel, Bourrier made plans to return to Martinique. Disposing of his holdings in Louisiana, he prepared to reside permanently in the Caribbean, thereby escaping the shame and disgrace he felt he might suffer if he remained in New Orleans.

Eventually, from some of his customers, Isaac learned that Étienne Bourrier had departed with Delphine in tow, headed for Martinique, where, it was said, he intended to reside permanently.

"What's he going to do, pass my child off as his own?" Jim speculated angrily when Isaac relayed to him what he had heard. Several times Jim had tried to get past the armed guards and into the hotel suite where Bourrier was holding Delphine prisoner, but there was no way he could devise to get around them and their weapons. He had even thought of going to the police and reporting the situation, but he knew that they would regard it as a personal matter and never interfere in what they would consider a love triangle involving a French planter, his quadroon mistress, and an outsider. He had tried to send messages to her secretly through an Irish bellboy who was living at Alphonsine's, but everything and everybody entering the room was carefully screened by both the guards and Bourrier himself. One day he ran into Darcie in the French Market, where he had gone to buy provisions, and tried to bribe her into taking a note to Delphine, but the maid, uncharacteristically, turned down his offer of gold, saying it would severely jeopardize the safety of her mistress.

"Marse Étienne is suspicious of everyone these days —most of all Miss Delphine and me," she said, her eyes wide with fear.

What Darcie neglected to tell him was that for much bigger stakes, namely her freedom, Bourrier had arranged for her to dress in Delphine's clothes and accompany him to the ship, in order to give credence to the story that Delphine had gone with him to Martinique. Later, under the cover of darkness, just before the ship was to set sail, Darcie would be spirited off the vessel with the precious documents, signed by Bourrier, proclaiming her a Free Woman of Color.

Anxious to verify the story told by Isaac's customers, Jim set about trying to locate Darcie once more and learned through persistent questioning that she had just opened a millinery shop on Rue Royal, which had caught on instantly and was frequented by Creole women and the colored mistresses of wealthy men.

Jim's entrance into the modish shop caused a stir among the women who were being fitted for fancy bonnets and elegant chapeaux decked with plumes, satin ribbons, and artificial flowers and fruits. Darcie, luxuriating in her new-found freedom, flitted about from customer to customer. Startled to see him, she asked, "Mr. Jim, now what's you doing in a ladies' shop?"

"I came to ask you a few questions," he said quietly.

"Me? Questions?" she said, feigning surprise.

"About Delphine."

"I don't know nothing about her," the former maid protested, assuming a defensive posture. "She's done gone to Martinique."

"I don't happen to believe that story," Jim said.

"Lots of folks seen her leave. Go ask anybody. They'll tell you," Darcie insisted.

"I'm asking you. I can't believe that Delphine would allow Bourrier to take her to Martinique of her own free will," he said.

"That's the way she went," Darcie assured him. "Under her own free will, just like you said, Mr. Jim."

"But she's carrying my child."

"Mr. Étienne's probably going to claim it for his own," she replied.

"I just can't believe the whole thing," he said, shaking his head.

Because of his obviously agitated state, the women present began to feel uncomfortable, and one by one they started drifting out of the shop, much to Darcie's consternation.

"It's true. Miss Delphine's done left New Orleans for Martinique," she assured him nervously. "Now why don't you run on and let me be? There ain't nothing more I can tell you."

By this time Jim was fairly certain that Delphine was no longer in New Orleans. For weeks he had spent most of his time searching for her, hoping for some clue as to her whereabouts, having left the operation of the mill in Roarke's competent hands, with Roger Guillon overseeing the mechanical details. Despite the eyewitness reports that Delphine had boarded the ship, Jim was still not convinced that she had actually gone to Martinique with Bourrier, although he had no real foundation on which to base his belief.

"Why don't you just forget about Miss Delphine," Darcie suggested.

"Because I love her and she happens to be carrying my child," Jim answered. "I won't rest until I find her."

"You won't never find her," the ex-maid predicted.

"I want my child," Jim declared. "I want to acknowledge him or her as my own."

"White men don't care nothing about their colored children," Darcie scoffed, her voice tinged with bitterness. "They sells them just like they sells any other slave. I seen it happen all the time. You is still a Yankee. You don't know nothing about how things is here. Things is different than where you come from in the North. You still green, Mr. Jim. Pretty soon you'll be like all the rest of the white folks—buying and selling us niggers like we was hogs or cattle."

"I care, but I see I can't convince you of that," Jim said, and left the shop.

When he was gone Darcie suffered transient remorse, wishing she had revealed Delphine's true whereabouts to him, but she feared Bourrier's retaliation too much to risk such a disclosure. She had seen what he had done to her mistress and she had no desire to suffer the same consequences, no matter how much her conscience bothered her.

When the grinding season finally ended, Jim was left with little to do except anticipate the next. Normally, once planted, cane could be harvested for three successive seasons before it had to be replanted. However, Roger Guillon suggested to Jim that he plant the hardier, frost-resistant ribbon cane instead of the ubiquitous noble cane, which could be permanently damaged, an entire year's crop ruined, by extended periods of cold weather.

In spite of the success of his enterprise, Jim was not content in his personal life. At night he lay alone on the pallet in his rustic cabin obsessed with the idea that Delphine might still be somewhere in the vicinity of New Orleans, in spite of the testimonies to the contrary. Night after restless night he tried to think of ways to track down her actual whereabouts, cursing himself for not storming the hotel suite when he had the opportunity, in spite of the guards and their weapons. Why had he stood passively by and permitted Bourrier not only to hold her prisoner but to abduct her to Martinique as well—if, indeed, that was what had happened? Why hadn't he had the courage or the foresight to confront the guards with weapons of his own if need be, kick the door down, and rescue Delphine? If he had fired that second barrel in the duel, Bourrier would surely have been dead now and Delphine with him instead of wherever she was. Jim shuddered to think what her fate might be. What torture speculation and hindsight were, Jim decided, getting out of bed in the inky darkness in search of the jug of bourbon, which he hoped would calm him, as it had so often lately, and help him to sleep.

Unquestionably, the mill was a success. In its first season, planters up and down the river succumbed, abandoned their own inefficient, aging sugarhouses, and brought their cane to Jim to grind. In fact, Mandragore's mill was the only one for miles around that was operating on any kind of a steady basis, and even it was grinding considerably less than in previous years. Cart after cart rolled into Jim's shed, and by lantern, torch, and moonlight the new mill operated around the clock throughout the grinding season.

The operation of Jim's mill was closely monitored by Placide Martinon, who smoldered over its unqualified success. Even the most loyal planters were bypassing Mandragore completely, leaving its mill, formerly the largest for miles around, with only the plantation's own crop to grind, and taking their cane to MacKay. The loss in revenue incurred by the switch, which he regarded as serious disloyalty, produced great consternation in Placide.

Breakfasting outside one morning, Odile watched her brother ride up to the gallery, dismount unsteadily, and stagger up the steps, looking uncustomarily disheveled and haggard. Romulus immediately put down the silver coffeepot and went to his master's assistance.

Unable to suppress her indignation, Odile rose and confronted her brother. "You're disgusting," she said. "Out all night gambling and drinking and carousing. You should be ashamed."

"What I do is no concern of yours," he said.

"It's my concern when this plantation faces ruin because of you and your debaucheries," she retorted. Although she knew it was a serious breach of ethics to discuss such matters in front of the slaves, she could no longer contain her emotions.

"Now you hold your tongue," Placide commanded, his face flushed with anger.

Fearful that he might strike Odile, Romulus tried to hustle him inside. "Don't you go get yourself excited, Miss Odile," he cautioned. "It's too warm for that."

Shaking a warning finger in his sister's face, Placide said, "Now you just hush up about the condition of things around here. Mandragore is just fine. I'm running things my way and I intend to continue to do so. When this year's cane crop comes in, we'll be the number one plantation in the state again."

"Hah!" she scoffed with a toss of her dark curls.

"I am going to plant more cane than we've ever planted before. We'll have the biggest harvest anybody's seen in these parts. Yes, sir, Mandragore will be on top again, mark my words," he declared as Romulus gently urged him toward the stairs. "Mark my words!"

🎜 21

Several weeks before Odile's nineteenth birthday, Verbena brought up the question of a party for her.

"That child's got to have her a party," the maid insisted to Placide as she watched him carefully fold the black perique tobacco leaves in the cigar-maker, preparing to roll some of his favorite cigars.

Looking up and scowling, he said, "I don't want all those traitors who took their cane to that Yankee to grind coming into this house and drinking my liquor, eating my food, and dancing to music I provide."

Undaunted, Verbena replied, "How you expect Miss Odile to get herself married if she don't meet some young gentlemens? It's time she was getting married. Pretty soon folks'll be calling her an old maid."

"Odile already knows every eligible gentleman up and down the river," he argued.

"I don't notice none of them busting down the doors coaxing to marry her," Verbena said. "Miss Odile needs to meet herself some new gentlemens. Shame a girl as beautiful as her has to sit around here with no beaux —least none with serious intentions."

"Odile could have all the beaux she wants," Placide asserted. "If she has none, it's her own fault. She remained in mourning for our father a ridiculous length of time. The only thing that got her out of those black widow's weeds was Narciso's ball."

"How come you so mean to her about her cousin when you know she's been sweet on Mr. Narciso ever since they was babies?"

"Narciso is a walking corpse," he said. "I have no intention of allowing my sister to marry a corpse."

"Mr. Narciso's probably going to outlive all the rest

of us," the maid speculated. "Folks been saying Mr. Narciso's going to die since the day he was born, and he ain't dead yet."

"In any case, a match between Odile and her cousin would distress me very much," Placide said, transferring a finished cigar to the humidor on his desk.

"You is mean, Marse Placide," she accused.

"If you don't watch that tongue of yours, Verbena, you'll find yourself picking cotton upriver," he threatened.

"You don't scare me." She chuckled. "Don't you forget, Marse Placide, I suckled you and both your sisters on my titties, raised the three of you just the same as if you was my own. On her deathbed your sweet mama pledged me to look after all of you. Don't you never forget that."

Finally, because of Verbena's persistence, Placide gave permission for a small celebration, striking Narciso's name from the list of proposed guests when it was presented to him. In defiance, Odile sent Narciso an invitation anyway and, for good measure, was tempted to send one to Jim MacKay as well. She knew that her brother was too well mannered to turn their cousin away, but she feared he might actually forbid MacKay to enter the house. Even Creole courtesy was not without its limits.

"Your brother thinks that Yankee is the very devil hisself," Verbena said. "Ain't no way he'll ever let him step through the door."

Resigned to not inviting MacKay, Odile sighed and said, "He probably doesn't know how to dance very well anyway."

Narciso, elegantly attired in green velvet, arrived with his mother and a pair of slaves on the afternoon of the party. It was obvious that he had expended great effort trying to look his best despite his thinness and chronic pallor. Under Placide's observant eye, he greeted Odile with a decorous kiss, presenting her with a book of compositions for the harp.

"Oh, Narciso, how can I ever thank you!" she cried with delight, rewarding him with a kiss on both cheeks.

"I anxiously await a recital of these pieces," he replied.

The party was a considerable success, with the guests playing a lively game of blindman's bluff (in which Narciso, as "it," was permitted to touch Odile in a way he would not have been otherwise permitted), rolling hoops on the lawn, and later dancing to a small slave orchestra. At midnight Narciso led everyone down to the batture on the river, the slaves lighting their way with torches, for what he called "a special surprise." There, a group of professional European musicians, Les Amis des Artes, serenaded Odile from an illuminated barge. Touched by the surprise gesture, she squeezed his hand as everyone sang "Happy Birthday" to their accompaniment.

Resentful that most of the guests at the party had patronized MacKay's mill during the past grinding season, Placide withdrew early from the festivities and sulked alone in the study, with only a bottle of cognac for company.

In the early hours of the morning, after the party had ostensibly ended, he was aroused by a knock on the door.

"Placide, it's Narciso," a voice called from the other side. "May I have a word with you?"

Walking somewhat unsteadily, Placide parted the doors and admitted his cousin, motioned him to the horsehair fauteuil, and poured a glass of cognac for him. Narciso's hand shook as he accepted the drink.

"What would you like to talk about?" Placide asked.

"I want to marry Odile," Narciso blurted out. "I've come to ask your permission."

Although the request did not come as a surprise, Placide chose to behave as though it did. "Marry my sister? Surely, Narciso, you must be joking."

Indignant, Narciso asked, "Why do you think I am joking?"

"Well . . ." Placide replied hesitantly. "This is somewhat difficult to say, but since you insist on an explanation—"

Narciso interrupted. "You **are** going to refer, no doubt, to my health?"

"Correct." Placide nodded.

"Then let me allay your doubts. My health permits me to marry your sister."

Placide gazed at him dubiously. Narciso was beginning to perspire.

"And does the good Dr. Zehner agree with this?"

The semi-invalid resented the mention of the physician's name. "What does that pompous ass know?" he scoffed. "He's been saying I was going to die for years."

"But you must admit, your health is precarious at best," Placide said.

"I admit no such thing," Narciso protested.

Growing impatient with him, Placide said, "Come now, cousin, you won't deny that certain marital obligations may be very difficult for you to perform in your present condition."

Instead of becoming angry at the inference, as Placide expected, Narciso smiled slyly and twirled the cognac glass between his flattened palms. "I will be able to perform my so-called marital obligations as well as any man," he asserted. "And perhaps better than some."

Ignoring the implications of the last remark, Placide continued, "Nevertheless, we must consider the eventuality that my sister may be widowed at a young age, were she to marry you—then what?"

"She will inherit my share of Florestal in addition to a sizable trust fund which will be established for her," he replied.

"And where will this trust fund come from?" Placide pursued.

"My father has promised to establish it."

The notion of a trust fund for Odile came as a surprise. Placide had heard rumors that Florestal cotton had suffered severely from weevil infestation in recent years; if it continued uncontrolled, it would soon bring the plantation to ruin. He was shocked to hear that his gouty old uncle Efrén had the means to establish such a fund at present. If true, Narciso's disclosure might cast a new light on the prospective union.

"This supposed fund . . ." Placide began, selecting his words carefully. "Perhaps it might be put to another use before the wedding?"

"Before the wedding?" Narciso questioned with a puzzled frown. "I'm afraid I don't follow you, cousin."

"Well, you see, I would like to modernize my sugar mill in order to compete with my neighbor, MacKay, who has not only stolen the business of the planters who formerly brought their cane to me for grinding, but because of his new method of sugar-making has also enabled them and himself to undercut the established price, squeezing my sugar out of the competitive market. At present, there is no way I can compete with sugar made by the process at his mill. It will be necessary for me to completely overhaul my mill in order to survive the competition. That, my dear Narciso, takes money."

"Have you gone to the banks?"

"It requires more money than our tightfisted bankers are willing to loan me," Placide said.

Narciso understood his cousin's strategy at once. Bribes were not foreign to him. "Perhaps such a loan can be arranged," he suggested. "I will speak to my father when I return to Florestal."

"Good." Placide grinned. "By the way, it may also interest you to know that this MacKay fellow has been looking at my sister in a manner of which I strongly disapprove."

Narciso was shocked. "He has?"

"But no matter," Placide assured his cousin. "Once my mill is refurbished, I will run him out of business —and out of the parish."

"Good," Narciso said.

Putting his arm around his cousin's bony shoulders, Placide rang for Romulus and ordered him to bring them another bottle of cognac. "You will have another drink with me, won't you?" he asked. "After all, if you're going to be my brother-in-law . . ."

❧ 22

Delphine awakened to what was surely the worst nightmare of her life. Her head throbbed so painfully she felt it would split in two. She felt weak and faint, and the waves of nausea which swept over her were worse than any she had experienced crossing the Atlantic in the severest storms. The most devastating symptom of all, however, was the terrible, burning thirst in her throat. When she tried to rise from the dirt floor on which she lay, she discovered, much to her horror, that her ankles were fettered together and chained to the stone wall of her cell. Her vision was blurred, and she blinked hard repeatedly in an effort to clear it, but to no avail. As best she could see, she was being held in a tiny cell with one barred window which gave onto an enclosed court filled with rubbish, piles of dirt, and a bare wooden platform at each end.

Am I in prison? she wondered, praying that if she was, someone would come and bring her some water. Even the lowliest of prisoners, she knew, was given bread and water. How she craved a few wet drops for her dry and aching throat.

In a short while a man appeared with a bucket of water. He allowed her two dippersful and no more, despite her entreaties.

"That's all for you, wench," he said, throwing the remainder of the water in the bucket into the courtyard.

"Where am I?" she asked. "How did I get here?"

The jailer grinned. "You mean you don't know?"

It was then that she began to suspect she might have been drugged. The last thing she could remember was sharing a toast of the liqueur called *le petit*

154

gouave with Bourrier. After that, everything was fuzzy. Perhaps whatever he had slipped into her drink was responsible for the horrendous thirst, blurred vision, nausea, and headache.

Delphine shook her head. "No," she answered.

"Well, I'll tell you where you are," he said. "You're in my slave pen. Permit me to introduce myself. I'm Nigel Pixley, slave trader." A stocky man of medium height, he had a wispy beard, rotten teeth and a big mole centered squarely between his tiny, squinty eyes that made him look like a Cyclops.

Slave pen! Slave trader! Delphine could scarcely believe her ears. "That's impossible!" she gasped. "I'm not a slave. I'm a Free Woman of Color. I've always been free. My mama was free. We've never been slaves!"

Pixley dipped into the pocket of his trousers and produced a document, which he read aloud, mispronouncing the French names it contained. In essence it declared Delphine Desforges to be a slave, the property of Étienne Bourrier and brought by him from Martinique to New Orleans for sale. It went on to say she was a woman of low character and loose morals, not to be trusted as a house slave.

"It's a forgery!" she cried. "That document is a forgery! I have papers that prove I'm free."

"If you do, dear, you'd better produce them mighty quick," the slave trader said. "You go on the auction block tomorrow."

"Tomorrow!" she repeated incredulously.

"You are one bad nigger, girl, and I want rid of you just as quick as I can," he replied. "No wonder Mr. Bourrier was willing to sell you so cheap. I'm going to let you go to the first buyer who'll take you."

For a long while after Pixley had left, Delphine lay on the floor in shock, scarcely able to believe his words. What a fiendish revenge Bourrier had wreaked! To be sold at auction as a slave! She could scarcely believe it. How could such a fate have befallen her, especially now, when she was pregnant with Jim's child?

She was weeping the following day when Pixley

brought her a blue calico frock and kerchief with which to wrap her head slave-fashion, as well as a basin of water and some soap.

"You get yourself washed up and dressed nice, hear?" he ordered.

"Why?" she asked.

"I told you yesterday, girl. You're going on the block."

"I'm not going on any block! I won't!" she said, recoiling in horror at the thought.

Fingering the menacing black whip attached to his belt, Pixley said, "You'll do what I tell you to do, girl, or you'll feel the sting of this whip on your hide!"

"No! No!" she begged.

Pixley lost his patience and slapped her across the face with the back of his hand. "You do as I say and not another word out of you! That's just a sample of what you'll get if I really lose my temper and get mad at you."

Around noon Pixley returned, pleased that she had followed his instructions and washed and dressed. He led her, still fettered at the ankles, out of the cubicle and into the courtyard, surrounded by three tiers of cubicles like the one she had been in, each holding one or more slaves. The cluster of buildings was arranged in such a way that the activities going on within were hidden from passers-by on the street. There were two entrances from the outside, one marked NIGGERS and the other VISITORS.

"You keep that mouth of yours shut today or you'll feel this whip so hard your life won't be worth a picayune when I get through with you," Pixley threatened. "Do you hear me, girl?"

Delphine merely glared at him silently.

"Do you hear me?" he repeated.

When she still refused to answer, he slapped her hard, as he had done earlier.

"I hear you," she murmured.

"Then you say, 'Yes, sir,' hear?"

"Yes, sir," she sniffed, rubbing her stinging face.

He conducted her to one of the two crude wooden

platforms, where she joined a half dozen other female slaves, all dressed alike in blue calico and arranged according to height. At the opposite end of the courtyard an equal number of male slaves were being closely inspected by prospective buyers, who felt their bodies, appraised their teeth as though they were horses, and stripped them, checking for telltale marks from the overseer's whip, the sure sign of a recalcitrant slave.

Pixley began the auction by holding a handkerchief over Delphine.

"This here is a mighty fine twenty-year-old mulatto named Dolly, a good strong field hand, obedient and a hard worker." Reaching down and pulling her skirt tight to reveal her protruding abdomen, he said, "And a good breeder."

Indignant, Delphine pushed his hands away from her stomach, and the buyers gathered around the auction block laughed.

"She's got spunk," one of them said.

"She'd make a good bed wench," his companion agreed.

The bidding began slowly, but when it picked up it became fiercely competitive, and ended with Delphine's being sold for nine hundred dollars, a high price for a female slave, to a badly pockmarked overseer with blue bracelets tattooed around both wrists. The bill of sale was signed "Munro Samples, Florestal."

᪥ 23

The announced engagement of Odile to her cousin, Narciso Valdéz, seemed to have greater impact on Placide than it did on either of the two principals. No longer was he sullen, moody, and ill-tempered, but instead outgoing and genuinely jubilant. He increased the slaves' daily allotment of cornmeal and pork, reduced the number of hours they spent in the cane fields—much to Davis's displeasure—curbed much of his excessive drinking and gambling, and spent more time with Denise.

"I wish you had more sisters to become engaged," Denise joked.

"Alas, I have but one other and she has chosen to marry Our Lord," he said with mock solemnity.

"Not such a bad choice." She laughed.

Then one day he suddenly reverted to his old ways, returning from the bank in one of the blackest moods anyone had ever seen, going so far as to beat his favorite horse unmercifully with his riding crop for an insignificant reason, and clouting Romulus when he tried to interfere.

Later, when she and the slave were alone, Odile asked him what had happened.

"Your brother and your Uncle Efrén had themselves a terrible row down at the bank," he revealed. "Mr. Efrén accused Marse Placide of all kinds of terrible things. Mr. Narciso was there, too, and when they started yelling and fighting he turned all blue and took one of them spells of his. The way they was cursing and shouting at each other made my ears burn. Oh, was they ever burning!"

Although neither Placide nor Narciso was so indelicate as to discuss the matter with her, Odile knew that a financial arrangement accompanied the announcement of the engagement—a reverse dowry, as it were, in which Efrén Valdéz had agreed to lend her brother a certain sum of money required to modernize the Mandragore sugarhouse. For days Placide had been cloistered in his study with draftsmen, engineers, and Abram, the plantation blacksmith, all of them prodding Abram to recall everything he could about the MacKay operation in an attempt to unlock the secrets of young Roger Guillon's revolutionary new sugar-making method. As Abram spoke, the engineers took notes and passed them on to the draftsmen, who eventually drew up plans based on the engineers' interpretation of the Negro's recollections. Placide seemed elated by the results of the confabulation, almost as much as he had been by the engagement itself, but Odile had no illusions about his feelings. So far as her brother was concerned her approaching marriage was purely expedient. He had traded his sister for a new sugar mill. The fact that the sponsor of the new mill happened to be a cousin with whom she was in love was purely incidental.

From Romulus's account, Placide's abrupt change in mood was linked to something amiss in the business transactions, and she greatly feared that her brother would break the engagement at any moment. After years of unyielding opposition, only the desperate straits in which the plantation now floundered had prompted him to consent to the match in the first place. If the Valdéz reneged on their promise to help him extricate Mandragore from its present plight by modernizing the mill, she was sure, the wedding would never take place. Odile bit her lip and fought back tears. She could not believe that she had come so close to something she had desired for so long only to see it slip through her fingers.

"It's not fair," she cried, flinging herself across the bed. "It's not fair!"

Several days after the altercation at the bank, Narciso came to call, alone and unannounced, looking troubled and unhappy. The moment Romulus informed Placide of his presence, the planter ordered the butler to lock Odile, who was gathering roses outside in the garden, in her room.

"Do it quickly," he commanded. "Narciso is not to lay eyes on her, do you understand?"

"Yes, sir, Marse Placide," the butler replied, with severe misgivings about imprisoning his mistress.

With great coolness and reserve, Placide received Narciso in the study and closed the sliding doors behind them tightly.

"I admire your courage in coming here today," he said.

"I had to speak to you," Narciso replied, his voice

trembling. "I suppose you blame me for my father's obstinacy at the bank? I cannot help the fact that he found your demands exorbitant and refused what you asked."

"He refused what we *agreed* upon—you and I," Placide reminded his cousin.

"Papa promised me he would keep his word about the loan. I didn't expect him to renege. It's his gout. When it acts up he becomes unreasonable," Narciso said. "We must approach him another time."

"I am without financing for the renovations in my mill," Placide said. "And you, dear cousin, are without a fiancée. I cannot wait for another time."

Tears welled in Narciso's great, dark eyes. "Please, Placide, you cannot do such a thing. You cannot deny me Odile. We have loved each other since childhood."

"Puppy love," he sneered.

"I will see you get your loan," Narciso assured the sugar planter. "Believe me, I will."

"Hah!" Placide scoffed. "The reason your father reneged on the loan had nothing at all to do with his gout. He was merely trying to save face in a desperate attempt to prevent the bankers from exposing the true state of his finances. Well, I don't blame him. No man likes to admit his plantation is about to go under."

"True," Narciso conceded, "Florestal is in some difficulty. Our cotton has been plagued by an infestation of weevils the past few years, but I am certain these destructive pests can be controlled. In addition, Munro Samples, the overseer, has been cheating on the cotton. Papa is too old and too crippled by his gout to run the plantation the way he used to and has given Samples too much authority. He now does all the purchasing—seed, tools, implements, even the buying of slaves. You see, I have not been able to involve myself in the running of the plantation as much as I would have liked lately, but I assure you, that will change. It's been because—"

Placide cut him off. "Because you are an invalid."

"I am *not* an invalid," Narciso asserted indignantly. "Perhaps I don't have the vitality of other men, but I am not an invalid."

"In any case, it's beside the point," Placide said. "You will not marry my sister—not now or ever. The engagement is broken. There will be no wedding."

With tears streaming down his face, Narciso pleaded, "Please, you can't do this. Without Odile I shall surely die. You will kill me just as though you took a knife and cut out my heart."

With an indifferent shrug, Placide curled his lip contemptuously. "Then die, you sniveling weakling," he said. "Die."

Following the emotionally charged episode with Placide in the study, Narciso suffered a severe seizure, turning blue, gasping for breath, clutching his chest, and frothing at the mouth. Romulus suggested Dr. Zehner, but Placide refused to send for the physician and instead ordered that his cousin be transported to his carriage and taken back to Florestal.

"Let Florestal suffer his antics," Placide said, believing the spell a trick. "I've had quite enough of him for one day."

Locked in her room throughout the excitement, Odile observed Narciso, writhing on a litter, borne by two slaves to the carriage, from her window. Alarmed, she pounded on the door and demanded to be released. "Unlock this door!" she cried. "I must go to Narciso. He needs me. Unlock this door and let me out at once! Verbena! Romulus! Lavinia! Somebody help me! Let me out!"

Only when the carriage had left the plantation and was well on its way north along the River Road did Placide unlock the bedroom door and release his sister.

"What did you do to him?" she demanded, her dark eyes ablaze with rage and indignation as she pounded on his chest with her fists. "What did you do to Narciso?"

"Less than I should have," he answered with a sneer, shoving her away. "I merely broke your engagement."

At that, Odile picked up her porcelain hairbrush and heaved it at him. Placide ducked, and laughed as

it struck the wall and shattered in a shower of porcelain.

Pushing him out of her path, Odile ran down the
narrow, winding stairs, through the lower hall, and out
the front door, with Verbena at her heels, imploring
the impulsive headstrong girl to return.

"Miss Odile, you get back here! You going to catch
your death without no shawl!" the maid exhorted.

Her dark hair flying behind her, Odile raced down
the carriageway to the River Road, but didn't stop
there. Turning on her heel, she headed upriver after
the carriage.

Distraught, Verbena turned to Placide, who stood
calmly at the armoire in the hall, selecting a riding
jacket. "Ain't you going to go after that child? Just
look at her running, skirts all aflying like some white
trash. I don't know how many times I done told her
ladies don't run like that. It just ain't fitting. Please go
and fetch her, Marse Placide. I don't know what you
did to get her so upset that way."

Sliding a fine calfskin glove over his slender hand, he
replied, "I saved her from throwing herself away on a
doddering fool."

For a considerable distance Odile ran along the top
of the levee until she sighted her favorite spot, a circle
of moss ringed by willows which, as a child, she had
believed enchanted. Crying and out of breath, she
threw herself down on the soft, green bryophyte and
listened to the sound of the river.

Lying on the soft moss, she fell asleep and awakened near dusk with a gasp to find a man standing
over her.

Jim MacKay doffed his hat and nodded to her.
"Good evening."

Embarrassed, Odile smoothed her skirts and said,
"I didn't know anyone was standing there."

"You looked so pretty asleep."

"You should have made your presence known," she
reproached.

"This is my favorite fishing spot," he said, sitting
down on the moss beside her, his fishing pole at his
side. "It looks like you've been crying."

"No I haven't," she said, wiping her eyes on the sleeve of her dress.

"*I'd* say you have been," Jim said, once again struck by her extraordinary beauty, now enhanced by an aura of sadness. "I hope whoever you've been crying over is worth it."

"He is," she blurted.

"So, it is a man who's reduced you to tears?"

"Haven't you ever cried over a woman?" she countered.

"Not exactly, but I have gotten a little choked up sometimes."

Goaded by her youthful curiosity, Odile boldly asked, "Was it over Étienne Bourrier's mistress?"

Not pleased to hear Delphine described in those terms, he said, "I prefer to think of her as just Delphine."

"Is that her name? She must be quite a woman— for a quadroon."

"She is."

"I guess you loved her?"

"I guess you loved that fellow you were just crying over?" he answered.

"Yes," she sighed sadly, and unexpectedly laid her head against his shoulder. Astonished but pleased by the intimacy, he slipped his arm around her. She took the move in stride.

"Well, Miss Martinon . . ." he started to say, gazing at her incredibly lovely face.

Pressing her fingers lightly to his lips, she said, "Please, don't talk now."

Jim suddenly found himself wrestling with several conflicting emotions. In spite of his strong feelings for Delphine, he was as attracted by this strange and unpredictable Creole beauty as he had always been, ever since their first encounter near Alphonsine's in the city. Wary of the motives behind this sudden intimacy and never entirely comfortable with her arrogance, he reminded himself of the vast difference in their backgrounds and social status.

Without warning, Odile threw her arms around his neck and buried her face in the hollow of his neck, obliterating instantly all his misgivings.

"I'm sorry," she murmured. "I just need someone to comfort me right now."

"It's all right," he assured her.

Raising her face, she smiled gratefully, almost as though she were inviting him to kiss her, and when he did, she gave herself fully to his embrace.

Excited, Jim slipped his hand inside the bodice of her dress and caressed the velvet skin of her breasts, feeling the nipples go hard under his touch. Unresisting, Odile turned her head to nuzzle Jim's neck, covering his skin with delicate kisses and bites. He slid his other hand beneath the voluminous folds of her skirt and petticoats, running his fingers across the silken skin of her full round buttocks. Odile began a sinuous undulation of her hips, and her breath came in tiny gasps of pleasure. She reached down, unbuttoned Jim's trousers, and slipped her hand inside, cupping his testicles and rubbing his rigid shaft.

"Odile, wait, what if someone should see—" Jim gasped.

"Quiet, Mr. MacKay." Odile giggled. "You just hush and allow me to demonstrate how Southern women are taught to ride." She straddled him so that his manhood rubbed up against her belly. Then, slowly, watching his face, she rose and moved forward, lowering herself so that he slid deep inside her. Back and forth she rocked, up and down, bringing both of them to the edge of climax many times before the final long, sweet fall.

As they kissed, embraced, and intimately explored each other, lying on the moss in the shimmering twilight, a tiny frog croaked nearby.

For a long time, neither of them was aware of the figure watching from atop the levee, until a horse's restless neighing disclosed its presence.

It was Placide.

Placide dismounted and strode over to the circle of soft moss. "So," he said, "this is how you dally with my sister, MacKay?"

Surprised and red-faced, Jim started to reply, but the Creole planter cut him off.

"I see you are not content merely to toy with the mistress of my friend Étienne Bourrier," he said, fingering his riding crop. "Now you must attempt to disgrace my sister as well. I can tell you, sir, the consequences of this act will be grave. I know nothing of your Northern women, but I can tell you that here in the South we regard our women most highly. A Southern gentleman is fiercely dedicated to protecting the good name of his family. As you know, I am my sister's guardian. Forcing your advances on her is a serious offense—far more serious than trifling with a quadroon wench."

Jim's initial embarrassment gave way to indignation when he realized Placide was alluding to Delphine as a "quadroon wench." "I beg your pardon," he said, instinctively clenching his fists. Rising to his feet, he assumed a combative stance.

Placide chose to ignore his aggressive posture and turned to Odile. "Get on the horse," he ordered her.

Compliantly, Odile did as she was told.

"I must leave now and escort my sister home," Placide said to Jim. "However, this matter is far from settled. You will be hearing from me shortly."

Jim watched in dismay as Placide and Odile rode off on the horse together. For a second she looked back, as though apologizing for the potential trouble she had inadvertently caused.

Back at Mandragore, Placide conducted Odile into the study, closed the sliding doors, and sat her in the horsehair fauteuil opposite his rosewood desk.

"You know, of course, the consequences of such shameless behavior as that in which you engaged today with MacKay?" he said in a surprisingly matter-of-fact tone.

Apprehensively Odile bit her lip and wondered what measures he intended to take. Would he pack her off to the convent? Confine her to her room for months? Engage Jim MacKay in a duel? Arrange a hasty, arbitrary wedding for her with a random individual?

"I'm sorry for my behavior," she said. "I was so distraught about your breaking my engagement to Narciso and the devastating effect it had on him that I temporarily lost my head."

"Excuses and apologies won't do."

"What then?" she asked.

Placide smiled and folded his arms. "Mr. MacKay will restore your lost honor by making you his bride," he said.

Odile was astonished. How could he have her marry anyone so soon after breaking her engagement to Narciso—especially MacKay, whom he had grown to despise since the construction of the new mill? Would he really permit a Yankee and an upstart who had pushed Mandragore to the brink of economic disaster to marry into the esteemed Martinon family? Surely he was trying to trick her, or was playing some kind of diabolical joke. Granted, she did find Jim MacKay attractive in an elemental kind of way—there was no denying that—and today, out of a desire to retaliate for her brother's cruelty to Narciso and herself, combined with the emotional turmoil she was experiencing, she had allowed things to go much too far.

"Marry Jim MacKay?" she said incredulously. "Surely you must be joking?"

"I assure you I am quite serious," he said, picking up a quill pen and twirling it between his fingers.

"You can't be."

"Oh, but I am," he said. "I saw everything that happened today—his hands . . . your hands . . . everything. It was disgusting for a woman of your station. Well, you may lie in the mud with pigs, but you won't drag the Martinon name down with you. I shall let MacKay make an honest woman of you, mud and all."

Odile leaped to her feet. "I will never marry him or anyone else under such circumstances," she declared defiantly.

Snapping the quill in two, he replied, "You will do just as I say."

"MacKay is a totally unsuitable husband. He's not even a Catholic—"

"You should have thought of all that before you permitted him to take such shameless liberties with you today."

Odile decided to try another tack. "What about *him?*" she countered. "How will you bend him to your will? You may order me to marry him, but you can't order him to marry me. Have you thought of that?" she said.

"I must concede, dear sister, that you have a point," he agreed. "There is a good possibility that MacKay may not see the advantages of making you his bride. I hear he is still mooning over that quadroon wench of Bourrier's. However, our friend has the choice of a wedding with you or a duel with me. And I can assure you that no matter what weapons or conditions he chooses—even if it's mallets in ten feet of water or daggers in a flour barrel—he will not emerge the victor. Nothing would give me greater pleasure than to put a bullet through his head or a rapier through his heart."

Confused and distraught, Odile said, "It's incomprehensible that you want to force me to marry a man whom you despise so much."

"It may be incomprehensible," he conceded, "but it's also expedient, a solution to a desperate situation —yours and the plantation's. Not a very agreeable solution, I admit, but a solution nonetheless."

Odile was stunned. Was he really bartering her in order to save the plantation? "I can't believe we are so desperate that you would stoop to such a thing as this," she said, shocked by the frankness of the revelation, to say nothing of its implicit callousness.

"Can't you?" Unlocking the top drawer of his desk, he shuffled through some papers, finally locating a letter which he directed her to read.

The language of the letter was formal and full of legal jargon, but the message was clear. The bank was about to foreclose on Mandragore.

"How is it possible?" she asked, her voice almost a gasp.

"Very simple," he replied. "When Papa died, he left a great many debts. Since then, they have continued to mount because of our poor crops in recent years. The past year was the most disastrous, because MacKay stole much of the outside grinding, the income which I was depending on to help stave off our creditors. The business of our mill has been usurped almost completely by our neighbor. For a while I had hoped that Narciso would be Mandragore's savior—so to speak—but alas, he was no savior at all. Now, MacKay is suddenly our hope. As distasteful as you may find the prospect—and I admit I like it even less than you—a union between you and MacKay may be the only way to save us from total ruin. And," he added, almost as an afterthought, "preserve your good name—or what's left of it."

"I can't believe you are so scheming," she said.

"A desperate man considers all avenues," he replied with a philosophic shrug.

"Just how, do you propose, will MacKay save Mandragore?" she asked.

"In the prenuptial agreements I intend to have drawn up, he will agree to unite his land with Mandragore once again—the amputated limb returned to the body. He will be in charge of the mill or mills—I hope to convince him to convert the old mill to Guillon's new sugar-making method—and I will be in charge of the planting, the slaves, and virtually everything else, just as I am now. All proceeds will be divided accordingly," he explained.

"And where shall we live?" she asked.

"This house is big enough for all of us. After all, I am counting on you to bind us into one big, happy family."

"What makes you think MacKay will be willing to live here?"

"I saw his face, the look in his eyes the first time he entered our door. He would give his eyeteeth to live as we do."

Still feeling the sting of resentment and indignation

at the way he was using her, Odile complained, "So I am the pawn in your game?"

"Why not?" he said indifferently. "It is time you marry anyway. What difference does it make to whom? If MacKay isn't to your liking, you can eventually take a lover, as Denise and many other worldly women have done. It's almost expected."

"Suppose you hadn't come upon us in that compromising situation today?" she speculated. "What then?"

"I know you," he replied. "You are my sister and a Martinon. The blood of our family courses hot through our veins. If it was not today, it would have been another day. We Martinons cannot go for long without—shall we say?—love."

"You're despicable," she said.

"I have been called worse."

"How can you use me in such a cruel and heartless way when you know I love Narciso?"

"Do you?" he said, raising a single dark eyebrow. "I wonder."

24

Dragging the heavy sack of cotton, made heavier by the secret addition of several rocks, to the end of the long row, Delphine felt faint and exhausted. Unaccustomed to such backbreaking work beneath the broiling sun, she was additionally burdened by being in her final weeks of pregnancy. If luck was with her, her cotton would be weighed quickly by the overseer and she could receive her day's ration of cornmeal and pork—determined by the amount of cotton picked—and return to the cabin she shared with a half dozen other slaves to rest.

Shortly before the noon bell, Delphine was feeling

taxed beyond her strength, noticed that she had ceased to perspire, a dangerous sign in the cotton fields, and fell to the ground, helpless. Andy, the driver, dragged her into the shade of the standing cotton and dashed a bucket of water on her. When she regained consciousness and began to perspire once again, Andy, a whip coiled around his neck, ordered her back to work.

Claudie, an older, maternal slave, came to her rescue and berated the driver. "Can't you see that child is sick? Now you let her be. She needs to rest."

Reluctantly Andy capitulated and allowed Delphine to rest a little longer in the shade of the cotton plants, but when Munro Samples came galloping down the row on his horse, followed by the overseer's usual pack of dogs, he was angry to see a slave idle and laid his whip across not only Delphine but Andy and Claudie as well.

"Get back to work, and don't let me catch you loafing again or I'll put all three of you in the stocks for a week," he threatened.

Because of her low productivity, Delphine's food ration was extremely meager and had to be supplemented by the others who shared her cabin, whose own rations were barely adequate. In other ways as well, they tried to make her as comfortable as possible within their scanty means.

In spite of her inefficiency and ineptness as a field hand, Delphine had yet to suffer a punishment more severe than an occasional lash from Samples's whip as he rode up and down the rows of cotton, following the various work gangs and their drivers. Other slaves had been staked to the ground and brutally beaten, or locked in the wooden stocks for days at a time. She wondered if she was being spared because she was pregnant, but Claudie assured her otherwise.

"You just lucky, that's all," the matriarch of the slave gang informed her. "That Munro Samples is the devil hisself. He'd whip his own mama if he got the chance. As it is, he done beat a couple of his own children half to death." She was referring to the offspring, all plantation slaves, the overseer had sired by his succession of slave mistresses.

As Delphine timidly stepped up to the scale, Samples grabbed the pitifully small sack of cotton out of her hands.

"You ain't worth your salt as a field hand," he disparaged her, immediately finding the concealed stones and tossing them aside. "You are worthless. I'll tell you one thing, that kid you got in your belly better be a better cotton picker than his mammy or else I'm going to sell both your asses downriver—and separate," he threatened, prodding her with the handle of his whip. "If you don't do better, bitch, you are going to feel the sting of my whip on your high-yellow hide."

The following day dawned especially hot and muggy, and Delphine could scarcely rise from the ragged quilt, on which she slept on the bare floor, and dress.

Later, when Andy rounded up his work gang and prepared to march them into the fields, Claudie informed him that Delphine was in no condition to work that day. "She sick," the maternal slave declared. "You better send Kitty over to tend her." In addition to running the main house and taking special care of Narciso Valdéz, Kitty, a tall, freckled, blue-eyed, light-haired mulatto, served as the plantation's unofficial doctor. A bright, clever girl who had been secretly taught to read by Narciso, Kitty had gleaned her medical knowledge from catalogues advertising the popular patent medicines of the day, whose ingredients she attempted to duplicate. Her favorite remedy for most ailments was a mixture of camphor, sassafras root, turpentine, molasses, and sulphur. Kitty wielded considerable authority around the plantation, and when she declared a slave too ill to work, Samples was obliged to honor her decree.

Before Andy could send Delphine—or "Dolly," as she was known at Florestal—to Kitty, he had to obtain permission from Samples.

Notified of her illness by Andy, Samples rode over to the work gang and seized Delphine roughly, jerking her around so that she faced him. "You ain't sick, wench. You're faking again. You get your yellow ass into that field, hear?" he commanded.

Snapping his whip over their heads, he personally herded the gang across the muddy barnyard, where cackling chickens, honking geese, and squealing pigs fled before him. Increasingly dizzy and lightheaded, Delphine suddenly fainted before a watering trough. Claudie immediately went to her aid.

Still on horseback, Samples trotted in a circle around the two women, fingering his whip, not altogether oblivious to the bitter, hate-filled looks displayed by the other slaves in the gang.

"Get that wench on her feet!" he shouted.

"She sick," Claudie protested, dipping her kerchief in the trough and applying it to Delphine's forehead.

Without warning he struck the older woman a powerful blow with his whip and sent her reeling backward into the drinking trough. One of the husky male slaves, fists clenched and face twisted with rage, started toward the overseer, prompting Samples to pull his pistol from the holster and point it directly at him.

"Stay where you're at, boy, or you're dead," Samples warned.

Knowing that the overseer wouldn't hesitate to shoot even the most valuable field hand, the man reluctantly backed off.

Anxious to clear the slaves out, to prevent trouble, Samples ordered Andy to proceed to the fields with them at once.

"I'll take care of this wench myself," he said, referring to Delphine.

Marched off with the other slaves, Claudie glanced backward at the overseer with smoldering hatred and watched as he picked Delphine up and threw her roughly across the back of his horse.

Never having made love to a woman in such an advanced stage of pregnancy, he was tempted to take her to the overseer's cottage and experiment, but, fearing the jealousy of his current black mistress, Samples took her instead to the slave infirmary, dumped her on a crude cot, and sent for Kitty.

"I want you to get her up on her feet," he said when the dignified slave arrived. "I need every hand I can get out there in the cotton."

When Samples was gone, coldly assured by Kitty that she would do her best, she came and sat on the edge of the cot, gazing down at her charge. "You sure are a pretty one, ain't you. My, my, how'd you ever get yourself in this fix? You ain't no field nigger. Not with them nice, delicate hands. If I didn't know better, I would think you was a fine white lady."

Kitty sent for a basin of water and with her big, bony hands carefully washed Delphine's face. Then, she removed her clothes and sponged down her body as well. "It looks like some fine white gentleman's been taking mighty good care of you. I don't know what you done to cross him, but it must have been pretty bad for you to end up here. You sure ain't had the life of no ordinary nigger—not with that nice smooth skin. I bet some maid creamed it for you every day, didn't she?"

Unable to answer, Delphine closed her eyes and began to cry. Tears soon seeped between her tightly closed lids.

Kitty smiled sympathetically and tried to brush them away with the tips of her fingers. "Don't you cry now, honey. Kitty's going to take good care of you and that young one you got in your belly there, just like she's been taking care of poor Mr. Narciso all these years," she promised as she kissed Delphine tenderly on both cheeks. "You're going to stay around the house until that baby of yours comes."

❧ 25

True to his word, Placide sought Jim MacKay out at his mill, and found the young Ohioan in the outer shed atop a cart of cane, wrench in hand, attempting to repair the stalled conveyor belt. None too pleased about the interruption, he nevertheless dropped the wrench and climbed off the cart, wiping his greasy hands on his trousers.

"I apologize if I have selected an inconvenient time for our interview," Placide said. "But what I have to say won't take long. Can we go somewhere more private and talk?"

Jim was certain the Creole had come to discuss the dalliance with his sister and was annoyed that he had selected such an inopportune time for it. The belt's breakdown had brought the mill to a complete standstill, while a steady stream of cane carts continued to arrive from the surrounding plantations.

"Hans!" he shouted to Oberdorfer, and instructed him to continue working on the belt until it was moving again.

"Shall we go to my cabin?" Jim suggested, wondering what alternatives Martinon was prepared to offer him. Would it be a duel? A shotgun wedding? Something more imaginative? So far as Jim could tell from the couple of years he had spent in Louisiana, all Creoles seemed to be overly emotional hotheads whose actions rarely had any rational basis. Although he had no actual fear of Martinon as an adversary, despite his considerable reputation as a swordsman and pistolier, he fervently hoped that the so-called insult to the family honor would not result in another duel. The last one, with Bourrier, had cost him too dearly.

Looking somewhat askance at the suggestion of the humble, rough-hewn dwelling as a meeting place, Placide nevertheless nodded his assent and headed his horse in the direction of the cabin.

Inside it was dark and refreshingly cool. Jim offered his guest a seat on an empty keg, which he hesitantly accepted, carefully folding his frock coat about his legs as he sat. Before they entered the cabin, Jim had drawn a bucket of water from the well outside the door, and now he offered the dipper to Martinon.

"No, thank you," the Creole said, watching with concealed disgust as Jim drank from the wooden scoop.

Wiping his mouth with his sleeve, Jim asked, "Now, what did you come to talk about?"

"Since I see you are quite busy, I will come right to the point. I am here to discuss a delicate matter—namely, the liberties you so boldly took with my young sister."

Jim glanced at him with poorly concealed annoyance. "I'm not sure I would describe it that way."

"In any event, I personally witnessed a highly compromising situation, one sufficiently scandalous to ruin my sister's reputation and chances for marriage," Placide said.

"If you'll pardon me for saying so, there are only three of us who know about it—you, your sister, and myself. I don't see how her reputation can be ruined unless one of us talks."

"There is no way to assure your silence, MacKay," he replied curtly.

"You have my word as a gentleman that I will say nothing," Jim said.

"If you were a gentleman the situation would not have come about in the first place. A promise of silence is not acceptable from a man who took advantage of the innocence of a young girl," the Creole asserted.

"Then what is acceptable?" Jim inquired. "A duel?"

"A duel would be the last resort," Placide said. "As much as I would personally like to confront you on the dueling ground for this most serious transgression against the honor of my family, at the behest of my sister I will seek another avenue of satisfaction."

"And what is that?"

"The alternative to my killing you," Placide replied, "is your marrying Odile."

Jim was stunned. Had this arrogant Creole really come to present such an ultimatum in the interest of his sister's good name? Surely there had to be a stronger motivation for such a rash move on Martinon's part. How could he be asking Jim to become a member of his family—one of the oldest and most prominent in Louisiana—under such circumstances? Jim suspected that there was far more involved in the ultimatum than the Creole would be willing to admit. What did he hope to gain with Jim as a brother-in-law? Rumor had it that Mandragore was in deep financial difficulties and in imminent danger of going under. Jim wondered how Placide figured he could bail them out. Then there was Odile herself—what were her feelings about such a marriage? Especially when it was common knowledge that she had been in love with her cousin for years, their engagement recently announced and then inexplicably broken. Jim was baffled.

Rising from the keg, Placide dusted off the seat of his well-cut trousers. "So, MacKay," he said, carefully replacing his high-crowned hat on his head, "you have thirty days in which to decide. At the end of that time there will either be a wedding—or a wake. I advise you to think it over carefully."

Leaving the mill in the care of Roarke and the others, Jim hopped onto his horse and headed into town to Isaac's store. When he got there Isaac was closing for the noon hour and invited Jim to accompany him to a waterfront restaurant for some fresh oysters on the half shell.

"So what brings you to town in the middle of the day?" the merchant asked, tilting his head backward and sliding the oyster from its shell directly into his mouth.

"Martinon is insisting I marry his sister," Jim blurted, anxious to unload the news to someone.

He was astounded. "What! Marry his sister?"

"It's true. He caught me dallying with her down by the river."

Isaac excitedly waved his tiny oyster fork at him. "You dallied with Odile Martinon?"

"Briefly," Jim admitted.

"So what do you mean he's 'insisting'?"

"It's either marry her or fight him in a duel. I have a month to think it over."

"Marry the sister," Isaac advised without hesitation, remembering the last duel.

"It's not quite so simple."

"Nothing's simple. Marry her. Why not? Who wouldn't want to marry a beautiful girl like Odile Martinon? But be careful," he warned. "Watch out for that Placide Martinon. He's a sly one. What's he got up his sleeve? He's not going to let you marry his sister just to save her good name. He's got something else in mind. Before you say yes, find out what it is he wants."

"I don't know what I have to offer. I'm not rich. I have only a few acres—nothing compared to his spread. My background is completely different. Frankly, I don't understand," Jim said, shaking his head.

Leaning close to him, Isaac ignored his oysters a moment and confided, "You know what you got? You got new blood, a good head, and a strong back. Martinon's not so stupid that he can't see the potential in a man like you. Let him look down on your lack of culture. Let him call you whatever names he wants, he knows you can do him some good. These Creoles have been here too long. With all their land and their slaves and their fine food and good wine and fancy clothes and fancy women, they've grown soft. They've forgotten how to work, how to run a plantation. After all, a plantation can't run itself any more than a store can. It takes somebody with some drive behind it, pushing, pushing, pushing. It's not easy. It takes your life's blood—every bit of energy you got. Martinon knows his plantation is in a mess. He knows he needs new blood, new spirit, new drive, new ideas to straighten it out and make it the place it used to be. He's been watching you. First he saw the way you drained the swamp and made a decent farm out of nothing but mud. Then he saw the mill and the success you made out of it. That jackal's eye of his misses nothing. He's a gambler. He's willing to risk his sister in order to save Mandragore from the wolves. Once you marry her, he'll begin, little by little, turning the duties and the decisions over to you, but he'll still remain in charge. You'll do the work and he'll live off the fat. Mark my words, Jim, I'm right."

"What about Odile? What about her part in all of this?"

"Her part?" Isaac laughed. "Her part is to do whatever her brother says. She has no choice."

Isaac blotted his mouth, wiped his hands with the large linen napkin, and then dipped into his pocket, producing a yellowed daguerreotype. Changing the subject, he asked, "Do you remember that marriage broker I mentioned in New York who thinks he's found me a bride?"

Jim glanced up from his plate. "Yes. Why?"

Isaac proudly passed the photograph to Jim. "She's coming from New York. A beauty, don't you think?"

Jim considered the photograph a moment without saying anything.

"Well, she's not Odile Martinon, but she's pretty, isn't she?" Isaac prodded.

"Yes, she's pretty," Jim finally agreed.

"And devout, too. She just arrived in America from the Sephardic colony in Amsterdam. I can tell she'll make a good wife." As he spoke, his face glowed with eager anticipation. "I can't wait until she gets here."

Jim continued to gaze at the photograph and wondered why he couldn't generate the same enthusiasm for his possible union with Odile. If he could only know for certain the fate of Delphine and his unborn child, perhaps he might feel differently. After all, Odile was beautiful and passionate, and she had given him reliable advice in the duel with Bourrier. Still, he knew that he could never be content married to her so long as he believed there was a possibility—no matter how remote—that Delphine still loved him and he could be together with her and their child.

The prospect of marriage to Jim MacKay was not altogether unattractive to Odile in spite of her long-standing adoration of Narciso, although she was hesitant to let her brother know her true feelings and protested vigorously whenever he mentioned the possible union.

She had no illusions that the marriage—if it did take place—would be a love match. If MacKay agreed to marry her, she felt, it would be merely to save her good name and avoid a duel with Placide. For her part, she would be sacrificing herself—if "sacrificing" was the correct word—in order to save the ancestral home. In essence it would be a marriage of convenience and nothing more. Such marriages were very common among the prominent families of the South, and, she supposed, the North as well. In these loveless unions it was customary, as Placide pointed out, for the husband to take discreetly a mistress, and the wife a lover. Appearances were preserved and desires satisfied. It was the ideal solution.

Earlier in her life, before romantic daydreams gave way to harsh reality, Odile had hoped for a love match, a whirlwind romance that would sweep her off her feet, but now the possibility of a marriage of convenience did not seem the terrible prospect it once would have.

One rainy day, as Odile and Placide sat in the parlor playing dominoes, he remarked, "You must admit MacKay is certainly healthier than poor Narciso."

Staring at the dotted black tiles before her, she conceded, "I suppose he is."

"He must be. Otherwise how could he work like a nigger the way he does?"

"I really think you shouldn't talk about Mr. MacKay like that," she scolded, astonished to hear herself actually defending him.

"Well, forgive me, my dear." He chuckled. "I had no idea you were so sensitive to remarks about your prospective suitor. Actually, if you must know, it's his capacity for work that I'm counting on to save us."

"He's really not such a bad sort," she said. "Even if he is a *Kaintock* and lacks the charm and polish of our Southern gentlemen."

"He's a boor and we both know it," Placide said impatiently. "But no matter. I have endured boors before. I shall be able to endure our friend MacKay if it means saving Mandragore."

Encouraged, Odile suggested, "I'd like to invite him to dinner soon. I think it's only fitting, being that he might be living here someday."

"Don't tell me I detect a thaw in your feelings for him?" Placide smiled.

"One's feelings for a person have nothing at all to

do with their suitability as a marriage partner. After all, one can have feelings for horses or dogs," she explained.

"I had the privilege of observing your feelings for MacKay down by the river—if you recall," he reminded her.

Choosing to ignore the innuendo, despite a slight blush which crept to her cheeks, Odile said, "The one thing that bothers me is the way he still pines for that quadroon hussy—Étienne Bourrier's mistress."

One day, returning from her weekly quilting session at Palmetto Place, the upriver plantation belonging to Henri and Victorine Pilette, Odile rode along the top of the levee. As she passed Jim's land she was surprised to glance over the side of the dike and see him sitting once again in the same mossy spot encircled by willows where Placide had earlier caught them together. On the edge of the bayou the sugar mill was going full blast, and she was surprised to find Jim away from his operation at such a busy time. Curiosity got the better of her, and Odile dismounted, leading her horse down the side of the levee to where he was sitting.

As she approached, he seemed embarrassed by her presence and turned away from her. Only as she drew close did she realize from his puffy, splotched face and red-rimmed eyes that he had been crying. She was stunned. Jim MacKay didn't seem the sort of man who would ever cry over anything. On occasion Creole men could weep openly without shame or embarrassment, but among Americans, such as Jim, it was practically unheard of. An unexpected surge of sympathy welled up within her, making her anxious to reach out to him, find out what was wrong and comfort him.

"Is something the matter?" she asked.

Attempting to pull himself together, he answered, "No, nothing."

"But you look upset," she persisted, noting for the first time that he was clutching a letter, which he had apparently been reading.

"I'm all right," he insisted.

Indicating the letter in his hand, she said, "Bad news?"

After a moment's hesitation, he passed it to her. "Decide for yourself," he said.

Sitting next to him on the old log she began to read, flattered that he had decided to take her into his confidence.

> My dear MacKay:
>
> Christian duty compels me to inform you that yesterday Delphine gave birth to a son. Shortly afterward both mother and child expired and were immediately buried because of the climate here in Martinique. Her last words to me were, "Forgive me, my beloved Étienne, and pray for my errant soul. You are truly the only one I have ever loved in all my life." Please excuse the brevity of this letter but my sorrow is too profound to permit further discourse.
>
> > Sincerely yours,
> > Étienne Bourrier.

Moved, Odile understood Jim's grief, although she was not altogether convinced about the veracity of the letter. Over the years her acquaintance with Bourrier had made her aware of the duplicity in his character. She was also cognizant of his longstanding friendship with Placide and the correspondence the two men carried on. Odile was sure that this letter had been instigated by her brother.

Laying her hand tenderly on his shoulder, she commiserated, "I'm so sorry, Jim." Despite the tragedy implicit in Bourrier's letter, Odile realized that at the same time it obliterated any possibility of a reunion between him and Delphine.

Much to her surprise, Jim suddenly put his arms around her and buried his face in her bosom.

❧ 26

Although Delphine had been experiencing slight, intermittent pain in the small of her back since early morning, she had no desire to spend the day in bed, and carried on with her usual household duties, one of which was to take a glass of port, prescribed by Dr. Zehner as a blood-strengthener, to Narciso in his room every afternoon. As she approached his book-laden quarters, she heard a loud commotion from within. The young man could be overly emotional at times and had had violent outbursts on occasion, but this one exceeded all others. Yelling at the top of his lungs, he was storming about the room in his night-shirt, knocking whole shelves of books onto the floor, kicking the harpsichord and other furniture, while his distraught mother looked on and tried to quiet him.

The din was so loud that neither mother nor son heard Delphine when she knocked and entered, nor was either aware of her presence.

As he waved his spidery arms at his mother, Delphine observed that his face was distorted and purple.

"She can't do this to me!" he was shouting. "I won't permit it! I won't permit it if it's the last thing I do—and it well may be."

"Please, dearest, calm yourself," Adela pleaded, wringing her tiny hands. "Calm yourself before you have another spell and I have to send for Dr. Zehner."

"I don't care if I do have another spell!"

"Don't say what you don't mean."

"But I do mean it. I *want* to have another spell!"

"Dr. Zehner said that someday one of those spells of yours is going to kill you."

"I don't care if it does!"

"Hush, darling, don't talk like that."

"I want to die!" Rolling his dark eyes heavenward, Narciso clasped his hands in mock prayer. "O God, please take me! Let me die! Release me from my misery!"

"Hush, dearest—"

"If I can't have Odile, I don't want to live!" he declared hysterically.

"She's no good for you, anyway," Adela said. "She's a wicked, nasty girl—as corrupt as her brother. I can't believe that either one of those children is the issue of my beloved sister-in-law. It must be the Martinon blood they have in their veins. The Martinons are all descendants of pirates, thieves, and whores. It's God's will that you shouldn't marry her. Don't you see that, my darling?" Adela attempted to put her arms around her son. "I never wanted her for you anyway—at least not after I realized the real reason behind her brother's desire for the union, after opposing it for so many years. Hah! What do they think we are, fools? He only wanted to use you to save his failing plantation from ruin. Well, he won't save it at the expense of my son. Let that Yankee upstart save them all."

Yankee upstart? The phrase caught Delphine's attention.

"Well, I say that if it takes place, that marriage will be a disaster," Adela predicted. "They'll all live to regret it—including that young Yankee lad. He'll rue the day he fell into that pit of conniving vipers."

Calmer, Narciso shook his head in dismay. "I still can't believe she would marry that MacKay," he said.

Hearing Jim's name and realizing the implications of the conversation, Delphine experienced a sharp spasm of pain deep within and let the tray with the single glass of port fall from her trembling hands. Clutching her belly, she collapsed.

Realizing for the first time that a third party had entered the room and probably overheard them, Adela cried, "These damned niggers! Just look what that wench has done—spilled wine all over. Damn her black hide anyway."

Narciso went immediately to Delphine's aid and attempted to drag her toward his bed.

"You're not going to put that nigger in your bed?" Adela asked, her eyes wide with horror at such a prospect.

Narciso looked at his mother with angry indignation. "I think she's in labor and about to have a child," he announced.

"Then get her out of here! We can't let any nigger go birthing babies in this room," Adela commanded.

Ignoring her protestations, Narciso attempted to lift the unconscious woman himself. Only when she saw him straining and purple did Adela condescend to help.

❧ 27

Foolishly—according to Verbena—Odile had decided to embroider details in the tapestry she was making with the so-called Chinese forbidden stitch, a stitch so tiny it put considerable strain on the embroiderer's eyes.

"You going to go blind sewing a stitch like that," the maid warned. "Just like all them poor Chinese."

Tired, Odile clipped the thread, stuck the needle in the pincushion, and rolled up the tapestry, a depiction of her ancestors establishing Mandragore. As she was about to leave the sewing room, opposite the parlor on the first floor, Placide wandered in in his stockinged feet. Out on the gallery she could hear the snap of the little slave boy's rag as he polished the master's boots.

"MacKay has only a few days left in which to decide. Foolishly I gave him an extension because of his grief over the death of his paramour and her child," he said. "Sometimes I think it was very stupid allowing him to humiliate us like this with his procrastination."

"You are the one who has humiliated us—or at least humiliated me—as much as he has," Odile retorted. "Treating me as though I was horseflesh, to be bartered and traded."

Placide shook his finger at her. "Let me remind you, dear sister, that this would not have come about if you had not conducted yourself like some common baggage," he said. "Well, either MacKay chooses a date for the wedding or he chooses his weapon. I'm getting tired of his stalling."

Later, alone in her room, Odile lay on the bed contemplating the situation. Although angry and resentful that she had been used as a pawn, she realized at the same time that if she didn't marry Jim MacKay and bring his managerial skills, drive, ambition, and new mill into the family, all that she cherished might be lost: the home which had housed four generations of Martinons, the plantation, the slaves, a whole way of life. Without a shred of pity they would be turned out by heartless creditors to face a life of shame and disgrace. It had happened to families older and more prominent than theirs. Women like Mademoiselle LeDoux were forced to become governesses and teachers of music. No, she would marry MacKay to save her family's future.

After a moment's consideration, Odile called for her coachman. "Cecil, do you know how to find the house of Nizilda Foucher?"

Both Cecil and Verbena were astonished to hear her utter the name of the woman who had the reputation of being the most powerful voodoo sorceress in New Orleans.

Verbena crossed herself. "What you doing talking about a woman like that?" she demanded.

"I ain't taking you there, Miss Odile," Cecil said. "No, ma'am."

"What you want with her anyhow?" Verbena asked.

"I need her help," Odile responded.

"You don't need nobody like that," the maid said, her eyes wide with apprehension.

"If you won't take me to her house, Cecil, I shall be forced to drive myself," Odile declared.

"I ain't going near there," Cecil refused. "That old witch spooks horses so bad they ain't no good for nothing but slaughtering."

"Marse Placide would skin us alive if we was to take you anywhere near old Nizilda," Verbena said.

"On the contrary," Odile replied. "I think in this case he might approve."

In all Kitty's years as a midwife at Florestal, Delphine's labor was the most difficult she had ever attended. She allowed the frightened, exhausted woman to labor nearly thirty-six hours before she became alarmed and went on horseback in the middle of the night to summon Dr. Zehner, leaving Delphine in the care of Claudie and some of the other slave women. By the light of the pale moon the tall, wiry mulatto jumped fences, crossed fields thick with cotton and corn, and forded streams en route to the physician's home. There, she pounded violently on the front door for a long time before Zehner himself in his nightshirt answered the door.

Thrusting the whale-oil lamp in her face, he demanded anxiously, "Is something wrong with Mr. Narciso?"

"No, sir," Kitty answered. "I got a girl in labor for thirty-six hours and still the baby ain't come. I'm scared—"

"What girl?" he interrupted impatiently.

"Her name's Dolly."

"You mean one of the *slaves?*" he said, seeming far less concerned once he realized she had not come about Narciso.

"Yes, sir."

"Damn it, girl, I don't go out to treat niggers in the middle of the night. You do the best you can for now and I'll see her in the morning."

"Please, Dr. Zehner, you got to come now," Kitty pleaded. "I'm scared something serious is wrong."

"Now listen here, Kitty, you have no right coming over here this way and waking me up. Miss Adela would have you whipped if she knew you were riding around in the middle of the night on some fool errand like this."

"This ain't no fool errand," Kitty insisted, raising her voice indignantly. "This girl is in a bad way. She going to die if somebody don't do something mighty quick."

"There's no emergency about a slave simply giving birth," he retorted.

"This ain't no matter of simply birthing a baby. Something's wrong," Kitty repeated. Somewhere nearby an owl was hooting. Kitty considered it a bad omen and increased the intensity of her pleas. "You got to come—please—"

"Now look here." Zehner bristled. "I told you that I'll see her in the morning, and that's that. You go on and get out of here before I take my cane to you."

Her light eyes blazing with anger and resentment, Kitty spat out, "If she was a white lady, you'd be on your horse and over there quicker than a flash."

"That's enough out of you!"

"Because she's black you're willing to let both her and the child die, ain't you?" she accused. "Don't you try to deny it because I know better."

Zehner waved his walking stick at her threateningly. "You get out of here!" he cried.

"I'm going, you no-account quack!" Kitty shouted as she ran for the horse as quickly as she could.

With Placide's approval, Odile sent Romulus over to Jim MacKay's with an invitation to dinner, and, much to her surprise, he accepted without hesitation.

"Just because he's coming here to eat don't mean nothing," Verbena cautioned. "He still ain't said nothing definite about no wedding. A man likes to eat good no matter what. Him living in that shack of his alone and cooking for hisself all the time most likely makes him hungry for a good meal."

Despite the maid's admonishment, Odile found herself excited at the prospect of Jim's visit. In recent weeks, since breaking her engagement, she had found herself—much to her surprise—thinking less and less of Narciso and more of MacKay.

At the appointed hour, Jim arrived dressed in well-tailored but more-conservative clothes than Placide or the more stylish Creoles might have chosen. Recently he had begun taking a greater interest in his appearance, seeking out the better tailors and barbers in town, anxious to improve the impression he made. His motivation for this did not spring from a desire to please the Martinons or imitate their tastes, but from a wish to establish himself as a successful member of the local community of planters and cease to remain on the fringes, as he had thus far.

For his part, Placide greeted his guest cordially, successfully concealing whatever animosity he might have felt, and complimented him on the cut of his coat.

After dinner Odile played several selections on the harp before Placide suggested to Jim that they retire to the study for brandy and cigars.

"She plays very well," Jim said of Odile.

"My sister is a girl of many talents," Placide agreed.

After a few minutes of small talk—planting, the weather, Jim's mill—Placide decided to boldly broach the subject about which he was most concerned.

"I trust you've made your decision now?" he asked.

"Soon." Jim nodded, but his expression gave no inkling as to what that decision might be. He wanted to stall as long as possible.

"Let me remind you, MacKay, that I'm not going to wait much longer," Placide said. "I've already been exceedingly patient."

Jim merely repeated, "Soon."

"Another week and that's all," Placide said firmly.

After a time Odile knocked at the sliding doors, interrupting.

"Shame on you, Placide, monopolizing our guest this way," she chided. Turning to Jim, she said, "I wonder if you would like to accompany me on a walk through the gardens, Mr. MacKay? I feel like taking some air."

"My pleasure, ma'am," he replied.

From the study window Placide watched anxiously as Odile linked her arm through the Yankee planter's, conducting him on a stroll down the garden path among the oleander, jasmine, and magnolias.

"I know this might sound immodest," she confided to Jim, "but even if Mandragore is my home, I still think it's one of the loveliest plantations in the entire South."

"It's the nicest I've seen," Jim agreed.

"My great-granddaddy imported plants and trees from all over the world, and the finest gardeners in Europe," she continued. "He wanted Mandragore to be a true showplace."

"He did a real good job," Jim said. "Tell me, how did it come by that name?" Most of the plantations had some sort of story behind their names. Several were named for plants found on the land—Palmetto Place, Laureldale, Briarwood—others for natural landmarks —Forest Point, The Cliffs, Rocky Hill. Still others were more exotic. Tezcuco was from an Aztec word meaning "resting place," and Houmas was named for the Indian tribe of the region.

Odile, proud of her heritage, was pleased that he had asked. "The story is probably more legend than fact, but I'll tell you what I know," she said. "My great-great-granddaddy, Theophile Martinon, was a pirate and associate of Jean Lafitte. He helped smuggle supplies to General Andrew Jackson through a secret channel in Barataria Bayou known only to Lafitte's pirate band, and thereby helped to defeat the British. However, before the war was over Theophile was captured by the British and hanged. At the hanging they forced my great-granddaddy, Jean Baptiste Martinon, Theophile's son, and just a child, to watch the hanging of his daddy. Well, as you might well imagine, it had a pretty strong effect on the boy. But instead of scaring him or anything like that, it made him more determined to fight back and make something of the name of Martinon. After a while Jean Baptiste himself went to sea, but he wasn't a pirate or anything like that, just a regular seaman. Pretty soon he established a shipping company of his own and became very prosperous. Eventually he decided to settle a short distance upriver from New Orleans, and started wandering around until

he finally came to a place where he remembered them
hanging his daddy. The awful memory riled him so, he
began crying and throwing himself down and pounding
the ground with his fists, carrying on until he got so
exhausted he fell asleep. While he was sleeping, his
daddy came to him in a dream and told him to buy all
the land in sight and eventually it would make him and
his descendants one of the wealthiest and most powerful families in the state. He also instructed him that he
must place the main house on the exact spot where the
hanging had taken place. Well, when Jean Baptiste
woke up he was pretty shaken, but he did as he was
told and bought up all the land. Still, it worried him as
to where to start building his house, because he had no
idea of the exact spot where the gallows were located.
He tried to recall, but he just couldn't. Finally one day
one of his slaves suggested he consult old Noémie
Foucher, a voodoo priestess. He did and brought her
to the land. Well, this old Negress marched right to a
certain spot and pointed to a mandrake growing there.
You see, the mandrake plant grows on the spot where
a man is hanged—at least that's the legend. This house
is built on that very place where the voodooienne
found the mandrake plant. 'Mandragore' means 'mandrake' in French."

Listening, Jim was fascinated by the story and by
the intense, involved, yet thoroughly charming way she
related it.

"That was very interesting," he said as they paused
beneath a rose trellis. Then, raising her chin with his
hand, he gently kissed her, unaware that Placide was
on the gallery and gazing in their direction.

❧ 28

W hen Kitty returned to the tiny room over the warming kitchen at Florestal, she was shocked to find a crowd of moaning, sobbing, and praying black women on their knees in a circle around the bed on which Delphine lay, covered from head to toe by a white sheet. The room was permeated by an ominous, fleshy odor she recognized as the smell of blood, and at the foot of the bed was a huge red stain, evidently the remnants of a massive hemorrhage mopped up by the slave women. Claudie, looking as though she were in a trance, held a tiny infant in her arms, gently rocking it from side to side.

Pushing the women aside, Kitty made her way to the bed and tore the sheet off Delphine. Her lovely face was horribly contorted, signifying that her death had been an agonizing one. Kitty gasped and clutched her throat.

"She gone!" Claudie wailed. "She gone, poor child. Cover her up."

One of the young slave girls spoke up. "But we got us a fine healthy boy. Just look at how beautiful he is. His pappy's got to be a white man."

Only hours later after Delphine's body had been removed from the room to be prepared by the women for burial did Kitty finally bring herself to look at the child, whom she ordered—against Claudie's wishes—to be left with her in the tiny cradle she had secured in anticipation of the baby's birth a few days earlier. Before taking Delphine away, Claudie had removed a medallion from around her neck and placed it on the infant. Kitty stared at the gold pendant, which seemed enormous on the tiny child, hanging nearly to his feet. She fingered it and wondered, with tears welling in her eyes, what the inscription, *"More than yesterday, less than tomorrow,"* meant and who had given it to Delphine. Even with her, Delphine had remained to the end secretive about her previous life.

Picking the child up in her arms, Kitty realized at once that the boy was not only husky and healthy but fair-complected, with a full head of tiny, tight blond curls. His eyes, too, were so light a shade of blue that Kitty felt certain they would remain that color.

"You got yourself a white pappy all right," Kitty said, kissing the baby's rosy cheek.

Later, when the question of a name for the child arose, Claudie insisted that Delphine had confided to her that she wished the child named James, after his alleged father.

"James," Kitty considered with a disapproving frown. "No. This is a fine boy and he needs a fine name worthy of him. 'James' is too plain, too ordinary, too much like the slave names we all been cursed with— he'll be called Jimmie for sure."

"Don't go giving him no slave names," one of the young girls protested.

"I want to give him a name that'll make him strong and proud," Kitty said. "I want this boy to grow up to be a man—a free man someday."

"He so light he could go up North and pass for white," another of the slave women pointed out.

"This boy ain't going to run nowhere," Kitty asserted. "If he's going to be a free man, he's going to be a free man right here."

"You talking like he your own," Claudie accused.

"I am fixing to raise him like my own," Kitty announced.

"You ain't even got you no husband," Claudie said indignantly. She was deeply resentful that Kitty had usurped the child from her, feeling he should have been hers to raise. "And from the looks of things, it don't look like you'll ever get none."

"I don't need none," Kitty retorted. There was a certain air of authority about her that the other slaves —male or female—seldom dared to challenge.

Taking the infant from his cradle, Kitty held him up by a single foot as though to demonstrate the child's strength to the assembled and somewhat disapproving women. The boy gurgled uncertainly but did not cry.

"I am going to name him Achille," she declared with a triumphant smile, recalling a powerful slave she had known in the past who had been lynched for his rebelliousness, the only man in her life who had ever truly stirred her.

29

Despite their strenuous objections, Odile forced Cecil and Verbena to accompany her to the infamous cottage on the edge of the French Quarter where the celebrated voodoo queen Nizilda Foucher resided.

"No self-respecting white woman would ever do such a thing," Verbena reproached.

"Some of the most aristocratic white ladies in New Orleans have availed themselves of Nizilda's services," Odile replied.

"She's the devil hisself," Cecil said, his eyes wide with dread. "She wears a scarf over her head to hide her horns. When decent God-fearing folks sees Nizilda coming, they crosses the street or goes around the block to keep from meeting up with her. No telling what kind of spell she's liable to put on you with them evil eyes of hers."

When the carriage stopped in front of the tiny ramshackle cottage raised high off the muddy ground on four stone piers, Verbena and Cecil tried to discourage her from going to the door.

"That's one house I ain't never going to set foot in," Verbena declared.

"Me either," Cecil agreed. "She's an evil woman. She takes babies not wanted by their mamas and hangs them up in her chimney and smokes them like they was hams or bacon. I even knows a man who had one of them smoked babies. It was black as coal and hard as stone. His wife made him get rid of it because as long as it was in the house they couldn't have no childrens. After they threw that thing out of the house, they done had theirselves five childrens."

"Nonsense," Odile scoffed. Ridiculing their superstitious fears, she flounced unaided out of the carriage and up the rickety wooden steps to the door.

In response to her insistent rapping, a cocoa-colored woman so thin her skin seemed to cling to her very bones eventually opened the door a crack, and Odile knew instantly from the shabby scarf, draped nun-like over her head and fastened beneath her chin with a rusty pin, that this was Nizilda herself.

"Nizilda Foucher?" she inquired politely.

The old woman narrowed her eyes suspiciously. "What you want with Nizilda?"

"I've come for help," Odile informed her.

Opening the door wider, the woman invited her to enter. "Come in, dearie."

A dirty gray dress hung from her bony frame, and her bare feet were stuffed into an old pair of men's shoes. A three-legged cat rubbed against the old woman's legs, purring.

The tiny room was almost bare except for a couple of broken chairs and wooden benches. Gaudy religious pictures adorned the walls.

Smiling, Nizilda displayed her jagged, yellow teeth. "How can I help you, dearie?" she asked.

In a roundabout fashion Odile finally explained that she had a procrastinating fiancé whom she wished to prod into marrying her quickly.

Without warning, Nizilda threw her head back and emitted a loud shrill screech of a laugh, which frightened Odile and sent the three-legged cat scurrying under the ragged curtain which separated the front room from an adjoining one in the rear.

"That's not an easy request," she cackled. "It takes

time to work good magic. You got to be patient even when you're in a hurry, dearie. I'll do my best to give you the best and strongest charms I got."

"Thank you," Odile said.

Taking her by the hand, Nizilda led her to a bench and sat down beside her.

"To make a marriage," she instructed, "you puts sand in front of a picture of Saint Joseph. Then, in the sand you must write the name of your beloved and your own. Around the names you places a circle of candles. When all this is done, get yourself two dolls—a male and a female—tie them together at the wrists with a piece of white satin, and put these dolls in the middle of the circle of candles. Now, every night at the same hour you must pray with all your heart to Saint Joseph to make this marriage for you. When he does—and he will if you follow what I say and do it right—you thank him by placing parsley and macaroni in the sand before his picture. Do you follow me, dearie?"

"Is that all there is to it?" Odile said. She felt disappointed, having expected the prescribed ritual to be far more complex and mysterious. This sounded too simple —no blood from a black rooster, no lizard's entrails to be buried beneath a dead tree at midnight, no earth from a fresh grave.

"That ain't all," Nizilda said. "I gots to make up a special love oil for you. You puts three drops between your bosoms whenever you're going to see your beau and it'll make him propose mighty quick. Now, while you're waiting for me to mix it, you go on in the other room and start your praying to Saint Joseph. The sooner we gets started, the better."

Without further ado, Nizilda parted the tattered curtains and led her by the hand into the back room.

In contrast to the bareness of the outer room, this one was cluttered with all manner of curious objects. Although it apparently served as Nizilda's bedroom— there was a cot with a ragged quilt in one corner—the room was dominated by a huge altar.

"You just kneel down there and pray," Nizilda directed, leading Odile before it.

The only light in the room came from seven candles,

each of a different color, burning in a holder on the altar, on which was displayed a bust of the Virgin Mary wearing an incongruous crown of thorns, as well as icons and pictures of various other Catholic saints.

As she knelt, Odile found it impossible to pray, so fascinated and taken was she by the exotic paraphernalia surrounding her. The low ceiling was hung with African fetish jujus, and in addition to the Catholic trappings on the altar, there was a black box containing a mummified heart stuck with cloves, the skull of a goat, molted snakeskins in a pile, a pelvic bone—probably human—placed in such a fashion that it resembled a bizarre face mask, as well as other mysterious objects which Odile was unable to identify, including a basket typical of the type woven by the Choctaws and sold by them in the French Market.

Curious about the contents of the Indian basket, Odile rose from her knees and decided to have a look. The room was too dark for her to see distinctly, but when she peered over the edge of the basket she saw, curled in the bottom, a thick black snake, which, Odile realized when it suddenly raised its head and hissed menacingly at her, had only one eye.

She let out a squeal and ran from the room.

"He's just a harmless pet," Nizilda laughed, knowing without asking what had frightened the girl. "If you had remained praying like I told you to, and not gone snooping around, he wouldn't have bothered you."

Still trying to catch her breath from the scare of the snake, Odile asked, "Is the love oil ready yet?"

Still chuckling, Nizilda handed her a tiny vial. "Remember what I told you—three drops," she instructed. "No more than that. It's very powerful."

"Thank you," Odile said, clutching the bottle. Still trembling, she pressed some gold coins into the woman's hand.

"Remember, dearie," Nizilda called after her as she hurried from the cottage, "pray. Pray real hard!"

Much to the consternation of Verbena and the other house slaves, Odile followed Nizilda's instructions to the letter—the sand, the circle of candles, the two dolls bound together with white satin, everything.

"Black magic in this house," Verbena moaned. "It's a good thing your mama ain't alive to see such goings-on. She'd be mighty upset with you."

"It's not black magic at all," Odile retorted. "I'm praying to Saint Joseph, just as any good Catholic prays to a saint for special intervention and favors."

"Ain't no self-respecting saint that's got nothing to do with Nizilda Foucher. Sometime—if I wasn't so scared—I'd like to tear off that old shawl she keeps over her head and show you those horns she's got underneath."

"She doesn't have horns," Odile scoffed.

"I knows folks who's seen them with their very own eyes."

"Nonsense!" Odile snapped. Inwardly she did worry from time to time about the wisdom of following the counsel of a voodoo practitioner. The part about praying to Saint Joseph gave her no pause, but the rest she found somewhat disconcerting. Once or twice she had been tempted to dismantle the secret altar she had assembled in an alcove of her room and getting rid of the sand inscribed with the names "Odile Martinon" and "James MacKay," along with the rest of the voodoo paraphernalia. Strangely enough, although she tried to ascribe it to coincidence, Jim's attitude toward her seemed to change significantly after she initiated the ritual. He seemed less distracted than in the past, and focused more attention on her whenever they met and exchanged a few words, making her recall the moments beneath the rose trellis and in the moss along the river. In fact, he had warmed toward her so much that Odile was sure that by the end of the week he would announce not only his decision but the date of the wedding as well.

As the days passed, Jim found himself, for some mysterious reason, thinking more and more of Odile and the prospect of marriage to her, and not just because the deadline for his decision was near. He sincerely liked her—but with reservations. Although most of the time she enjoyed playing the role of coquette, he believed that deep down she had the capacity to be sincere, loyal, decent, and compassionate. He hoped that if they were married and she were removed from the corrupting influence of her brother and friends, she would abandon her frivolous, artificial ways and allow the more substantial qualities within her to emerge.

One day when Jim dropped by Isaac's store he was surprised to find his friend out front, dressed in his finest clothes and seated in one of the livery stable's finest carriages.

"Hey, what are you doing all dressed up in the middle of the week and in that fancy carriage?" Jim asked as he tied his horse to the hitching post in front of the shop.

"I'm on my way to the wharf to pick up my bride," Isaac answered nonchalantly. "Come, get in the carriage and go with me."

"I'm not dressed very well," Jim said. He was wearing his usual work clothes.

"So what? Who's the groom, you or me?"

With that Jim hopped in the carriage and they were off to the waterfront.

The wharves, piled high with endless bales of cotton and hogsheads of sugar and molasses, were bustling with activity, evidence of New Orleans's ascendancy as the most important port in the South and one of the most important in the new United States. Commercial trade as well as the produce from the fertile surrounding countryside was rapidly making the area one of the most prosperous and thriving in the entire nation.

There were several slave ships in port, and Jim witnessed the same spectacle he had seen when he first arrived: a coffle of blacks from Africa, chained into submission, disembarking under the wary and watchful eyes of the slave traders, armed with their guns and whips. The sight of these bewildered yet proudly defiant Africans, manacled in iron collars and chains, dismayed Jim and made him wonder if surely there wasn't some alternate system of labor under which the economy of the South might function equally well. The massive conversion to cotton throughout the Southern states, making the region virtually dependent on a single crop, had greatly stimulated the demand for slaves, and it was inevitable that New Orleans, the largest Southern seaport, would become the center of the slave trade. Although it was accepted throughout the South with little qualms, slavery was the one aspect that made Jim pause and wonder whether plantation life—no matter how benevolently the slaves were treated—was ultimately for him.

As they rode along the docks, Jim decided to tell Isaac for the first time about his present situation with the Martinons.

"I might get married soon too," he announced casually.

"To Martinon's little sister?" Isaac guessed correctly, with his usual canniness.

"Yes. To Odile. I've decided to go through with it."

Slapping the horse on the back with the reins, Isaac said, "Be careful of those Martinons. They are sharks and will eat you alive."

"If you mean Placide Martinon, I have no fear of him," Jim assured his friend.

"I mean both of them," Isaac replied. "The same blood is in the veins."

"No. Odile isn't like her brother at all. She's been very kind to me. She's helped me get over the grief of Delphine's death and the loss of our child."

"Don't be fooled," Isaac cautioned. "She does whatever her brother orders her to. He's a cunning weasel, and that girl is in his power."

Jim laughed. "Not Odile. She has a mind of her own, believe me."

"Mind of her own?" the merchant scoffed. "If she's agreed to marry you, it's because he's told her to."

"Why would he pick me out? There are lots of other men she could marry."

"I told you before," Isaac reiterated impatiently. "Martinon's smart enough to know you'll put life back into that dying plantation. He knows you'll break your back to save it and at the same time make him the most powerful planter along the river again. That's all he wants. That's what they both want."

"Suppose I do save the plantation—as you say—

how will that make *him* the most powerful planter when he's sharing the place with me? It's all in the marriage contract. I read it," Jim said.

"Once the place is saved, he'll look for a way to get rid of you," Isaac predicted. "You'll see."

"I'm ready for anything Placide Martinon may have up his sleeve," Jim asserted.

"Maybe," Isaac said as they passed a line of black stevedores rolling hogsheads of sugar aboard a waiting ship. Jim noted that the barrels were marked MANDRAGORE. "And maybe not . . ."

Because she was from a genteel and aristocratic, though impoverished, old Creole family, Mademoiselle LeDoux was engaged in many capacities. In addition to instructing the children of the affluent in the harp, singing, mandolin, guitar, ballroom dancing, deportment, French, and etiquette, she was frequently retained to oversee wedding arrangements as well.

"Ah, my dear Odile, this will be the most splendid, the most brilliant wedding New Orleans has seen in ages!" the elderly woman exclaimed, her thin hands aflutter with excitement when Odile informed her that she and Placide had decided to engage her to supervise her upcoming nuptials.

However, when Odile laid out some of the spinster's plans before Placide, he became irate.

"Not only will this be the most brilliant and splendid wedding, it will be the most costly. The fiscal state of this family cannot permit such extravagance," he declared. "What the hell is this item, 'Chinese spiders'?"

"They are special spiders imported from China," Odile explained.

Placide was aghast. "Spiders? At a wedding?"

"A few days before the ceremony millions of these spiders are set free on the plantation to weave their webs in the trees and shrubs. Then on the morning of the wedding the slaves go about spraying the webs with gold and silver dust. When the sun hits these dusted webs, they shimmer and shine and glisten in the most beautiful way! It's a lovely sight. Don't you remember, Placide, the Roquet family did it for the wedding of

Victorine and Henri? I shall never forget how all those trees looked. It was like fairyland."

"Yes, I'm sure it was," Placide said dryly as he picked up his pen and crossed "spiders" and "gold and silver dust" off the list Mademoiselle LeDoux had submitted for his approval.

Odile's face registered her disappointment. It was increasingly clear that the wedding was not going to be the huge, romantic affair of which she had dreamed since earliest childhood. First, Narciso had been dispensed with as groom—a serious blow to her fantasy. Then, the plantation chapel had been substituted for St. Louis Cathedral—another blow. Now the spiders were gone. Little by little, Placide was chipping away at her dreams.

A few days later Odile got the list of persons to whom wedding invitations would be sent, intending to take them to a scribe in the French Quarter who specialized in such things when she went for a fitting of her wedding gown with Olympe, the seamstress, and showed it to Placide.

Scowling, he slapped it down on the desk before him.

"My God, Odile, how could you possibly make up such a list? Some of the people on it are entirely unsuitable," he reproached her. "I will not have them in my home. Not only has MacKay included that rabble who work in his mill, but that Jew peddler, DaCosta, and his new wife as well—to say nothing of that half-nigger Roger Guillon. And what about this person, Roarke? Didn't he used to be one of the Boisblanc niggers before the old man died and set the slaves free?" Placide jumped to his feet, his face red with rage. "Don't tell me that you are planning to allow MacKay to invite *niggers?*" he shouted.

"I didn't see the list before," she said. "Mademoiselle LeDoux asked him for the names of friends he wished to invite, and these are the names he gave her. I'm no happier about it than you are."

Placide, agitated, began to pace back and forth across the study. "I can't believe that even MacKay is

capable of such an affront. Imagine, the nerve of him
expecting us to endure such trash in our own home. I
can't believe it," he railed.

"What can we do?" she asked.

"I don't know, but we must do something," he conceded. "You don't want niggers at your wedding—perhaps even bold enough with liquor in them to dare to
ask you to dance."

Odile shuddered. "Of course not. The thought of
that German Oberdorfer is revolting enough, and he's
white," she said.

"We simply have to do something about this list,"
he insisted.

"But what?"

"There is no easy answer," he replied. Then, snapping his fingers and breaking into a grin, he said, "I
have it! We will use the chapel as an excuse—say it
was much too small to accommodate so many people
and some had to be dropped. We will put the blame on
Mademoiselle LeDoux and say she arbitrarily dropped
names unfamiliar to her."

"But we'll be dropping all his friends," Odile reminded him.

"Magnificent," Placide said, reaching for his pen to
begin crossing off names. "Actually, I wish there were
some way to eliminate MacKay himself and still have
the wedding, but I suppose that is asking too much."

The chapel at Mandragore stood amid a grove of
sycamores several hundred yards from the main house
and directly behind the cemetery, whose above-ground
burial vaults held the remains of four generations of
Martinons. Although it was larger than the usual plantation chapel, Father Daubigny not only thought it was
inadequate for the wedding but felt that his dignity had
been insulted by Placide's request that he perform the
ceremony there instead of at St. Louis Cathedral,
where he firmly believed such nuptials rightfully belonged.

"But as one of the state's leading families, you have
a certain obligation," he protested when Placide in-

formed the cleric of their choice for the site of the wedding.

"We are still in mourning for the death of our father and feel a large affair would be in poor taste," Placide replied.

"But your father died several years ago," Daubigny said.

"Ah, that only proves the depth of our grief," Placide replied solemnly.

The promise of a generous gratuity and food prepared under Verbena's supervision were the two factors which changed the plump priest's attitude toward the service he consented to perform.

In keeping with the small scale of the planned nuptials, Odile was permitted a single attendant. Her first choice was naturally her sister, Eugénie, but permission could not be obtained from her order, so Louise Boisblanc Chardonnier was selected, because she was Odile's closest friend—a relative term, since Odile had really not formed a close friendship with anyone while growing up except her cousin Narciso. Jim's best man was none other than Placide himself. At first Jim had wanted Isaac, but Father Daubigny was scandalized by the suggestion that a non-Christian participate in a Catholic sacrament. The priest suggested Placide— hardly a satisfactory choice for Jim, but he decided not to fight it, wanting to conserve his energies for more important issues.

Because of the chapel's limited seating capacity— several dozen worshippers at most—the guest list was very carefully prepared. Most of the names on it were Martinon relatives and close friends, including the Valdéz of Florestal. In a terse note Adela declined, stating that Narciso was much too ill to attend and neither she nor Efrén cared to leave him.

With poorly concealed anger and resentment, Adela wrote: "There is no use in hiding the fact that this wedding was a severe blow to Narciso and is responsible for a setback in his delicate condition."

In answer to Jim's demands to see the final guest list, Odile, Placide, and Mademoiselle LeDoux were vague and evasive, all three denying knowledge of it, shift-

ing the responsibility for its preparation from one to
another.

"But I want to see if anyone's been left out," Jim
insisted.

"No one important," Odile assured him.

For a transient moment at the altar, Odile thought of
Narciso and wondered how it might have been if he
were standing beside her instead of Jim MacKay. She
felt curiously numb and a little sad, as though the ceremony were a disappointment, something to endure
rather than enjoy. As a child she had hoped her wedding would be the supreme joy of her life, but now the
only emotion she experienced was indifference.

For his part, Jim was more relaxed than he had expected to be, but experienced no elation. In fact, as he
slipped the gold band on Odile's finger he flashed for a
moment to the day he placed the gold medallion
around Delphine's neck for the first time, and felt a
sudden pang of remorse.

Later, as Jim surveyed the faces in the chapel, he
realized at once that not just the DaCostas but all his
friends had been excluded by the Martinons. He
smiled inwardly, knowing—as the Martinons did not
—that he had personally invited all the absentees to
the reception, which was scheduled to be held outdoors
on the Mandragore grounds. Lack of space could no
longer be an excuse. Jim consoled himself with the fact
that the wedding ceremony would have bored them
and thus he didn't mind their exclusion from it. Nevertheless, it was important to him that his friends attend
the celebration afterward. He was anxious to see the
reactions of his bride and her brother and Mademoiselle LeDoux when not only the DaCostas but Roarke,
Roger Guillon, Iris, Alphonsine, Hans Oberdorfer, and
the mill hands all arrived. By then the vows would
have been exchanged and the marriage contract put in
effect, giving Jim far more say in matters concerning
Mandragore.

The men at the mill had not reacted favorably when
he finally announced his intention of marrying Odile

Martinon. In fact, Roger Guillon, always outspoken, went so far as to register his dismay.

"I don't understand, Jim—why?" he asked, his eyes flashing questions he was far too polite to ask.

"Sometimes, Roger, I don't even know for sure myself," he admitted as he looked over his modest farm to Mandragore's vast acres beyond, seeking the answer.

When Jim first proffered the invitation to the reception, some of the millworkers were reluctant to accept, although pleased and flattered by the gesture.

"I couldn't go there with all them high-class white folks," Roarke said.

"I want you there," Jim insisted.

"I can't do that, Mr. Jim."

"You'd better if you want to keep working for me, Roarke."

To be certain that there would be enough food and drink for his friends, Jim, on his own, ordered extra barrels of whiskey and champagne, as well as additional roast pigs, chickens, and a side of beef.

"It's my wedding too," he assured his friends. "And I want you all to come and enjoy it, damn it."

The Catholic ceremony, spoken mostly in Latin, was difficult for Jim to follow, but briefer than he had anticipated. He had steadfastly refused to abandon his Presbyterian faith and convert to Catholicism, despite pressure from Odile and Father Daubigny on the issue.

Afterward, the guests drifted out of the chapel and onto the lawn, where they were serenaded by slave musicians and entertained by the field hands, who— much to Davis's chagrin—had been given the day off, and joyously danced the African-inspired Bamboula, Counjala, and Cadja.

Beneath the shade of a stately magnolia, the bride and groom, flanked by Louise Chardonnier, Placide, and the priest, formed a receiving line and individually greeted the visitors.

Looking radiant and more beautiful than ever, Odile, stunning in yards of satin and rare Belgian lace, greeted each guest with a kiss or extended hand. Only when she caught sight of Isaac and his new bride,

Silvia, a slim, pretty blonde, in the line did her smile vanish.

"What are they doing here?" she demanded of Jim.

Ignoring her, Jim stepped forward and genially shook Isaac's hand and kissed Silvia on both cheeks.

"So glad you could come," he said. As he started to present them to Odile, she abruptly turned her back and engaged in a conversation in French with an elderly aunt from Baton Rouge.

Tapping her on the shoulder, Jim said, "Surely you remember Mr. DaCosta, dear—"

Furious at Jim's attempt to embarrass his sister, Placide sprang to her aid. "I'm afraid there's been some mistake," he intervened. "We aren't seeing peddlers today."

"There's no mistake," Jim asserted, struggling to control his anger. "Mr. and Mrs. DaCosta are my friends and, as such, I welcome them."

"See?" Isaac said with a triumphant grin to Placide. "I always said some day I'd be welcomed back, and here I am."

Odile was outraged by the presence of what she termed "undesirables" at the reception—not just the DaCostas, but Roarke, Alphonsine, Iris, Oberdorfer— to say nothing of Roger Guillon, who, eager to defy established conventions because of his liberal European education, actually went so far as to request a dance with her, a move which upset her so much that she abruptly left the guests to dash into the house and upstairs to her room, where she threw herself across the bed, sobbing.

Jim, who was engaged in conversation with Iris at the time of his bride's sudden departure, excused himself and followed her.

Entering the room quietly, he crossed to the bed and laid his hand on her shoulder.

"Don't touch me, you lout!" she cried. "Get away from me!"

"What's wrong with you, Odile?" he asked impatiently.

Raising her head from the tear-stained pillow, she

said, "As if you didn't know! How dare you pretend you don't?"

Sitting on the edge of the bed, covered with the special nuptial spread decorated with blue and white satin bows in honor of their wedding night, he said, "It's because I invited Isaac and Silvia and Roger and all the others, isn't it?"

"You invited that scum, that horrible trash, behind my back to deliberately humiliate me," she accused. "That was a low, mean, vicious trick!"

His voice taking on an irritated edge, Jim retorted, "Those 'scum' and 'trash,' as you call them, happen to be my friends—people I can depend on for help when I need it."

"Some friends!" she berated him contemptuously. "Niggers, white trash, and whores. How do you think it looks to our slaves when they see us entertaining rabble like that, accepting them as equals? That's all they need to get uppity and step out of line. The house slaves speak their minds too much as it is. How do you expect us to command their respect when they see us consorting with that low-life?"

"Now just a minute," Jim said angrily. "I don't happen to like you referring to my friends that way. As of now, you are my wife, and I expect you as my wife to treat my friends with the same courtesy and respect that I extend to the Chardonniers, and the Seguins and the Pilettes and the Anspachers and all your other friends here today."

"My friends are decent people, not niggers and riffraff."

Speaking calmly but firmly, Jim said, "I want you to stop this nonsense and go back downstairs and act as if nothing has happened."

"I can't do that," she protested.

"Yes, you can. You will be civil to everyone at this reception, be the lady you're supposed to be," he directed.

"I will not leave this room until all that rabble is off this property," she declared defiantly.

"As your husband, I order you to get up off this bed

and go downstairs and conduct yourself as a lady and stop acting like a silly ninny."

"I don't care if you are my husband, I'm not taking orders from you."

"You will obey me just as you promised to do in front of the priest only a short while ago," he said.

"Those vows give you no right to humiliate me."

Taking her firmly by the arm, he said, "You will do as I say."

"Take your hands off me! You have no right to treat me like that half-nigger wench you used to sleep with. I know you still think about her. When you were talking to that Iris creature, I heard you mention the name 'Delphine.' You thought I wasn't listening when you were talking about her, but I was."

"Stop this nonsense and get downstairs," he commanded.

"How dare you order me around!"

"You are my wife now. You will do as I say."

"The ceremony may be over, but so far I am your wife in name only, and don't you forget that," she said. "And if you aren't careful, mister, that's all I may ever be."

Angry at her persistent display of defiance, Jim struggled to control his temper. "Now is that a fact?" he said.

"Yes," she affirmed, with a contemptuous half smile on her lips.

Jim reached down and grabbed the bodice of her gown. As she tried to struggle free, the fine white satin ripped, exposing her breasts.

"Look what you've done!" she cried, clutching the torn fabric. "Just look, you beast! You've ruined my beautiful wedding gown!"

Giving vent to her anger and resentment, she flew at him, attempting to dig her fingernails into his face, but Jim caught her wrists. As he held her, she kicked his shins repeatedly. In an effort to restrain her, he forced her to the floor and threw himself on top of her, trying to calm her fury. As she struggled beneath the weight of his body, the satin wedding gown, unable to withstand such stress, ripped further.

"Let me up, you dog!" she cried. Then, wiggling her knee into position, she managed to poke it into his groin, temporarily stunning him.

"You little hellcat!" Jim gasped, clutching his genitals in agony.

Taking advantage of her surprise maneuver, Odile squirmed out from under him, staggered to her feet, and made a desperate escape from the room in the ripped and tattered wedding gown.

At the foot of the winding stairs Odile threw herself into Verbena's waiting arms, the maid having come out of the warming kitchens to see what was the matter when she heard the commotion upstairs.

"Help me, Verbena!" she cried. "I've married a madman!"

Recovering from the knee in the groin, Jim was up and down the stairs after her.

Enfolding Odile in her protective arms, Verbena pleaded, "Please, Mr. Jim, don't you hurt this poor child."

Wordlessly, Jim grabbed Odile by the arm and attempted to yank her out of the slave's clutches.

Realizing that Verbena was poor protection against Jim's strength, Odile broke loose and ran outside, screaming, through the assembled throng of startled guests.

With Jim in close pursuit, Odile, in her tattered bridal gown with most of her lacy undergarments exposed, dashed for the safety of the chapel. Once inside, she threw the bolt across the doors and then for good measure began piling benches and chairs in front of it.

"Come out of there before I break the door down!" Jim shouted, pounding violently on the doors.

Witnessing the shocking scene, Placide sought out Father Daubigny and asked him to intervene.

"Please, my son," Daubigny said, taking Jim by the sleeve, "you must not violate the sanctity of this holy building. Even though it is not a church or a cathedral, it is the house of our Lord nonetheless. You must respect it as such and stop."

Turning indignantly to the cleric, Jim said, "My wife has locked herself in there."

"Nevertheless, my son, you must not threaten to destroy a dwelling place of our Lord," the rotund priest cautioned.

"Father Daubigny is right, MacKay," Placide agreed. "You'd better listen to him."

"You must be patient with Odile," the cleric continued. "Today has been one of great stress and excitement for her. After all, it isn't every day a young girl gets married. She will come out in time if we let her alone."

Putting his arm paternally around Jim's shoulder, the priest urged him away from the chapel. Only with great reluctance did Jim abandon it, feeling foolish and embarrassed when he realized that he was the focus of everyone's attention.

"I think you like making scenes, MacKay," Placide said with a sneer, holding his glass out for Romulus to refill it with champagne.

Inside the chapel, Odile gave no indication that she had any intention of leaving.

Much to Jim's chagrin, and to the amusement of Placide and the slaves, Odile spent her wedding night locked in the chapel, refusing all exhortations, including Father Daubigny's impassioned pleas, to come out.

After midnight, when it was clear that she had no intention of abandoning her refuge, Jim, still in his formal wedding attire, refused all urging that he spend the night at Mandragore and strode off on foot across the cane fields, to sleep alone in his rude cabin.

The honeymoon which was to have begun the following day—a trip by steamboat to Natchez—was canceled. Together, Jim and Odile had succeeded in creating the season's juiciest scandal.

No longer amused by his sister's antics, the following day Placide forced her to unbar the chapel door and come out, insisting that she apologize for her outrageous behavior and persuade Jim to return to Mandragore, where, prior to the wedding, it had been agreed the couple would reside.

"If you do not do this," Placide informed her, "he

has grounds for an annulment. God knows, there were enough witnesses to your actions."

"I don't care." She sulked.

"Let me remind you, dear sister, that if he does annul this marriage, my working agreement with him is finished as well, and you know what that means. It means all is lost—this house, this plantation, the slaves, everything. Our lives will be destroyed. You will end up by teaching etiquette and the harp to children of the rich, like Mademoiselle LeDoux."

"I don't care," she snapped, but her tone was unconvincing. Placide's words had struck their mark.

"Think it over and you will."

Later in the day, Odile decided to swallow her pride for the sake of survival. She dressed carefully and rode over to Jim's cabin, where she found him sitting on the porch in his work clothes, whittling a piece of wood.

"Jim . . . ?" she said tentatively.

Without looking up, he said, "What do you want?"

"I'd like to talk to you." She did her best to make her voice sound quiet and contrite.

"All right," he said after a few thoughtful moments. "Get down off your horse and we'll talk."

She dismounted, tied her horse to a hitching post, and strolled over to the porch.

"I'm sorry about yesterday," she said.

"Are you?" he replied, keeping his eyes on the stick in his hand as he whittled.

"Yes. I want you to come home."

Meeting her gaze, he responded coldly, "I am home."

"I mean to Mandragore."

"That's your place, not mine."

"It's our home now. I want you to come live there with me, as we agreed."

"My home is here," he asserted.

"But we're married. Mandragore is as much your home as it is mine or Placide's. It was all in the prenuptial agreement," she reminded him. "In the eyes of the Lord we're husband and wife."

"Speaking of the Lord," he said, "He says a woman's place is beneath her husband's roof. This is my roof."

Appalled at the thought that Jim might dare to sug-

gest that she live in such a primitive hovel, she decided
to treat the inference lightly. "Oh, Jim, stop joking,"
she chided.

"I'm not joking. I'm serious."

Deciding this was one more attempt to humiliate
her and force her to submit to his will, Odile struggled
to control her indignation. She was afraid an outburst
of temper might doom the marriage for good. Groveling
this way before him was humiliating enough, but nothing in comparison to the disgrace and shame she and
Placide would suffer if Mandragore were lost for good.
Nothing could be worse than that.

"I don't believe you," she said.

Jim laid the piece of wood down and closed the
blade of his knife. "If you intend for this to be a real
marriage," he said, "you go get your things and bring
them over here. This cabin will be our home until I
decide otherwise. Don't argue, because that's all I've
got to say on the subject."

❧ 30

Odile did her best to endure the hardships and
humiliations of living in the primitive cabin, even
though some of her difficulties were ameliorated by the
fact that she not only surrounded herself with Verbena
and some of the other slaves but also spent much of
her day at Mandragore, even though Jim decidedly
disapproved and discouraged the practice. "*This* is
your house. I want you to stay here."

"I don't see how the two of you sleeps in this tiny
little old bed," Verbena said one morning as she made
up the narrow pallet on which Odile slept alone.

"Jim sleeps outside in the hammock," Odile revealed.

"A man can't get proper rest in no hammock," the

maid said. "His place is right here in this bed with you. You is his wife."

Sighing, Odile admitted what the slaves had suspected. "Wife in name only. Jim is still hurt and angry about the way I treated his friends at the reception and for embarrassing him by locking myself in the chapel on our wedding night."

"I don't see how a fine, healthy young man like Mr. Jim can keep away from a pretty girl like you," Verbena said, shaking her head. "It just ain't natural."

"Besides being angry with me, he's absolutely exhausted when he comes in at night from the mill or the cane fields," Odile said.

"I declare," Verbena said. "A man would have to be almost dying not to want to bed down with a good-looking wife like you, Miss Odile."

"So one would think," Odile agreed wistfully.

At the end of her first miserable week in the cabin, a fierce thunderstorm struck, bringing with it torrents of incessant rain. Although disconcerted by the violent storm, Odile welcomed it as an event that surely would bring Jim out of the hammock and into the cabin to sleep, but instead he was forced to remain in the mill far into the night when the torrential rain brought about a serious breakdown in the machinery.

Frightened by the rolling thunderclaps which shook the crude building, Odile huddled alone in the corner of the bed and pulled the covers over her head to shield her eyes from the flashes of lightning, praying aloud to every saint she could think of. All at once, without warning, the roof sprang a leak and a torrent of water poured onto her and the bed. With a shriek, Odile leaped from the pallet and ran to the door, emitting a second, louder shriek when she nearly collided with Jim, who was returning from the mill.

"What's the matter?" he demanded.

"Look at me!" she cried, holding the lantern up. "Just look at me—I'm soaked! The roof just caved in. The bed is soaked, too. And where were you?"

"I told you earlier. There was trouble at the mill."

"You're never here when I need you."

"I couldn't help it—"

"I hate this place! I hate it! I'm leaving here and I'm never coming back. I don't care what happens."

"Calm down," he said. "I'll get a bucket and put it under that leak."

"I don't care about any bucket. I'm getting out of here!"

With that, she yanked the quilt off the bed, wrapped it around her, and headed for the door. Before Jim could stop her, she was outside and running through the muddy cane fields.

"Damn your silly, spoiled hide," he muttered, and started after her.

Eventually catching up with her, he seized her by the arm. "You get back in that cabin before you catch your death of cold," he ordered.

"*You* get back in that cabin," she shouted, raising her voice over a thunderclap, her dark hair plastered to the side of her face by the rain. "I'm going home, where I belong. I've had enough. I don't care what happens, I refuse to spend one more minute in that pigsty of yours."

Releasing her, Jim said, "All right, do what you want."

"I intend to," she declared. Turning her back on him, she marched, ankle-deep in mud, through the black, stormy night, illuminated only for seconds by brilliant flashes of lightning.

As a result of her night flight through the rain and mud, Odile, who had seemed particularly disposed to respiratory infections since childhood, came down with a severe chest cold, which worsened into pneumonia.

Gravely concerned about the health of his sister, Placide sent Romulus to inform Jim of his wife's serious condition.

"Miss Odile keeps asking after you, Mr. Jim," the butler said, doing exactly as he was instructed.

Because of the seriousness of her illness—pneumonia frequently was fatal—Jim put aside his rancor and called on his bride of a few weeks, who lay, pale and feverish, beneath the carved rosewood canopy in what was to have been their connubial bed. Seeing her so ill and frail, Jim dismissed her willfulness and arrogance and realized that, unlike him, Odile was a true aristocrat, pampered and sheltered since infancy, and not equipped to endure a life of rugged hardship and deprivation. Looking small amid the mounds of pillows and the bulky coverlet, Odile seemed a delicate, exotic bird which would surely perish if removed from its native habitat. Feelings of sympathy and affection stirred within him, replacing old resentment and anger.

When she saw him, Odile smiled weakly and extended her delicate hand to him. "I'm so glad you've come," she said, in a whisper barely audible above her labored breathing. "I was so afraid you wouldn't and I'd never see you again. Please, sit close to me."

Jim sat gently on the bed and, bending forward, kissed her on the forehead, which was covered by a light film of perspiration. Her skin felt hot beneath his lips.

"Stay close to me, Jim," she pleaded, tears rolling down her cheeks from beneath her half-closed eyelids. "Don't leave me—at least not now, while I'm so sick."

He was tempted to remind her that she was the one who had left him, but decided to remain silent on the matter. "I'll stay until you get better," he assured her.

Jim's consenting to stay temporarily at Mandragore was the signal for Verbena to order the younger house slaves to prepare the former attic nursery for him, and Romulus was sent to fetch his clothes and personal belongings from the cabin.

On his way to Jim's former residence with the horse-drawn wagon, the butler encountered Placide returning from a night of carousing in the French Quarter. Much to Romulus's surprise, his master, despite his exhausted appearance, insisted on accompanying the butler when he found out where he was heading.

Stumbling inside, the Creole planter looked over the tiny house for the second time. His face screwed up in disgust, he muttered, "My God, to think that my sister had to endure this hovel. No wonder she's sick."

As soon as Romulus had loaded all of Jim's possessions in the wagon, Placide asked, "Is that everything?"

"Yes, Marse Placide. I think so."

"Better be certain."

Romulus surveyed the cabin and, satisfied that nothing had been forgotten, said, "That's everything, Marse."

With that, Placide took a match from his pocket and, as the butler watched in horror, applied it to the straw mattress of the pallet on which Odile had so chastely slept.

"What you doing, Marse Placide?" the slave asked, wide-eyed, as the pallet burst into flames.

"Come, let's get out of here," Placide urged.

Sending Romulus on ahead with a stern warning not to breathe a word of what he had witnessed, on pain of death, Placide remained behind. From a concealed location he watched the cabin burn to the ground despite the frantic efforts of the millworkers to extinguish the flames.

When Jim learned of the destruction of the home he had built with his own hands from timbers which had accompanied him all the way from Ohio, he immediately accused Romulus of starting it, since the outbreak of the fire occurred almost simultaneously with his presence there.

"I swear, Mr. Jim, I don't know nothing about it. I done left a long while before it started," the butler insisted, looking nervously to Placide to corroborate his story.

Dependably, Placide came to his rescue. "Romulus is completely innocent. If I thought for a moment he had anything to do with that fire, I'd string him up and skin him alive myself," he declared. "Probably the fire was started by field rats chewing on matches."

"I keep my matches in a metal box," Jim replied.

"Nothing is safe from rats." Placide chuckled.

For the sake of Odile, and having little alternative except to return to Alphonsine's after the destruction of the cabin, Jim agreed to continue to live at Mandragore permanently. The moment he informed her of his decision, Odile's fever broke, and Dr. Zehner announced that she was finally on the road to recovery, news which brought considerable relief to the entire household.

Taking Jim's big hand in hers, she pressed it to her fever-cracked lips and said, "As soon as Dr. Zehner says I'm well enough, you can move out of that old nursery in the attic and into this room. I'm so anxious for us to live as husband and wife." She looked to Jim, anticipating a response, but he remained silent.

At dinner that evening, Jim found himself alone at the table with Placide. A certain amount of tension was generated whenever the two men encountered one another, especially since the reception. Neither felt truly comfortable in the other's presence, and the fact that they were now brothers-in-law had not changed that. Nevertheless, over the meal of roast duckling—game birds Placide had shot himself in Mandragore's own marshes—they treated each other civilly.

As Romulus held the tray for Jim to serve himself, Placide slipped his linen napkin out of its silver ring and laid it across his lap. In the corner one of the little Negro boys operated the overhead fan, his eye on a fly buzzing around the etched-glass fly-catcher filled with molasses on the corner of the table, wondering if the insect would be attracted to the sticky bait and trapped.

"I am relieved that Odile finally seems to be recovering," Placide said.

"Yes." Jim nodded.

"She tells me that as soon as Zehner pronounces her well enough, you two will be sharing the master bedroom."

"Perhaps," Jim replied, lifting the wineglass to his mouth.

"It's odd how often good things can come out of adversity," Placide mused.

"How's that?" Jim asked.

"Well, if your cabin hadn't burned, you might still choose to be living there and you might not have reconciled with my sister—pneumonia or not."

"Possibly," Jim agreed.

"In which case our agreement would have been null

and void, and instead of your being associated with one of the finest plantations in the South, you would have been stuck on that little insignificant farm of yours," Placide speculated.

"I wouldn't call my farm insignificant even though its acreage is admittedly small. My mill has ground a lot of sugar in its short life. Besides, local talk has it that Mandragore is so debt-ridden that it is about to go under, in spite of its illustrious past," Jim said.

Raising his eyebrows, Placide replied, "I wasn't aware of such gossip."

"It's common knowledge," Jim assured him. "You aren't fooling anyone with your airs. Everybody around these parts knows that the banks are getting ready to foreclose on this place."

"I won't try to deny that Mandragore is in some fiscal difficulties," Placide conceded.

" 'Some fiscal difficulties'?" Jim repeated. "You mean you are facing total disaster."

"I can assure you that things are not as bad as that," Placide replied, struggling to retain his composure. "The situation certainly is not hopeless. I have every expectation that Mandragore can be saved and restored to its former position as a leading, if not *the* leading, plantation."

Meeting his eyes, Jim added, "With my help."

"With our combined efforts," Placide corrected.

"We both know that my mill is the most valuable asset of our merger," Jim said. "What exactly are you contributing, Placide—I mean, personally?"

"My experience as a planter, my expertise," the Creole answered, looking a bit offended by the question.

"Your so-called expertise, my dear brother-in-law," Jim said, setting his wineglass on the linen tablecloth, "is worthless."

Placide was aghast. "What!"

"Yes, that's right—worthless. If you knew the first thing about running a plantation, Mandragore wouldn't be in the predicament it's in," Jim asserted.

"How dare you!" Placide said, slamming his knife and fork against the delicate china plate.

Ignoring the Creole's indignation, Jim continued in a quiet, serious tone. "This place has tremendous potential, and it galls me to see it squandered under poor management. I'd like the chance of putting it back on its feet again, and I want you to give it to me—but only under one condition."

"Do you have any idea how presumptuous this is?" Placide said.

"Of course it's presumptuous, but I want the opportunity to try to run things around here," Jim continued, undaunted. "Completely."

"What is your condition?" Placide asked in a skeptical tone.

"That you stay out of things."

Placide threw his napkin on the table and stomped out of the room.

Once he had calmed down and recovered from his indignation, Placide finally agreed to turn the running of Mandragore over to Jim, agreeing to the very condition his Yankee brother-in-law demanded. To all intents and purposes Placide would remain the nominal head of the plantation, receiving a generous income for which he had little to do except stay out of the way. His new life, he soon found, was not at all difficult to accept. His days and nights were now free for the pleasures so dear to the heart of every Creole gentleman: gambling, drinking, dancing, gossiping in the cafés with his friends, attending cockfights, fishing, shooting, riding, and—last but scarcely least—visiting with his mistress.

From earliest childhood Placide had known that someday he would have to take over the running of the plantation after his father died. Secretly he detested the planter's life, hating its helpless dependence on the soil, whims of weather, recalcitrant slaves, difficult overseers, capricious fluctuations in the market, temperamental bankers, and all the rest of the irritations that went with it. Inwardly he yearned to free his life from the soil to which it was chained, but it was a yearning he never dared reveal to anyone. In fact, it was his wish that everyone believe he had relinquished his duties under protest, and then only with the greatest reluctance.

"Do you have any idea how it feels to be giving up my authority around here?" he remarked to Jim as he turned over to him the key ring containing the plantation's important keys. "I feel like a bull that's just been castrated."

Jim was aware of the enormous responsibility ahead of him—making Mandragore solvent once again—but somehow he felt he could handle it.

"The first thing I want to do is switch from noble to ribbon cane," Jim said. "Then we'll no longer have to live in fear of being wiped out by a severe frost."

"A very bad idea," Placide criticized. "The yield of sugar from ribbon is much too low."

"But if we plant more acreage, we can equal our old yield of noble. I still have nearly three hundred acres that can be reclaimed."

"That's hardly enough."

"It's a start," Jim said. "The slaves can begin work on the back swamp during the off season."

Jim could not believe he was talking so casually about slave labor, accepting it as an inescapable fact of life, the way Southerners did. It was the one aspect that stirred Jim's misgivings and dulled his enthusiasm for taking over the stewardship of Mandragore. With the present state of agriculture, one could not grow any of the large money crops—cotton, sugar, tobacco, indigo, and rice—without slaves. Mandragore had had slavery for more than a century, and Jim was forced to accept it as a necessary evil, recognizing pragmatically that within the present system there was no other feasible way to be competitive. He realized that the "peculiar institution," as the abolitionists called it, was so firmly entrenched, so intricately interwoven into the very fabric of the Southern economy, that it couldn't be eradicated without devastating consequences.

One thing he did vow, however, was that at Mandragore the slaves would be treated as decently and humanely as possible, and on that point he had no intention of wavering. One of his first duties as manager of the plantation would be to make sure that Hiram Davis understood this.

Davis resented Jim's new authority. He had disliked the Yankee from their very first meeting, and he had no intention of making things easy for him.

"I've been handling niggers ever since I was a kid, and I can tell you that there's only one thing them burrheads understand and that's the sting of a bull-whip across their black hides," the overseer expounded, spitting a stream of tobacco juice at a butterfly poised on a dandelion.

"No slave will be mistreated on this plantation," Jim decreed.

"A good lashing now and then ain't mistreatment."

"There will be no whippings," Jim said. "Is that clear?"

Hands on hips, Davis stared at Jim in disgust with his single eye. "Now how are you going to keep niggers in line without a whip? You must be crazy, mister."

Struggling to control his temper, Jim repeated, "There will be no whippings."

"I never heard of such a thing. A little touch of the whip now and then does them good," Davis asserted. Turning to his ever-present companion for affirmation, he said, "Don't it, Willie?"

Grinning, Willie nodded his head. "Sure do," the black youth agreed.

"This is the last time I'm going to say this, Davis," Jim said. "There will be no more whipping, and that is final."

"I'll have to talk to Mr. Martinon before I could go along with an order like that," Davis replied, shaking his head.

"Mr. Martinon agrees one hundred percent with me on this."

"That's hard for me to swallow."

"I believe Mr. Martinon has told you that I now have the same authority as he has," Jim asserted.

"He didn't say nothing about no whippings any more, I can tell you that."

"You either comply with this order or you look for a position on another plantation. Is that clear?"

"You know what you're going to have? You're going to have these niggers running wild. You're going to have yourself a slave rebellion, that's what. Once them niggers get word they can do anything they damn well please without fear of whipping, you're going to have yourself one unholy goddam mess. You're a newcomer around here," Davis said, obviously agitated. "You got no right fooling around with things that you don't know the first goddam thing about."

❧ 31

Odile recovered slowly from her bout of pneumonia, but eventually she was permitted to leave her room and take the air on the second-floor gallery for a short period each afternoon, weather permitting, carefully wrapped in shawls and afghans by the ever-attentive Verbena.

For her part, Odile was glad that Jim had moved into the main house and taken over the management of the plantation, not only because she felt he could rescue the ancestral home from the avaricious bankers but because his new authority released her from her brother's tyrannical domination.

On the other hand, all was not well with her. She was bothered by the fact that their marriage still had not been *officially* consummated, and would have been profoundly embarrassed had the situation become common knowledge among her social peers, although she felt sure the slaves, who knew everything, suspected that husband and wife had yet to share the same bed.

One day, as Dr. Zehner was listening to her chest through negligee and wrapper, while Verbena stood by decorously chaperoning, Odile asked, "When can my husband and I resume sharing the same bed?"

"Very soon." He nodded. "Very soon indeed."

After dinner every evening Jim made it his business to visit Odile in her room, where they chatted about the events of the day and happenings on the plantation before he retired to his room overhead in the attic nursery. Now that Dr. Zehner had assured her that it would soon be all right for them to share the same bed, Odile wondered how she might convey this news to him without seeming too bold. Feeling that it might be helpful to appear especially alluring, she ordered Verbena to have the huge copper bathtub brought into her room and filled with hot water carried up from the cookhouse. After helping her bathe, the maid arranged Odile's hair into a series of soft black curls which framed her lovely face in a most attractive manner. From the cedar chest at the foot of the bed Odile selected a nightgown, part of the trousseau she had originally intended to wear on her honeymoon voyage up the Mississippi to Natchez.

"I wish we could still have our wedding trip," Odile mused wistfully.

"The way Mr. Jim's been working hisself, he ain't got scarcely time to breathe, let alone go on no honeymoon," Verbena declared. "He just keeps pushing hisself from dawn to dark. Ain't no nigger who works as hard as that man."

"I know," Odile conceded regretfully.

Before the maid left, Odile told her to light several scented candles and put them about the room. She hoped to imbue it with a soft, romantic glow and at the same time fill the air with the heady aroma of sandalwood.

As usual, when he came upstairs Jim sat on the edge of the bed and tenderly kissed his wife's forehead. "How are you feeling?" he asked.

"Dr. Zehner says I'm almost cured. Isn't that wonderful?" She threw her arms around him and squeezed him tight. "Oh, dearest, I've been waiting so long for him to say I was well again."

"Me too," he said.

Casually she allowed a sleeve of the nightgown to slip off her shoulder, exposing her pale skin.

"I'm so glad that hateful pneumonia's over with," she said.

"Me too," Jim agreed, kissing her exposed shoulder. "Now that you're well, there's something I want to ask you to do for me," he said.

"Ask and your every wish shall be granted, sir," she replied coquettishly as her fingers slipped playfully between the buttons of his shirt.

"I want you to go and call on Isaac and Silvia and personally apologize to them for the shabby way you treated them at the reception," he said.

His request was hardly what she was expecting. "What?" she cried. "I can't believe my ears. Surely, Jim, you aren't serious?"

"I assure you I am," he said. "You can begin with Isaac and Silvia, because they will be the easiest. As you get stronger and more adept at apologies, I want you to call on Roger Guillon, Hans Oberdorfer, Iris and Alphonsine, and Roarke—in short, everybody you insulted."

At the recitation of the names, Odile's eyes grew wide with horror. "Have you lost your mind?" she asked.

"If you want to call yourself my wife, this is what you will have to do," he informed her.

"This must be some kind of joke."

"I've never been more serious in my life."

"Is there no end to the ways you can think up to humiliate me?" she said.

"There's nothing humiliating about apologizing to people you've offended."

"There is when they're nothing but rabble and trash and so far beneath you that they're not worth giving the time of day," she retorted angrily.

"Very well," he said, rising from the bed. "Do as you see fit. But let me warn you that you sleep alone in this bed until you do what I've just asked."

"You can't do this to me," she protested.

"I'm afraid I can."

Suddenly Odile began to cough violently, so hard in

fact that she extinguished several candles close to
the bed. "You're giving me a relapse," she gasped.

Jim shrugged indifferently and left the room, leaving
her to thrash about angrily in the great bed, ringing
desperately for Verbena to come and soothe her, as
she always did.

With Jim completely immersed in the running of the
plantation, totally rejecting her, and Placide spending
more and more time away in town with Denise and his
pleasure-seeking cohorts, Odile grew increasingly restless and lonely.

One night, Jim sat poring over the plantation's account books in the study, a room which had once been
the Creole planter's exclusive domain but had now
been more or less appropriated by his brother-in-law.
Romulus kept him supplied with hot tea from the teapoy.

"These books look like they were kept by chickens,"
Jim remarked as the butler filled his cup. "Look at this
chicken-scratch."

"Yes, sir," Romulus agreed automatically.

"How can I possibly figure out something that looks
like this?"

"It looks like it'd be mighty hard, Mr. Jim."

" 'Hard' isn't the word for it."

"Maybe Marse Placide wrote it like that so's nobody
never could understand," Romulus suggested.

Recalling the financial state of the plantation and his
brother-in-law's turbulent dealings with the New Orleans banks, Jim decided the old Negro might have a
point. "I think you might be right, Romulus."

"Yes, sir," he said, putting the lid back on the tea
compartment within the teapoy.

Later, without knocking, Odile slid the doors apart
and entered the room. Jim looked up from the ledgers
before him with a mixture of surprise and annoyance.
"What is it?" he asked brusquely.

"I have decided to go and spend a few days with
my Aunt Adela at Florestal," she announced, and
waited for his reaction.

"You have, have you," he remarked, rocking backward in Placide's desk chair.

"Yes," she replied. "I'm becoming rather bored here."

"Really? Perhaps getting out and making some new friends might brighten your life a little," he said in a sarcastic tone. "I could give you a list, if you like."

"I need a change," she said, ignoring his suggestion, knowing perfectly well what he was referring to.

"A change might do you good—a change of heart, rather than a change of scene, however."

"I prefer a change of scene, frankly."

"Bored, are you?"

"Bored to death," she answered.

"Perhaps you haven't got enough to do. Maybe you need more work, more responsibilities. I think you rely entirely too much on Verbena to run this house and oversee the other servants."

"Verbena does things very well. It's not necessary for me to interfere. I need a change of scene—nothing else," she repeated.

"Have you informed your aunt of your coming?"

"Yes."

"And if I say you can't go?"

"Then I shall be most disappointed. And so will my aunt."

"To say nothing of your cousin," Jim added.

"Narciso always looks forward to my visits. We've been close since childhood. His health has been poor lately. I feel it is my Christian duty to call on him and the others."

Jim arched his eyebrow. "Christian duty?" he repeated skeptically.

"To visit the ill," she clarified.

"If I were to forbid you to go, you would defy me and go anyway, wouldn't you?"

"Naturally, I prefer to go with your permission," she said. "But should you withhold it—yes, I would go anyway."

Jim scratched his chin a moment. "What is the punishment for disobedient wives under your Napoleonic Code here in Louisiana?"

"Probably whipping, but that would be difficult to administer, since you have expressly forbidden such punishment on this plantation," she reminded him.

"For slaves," he answered. "Not for wives."

Odile was not amused by his attempt at humor.

Turning his attention once more to the ledger, he dismissed her with a wave of his hand. "You have my permission to go anywhere you like," he said indifferently. "And stay as long as you want."

Looking somewhat hurt by his casual dismissal, Odile turned abruptly and left the room.

A flurry of excitement greeted Odile's arrival at Florestal, and everyone except Narciso ran out to the carriageway to greet her. Although initially bitter and resentful about her wedding to Jim MacKay and its devastating effects on their son, Efrén and Adela Valdéz welcomed her warmly, wondering whether her visit—especially since she arrived alone—signaled trouble in the new marriage. They had heard rumors to that effect and were curious to learn the details firsthand.

Embracing her, Adela apologized, "I'm so sorry not to have been able to attend your wedding, dear, but you don't know how ill Narciso was at the time. I was so frightened we might lose him. But I heard it was quite lovely, in the chapel and all. That chapel was your mama's favorite, that blessed saint."

Later, when they were alone in the parlor, Adela reported in great detail the current state of her son's health. "He's been so sick. He's had to sleep sitting up against five pillows. The most he ever needed before was four. He turns blue at the drop of a hat. Sometimes he becomes confused, and once he was in a coma for half the day," she recounted in highly emotional tones. "I'm certain the end can't be far away. I'm so happy your new husband has allowed you to come visit us so poor Narciso can see your lovely face once again. You mean so much to that sweet, gentle boy."

Odile had scarcely been at Florestal forty-eight hours when Narciso rallied so remarkably that everyone was astonished and the word "miracle" was bandied about. Not only was he out of bed and dressed for the first time in weeks, breathing without the usual effort, but he went so far as to actually accompany Odile on her morning ride along the river.

In a willow glade they stopped and dismounted, allowing the horses to drink. Eagerly Narciso took Odile's hand in his and pressed it to his purple-tinged lips.

"Gazing at your beautiful face is better for my poor heart than all the medicines in the world. You only have to look at me for a single moment with those fantastic Spanish eyes of yours, my Moorish princess, and I feel strong enough to swim this river or to run a race. I feel that you are the Christ and I am the hopeless, abandoned leper waiting to be cleansed and healed."

Accustomed to her cousin's florid speeches, Odile nevertheless feigned shock. "Hush, Narciso, that's blasphemy," she reproached him.

Ignoring her admonitions, he reached out and embraced her fervently, covering her face with eager kisses.

"I would abandon God for you, my darling," he declared.

Horrified by such an oath, Odile tried to squirm out of his arms, but he held her with surprising strength.

"Please, Narciso, you must let me go," she begged. "Remember, I am a married woman now."

"How could I ever forget that?" he said in a resentful tone. "I can't forget either that were it not for your ruthless and greedy brother, you would be my bride and not the wife of someone else."

"You mustn't say that," she said.

"Every time I think of another man making love to you—you who rightly belong to me—I can't bear it."

"Making love?" she repeated.

"Yes, of course."

"Would it surprise you to know that my husband has yet to share my bed?" she asked him, well aware of her deception. She and Jim had never shared a bed, but that fateful day at the riverbank . . .

"Don't poke fun at me with such ridiculous lies."

"It's not a lie. It's the truth. Jim has never touched me. You are still the only man who has."

He stared at her in disbelief. "I don't believe you."

At that, she went on to relate to him the details of the situation while he listened with amazement.

When she concluded, he was so moved by her story of hurt and indignation at the hands of an insensitive husband that he embraced her passionately. "Then it is true! I am still the only man who has known you?"

"Yes," she said.

"My love, my love," he murmured into her ear between kisses. "My only love. God, how I love you, Odile!"

Although the sudden apparent improvement of Narciso's health made it possible for him to join the rest of the household in the dining room, he chose to continue taking his meals in his room, and requested that Odile dine with him for company.

In the evenings they frequently played duets— she on the harp, he on the harpsichord—or Odile sang French songs she had learned when very young, while Narciso accompanied her on the guitar. When their evenings weren't musical, they were devoted to sixteenth-century Spanish poetry, Narciso reading aloud in elocutionary tones, Odile at his knee, listening with rapt attention. While engaged in these mutual interests, they were seldom interrupted, except by Kitty, who personally looked after Narciso, bringing him his tonics and medicines at the prescribed hours.

One night, much to Odile's amazement, Kitty appeared with an infant in her arms, a startlingly beautiful child with luminous blue-green eyes and a mass of tight blond ringlets. Because Kitty treated the child with such total adoration, it was only natural for Odile to assume that it was her own, although she could scarcely believe that such a lanky, graceless woman so utterly lacking in basic femininity could have borne such a child, especially when she speculated that the father was undoubtedly Munro Samples, who had sired a great number of the mulatto slaves on the plantation.

"You are mighty fortunate to have such a lovely child," she said.

"Oh, no, ma'am." Kitty chuckled, flattered by Odile's assumption. "He ain't mine, though I wish he was. His mama done passed away and the Lord gave him to me to raise. I feel like he's mine, I got to say."

"I'm so sorry to hear about his mother," Odile said, sincerely moved by the disclosure that the child was an orphan, slave or not. "His daddy must have been quite fair."

"Yes, ma'am," Kitty affirmed. "His mama claimed his daddy was as white as you, Miss Odile. His mama wasn't no ordinary field nigger, neither. She was like a fine lady, a beautiful high-yellow gal."

Odile smiled at the infant. "I can tell you love him very much."

"Just like he was my own flesh and blood," Kitty asserted proudly.

Chucking the baby under the chin, Narciso added, "And she's spoiling him outrageously."

The infant responded by grabbing Narciso's aquiline nose playfully with his tiny fingers and gurgling happily.

"What's his name?" Odile asked.

"I calls him Achille," Kitty answered.

"What a splendid name," Odile said.

"Kitty favors the classics," Narciso commented wryly.

Watching Kitty holding the robust infant with such obvious affection stirred Odile's own maternal yearnings and made her long for a child of her own one day. If she were so blessed, she hoped it would be a fine, sturdy boy like this. Boys were lucky. They had mobility and independence and were free to assert themselves without censure. Girls were dependent and helpless and stifled from the start. As a child she had often wished she had been born a male. How different her life might have been.

At bedtime Odile returned decorously to her room, made certain she said good night to her aunt and uncle, allowed one of the slaves to help her undress, and got into bed—and then, when all was silent in the great house, crept quietly back to Narciso's room, where she spent the night cradled in his wiry arms.

Her clandestine nightly excursions did not go undetected by Adela and Efrén Valdéz. Adela, whose hearing was especially keen, heard her soft footsteps tiptoeing past their door one night. Laying her hand on her husband's shoulder, she whispered, "There she goes."

"Who?" Efrén snorted impatiently.

"Odile. She's going into our son's room."

"What for at this hour?"

"To sleep with him," Adela revealed, smiling in the darkness.

"The brazen hussy—"

"Hush, dearest," Adela admonished her husband.

"The adulteress. Only married a few months and already betraying her husband. She ought to be publicly stoned."

Adela laid her tiny fingers across his mouth. "Hush, Efrén," she repeated in a whisper. "Just remember, every night she spends with our Narciso gives him another day on this earth with us."

Eventually Odile resolved to end her visit to Florestal and return home, though she knew Narciso would be devastated when she broke the news of her impending departure to him.

His great dark eyes brimming with tears, he said, "What shall I do without you? I'm sure I will die. This time I shall surely die when you leave. I have felt closer to you than we have ever been. How can I pass nights alone in that great empty bed without you at my side, listening to your breathing, seeing the moonlight on your lovely face . . . ?"

"I will miss you, too, my dearest, but I must go home. I have no other choice," she said. Narciso was right. She also felt closer to him than ever before. Perhaps it was because she was now married and the forbidden aspect of their love made it even more intense. For the first time she realized how many things they shared and loved that she and Jim could never share:

a common heritage, a common culture, a mutual empathy and understanding. On the other hand, she was aware that Jim possessed a strength, a vigor and vitality, a determination to succeed, an ambition that she needed as much as the tenderness and passion that Narciso offered. It was, as it always had been, an insoluble dilemma. If only the qualities of the two men could have been combined in one . . .

"You'll live," she assured him, caressing his pale cheek. "You've got to live—for my sake. I need you, Narciso. What would I do without you? We'll see each other again."

"What do you care?" He sulked. "You have your husband. The moment he takes you in his arms, you'll forget me."

"I care very much," she said, brushing his lips with her own. "I always have—since we were children. Remember? And I always will."

"I wish I could believe that."

"What more can I do to prove it? I've risked my good name, my reputation, my marriage, everything, by coming here like this. What more could you possibly ask?"

"When will you be back?"

"Soon. Until then, you must be patient and wait for me."

"Will you think of me?"

"Every day."

"Even when you're with him?"

"Always."

Unable to control himself any longer, Narciso reached out and pulled her into a desperate embrace. "Don't you see how much I love you?" he said.

"Yes, I *see*." She sighed. "But what can I do?"

❧ 32

Not long after she returned from Florestal, Odile began to be aware of certain vague but definite changes taking place within her body. For one thing, her breasts had mysteriously begun to swell, and strained against the fabric of her camisole to the point where wearing it was uncomfortable. Too, they were lined with prominent tortuous blue blood vessels, and the nipples were tender and tingly. To add to her dismay, she was awakened from sleep several times a night by an urgent need to use the decorated porcelain chamber pot in a drawer of the night table beside the bed. Another change was in her appetite. In spite of her slender, delicate appearance, Odile had always had a good appetite, but since coming back to Mandragore she had felt positively ravenous and was eating more than ever. Naturally, these changes had not escaped the observant Verbena.

"Lord, child, something done happened to you while you was at Florestal," she commented as she struggled to lace Odile's corset over her expanded waistline.

"What do you mean by that?" Odile asked apprehensively.

"You the one who knows that, Miss Odile," the maid answered ambiguously. "I ain't got to tell you."

When Odile's time of the month came around, nothing happened, and she was forced to slyly dispose of the daily supply of carefully folded linen pads, as fresh and unsoiled as when Verbena prepared them for her. With dread and apprehension, Odile now knew that she would have no need for the pads for the next nine months. She was sure she was pregnant. Riding along the river bank, she stopped at the familiar mossy patch ringed with willows, dismounted, threw herself down on the soft moss, and wept.

"Oh, my God, what will I do? What will I do?" she said to herself over and over. "Narciso . . . Narciso . . ."

Once she had managed to accept the fact that she was indeed pregnant by Narciso, she knew that the obvious problem was to decide what to do about it. Since her marriage to Jim had yet to be consummated, she could seek an annulment and marry Narciso, but that would be a long procedure with an outcome uncertain at best, to say nothing of the scandal and disgrace that would undoubtedly accompany it. In addition, there was the chance that the baby would be born before the annulment was granted and stigmatized for life as a bastard. She had no desire for her child to suffer for her own error. On the other hand, she could try to preserve her marriage and convince Jim and everyone else that he was the father of her offspring. That would involve serious deception and compromise, as well as immediate action, but seemed to assure a more promising future for both her unborn child and herself. There was really little choice. The major objective was to get Jim into her bed.

For a single day Odile contemplated how she could get Jim to abandon his attic roost and sleep with her. One of the easiest solutions would be to swallow her pride and capitulate to his demand that she accept the riffraff he called friends. Unwilling to humiliate herself to that degree if it could be avoided, she decided that a more appealing alternative would be to call once again on Nizilda Foucher. Her sorcery, or whatever it was—Odile felt uncomfortable with that term—had been successful once. Perhaps it would be successful again. At any rate, she decided, it was at least worth a try, considering the alternatives.

Neither Nizilda nor her shack had changed much since Odile's last visit. If anything, the old woman had become even uglier and more sinister-looking. Clutching the scarf which invariably covered her head, she greeted Odile with a cackling laugh. "Come in, dearie," she said, pleased that her initial magic had been sufficiently successful to bring the young, aristocratic client back again. The three-legged cat brushed back and forth against Nizilda's scrawny legs.

Without wasting time on pleasantries, Odile decided to come right to the point of her visit, having no desire to remain in the dingy, eerie, foul-smelling shack longer than necessary. "I want something to entice my husband to sleep with me," she said.

Nizilda threw back her head and let out one of her bone-chilling screeches. "What? A beauty like you can't get her man to sleep with her?" she asked incredulously.

"It's true," Odile admitted uncomfortably. "I need a charm or a potion or a gris-gris right away."

The desperation implicit in Odile's tone was not lost on the sorceress. After considering a few moments, she replied, "What you asking, dearie, ain't going to be so easy."

"You helped me before."

"That was different."

"I know you can help me again, Nizilda."

The old woman shook her head. "It might take some time," she cautioned.

"I need something fast. Very fast."

"Good magic don't work fast."

"I'll pay you anything you want."

Nizilda looked at her askance. "I don't accept pay from folks. If I takes money for my work, then pretty soon I would lose my power."

"What about the last time?" Odile reminded her, thinking of the gold coins the voodoo practitioner had gladly accepted, without qualms.

"If folks wants to give me a donation, an offering, that's different, but I don't set no prices or charge nothing. That's how come I'm so good," Nizilda said.

"I'm sorry," Odile apologized. "I didn't mean to insult you."

"You young folks is always in such a hurry. You all wants everything fast, fast, fast," Nizilda disparaged.

"I'm desperate," Odile blurted.

"I can see you are, dearie. I ain't blind." Narrowing her eyes, she stared at Odile suspiciously. "You done got yourself a baby on the way, don't you?"

"Yes," Odile admitted.

"And the father ain't the man you married to, is he?"

"That's none of your business!" Odile snapped defensively.

"Ain't no way I can help you if you don't tell me the truth."

"All right, he's not."

"I knew that right along. Ain't no way nobody can fool old Nizilda. I knows everything before folks opens their mouths," she boasted. "Well, dearie, this is a special case. It means I'm going to have to work extra hard for you."

"Whatever you have to do," Odile urged.

"I gots to mix you up a special powder—one you better be mighty careful with."

"I'll do whatever you say," Odile agreed.

Shuffling across the bare floor in her oversized men's shoes, Nizilda ushered Odile into the adjoining room. The ceiling seemed even more cluttered than before with African jujus, and what looked like the same seven candles burned on the altar before the Virgin crowned with thorns. The Indian basket was in its place.

Just as on her previous visit, Nizilda directed Odile to kneel at the altar and pray while she mixed the powder. Remembering the snake in the basket, Odile was hesitant to comply.

"Don't you worry none about old Legba. He won't bother you if you don't bother him. With only one eye, he can only see half as much. Besides, I'll be right nearby, dearie."

While Odile knelt, her mind was hardly on prayer. In the front room the sorceress busied herself mixing powders, oils, and solutions from bottles and jars marked "Love Powder," "Drawing Powder," "Delight Powder," "Goddess of Love," "Vantine," "High John Root," "Controlling Drops," and the like.

Just as Odile's knees were aching beyond endurance

Nizilda finally announced from the other side of the ragged curtain that she was finished.

Presenting Odile with a cloth packet containing an innocent-looking white powder, she instructed her in its administration. "You got to feed it to your man for a week. Put it in his food—mashed yams is best. It'll make him sick, so sick you going to think he's dying, but he won't die. When he gets better, dearie, ain't no way he will be able to keep away from you. He'll be wanting to love you to death."

With so many slaves present, especially during meals, it was especially difficult to doctor food, but Odile did finally manage to slip some of Nizilda's white powder into Jim's mashed yams when no one was looking.

After consuming every bite of the yams—which, Jim noted to Verbena, tasted slightly bitter—he retired after dinner to the study, where he struggled once again to try to get the plantation's books in some kind of order. Since taking over the management of Mandragore, Jim had found himself in charge of virtually everything. Much to Denise's joy, Placide practically lived at the Couronneau town house, and with Victor's tacit approval. Only the butler, Valcour, seemed to resent his presence. In exchange for free rein over the plantation, Jim was only too happy to supply Placide with a generous allowance with which to indulge his pleasures. With the Creole planter out of the way, Jim could run the vast enterprise as he saw fit without interference.

The only fly in Jim's ointment was the overseer, Davis, who bitterly resented his authority and sought to frustrate and oppose him every chance he got. Jim was particularly strict in his proscription against corporal punishment, and found it necessary to repeat his warning to Davis that if the mistreatment and abuse of the slaves continued, the overseer would be dismissed.

One day, as he was riding through the cane fields, he had come upon the overseer thrashing one of the slaves for sleeping among the high cane when he was supposed to be hoeing, while Willie and the other slaves in the work gang looked on. Every time the downed slave tried to move, Davis's hounds automatically set upon him, snarling and ferociously baring their teeth.

"All right, Davis, give me that whip," Jim commanded.

Davis acted as though he failed to comprehend the order. "What did you say?"

"I said, give me that whip."

"This here's my personal whip and I ain't giving it up to nobody," the overseer said defiantly.

"You'll either give me that whip now or you'll get off this plantation and stay off," Jim said angrily.

Reluctantly, with a look of smoldering resentment, Davis relinquished the whip.

Jim tried to dismiss the episode from his mind and concentrate on the account books, but he felt ill. His dizziness and nausea steadily increased, finally forcing him to put the huge ledgers aside and go to bed.

In the middle of the night, he awoke deathly ill and, racing to the window, stuck his head outside, vomiting uncontrollably on the roof.

Hearing Jim's distress from his room over the warming kitchens, Romulus climbed the steps to the attic nursery and went to his aid. Holding the porcelain wash basin while Jim continued to vomit, the slave was shocked to see it fill with deep-red blood.

Leaving Jim a moment, Romulus roused Cecil and ordered him to go get Dr. Zehner at once. "Look like Mr. Jim is going to die."

For nearly a week Jim lay desperately ill while Odile spent many hours each day in the chapel, frantically praying for his recovery, promising every saint in heaven she would never again resort to any of Nizilda Foucher's potions or powders no matter how desperate she was.

At Odile's urgent request, Placide was summoned back to the plantation from the Couronneau residence in New Orleans. Looking quite concerned over Jim's condition, he said, "He looks as if he's been poisoned."

Later, when he and Odile were alone in the parlor, Placide remarked, "You know, my dear, there are other ways of getting rid of a husband, if you are really that eager."

Horrified by such a suggestion, she said, "How could you say such a thing? Shame on you, Placide! I don't consider that humorous in the least."

"It wasn't meant to be," he replied.

Eventually Jim recovered, but he was in a profoundly weakened condition for several weeks and confined to the house, where Odile showered him with attention, still praying fervently for the return of his strength. Despite the ever-present animosity between them, they did grow somewhat closer because of the daily association.

One day, taking his big hand in hers, Odile pressed it against her cheek. "You know, Jim, I've decided that Sunday might be a good time to ask Isaac and his wife to come to dinner. That is, if you feel up to visitors . . . ?"

Jim could scarcely believe his ears. Had she really, on her own initiative, suggested inviting the DaCostas to Mandragore? Since taking over the plantation he had had little time for his old friend, and he longed to see Isaac again. But, better than that, this suggestion of hers represented a definite capitulation, a complete turnaround, a break in the impasse between them. Reaching out, he put his arm around her waist and pulled her to him, surprised at how much thicker her tiny waist had become lately. "Do you mean that?" he asked.

"I suppose I do," she answered, smiling sweetly. Odile still considered the DaCostas socially far beneath her, with their funny accents, unstylish clothes, and lack of the more subtle graces, to say nothing of the fact that they weren't Christians. But at least, unlike some of Jim's other so-called friends, they were white. All in all, Odile felt reasonably comfortable and not overly compromised with the solution to her increasingly desperate situation.

"I'm glad," he said, kissing her cheek.

That night he ordered Romulus to transfer his belongings from the nursery into his wife's room on the lower floor.

Overhearing the order, Verbena commented, "It's about time, that's all I got to say."

Odile had made the supreme gesture and so had Jim, each in their own way. At last the connubial bed was shared by both parties. Because of the pent-up frustration they both felt after weeks of the stalemate, their first night was a marathon of activity.

"I had no idea you were so passionate," Jim said as he lay on his back, trying to catch his breath.

"Now do you see what you've missed?" she said, smiling slyly in the darkness.

On Sunday afternoon, as planned, Isaac and Silvia arrived for dinner, which Odile decided to have served outside on the gallery. The thought of entertaining the DaCostas in the dining room in which some of the most illustrious and fashionable people in the state had been guests was unacceptable to her.

"I think it's so lovely to dine outdoors when all the trees are in bloom," she said to Jim, who suspected nothing, so glad was he that she had finally capitulated and invited his best friends to the house.

The DaCostas, looking the very picture of bourgeois respectability, arrived in an elegant carriage, which Isaac was quick to inform them was his own and not rented from a livery stable. "The horse is mine, too," he added, and later in the evening he announced that he was negotiating for the purchase of a house on the Esplanade, one of the more elegant streets in the French Quarter.

Although somewhat more reserved than usual, Odile was nevertheless cordial and courteous throughout the visit, and especially sympathetic to Silvia, who she learned was also expecting her first child.

"The winter that comes," she revealed to Odile in her charmingly awkward English, referring to the baby's expected time of arrival.

Odile found herself wishing she could disclose her

own condition to Silvia so the two women could share the mutual experience, since she felt they shared little else, but instead she found herself saying, "How do you find New Orleans?"

"I like it very much." Silvia smiled. "The last week Isaac took me to the French Opera. Ah, I love it so much! *Les Huguenots*—so beautiful."

"We heard Julia Calvé," Isaac added. "What a glorious voice!"

After dinner the two women retired to the parlor, where Odile showed Silvia the needlepoint tapestry on which she was currently working, while Jim and Isaac elected to stroll across the lawn under the moss-laden oaks.

"I can tell you one thing," Jim said. "It's certainly a lot more work running this place than merely looking after a mill and a few acres of cane."

"But you like it? You're happy with the arrangement?" Isaac questioned.

"I'm happy," Jim assured him, his voice full of enthusiasm for his new undertaking. "The only thing that gives me trouble is the matter of slaves and the overseer. I don't like the institution in general, and I dislike the current overseer in particular."

"Is he the one we tangled with that first day on Martinon's land?" Isaac asked. "The tobacco-spitter with only one eye?"

"Yes," Jim affirmed. "His name is Davis. Hiram Davis."

"I don't like him either," Isaac agreed. "But as for slavery, what can you do? It's the system."

"I wish there were some way to free the slaves and yet have them stay on as workers and pay them a regular wage, like the men at the mill," Jim said.

"The mill's a whole different proposition," Isaac pointed out. "It's an industry, like they have in the North. You can pay men wages in industry and still make a profit. If you do that in agriculture you go broke in a minute. As it is, you American sugar growers have all you can do to compete with the cheap sugar coming in from Cuba. If it wasn't for the market in the Western states, Cuban sugar would wipe you out."

"I know." Jim nodded in agreement.

Later, the two men rejoined their wives on the front gallery, sipping coffee and watching fireflies flickering on the lawn. Some distance away, slaves burned kerosene-soaked rags and fanned the air to discourage mosquitoes.

"I'm planning some major changes soon in my chief personnel," Jim informed Isaac, continuing the conversation he had started earlier.

"Such as?" Isaac questioned.

"For one thing, I'm getting rid of Davis as overseer," Jim announced.

Startled by the news, Odile turned away from Silvia, with whom she had been discussing china-painting. "You can't do that," she protested. "He's been here for years."

"That's the trouble," Jim said. "He's been here too long."

"Who would oversee the plantation?" she asked anxiously.

"I'm thinking of moving Hans Oberdorfer out of the mill and putting him in charge," Jim answered.

"Oberdorfer?" Odile said. "What on earth does he know about handling slaves and raising sugar? He's a German, an immigrant. He's hardly been in this country more than a couple of years."

"Hans learns very fast," Jim assured her. "He's a very intelligent fellow."

Reaching out and patting her hostess's hand, Silvia smiled and said, "Many immigrants learn fast."

Odile drew her hand away.

True to his word, Jim moved ruddy, jovial, big-bellied Hans Oberdorfer from the mill to Mandragore, where he installed him in the overseer's cottage, formerly the domicile of Hiram Davis. Davis had resentfully vacated the premises a few days earlier, taking his few meager belongings with him. Before he left, he tried to buy Willie, but Jim refused his offer and, as a compensatory gesture, granted Willie his freedom, allowing him to go with Davis as a free man.

"I'm sure you'll find another overseer's post," Jim said to Davis.

"I ain't looking for none," Davis replied sullenly. "When I come back to a plantation again, it's going to be as the master. I'm finished with overseeing. Who knows? I may even end up with this one someday. You never can tell . . ."

When Odile learned that Jim had given Willie his freedom, she was furious.

"Simple-minded as that boy is, he's worth at least five hundred dollars," she said.

In actuality, Odile's only real interest in the plantation was to see that it continued to provide her with the lifestyle to which she had always been accustomed. She had no real concern for Davis or loyalty toward his stewardship, but she did know that he was capable of driving the slaves to produce the necessary crops, and that was what was important. With Davis gone and Hans Oberdorfer an unproven quantity as overseer, she was uncertain how things would continue, especially since her brother had so completely and readily relinquished his authority to Jim. Her well-being was clearly in Jim's hands, and in a way she had not anticipated.

In spite of the sometimes antagonistic nature of their relationship, Odile and Jim managed to get along reasonably well considering the vast disparity in their temperaments, values, backgrounds, and attitudes. Surprisingly, they were more compatible in bed than anywhere else, perhaps because all external trappings were quickly abandoned in the face of the sheer physical pleasure they took in each other. Jim was an ardent lover, and what he lacked in sensitivity and subtle nuance he compensated for in vigor, endurance, and unflagging interest in her. As best she could, Odile tried to put Narciso out of her mind, but there were moments when she longed for a whispered line of verse from Calderon de la Barca or Rojas-Sorrilla, or a French love song hummed sleepily into her ear.

During her years growing up on the plantation Odile

had gleaned enough knowledge from the remarks of Verbena and the other slaves to know that physical passion between two people dissipated quickly and was scarcely enough on which to base the foundation of a lifelong union. Her only hope was that it would continue until the baby arrived. This unborn child, she believed, would cement the relationship and provide her with the necessary leverage for dealing with Jim in the future.

For a while Narciso had besieged her with desperate, impassioned declarations of love and pleas to return to Florestal, which she found most disconcerting. Carefully destroying the letters, she sent him a single reply, in which she pleaded that if he truly loved her as he professed to, he would cease all contact of such a nature as to possibly seriously jeopardize her marriage. She also informed him that she was expecting a baby and that Dr. Zehner had cautioned her against any undue stress or exertion, so making trips to Florestal would be out of the question until after the baby's birth. She was careful to point out that the pregnancy had only very recently been diagnosed and that Jim was thrilled with the prospect of fatherhood; she hoped thereby to discourage any ideas Narciso might have about the possibility of his being the baby's father.

Because of her confinement, Odile had few visitors besides her three old friends, Louise Chardonnier, Anais Seguin, and Victorine Pilette, all of whom abandoned their quilts and embroidered tapestries to concentrate on clothing and accessories for the expected baby's layette.

"Oh, we're all just so excited for you—having your very first baby!" Victorine, herself the mother of three small children, rhapsodized.

Balls, late-night parties, and extended excursions were ruled out by Dr. Zehner, although she was allowed to attend occasional barbecues or other festive celebrations at nearby plantations for a few hours at a time. Even then Jim was none too happy with the prospect of her riding over the badly rutted River Road in a bumpy carriage. "I don't want anything happening to this baby of ours," he said.

"I never felt better in my life," she said, giving his arm an affectionate squeeze. She truly appreciated his protective concern and the assurance it gave her about the future.

Since the announcement of his sister's pregnancy, Placide had called at the plantation much more frequently than had been his custom since Jim had taken over, although Odile wasn't sure whether her brother came to see her or to admire the changes in the old mill, which was receiving a complete overhaul under Roger Guillon's supervision.

"When this mill is completed we will have the capacity to grind all the sugar up and down the Mississippi for miles," Jim informed his brother-in-law. "A virtual monopoly. None of the mills in any of the surrounding parishes can begin to compete with us."

The conversion of the old mill required not only the technical services of Roger Guillon but significant and frequent contributions from Roarke as well. The latter spent considerable time with Jim, who informed him that he would play a vital role in the operation of both mills when the renovation was completed.

Because Jim's time was precious and had to be wisely apportioned as the plantation activities expanded, he decided to combine meals with business conferences, discussing progress in various areas with Guillon, Roarke, and Oberdorfer. He insisted that they dine with him daily in the great house.

Roarke was shocked by the suggestion. "Oh, Lord, Mr. Jim, I could never do that. A black man sitting at the same table with a white man in his own house!"

"You're not an ordinary black man, Roarke," Jim said. "You're the best damned sugar-maker in this or any other parish."

Unconvinced, Roarke shook his head. "But your wife, Mr. Jim, she ain't going to like that one bit. No, sir."

"My wife doesn't run this plantation, I do," Jim asserted. "You just come to dinner, and let me worry about her."

He instructed Romulus to set three additional places at the table for his right-hand men.

Romulus was aghast. "You ain't going to have blacks and mulattos at *this* table?" he asked. "It ain't fitting, Mr. Jim. What would Miss Odile say?"

"We'll find out when she joins us," Jim replied.

"She won't never join you when she hears who's coming to dinner," Romulus said.

"She will if she knows what's good for her," Jim declared. "You tell Miss Odile that I expect her at this table."

When the butler conveyed the message, Odile exploded. "If he expects me to humiliate myself by sitting at the same table with that rabble, he's crazy!" she said.

"I'm only repeating what Mr. Jim told me to tell you, Miss Odile."

That evening Odile took to her bed and sent word to Jim that she was much too weak and tired to join him for dinner.

Angrily confronting her in their bedroom, he demanded, "What is this nonsense?"

"I'm feeling very poorly," she murmured.

"You look fine to me," he countered. "I want you to get up out of that bed and come downstairs."

"I couldn't possibly."

"Are you going to get up or do I have to drag you out of bed?"

"Please, Jim, I told you I can't," she protested.

Without further ado, he grabbed her roughly by the arm and jerked her to her feet, throwing the bedcovers askew in the process.

"Be careful—the baby!" she cried.

"That baby is a MacKay," he said. "MacKays are tough. They can take a lot. I want you dressed and downstairs at that dinner table in five minutes. Is that clear? You have guests, whether you like it or not."

❧ 33

As Mandragore prepared for the first fall harvest season in which both Jim's mill and the old refurbished one would be in operation, Placide began spending more time at the plantation than in the French Quarter. There was still too much of the planter in the Creole for him not to be moved by the sight of the tall, waving green cane that stretched as far as the eye could see. Soon it would be time for Father Daubigny to pay his annual call and pronounce his blessing over the incipient cutting season. Planters up and down the Mississippi for miles had negotiated with Jim to have their cane ground at Mandragore. The plantation had a virtual monopoly on sugar production in the area, since no one else had access to Roger Guillon's patented extraction method and even the most efficient of the older mills could not begin to compete. In essence, Jim had cornered the market.

"There is really no competition, is there?" Placide remarked as he and Jim rode together along a cane-break watching the slave work-gangs cutting the first stalks with their gleaming machetes.

"Not that I know of," Jim replied. "And I hope it stays that way for a long time to come."

"How's that German doing?" Placide asked.

"Oberdorfer?" Jim said. "Fine. There was a little trouble at first—some of the bolder slaves tried to assert themselves and challenged both him and me. Once they learned who's boss and that kindness isn't necessarily weakness, there's been no real trouble. Between the two of us, Oberdorfer and I are managing pretty well."

It was true. After some initial difficulties, most of

the slaves had settled down nicely, having grown accustomed to the benevolent authority of the big-bellied German immigrant, who tried to deploy the slaves as fairly and efficiently as possible. In addition to the ban on corporal punishment, Jim had promised that families would not be broken up by the sale of individual members to other plantations, food rations would be increased, and—most astounding of all—all babies born on the plantation from then on would be free on their twenty-first birthday.

The first time Jim revealed these radical innovations to Placide, the Creole was shocked. "The first two conditions I can perhaps accept, but the last never," he objected. "We will lose all our slaves by attrition."

"I understand your reaction," Jim said, "but what I am counting on is that in the future farming methods will be sufficiently improved and mechanized to the point that there will be no need for slaves at all."

"That is a foolish dream," Placide scoffed. "The South is not like the North, all small farms instead of giant plantations. The South will always have to have slaves. It is our system. There is no way our economy can survive without them."

"I disagree," Jim said. "Men like Roger Guillon have many ideas which could revolutionize agriculture in the South, eliminating the need for much of the hand labor."

"Our present methods have worked for us for over a hundred years," Placide argued. "Why should we change?"

"Someday we may have to," Jim replied. He urged his horse toward a stream where it could drink.

As Jim and Placide toured the vast plantation, they eventually came to the levee at the end of a canebrake. Jim was surprised to see Roger Guillon and Hans Oberdorfer intently examining the huge earthen dike. Generally Roger took little interest in the cane fields and seldom left the two mills, in which he had an intrinsic as well as a substantial financial interest.

"What are you doing out here, Roger?" Jim asked as he and Placide approached.

"Hans asked me to come and take a look at this levee," the young engineer replied.

"What's the matter with it?" Placide questioned.

"I think a crevasse is developing," Roger replied.

Any crack in the levee was regarded with alarm by most local planters. What was only a small leak could be quickly enlarged by the pressure of the water behind it into a major rent in the dike, resulting in a massive flooding of the fields, destroying acres of crops.

"What do you suggest?" Jim asked.

"I suggest correcting the defect right away. If something isn't done quickly the entire levee could give way," Roger announced.

"I doubt this levee would ever give way," Placide scoffed.

"I have inspected it and found several serious defects in the structure that pose a great threat," Roger said. "We must bear in mind that this is the hurricane season. If we get a severe storm with lots of rain and wind, the river could crest high enough to put such a severe strain on the wall that it gives way. My advice is to repair this crevasse as soon as possible. I suggest you use every available hand you've got."

"This is the cutting season, Guillon," Placide said. "We can't spare men for this kind of nonsense."

"If that levee gives way," Roger warned, "there won't be any harvest, Monsieur Martinon."

Jim knew instinctively that Roger's priorities were the right ones. "I'll see who we can spare," he said. "There must be a few available workers—perhaps some of the house slaves."

"It's a big job—bigger than I think you all realize," Roger asserted. "You need more than house slaves."

"I think you are being hysterical, Guillon," Placide said. "My family built these levees more than one hundred years ago. There has never been any trouble. Certainly there have been minor problems and repairs, but that's to be expected. Suddenly pulling all the slaves from the cane fields for major repairs at this time is absurd."

"This relatively small leak could develop into a major catastrophe," Roger insisted.

"I think you exaggerate," Placide chided him.

Jim felt the need to step in. "Roger's an engineer—a professional. I trust his judgment. If he says the levee won't hold in a big storm, I'm prepared to take his word for it."

"Monsieur Guillon may be a professional, but I think he is also an alarmist," Placide said.

Annoyed at Placide's persistent opposition, Roger replied, "You won't think I'm such an alarmist, Monsieur Martinon, if you suddenly find your grand plantation under ten feet of water."

Making it plain that he had heard enough of what he considered impudent effrontery, Placide urged his horse around and started to ride off. Jim finished his exchange with Guillon and Oberdorfer and then caught up with his brother-in-law.

"I do feel we'd better heed Roger's advice, even if it does mean falling behind a day or two in the harvest," Jim said.

"When you're dealing with cane, a day or two can be vital. In any case, I'm not going to worry about it," Placide replied. "I've decided to return to the French Quarter this evening."

"I wish you'd stay around. We're going to need all the help we can get on that levee," Jim said.

Placide stared at him in surprised indignation. "You aren't suggesting that *I personally* work on that levee, are you?"

"*I* intend to," Jim assured him.

Placide was aghast. "You mean digging in the dirt?"

"With pick and shovel."

Placide's normally pale face grew flushed.

"There is certain work which a gentleman does not perform. Digging in the dirt with niggers is just such work. You may lower yourself to such endeavors, but I do not."

With that, he dug his spurs into his horse's flank and galloped down the road ahead of Jim.

✢ 34

In the morning Odile rarely awakened before Jim, but as her pregnancy entered its final days she found herself rising early, increasingly restless and uncomfortable, anxious to get out of bed and walk around. Since the original crevasse in the levee had been uncovered by Roger Guillon, more extensive investigation had revealed additional serious defects in Mandragore's entire levee system, a result of many years of neglect. Jim had been involved night and day in the repair of the dike, a frantic project in which every available person on the plantation, white or black, had been enlisted, including all the house slaves except for Verbena, and she had escaped only because Odile protested that in her present condition she needed the maid in the house with her at all times. She knew the baby was due at least a month earlier than anybody suspected, and hoped she could convince everyone that its birth was premature. As for Verbena, she was grateful for her mistress's intervention, because it saved her from the pick-and-shovel brigade which had enlisted Cecil, Romulus, and Lavinia, as well as all the other house slaves.

Trying not to wake Jim, who was still sleeping soundly, exhausted from the previous day, Odile slipped out of bed and walked through the floor-to-ceiling window to the gallery, hoping that if she could stir around and get her circulation moving, she might relieve the cramps in her legs. Leaning against the balustrade, she gazed over the moss-laden oaks toward the river. The air seemed still and heavy, and the morning had an expectant quality about it. Raising her eyes to the sky, she found it filled with dark clouds in strange, ominous shapes, streaked with greenish, yellowish, and violet shafts of light.

As she walked along the second-story gallery toward the rear of the house, she could hear the slaves grumbling as the drivers loaded them into wagons with their rakes and picks and shovels for another day of construction on the levee. Oberdorfer, riding his horse down the middle of the dusty alley running between the opposing rows of slave cabins, looked up and, when he saw her, took off his wide-brimmed straw hat and waved. Being a European and accustomed to a rigidly stratified society, Oberdorfer respected Odile and her family as the landed gentry—the aristocrats, as it were, in a classless democracy—and kept to himself most of the time. He was not at all aggressive, unlike Roger Guillon, who eschewed any sort of obsequiousness. Odile detested the engineer for his impudence in daring to treat her as an equal, although Jim persisted in reminding her that the inventions and astuteness of this son of a quadroon whore—as she referred to Iris— were responsible for Mandragore's salvation. Odile waved back, returning the new overseer's greeting. In retrospect, she wondered why she had ever protested Davis's dismissal. Oberdorfer, once learning the routines of the plantation, was doing an excellent job— just as Jim had assured her all along—and she certainly had no fondness for Davis.

When she returned to the bedroom, she saw that Jim was not only awake and out of bed, but half dressed as well.

"What's going on out there?" he asked, referring to the peculiar colors and cloud patterns in the sky.

"I don't know," she replied.

"Well, you've lived here all your life. I'm just a newcomer from Ohio. We depend on you natives to keep us informed," he joked, brushing her cheek with his lips as he headed for the shaving stand. Splashing cold water from the pitcher into the porcelain basin, he asked, "You don't think it means anything bad, do you?"

"Bad?" she repeated.

"A storm or something?" He had heard of devastating tropical storms and hurricanes in the past, although none of any serious consequence had struck the area since his arrival. "Well, we only have one more bad place in the levee to fix, but something tells me we'd better get it finished quick. I've got a feeling there might be trouble brewing up there in that sky, and it's heading our way."

When he finished shaving, he sat on the edge of the bed and pulled on his boots. Wordlessly, Odile sat down beside him. He put his arm around her, kissed her cheek again, and placed his other hand on her bulging abdomen. "How are you both today?" he asked.

"The baby and I? We're both fine."

"Are you sure you'll be all right with just Verbena here?"

"Yes."

"Don't forget, if you have any problems, just tell Verbena to get out there and ring the plantation bell," he instructed her as he slipped into his jacket. "I'll come right away." With that, he kissed her again and was off to the levee with the rest.

Although the sky looked threatening all day and various dire predictions were made by the slaves with regard to a possible storm, the rain didn't actually start until late morning, and only by mid-afternoon was the steady downpour accompanied by high winds.

Because of the impending storm, Jim knew the crevasse had to be repaired as quickly as possible, and arranged with the city prison authorities for about thirty prisoners to augment the plantation labor force. The prisoners, chained together at the ankle, arrived in wagons escorted by half a dozen armed guards. Most of the convicts were runaway slaves who had been caught and sentenced to hard labor. The Mandragore slaves seemed frightened of these convicts, whom they, like the Creoles, referred to as *"Negres Marrons,"* and were disconcerted at having to work close to them on the repair of the levee.

At nightfall Jim felt relieved that the crevasse was finally sealed and the job completed, knowing that the levee would hold if a true hurricane struck during the night.

In the house, Odile stood at the bedroom window watching the slaves returning from their toil, knowing that Jim—always the last to leave—would soon be home. She had tried to ignore the pains, which had begun about mid-morning and continued steadily throughout the day, but they were now so frequent and severe that she wondered how much longer she could stand them without some opium from Dr. Zehner. As she stared out the window, the intensity of the wind and rain seemed to increase with the intensity of her pains, as though nature and her body were acting in concert.

Alone in the room, with the only light a flickering whale-oil lamp on the night table, she reached for the hand-carved rosary her mother had brought back from a visit to Cuba and began praying for the safe delivery of her baby, which she knew was imminent.

Downstairs, Verbena, still the only slave in the house, went around the gallery closing and bolting all the shutters, well aware of how easily they might be torn off their hinges and flung about if the storm continued to rise during the night. From years of experience delivering many babies, she knew that Odile's labor was progressing rapidly, and she wanted to have the house secured before returning upstairs to begin her vigil, which would continue until the baby arrived.

As Odile prepared to return to bed, a sudden gush of fluid burst forth from inside her and ran down her legs. Odile let out a cry and called for Verbena. "Come up here quick!" she yelled, frightened. "I need you! Verbena! Verbena!"

When the maid arrived, breathless, at the top of the spiral stairs, she knew instantly what had occurred. "Good Lord, child, your waters have done broke," she said.

"Help me, Verbena," Odile pleaded, looking apprehensive as she clutched at her swollen abdomen. "Help me. I'm so scared."

"There ain't nothing to be scared of. You just go lay

down and don't you get up, hear?" the maid said, escorting her back to bed.

"Don't leave me, Verbena."

"I got to go summon Mr. Jim," Verbena said, starting to leave the room.

"No! Come back!" Odile cried. "Don't leave me alone!"

"He told me to ring the bell if we needs him and I gots to go do that," she replied. "If I don't, he'll skin me alive."

She went downstairs and, covering her head with a shawl against the rain and wind, ran out to the yard and rang the plantation bell.

Dozing between pains, Odile awoke with a start when Jim, summoned by the bell, entered the room. He went straight to the bed and, sitting on the edge, clasped her hand in his.

"I came the moment I heard the bell," he said, his blond hair falling in wet locks over his eyes.

"Listen, Jim, I think you'd better send for Dr. Zehner," she said, in a series of whispery gasps.

He pressed his finger tips into her abdomen and felt it go steely hard beneath them. "You're having good strong pains," he said. "I'll go for him right away."

"No," she objected. "Send Cecil. I want you to stay here with me. I'm frightened, Jim. Don't leave me."

"Cecil's exhausted. I've had him working on the levee all day. He's not used to that kind of hard labor."

"Then send one of the other slaves."

"They're all exhausted."

"I don't care. Send them anyway."

"No. I'll go myself."

"No, Jim, I want you *here*."

"Verbena will stay with you until I get back."

"No!"

"I don't trust a slave to ride through this storm. They'll hide out under a bridge somewhere until it's over," he said, rising from the bed and starting for the door.

"Jim! No!" she shouted after him, beating her fists against the bed in frustration as he left the room.

As Jim opened the front door, the wind tore the knob out of his grasp and banged it furiously against the wall of the house, rattling the chandelier in the receiving hall. Verbena, summoned by the noise, caught up with Jim and threw a poncho around his shoulders.

"You better not go for no doctor, Mr. Jim. Not in this storm. You stay here. You and I can deliver that baby ourself," she advised.

"I've got to go, Verbena," he insisted as he headed across the rain-swept gallery toward the steps.

At first Jim elected to ride atop the levee in spite of the piles of sandbags, which made footing precarious for his already skittish horse, but eventually the wind forced horse and rider back onto the muddy River Road. By sheer force of will Jim urged the animal through the swirling wind and lashing rain, guiding it around fallen trees and other debris blocking the path. His greatest worry was that he might have to finally dismount and lead the horse on foot all the way to Zehner's house. The thought that the physician might be unwilling to venture out in such a storm never entered his mind.

As Jim reached the north bend in the river, a point which demarcated his original farm from Mandragore, he thought he discerned a lantern in the distance, and as he approached he saw that it was indeed a lantern— Roger Guillon's.

"What in God's name are you doing here?" Jim asked.

"I came to check a place in the levee I've been suspicious of," Roger replied. "It seemed all right, but the only way I could test it for sure was in a storm."

"And?" Jim asked anxiously.

"See for yourself." Roger held the lantern close to the dike, and Jim watched in horror as he observed a stream of brown river water seeping through a crack.

"Another crevasse!" he said.

"Yes, and if we let it go this whole section of levee will give way," Roger declared.

"Go get Oberdorfer," Jim directed. "Tell him to bring out a work crew right away."

"The slaves are all exhausted," Roger replied. "Besides, there's no time for that. By the time I reach Oberdorfer's cottage and he rounds up a work gang, it'll be too late. The river's cresting higher by the minute. The higher the water rises, the more pressure there is against the levee and the more likely this crevasse will give way. If it does, all of Mandragore will be underwater."

"Odile's in labor. I'm on my way to get the doctor," Jim said.

"This crevasse has got to be plugged up now and you and I have got to do it ourselves," Roger declared.

"I can't," Jim protested. "My wife—"

"You haven't got time to worry about that."

"But I must—"

"One of the slaves can deliver her. There's really nothing to it," Roger said.

"Odile wouldn't want a slave to deliver her baby," Jim said. "She'll never forgive me if I don't go get Dr. Zehner."

"If the plantation is destroyed it won't matter whether she forgives you or not," Roger reminded him. "When it comes to babies, white or black, it doesn't make much difference who delivers them. They all come out the same way."

"I know but—" Jim anguished.

"No 'buts' about it, man!" Roger said, becoming a little exasperated with Jim. "It's *your* land. I don't know why the hell *I'm* getting so excited."

With that, Roger headed for his horse, which was tethered to a nearby sycamore. Frightened by the wind, which ripped branches loose and scattered them around, the animal danced about as the young engineer unpacked two shovels fastened to the saddle.

Returning, he held one out to Jim. "Well?" he asked. "Are you going to join me?"

With scarcely a moment's hesitation, Jim took the shovel, and they began to dig.

✍ 35

Outside the elegant Couronneau town house swirling winds accompanied by torrential rains toppled chimneys and weather vanes, tore shutters off their hinges, and ripped shingles from roofs. Inside, in the secret windowless attic chamber, Placide lounged in a velvet chair, feet propped on an ottoman, puffing on an elaborately carved opium pipe, which he occasionally passed to Denise, perched on the arm of the chair beside him. Both anxiously awaited the start of the performance she had arranged for her lover.

Below them, on the second floor, Victor Couronneau slumbered, unaware of the storm raging beyond his shuttered windows, nudged to sleep by the sedative powders his wife had secured from Nizilda Foucher and slipped into his bedtime chocolate. A single lamp burned with a low flame at his bedside.

One of Denise's favorite themes was the circus, and it dominated the evening's entertainment. In a spangled suit and glittering cape, Valcour, whip in hand, acted as ringmaster, signaling for two voluptuous masked slave girls dressed as cats to bring in a naked, muscular black man trussed in a leather harness in such a way that he was compelled to walk, like an animal, on all fours.

"And now, *messieurs* and *mesdames,*" Valcour announced in a resonant, theatrical voice, "we have Samson, the strong-man, and his two Delilahs to thrill and entertain you."

Prodding the harnessed slave with the whip handle, Valcour forced him to lie spread-eagled on a table, to which he was shackled with iron cuffs and chains.

258

"What are they going to do?" Placide asked with eager anticipation.

"You'll see, darling," Denise replied, smiling.

When the man was fully immobilized the two girls went to work on him, caressing his body slowly and sensuously at first, gradually accelerating their efforts. Eventually they progressed to pulling at his hair, kissing and licking him from head to toe, biting his fingertips, toes, and nipples until he was fully aroused. Then, as one girl rubbed his cheeks with her bare breasts, the other knelt between his spread legs and made love to his distended genitals. Alternating positions, the two girls succeeded in exciting their captive to a feverish state. It was then that Valcour entered the scene with a lighted candle. As the girls intensified their erotic efforts, Valcour tilted the taper and allowed the hot wax to drip onto the prisoner's scrotum until he cried out from the exquisite mixture of pleasure and pain.

Excited, Placide puffed harder on the opium pipe and rubbed himself between his legs.

"Delightful, isn't it?" Denise grinned.

Eventually, exhausted and spent, the male captive, still shackled to the table, his genitals caked with wax, was abandoned for a mulatto girl, barely in her early teens, tied to a child's gaily painted rocking horse.

"And now, *messieurs* and *mesdames,* for our second act of the evening we have Ninetta, the bareback rider," Valcour announced in a loud voice, to compensate for the howling wind and pounding rain beyond the solid-brick walls of the attic room.

At the butler's signal, the two cat-girls went to work on little Ninetta in much the same way: kissing her mouth and budding breasts, licking her limbs, which were secured to the four legs of the rocking horse by leather thongs.

"That little one, on the rocking horse," Placide said, handing the opium pipe back to Denise, "she must be quite badly behaved if Valcour had to tie her to her little horse. Have him bring her to me right now."

Denise gave the order, and the butler untied the pubescent girl and marched her to Placide. She trembled with embarrassment, and tried to cover her nudity with her hands.

"You must be disciplined, Ninetta," Placide slurred, obviously deep under the effect of the opium's sweet fumes. "You must be spanked," he continued; with that, he pulled the young girl across his lap and began to slap her naked bottom.

Denise giggled at Ninetta's yelps of pain and pleas for mercy. Denise, her blood pounding at the sight of the squirming girl's bared buttocks receiving Placide's spanks, ordered Valcour to disrobe and bend over the rocking horse. She went to the wall, where whips, handcuffs, and the like were hanging, and selected a small "house" whip, commonly used for disciplining domestic slaves.

"Now, Valcour," she began, smirking at the hapless slave's naked buttocks, high in the air across the rocking horse's saddle, "I shall not stop until you've cried out in just the manner of that delightful minx across the master's knee." Soon the rhythm of her stinging whip matched that of Placide's palm, and both Valcour and Ninetta were howling in unison.

The two cat-girls watched the scene, eyes wide with wonder, particularly at Denise's treatment of her unfortunate butler. They began to caress each other as Valcour begged for mercy and was allowed up by his severe mistress. Placide also had tired of his game, and watched as Ninetta danced around the room, sniffling and rubbing her sore rear.

Meanwhile, on the floor below, Victor Couronneau, somewhat stuporous from the sedative, was awakened by the shattering of glass—a shutter torn loose by the wind was hurled against the window opposite his bed. Getting up to investigate, he reached for the lamp on the night stand and accidentally knocked it to the floor, breaking the glass chimney. The exposed flame, fanned by the high wind through the broken window, ignited the flailing drapes, which in moments burst into flames. His eyes wide with horror, Victor fled the room and stumbled into the hall.

Upstairs in the attic room, the performance continued. As the cat-girls caressed and soothed the mulatto nymphet, now bound spread-eagled to the floor, Valcour straddled her. It had been long rumored in the French Quarter that the Couronneau butler was endowed with spectacular proportions, and Placide observed, through the opium haze, that those rumors had not been exaggerated. While the cat-girls lubricated him and Ninetta with a vial of viscous oil, he slowly inched his way into her as she tugged at her restraints, screaming with pain and terror.

Turning to Denise, whose attention was raptly focused on the bizarre scene before her, Placide protested, "He'll tear her apart."

"Hush, dearest," Denise admonished him, fascinated by the display.

Because the windowless room was already filled with thin, gray smoke from the burning opium, it was some time before anyone noticed the ominous thick, black smoke easing under the bolted door. The little mulatto girl was the first to cough, and she was soon joined by her tormentors. Alarmed, Placide got up to investigate. Unbolting the door, he was assailed at once by huge billows of smoke rising up the stairwell. Frightened and nearly overcome, Placide, followed by Denise, Valcour, and the two slave girls dressed as cats, hurried down the spiral stairs, coughing and gasping, leaving the black man used earlier and the mulatto girl behind, still bound and helpless.

Seeing the entire second floor engulfed in smoke and flames, Placide smashed a shuttered French window and led them out onto the gallery above the central courtyard.

"Jump!" he commanded.

"I can't!" Denise protested. "It's too high!"

"You have no choice," he said, the heat from the flames already searing his back. Together, Placide and Valcour picked Denise up and threw her over the wrought-iron railing into a clump of bushes below. She was followed by the two cat-girls, and then the two men jumped over and fell.

Victor Couronneau appeared on the gallery in his nightshirt. Realizing there was no alternative, he closed his eyes and plummeted into the courtyard after them. Missing the shrubbery, the old man landed on the flagstones and emitted a cry of agonized pain.

"My God, he's injured!" Denise cried, running to her aged husband's aid.

"My hip! My hip!" he repeated, writhing in pain.

Amid the pelting rain and howling wind, the escapees from the attic huddled together, attempting to shelter the injured Victor while all around them the town house and its attached slave quarters were consumed by crackling flames. Eventually, with a terrible roar, the walls collapsed and it crashed in on itself. Only the petrified screams of those trapped inside could be heard.

❧ 36

Odile, her brow covered with perspiration, clutched the bedposts and bit her lip to keep from crying out in pain. The contractions were harder now, lasting longer, and the periods of relaxation between shorter and less frequent, so that she scarcely had time to catch her breath.

Realizing that the baby's arrival was imminent, Verbena made preparations for the birth, all the while attempting to comfort the frightened Odile. Wiping the sweat from her mistress's face with a damp towel, she said, "Don't you worry none, child. Everything's going to be all right, hear?"

While she spoke so reassuringly, the wind outside roared with such ferocity that Verbena marveled that the roof remained on the great house.

"Why doesn't Jim come back with Dr. Zehner?" Odile asked anxiously.

"I doubt if the good Lord hisself could get here in this storm," the maid answered.

"Oh, Verbena, I'm so afraid," she whimpered,

reaching out and clutching the black woman's hand.

"Now you hush and don't you worry about nothing," Verbena admonished.

"I'm worried about Jim and the doctor."

"They'll be here bye and bye."

"But I need them now."

"You got me, honey, and you don't need nobody else."

"I want my husband. I want the doctor," Odile whined.

Verbena didn't have the heart to tell her that she doubted that they would see either one before the baby came. "You just try to relax, honey, and save your strength," she admonished her. "You going to need all the strength you done got when it comes time for pushing."

The high winds had torn shingles from the roof, resulting in leaks in various parts of the house. Lavinia, Romulus, and the rest of the house slaves, back from their day of manual labor on the levee, went from room to room attempting to place pails, basins, pans, and chamber pots so as to catch the dripping water. Wishing to check on the other house slaves and any possible damage to the house or furnishings, Verbena took advantage of one of Odile's brief naps between pains to slip out of the room.

Awakened by the start of a new and even harder contraction, Odile was panic-stricken to find herself alone.

"Verbena! Verbena!" she cried.

All of a sudden there was a horrendous crash out on the gallery just beyond the shuttered window, and Odile, frightened, let out a scream.

Verbena abandoned the great-grandfather clock she was trying to move from beneath the dripping ceiling in the hall and rushed to her mistress's side.

"Verbena—out on the gallery—" Odile said, massaging her abdomen.

Peeking through a crack in the shutters, Verbena replied, "Just a branch off one of them old oak trees the wind must have tore loose and blown against the house. It's nothing. You just rest, honey."

But Odile could not rest. A contraction stronger than any she had so far experienced suddenly gripped her and, fearing her back would split in two, she let out a terrified scream. "Help me, Verbena! Help me!"

Verbena took the veilleuse off the night table and, lifting the covers, peered between Odile's raised knees. For a moment she could scarcely believe her eyes. The baby was crowning. A couple more contractions and it would be out. At once she summoned Lavinia and told her to forget about everything else and bring supplies at once. "And don't you be dillydallying none or I'll whip you myself," she warned the young slave.

"Help me, Verbena!" Odile cried. "It's coming! I can feel it. It's coming out! What am I going to do? It's coming! It's coming! Help me, Verbena. *Help me!*" Odile shrieked, her knees raised and wide apart, biting the hand-carved rosary.

Unconcerned, Lavinia shuffled back into the room with the sheets, clean towels, basin of hot water, string, and sharp knife that Verbena had requested.

"Took you long enough, girl," the older slave chided.

"We ain't got no bucket for the afterbirth," Lavinia announced. "They's all being used to catch the leaks."

"I ain't got no time to worry about buckets now," Verbena said. "You just do what I tell you. Come on around here and give me one of them towels to catch that baby with."

"Catch the baby?" Odile repeated in a panicky tone.

"That's right, Miss Odile." Lavinia chuckled. "The baby's almost here."

"When you gets your next hard pain I wants you to push just as hard as you can, honey," Verbena directed. "I wants you to push this baby right on out of there."

In moments the new pain began, and Odile, frightened and screaming, nevertheless did as she was instructed. Without difficulty the baby's head popped out, and a few moments later, with skillful manipulation, Verbena extracted the rest of the infant and held it up.

"It's a boy!" Lavinia cried, clasping her hands together excitedly.

"Is it over?" Odile asked.

"Yes, and you got yourself one fine son." Verbena smiled.

"Is he all right?" Odile asked anxiously.

"He just fine," Lavinia replied.

"Thank God," Odile murmured, relaxing her grip on the bedposts. "Thank God."

❧ 37

Jim and Roger struggled not only against time but against the elements as well—rain which lashed at them in stinging sheets and winds which blew with such force that merely standing and maintaining one's balance was a feat. The unceasing torrential rains combined with the high tides invariably accompanying tropical storms had raised the river to dangerous heights. This further stress to the sides of the levee made the two men fear that the trickle now seeping through the earthen breastworks could at any moment give way to a demolishing flood.

Though both soaked to the skin, Roger held the bags, while Jim filled them with sand, now so wet that the filled bags were as heavy and as hard to lift as slabs of stone. One after another, they piled bag on bag until they felt sure they had a seal. Standing back, Roger raised the lantern and tried to decide whether or not the last bag had finally stemmed the leak.

"I hate to say this," Roger began, "but what we're doing now is like placing a tiny bandage over a great, festering wound. Inside this levee, behind the crack, there's massive erosion going on."

Hoping the young engineer would come up with a

bright, almost miraculous solution he himself had not foreseen, Jim asked, "What do you think the next step should be?"

"Complete reconstruction of the levee."

"I was afraid you'd say that," Jim admitted ruefully.

Roger shrugged. "It's the only answer."

"Well, we'll have to wait until after the storm for that," Jim said.

Although their backs and legs felt as though they might give out at any moment, they decided to fill more sandbags and stack them over the leak, just to be on the safe side.

As they feverishly worked, Jim listened to the terrified whinnies of the horses as they strained against their tethers and nervously pawed the mud in which they were forced to stand. At times the fury of the wind bent the trees to which the horses were tied almost to the ground, and Jim fretted that the trunks might snap and the frightened animals run away.

Finally Roger said, "I think that's enough."

Hoping he still had time to go after Dr. Zehner and bring him back before Odile gave birth, Jim said, "I agree."

Hoisting his shovel over his shoulder, Jim started for the clump of trees where the horses were and noticed that all at once there was a lull in the wind. Staring up at the night sky, he was astonished to see a star or two twinkling among the heavy clouds. "Is it over?" he asked Roger.

"We'll have to wait and see," Roger replied. "It might just be the eye of the hurricane passing over."

They packed their tools on the still-skittish horses and prepared to leave.

"I want to check that crevasse one more time," Jim said.

"It'll hold," Roger assured him, anxious to get home to bed.

But Jim prevailed, and they together rode along the levee. With the handle of his shovel, Jim probed among the sandbags, searching for new leaks and testing the results of the day's efforts. "Seems fine," he said.

Just as they prepared to leave for good that night, the wind suddenly returned, blowing this time from the opposite direction and with an even greater force than before, accompanied by the same pelting rain.

"I was right," Roger said, pointing to the now-black sky. "It was just the eye passing over."

Hearing the dreaded sound of gushing water somewhere nearby, Jim and Roger exchanged apprehensive glances. Without a word, both knew what had happened: The levee had sprung a new leak.

Rushing to the spot where the sound of rushing water told them that the river had succeeded in penetrating the earthen wall, Jim realized instantly that there was no time to plug this new crevasse in the usual way. Leaping off his horse and tossing the reins to Roger, he threw himself over the stream pouring from the hole in the eroded dike. From the pressure against his body, Jim knew he had landed in the right place. The problem was going to be to stay there. His body was the only shield between the plantation and the river.

Roger, too, realized that there was no other way to stem the new crevasse. Feeling helpless just standing by, he tried to think of some way to relieve his friend.

"Let me take your place," he said.

"No," Jim refused. "Start putting sandbags all around me. That's the best thing you can do right now. Go on. Don't hesitate. Don't worry about me. There's no way I'm going to let this damned river ruin everything I've been working so hard for since I took over Mandragore. Odile will just have to let Verbena deliver the baby."

"You might have to lie there all night," Roger said.

"Goddamn it, I'll lie here forever if it means saving Mandragore!" Jim declared.

At dawn the sun rose on a sky streaked with yellow, green, and violet. The air was fresh and clean. The hurricane had vanished as suddenly as it had arisen, leaving in its wake high water, boats ripped from their moorings and drifting aimlessly about, fallen trees, houses without roofs and windows, washed-out bridges, swollen streams, and all manner of debris strewn about the countryside.

Throughout the harrowing night, Jim had insisted on lying against the side of the levee, a human plug in the leaking dike. Roger had remained at his side, bolstering his spirits and keeping him surrounded with sandbags.

As soon as it was light, Hans Oberdorfer arrived with a wagonload of slaves. The portly German, seeing Jim lying in the mud, was astounded to learn that all that had lain between the plantation and disaster was one man's body.

"Mein Gott!" he exclaimed. "This I cannot believe!"

Together, Oberdorfer and Roger helped Jim to his feet. When he attempted to take a few steps, he was so stiff and weak from the night-long ordeal that he tumbled to the ground.

"Put him in the wagon and take him to the house," Roger directed.

Preferring to ride his horse, Jim started to object, but, soaked, aching, and exhausted, he knew he wasn't able to and allowed his friends to lift him over the side of the wagon onto the straw covering the floorboards.

The wagon and team plodded through the mud, and, unable to restrain his curiosity, Jim raised his head to survey the damage done to Mandragore by the storm. The plantation seemed to have escaped serious harm. Although several trees had been uprooted and many were missing major branches, the bulk of the cane withstood the onslaught of wind and rain better than he had expected.

As the wagon headed up the alley between the rows of slave cabins, he observed that most of the buildings had survived remarkably well, losing only chimneys, shingles, doors, windows, or shutters, although one or two of the older slave cabins and a wagon shed were completely demolished. The driver of the team assured him that no one was seriously injured and most of the livestock were unaffected, except for a few pigs and chickens and a single calf, all of which drowned. Thus, it appeared that the plantation had come through the hurricane relatively unscathed, and Jim was grateful.

His big concern, as it had been all night, was for Odile and the baby. He seriously doubted that the infant had been born yet. First babies were usually a long time in coming.

Halfway across the muddy barnyard, Jim heard the plantation bell ringing wildly and saw Romulus running excitedly toward the wagon.

"Mister Jim! Mister Jim!" the butler cried.

Jim sat up in the wagon. "What's the matter?" he asked anxiously. "What's the bell ringing for?"

"For your son," Romulus answered. "He was born during the night. You gots yourself a son, Mr. Jim. Born right in the middle of that storm."

"How is he?" Jim asked, scarcely able to believe his ears.

"He fine," Romulus answered. "A fine, healthy boy."

"And my wife?"

"Miss Odile, she fine too."

Despite the bone-wrenching fatigue throughout his body, Jim climbed over the side of the wagon and ran to the house. Inside, he headed upstairs, almost colliding with Lavinia, who was on her way down with a basin of water.

"Congratulations, Mr. Jim," she said.

Excitedly throwing open the bedroom door, he saw Odile, looking tired but lovely, sitting up against the pillows, a tiny infant cradled in her arms. She looked up and stared at him, stunned, as though he were some sort of apparition.

Wordlessly, he went to her and kissed her. Then, gazing down at the infant in her arms, he said, with awe in his voice, "I can't believe it."

Huddled in one corner of the room was a timid-looking slave girl whose huge, engorged breasts indicated that she, too, had recently given birth; she would probably be used as wet-nurse for the new Mac-Kay baby. Verbena commanded, "Open your dress and let me see them titties. I want to make sure you is healthy. I don't want no dirty titties going in this here child's mouth."

Obediently the girl did as she was told, and once

she had passed approval, Verbena turned her attention to Jim. "You going to catch your death of cold, Mr. Jim, if you don't get out of them wet clothes."

Oblivious to the maid's admonitions, Jim continued to stare at the baby. For an instant he allowed himself to wonder what his and Delphine's baby might have been like. "Look how big he is," he said.

"Yes, he is," Odile agreed, carefully adding, "considering he's come early."

"He's going to be big and tall, like his daddy," Verbena predicted.

"He has his mother's coloring," Jim said, indicating the baby's cap of fine black hair and eyes that were almost a purplish hue and sure to turn brown.

"You never went for the doctor, did you?" Odile asked Jim in a cold, reproachful tone.

"I couldn't," he admitted. "I started out for Zehner's place, but—"

Odile interrupted, "But you decided the levee was more important. I've already heard from the slaves how you spent the night there."

"If I hadn't, Mandragore would probably be under ten feet of water right now," he replied.

"That's just an excuse. You didn't want to go for the doctor," she accused.

"I did—"

"We could have died, the baby and me."

Embarrassed by the scene she was making in front of Verbena and the wet-nurse candidate, Jim said, "Well, everything came out all right, didn't it?"

"No thanks to you," she persisted bitterly. "You didn't care enough to go for the doctor, as you promised. All you care about, Jim MacKay, is your cane and your mills. You don't care a thing about me or this child."

"I love both of you," he assured her, uncomfortable at such accusations.

"No you don't."

"I do."

"The hell you do," Odile said.

Deciding she'd better step in, Verbena said, "Now you hush, Miss Odile, hear? Don't you go talking to

Mr. Jim that way. Shame on you. When a woman starts talking that way, it means she's tired and needs a rest. You shouldn't be doing a lot of talking and saying things you're going to be sorry for later on."

"I'm not going to be sorry for anything," Odile said, transferring the baby from one arm to the other, away from Jim. "He's the one who's going to be sorry."

In the days following the baby's birth Odile's attitude toward Jim softened, somewhat, but an undercurrent of resentment persisted, resentment engendered by her insistence that he had given the levee repairs precedence over the health and safety of the baby and herself.

Recovering with amazing speed from the delivery, she was on her feet in a couple of days, defying everyone's urging that she remain in bed.

"You going to get yourself a case of the 'milk fever' up and walking around that way," Verbena warned.

Odile ignored the maid's admonitions, and even mentioned the possibility that she might nurse the baby herself instead of relinquishing him to the black wet-nurse, as was the custom. Needless to say, Verbena was outraged by this suggestion. "Have you done gone and lost your head, child?" she said. "You know it ain't proper for a white lady to nurse her own child when she got slaves to do it for her. Only poor white trash nurse their own babies."

Although she longed to see Placide and show him the baby, Odile did not think it particularly strange that her brother had not as yet called at the plantation. The River Road leading into the city had been badly gutted by the storm and was so clogged with debris, not to mention the fact that several bridges were out, that travel was hazardous.

Later, when she received news that the road was once again passable, she became anxious when Placide still neither came nor sent congratulations.

"I don't understand it," she said to Verbena. "Everyone has come to see the baby—the Pilettes, the Chardonniers, the Seguins, the Anspachers—except my own brother."

"He'll be here by-and-by," Verbena assured her.

"Perhaps I should send Cecil after him," she said.

Overhearing her as he entered the bedroom for a midday peek at the baby, Jim volunteered to go to the city and seek out Placide himself, wanting to make amends for his supposed thoughtlessness during her labor. "I'll go round him up and tell him to get on out here and meet his nephew," he said.

Hesitant to go right to the Couronneau home and ask to see Placide, Jim decided it would be wise to stop off at Isaac's store opposite the French Market first and find out if Isaac had heard any news of his brother-in-law. This store, like the new one on Canal Street, which was run by Silvia, was patronized by a broad cross section of the New Orleans populace, bringing with them all sorts of tidbits of gossip and information.

Isaac was delighted to see his old friend, and they exchanged warm greetings and cigars. Both men's wives had given birth to sons just days apart.

"How can that be?" Isaac asked, staring at his cigar in amazement. "Silvia was pregnant a whole month before Odile."

"The baby came a month early," Jim replied.

"Small, then?" Isaac asked anxiously.

"No. He's big and husky." Jim chuckled.

"Silvia and I named ours 'Daniel.' What's yours?"

"We haven't decided yet. Odile wants to call him 'Martinon'—you know, the family name. I think that sounds too formal. I want him to have a regular first name."

"Such as?"

"Odile suggested 'Antoine,' after her father."

"A French name, huh?"

Jim shrugged. "If that's what she wants."

"They get what they want, these women," Isaac nodded. "But I got to admit, 'Daniel' I like. He'll be eight days old on Sunday. You've got to come to his *brith*—circumcision. We're going to make a big party, Silvia and me. Bring Odile."

"I don't know if she's strong enough yet," Jim said, knowing his wife would never attend such a function.

"Then come by yourself."

Turning to the real purpose of his visit, Jim said, "Listen, Isaac, what I've come about is my brother-in-law. We haven't heard a word from him in days."

Isaac stared at him in amazement. "You mean you don't know?"

"About what?"

"The fire. The night of the big hurricane the Couronneau house burned. Placide Martinon was there at the time."

"Is he all right?" Jim asked anxiously, hoping nothing serious had happened to his brother-in-law which might upset Odile.

"It depends on how you mean 'all right,'" Isaac replied. "He wasn't hurt in the fire. He and his lady friend, Denise Couronneau, escaped by jumping from the second-story gallery along with three slaves and her husband. The old man suffered a broken hip and died a few days later as a result. There was more trouble, though . . ."

"Such as?" Jim asked.

"Such as what they found in the rubble."

"What?"

Avoiding Jim's eyes, Isaac muttered, "Things I don't like to talk about."

"Tell me, for God's sake," Jim insisted.

"In a secret room in the attic they found—how can I say it?—torture equipment from out of, God forbid, the Spanish Inquisition. Racks and wheels and all kinds of other terrible devices. For her pleasure, Madame Couronneau and her butler used to torment the slaves and force them to take part in orgies like the Romans and Greeks had. Two slaves' bodies were found in the weckage of the fire. A man and a woman, both tied-up, I heard."

Jim shook his head. "I can't believe it."

"I'm only telling you what I heard," Isaac said.

"Where are they now—Placide and Denise?"

"After the fire, when the people in the French Quarter realized the terrible things that were going on in the Couronneau house, they stormed it and found the butler and two women slaves living there among the ruins and took them to jail. Your brother-in-law and his lady friend were staying at the new St. Louis Hotel, but when they heard an angry mob was coming to get them—maybe to hang them—they escaped," Isaac related.

"Where did they go?"

"Rumor has it they took the first ship out of here headed for France."

Shaking his head in disbelief, Jim repeated, "My God . . . My God . . ." over and over. All the way back to the plantation he agonized how he would tell Odile about the scandal surrounding her brother and his desperate flight to France with Denise Couronneau. With the birth of the baby so recent, he wanted to spare her any sort of upset, and yet he was obliged to explain why Placide had not come to call. There was simply no way he could keep the news from her. If he didn't tell her, someone else surely would.

Isaac's bizarre tale wasn't completely a surprise to Jim. He had known for some time that Placide and Denise and their friends were involved in all manner of vice, although he had no idea they embraced such extremes. The story of the torture of slaves appalled him.

From a purely selfish point of view, Placide's flight and his probable exile in France—warrants had been issued for his arrest in Louisiana—might not be such a bad thing. Although his brother-in-law had had little to do lately with the management of the plantation, he was still the legal half-owner. Perhaps he could work out an arrangement with Placide to buy out his share; then Mandragore would be exclusively MacKay property. Of course, there was always the possibility that Placide would refuse to sell, but Jim doubted that. His brother-in-law was too shrewd to pass up a good offer. Through his mother, little Antoine Martinon MacKay was bound to inherit half the planta- tion, but for Jim that wasn't enough. He wanted to assure Mandragore's passing into the hands of his de- scendants in its entirety. In short, he wanted it all.

Part Two
1859

❧ 38

Although only one year away from his fiftieth birthday, Jim felt little changed from a decade earlier—or even two or three decades earlier, for that matter. One thing was clear to him, however, and that was that no matter how slight the changes time had wrought in a man, the biggest change was in the way those around him treated him. That treatment might range from respect and deference to impatience and disdain, often causing him to alter his behavior and attitudes according to the perceptions of others. Age, Jim concluded, was more a question of how one was treated, rather than how one felt. *Others convince us we're growing older,* he thought, *even if we don't feel it.* Inside, Jim firmly believed he was still the same brash, eager young Ohioan who had drifted down the Mississippi on a flatboat a quarter of a century earlier.

Physically, Jim decided, he had not aged all that much. Granted, his once-thick, unruly blond hair had grown thinner and generously streaked with gray. His eyes didn't quite exhibit the same youthful luster they once had, and his face showed a few creases—as much from years spent outdoors in the subtropical sun as from age. His trunk had thickened a little, especially at the waist, and his belly was not as flat as it once was, but most would have considered him reasonably trim. Fortunately, one thing which had not diminished was his stamina. When necessary, he could still put in a sixteen-hour day, although in later years his duties had become far more managerial and less physical, requiring him to spend more time in the study and less in the fields and mills, a change he didn't necessarily welcome. Operations at Mandragore had expanded considerably and in many directions. The farmer had gone from planter to business entrepreneur.

Much to everyone's amazement—not least of all to Odile and himself—their marriage had endured. Stormy and uncertain from the very beginning, it had continued on an often shaky, precarious course, held together by Odile's personal determination to make it work at all costs as well as her Catholicism and Jim's willingness to accept a relationship that was less than ideal. It could hardly be described as a marriage made in heaven. If there was not and never had been a great deal of romantic love, there was at least mutual respect and tolerance. Friendship, loyalty, affection, and a desire to achieve common goals had successfully supplanted more intense emotions, so that if Jim and Odile were less than lovers, they were certainly friends. Probably the union's strongest cement was their devotion to their son, Antoine, as well as to the plantation.

As the mother of a young man soon to reach his majority, Odile, just over forty herself, still retained much of her youthful beauty, now enhanced by a certain mellowness imparted by experience and understanding, which gave her a decided edge over younger rivals. At social gatherings it was not at all uncommon to find her surrounded by men of all ages, the center of masculine attention, while younger, perhaps prettier, women were neglected.

"Odile, honey, I do believe you are still the belle of the ball," Jules Seguin said as they whirled about the floor at the Osiris Ball, one of the most spectacular of the many festive dances attendant to Mardi Gras.

Physically, nature had been most kind to her. If a few strands of gray invaded her jet-black locks and a tiny line or two crossed her ivory complexion and her bosom and hips were perhaps a trifle more ample than they once were, it only added to her attractiveness.

Following the birth of Antoine, she seemed to grow

quieter and more contemplative, acting less from impulse than from careful deliberation. Her life focused more on her son than on herself, although, for a woman of such extraordinary beauty, she had never been as selfish or vain as others would have given her license to be in light of her exceptional attributes. As to her relations with Jim after the boy's birth, they seemed much the same as always, vacillating unpredictably between warmth, loyalty, and affection and contemptuous, willful antagonism. Somehow managing to maintain a healthy sexual interest in each other, they shared the same bed for more than twenty years, except during periodic spats when either Jim or Odile moved to the attic or the divan in the study. Both of them desired additional children, but after the birth of Antoine Odile had not been able to carry a baby past the first few weeks of pregnancy, a situation she found disheartening, especially since she was anxious to present Jim with a child which was truly his own. Sadly, the fulfillment of such a wish did not seem to be her fate.

Shaking his now-white head, Dr. Zehner said, "I don't understand it. You were able to carry a child for the full nine months once, why not again?"

From time to time Odile wondered if the paternity of the child was related to the viability of the pregnancy, but unequivocally dismissed the possibility of having anyone except Jim father another child. A person could be forgiven one such error, but not two. Despite a desperate desire for other children, both she and Jim resignedly accepted the fact that Antoine seemed fated to be their only issue.

At twenty, Antoine was both the joy and the trial of his parents' lives. Tall, slender, with a strikingly handsome face, dark eyes, black hair, and ivory skin, the boy decidedly favored his mother in appearance.

"The only thing Scottish about that boy is his name," Jim would often remark. "And only his last name at that."

Not just in looks, but in temperament as well, Antoine favored his Creole antecedents. Variously described as impetuous, fun-loving, sensuous, and volatile, he disdained serious involvements—most distressingly, the operation of the sugar mills and the growing of cane, as well as the many new enterprises in which Jim was now engaged. Although Jim adored his only son, he was severely disappointed by the boy's lack of interest in the affairs of the plantation he would someday inherit. In fact, the only aspect of life at Mandragore for which he displayed any enthusiasm at all was the stable. At a very young age he was considered the finest horseman in the parish, winning major ribbons in every horse show, much to Odile's great delight. When he wasn't galloping across the fields or jumping hurdles in the pastures or otherwise engaged with his horse, Pegasus, an offspring of his mother's horse, Comet, Antoine participated in the other pleasurable pastimes available to the sons of the wealthy and privileged: hunting, fishing, dancing, partying, drinking, serenading attractive young girls beneath their windows, playing billiards, dominoes, euchre, fiddle-playing, attending oyster suppers, and generally carousing with his friends.

"That boy is just like his uncle, Placide," Verbena would say, shaking her gray head.

As much as it dismayed Jim, he had to admit that she was right. Antoine's similarity to his uncle was most apparent one day when the boy came to Jim and asked for an allowance with which to support an octoroon to whom he had recently taken a fancy as his mistress. Indignant that the boy dared to make such a request, Jim flatly refused, berating Antoine for his lack of interest in the plantation and other serious matters, forgetting for the moment his own youthful passion for Delphine.

"Shame on you for proposing such a thing," he reproached him. "What do you think your mother would say if I should tell her about this—you wanting to keep a mistress?"

"But you won't." Antoine grinned, knowing very well that the subject of colored mistresses was rarely broached with well-bred women like Odile and would have been considered insulting. The fact that nearly every Creole man of means had at least one colored mistress was never acknowledged in polite circles.

There were few things which Jim could bring himself to deny his son, but a mistress was one of them. "If you want a mistress, young man, you'll have to use your own means to maintain her," he declared. "I have no intention of sponsoring such an indulgence."

"Perhaps if I displayed more interest in the plantation?" Antoine suggested.

"I doubt that I would be inclined differently," Jim said. He was well aware that Antoine and his friends regularly visited Xenia's, and although he didn't exactly disapprove on moral grounds—he himself had done the same thing, at a slightly older age—he did worry that the boy might contract a venereal disease and impair his ability to procreate. The only way of stopping such diversions would be to withdraw his allowance, but if he did, Jim was sure, Antoine would manage to wheedle money from Odile. Like the boy's mother, Jim wished to see Antoine married, with children, and settled at Mandragore, but the youth seemed so wild, irresponsible, and pleasure-seeking that at times Jim wondered if such an aspiration would ever come to pass.

"The right girl will change him," Odile assured Jim one night as they were lying in bed listening to the crickets and frogs in the warm spring night. "Wait and see."

"Who is 'the right girl'?" he asked.

"Well, there's Valentin and Louise's daughter," she suggested.

"Jacqueline Chardonnier?" Jim scoffed. "Antoine would never marry her. He considers her far too homely."

"Or Heidi Anspacher."

"She's too poor a horsewoman."

"What about Felicité or Angeline Pilette?"

"Antoine accuses Felicité of having two left feet on the dance floor," Jim answered. "And Angeline at twelve is much too young for a boy his age."

"Eight years is nothing. After all, you're eight years *my* senior," she reminded him.

"Yes, but that's different," he said. "Why are we fooling ourselves? Antoine would have none of these girls."

"The trouble is he's known them all since childhood. They've grown up together. There's no mystery." Odile sighed. "What we need in this parish are some new girls, some fresh faces."

If, over the years, the changes in Jim and Odile were relatively slight, the changes in Mandragore were not. Not only had Jim drained several hundred additional acres of swamp, now planted with cane, and continually modernized both mills, he had expanded his interests into cotton as well. Although there was too much rainfall in the region to raise cotton successfully at Mandragore, he had negotiated with Narciso Valdéz to manage much of Florestal's cotton-raising, and frequently dispatched Hans Oberdorfer to that more northerly plantation to supervise the new undertaking, promoting him from overseer to his special assistant.

The contracted cotton from Florestal was shipped directly to textile mills Placide had established during his exile in France, under a complex arrangement between Jim and himself, part of which called for Jim's gradual purchase of his brother-in-law's share of the plantation. Since Placide was now a resident of France, and would likely remain so permanently, he had little interest in Mandragore and offered no resistance when Jim offered to buy out his holdings. He had married Denise and settled outside of Paris. Although more than twenty years had passed since the fire and the scandal surrounding it, their names were still mentioned with loathing and revulsion.

In addition to the domestic problems at Mandragore, the slave issue was one with which Jim, as well as the United States, was growing increasingly uncomfortable, a seemingly insoluble problem. Despite the rallying of the vociferous abolitionists, the United States Supreme Court reversed an earlier decision handed down by the Wisconsin Supreme Court and declared that slaves who had fled to free states could be returned to their masters under the Fugitive Slave Act. In addition, Kansas was soon to vote on a state constitution which would declare it either a slave state or a free state, and a wild-eyed radical named John Brown wanted to establish a republic in the Appalachians from which to fight slavery with a coalition force of fugitive Negroes and abolitionist whites. In Illinois, an increasingly powerful politician, Abraham Lincoln, was speaking out ever more strongly against the institution and the divisive effect it was having on the Union, causing a furor among the big planters of the South. Secretly Jim was morally in accord with many of Lincoln's views, but it would have spelled personal disaster for him to dare to voice his sentiments.

"If only clever men like Roger Guillon would find ways to mechanize farming so we could get rid of this abomination called slavery," Jim said one day to Oberdorfer as they were standing on the docks watching a shipment of cotton being loaded aboard a vessel. Because the big German's background made him an outsider, Jim knew such confidences were safe with Oberdorfer.

True to his word years earlier, Jim freed the first group of slaves born under the new regime at Mandragore on their twenty-first birthday, but induced most of them to stay on by pointing up their ties to the remaining slaves and offering them an actual share in the plantation's profits—a revolutionary innovation at the time.

"This slavery business is becoming a bigger issue every day," Jim said to Oberdorfer.

"And it'll become even bigger if Mr. Lincoln gets into the White House," the German predicted.

"I don't think he has a chance," Jim said, echoing the consensus of his fellow planters.

"I'm not so sure he doesn't," Oberdorfer countered.

"If he does become President, there'll be trouble," Jim asserted. "That's for certain."

"*Ja,*" Oberdorfer agreed. "Big trouble."

39

Tolling at noon, as it had for years, the plantation bell signaled the dinner break for the slaves, drivers, and overseers, a welcome relief from toil in the mill and cane fields. For Odile it announced a time of prayer and meditation, much as the Ursuline convent bells did for Eugénie. Instead of joining Jim and whatever men he decided to confer with over the noon meal, Odile would retire to the chapel to pray for the souls of the departed and the living. Most of all she prayed for herself, hoping to expel the feelings of guilt and inexplicable dread which lately seemed to afflict her.

"O Lord, please forgive this humble sinner who kneels before you," she intoned. "Cleanse my soul and give me the strength I need to overcome my weakness."

One day, almost in a trancelike state, so fervent were her prayers, she was startled by a knock at the chapel door—startled because the slaves had been given strict orders not to disturb her except for the most urgent matters. Rising from the prie-dieu, she opened the door and received Romulus, now crippled by arthritis, cataracts beginning to cloud his vision.

"What is it?" she asked impatiently.

"Begging your pardon, Miss Odile," he said, his tremulous white-gloved hand holding out a letter, "but this just arrived from Paris, France."

She immediately recognized Placide's handwriting, and snatched it from the aged butler, saying, "Thank you, Romulus," and dismissing him.

Eagerly, she tore open the envelope. It had been months since she had heard from her brother, and she had begun to fear that something serious might have

happened, although she knew perfectly well that trans-
atlantic mail service was erratic at best, even in a leading port such as New Orleans. Her breath came in
excited half-gasps as she read.

Dearest sister,

You must forgive me for having delayed so long
in writing you, but I have been extraordinarily
busy of late. I know you must think me an un-
grateful wretch not to have written you for such a
long time. I received the latest bank draft arranged
by your husband and had no difficulty with the
transfer of funds. In other words, all went well,
just as it has with the other payments Jim has
made in the past. Soon, Mandragore will be completely his and, alas, mine no more. I assure you
the thought saddens me but my grief is assuaged
by my now thriving chain of textile mills, which,
of course, would not have been possible without
the sale of my share of the plantation. God only
knows what fate might have befallen Denise and
myself in this difficult but thoroughly beguiling
nation if capital had not been provided me with
which to start a business.

I cannot believe that my beloved nephew is
almost twenty-one. Have I truly been away from
my cherished New Orleans that long? It is my most
fervent hope that some day you and Jim and my
dear nephew may come to France for a visit.
Nothing would give me greater pleasure than to
see you again. Denise and I speak of you all often
and always with great affection.

My dear wife is fine and seems to thrive here in
Paris. Lately, she has had a peculiar passion for
the circus. Many abound in this City of Light and
she fills our salon nightly with all manner of
performers—acrobats, animal-tamers, jugglers,
clowns, gypsies, and especially poor creatures of
curious aspect called "freaks." Ah, Denise!

Needless to say, my life in Paris is quite different from my life at home, as you might well have
guessed. In my middle—nay, aging—years I have

become quite a sober man of business. I believe your husband would now be proud of his brother-in-law. I must say that the role seems to fit me rather better than I anticipated and I am surprisingly comfortable with it, spending my days either at my office or in my factories, where your American cotton is woven into the cloth these Europeans prize so highly.

I shall write Jim separately, as is always my custom, regarding the new arrangements for the cotton shipments. I trust that things are still going well at my beloved Mandragore and this year's cane crop will be abundant.

Denise sends her love, as do I, to all of you. Receive a fervent embrace from your loving brother,

Placide

Sighing, Odile folded the letter and slipped it back into the envelope. How often she wished she could go to Paris—not that she was all that anxious to see her brother again, but simply for a change—to observe the fashions, the people, attend the opera, visit the museums. Her feelings for Placide himself could best be described as ambivalent. When he was in charge of her life, he had been domineering, almost a tyrant, and she had neither forgotten nor forgiven that. Yet she had aided him in his exile, perhaps more from a feeling of family loyalty than from anything else, and had encouraged Jim to continue sending payments to him even when times were difficult. Mere money seemed an insignificant exchange for the proud heritage and majesty of Mandragore.

With that thought nestled in her bosom, Odile returned to the altar and continued her prayers.

❧ 40

Six years earlier, in 1853, a yellow fever epidemic
swept through New Orleans, killing eleven thousand, or roughly ten percent of the population. Few
families were left intact by the dread disease, hospitals
were jammed, and convents and orphanages throughout the city filled with parentless children. Few measures could be taken to prevent the pestilence. Pots
of tar were burned on street corners and cannons were
fired periodically to "cleanse the air." Parents administered camphor to their children and sprinkled
pinches of prophylactic quinine in their daily black
coffee—and prayed. In spite of the precautions, the
daily mail invariably brought to every home at least
one black-bordered envelope announcing the latest
death. Tables all over the city were set with special
"mourning" china, edged in black.

One of the victims of the "Bronze John," as it was
sometimes called, was Silvia DaCosta. Ignoring the
warnings of her friends to stay indoors and avoid
breathing the deadly miasma in the air, as women
were advised to do, she scoffed at such precautions
and staunchly insisted on making the trip every morning from the stately house on Esplanade to the store
on Canal Street in an open carriage.

One day the deadly fever struck, Silvia became
jaundiced, and in a matter of days she was dead.

Isaac's grief was tremendous. He totally neglected
not only his burgeoning business enterprises—in addition to the original two stores, he had subsequently
acquired an entire block of stores and offices on Canal
Street as well as other holdings throughout the city—
but his two children as well, Daniel, then thirteen and

fresh from his bar mitzvah at the temple of which Isaac was president, and Raquel, eleven. If it had not been for Jim's moral support and Iris's jumping in and supervising the children, servants and household, Isaac might not have survived, so great was his grief. It was Jim who forced him to leave his room where he thrashed about day after day, sobbing, and to rejoin the living.

The first place he insisted Isaac go one Sunday was the riverfront café where the two friends had often breakfasted in the past.

"How can I eat?" Isaac complained. "How can I even think of food?"

"Start with coffee," Jim said, hailing the waiter.

A custom was started that Sunday, and maintained every Sunday thereafter. Jim looked forward to breakfasting with Isaac, the only time during the hectic week he could totally forget his responsibilities at the plantation. Even in the busiest of times, such as the fall sugar-making season, he tenaciously managed to keep Sunday mornings free, leaving Oberdorfer in command.

Among the Creoles, the Sabbath was a day the family spent together, usually visiting friends and relatives after mass, but for Jim and Odile it was a day each was free to pursue independent interests. Throughout their marriage, Jim's persistent refusal to convert to Catholicism remained a point of contention. Forced to attend mass without her husband, Odile swept down the aisle on Antoine's arm, to the pew bearing the Martinon family crest, her extraordinary beauty still turning many heads. Recently, however, Antoine had refused to accompany her, and she was forced to go alone. The youth's Saturday night carousing brought him home in no condition to leave his bed before late Sunday afternoon—and that was only if he returned home to sleep. Frequently, no one saw him until Monday or later.

On one particular Sunday, as Jim drove along the waterfront to the café to meet Isaac, he looked over the huge oceangoing ships crowding the busy harbor, their white sails billowing in the wind as they glided up and down the wide river from the gulf. At dockside one boat in particular caught his eye as it was being loaded with bales of cotton bound for France, all stamped *Mandragore*. He felt a sudden twinge of pride as he recognized the vessel as one of the sailing ships in which he had recently acquired a financial interest at Isaac's urging.

"Buy interest in a few ships," the successful merchant had advised. "Ship the cotton and sugar on your own boats. With your brother-in-law's mills on the other end, how can you lose? Why should someone else get rich from your shipping costs? You ship enough to warrant buying a few boats."

It had been good advice. Not only did Jim save considerably in shipping the cotton and sugar to Europe, but he also realized a nice profit on the return voyages from the manufactured goods from the Continent that the newly affluent Americans craved. Although Jim knew little about shipping and even less about ships, it was quite clear that the new venture would be a decidedly worthwhile and profitable enterprise.

As he entered the café, Jim saw that Isaac was already seated and waiting for him, accompanied by his son. Daniel, who had inherited his mother's sharp, angular features, had little interest in retailing or real estate which disappointed his father, who did his best to conceal his chagrin. Instead, the boy, who was almost exactly the same age as Antoine, had a keen curiosity about living things and had established an elaborate vivarium in back of the house on the Esplanade. There he kept all kinds of local specimens of reptiles, amphibians, and mammals whose habits and characteristics he exhaustively studied, keeping detailed records of his observations. Whenever an animal died, the boy would perform an autopsy on it, using various veterinary texts as a guide. Much to the servants' consternation—they regarded such practices as ghoulish—he examined all the creatures' internal organs, obsessed with determining each cause of death.

"Good morning," Jim said.

"Good morning, Jim," Isaac replied.

"Good morning, sir," Daniel echoed, rising politely and pulling out a chair for Jim. "Where's Antoine? I thought perhaps he might accompany you this morning."

Daniel's inquiry after Antoine was merely a courtesy. The two boys had little in common and, although Daniel had made repeated overtures of friendship, Antoine, steeped in his mother's prejudices and snobbery, persistently rebuffed them.

"That wastrel son of mine was still sleeping when I left home," Jim replied.

With a shrug Isaac said, "So, let him sleep."

"All he's interested in is amusing himself—that, and horses," Jim complained. "I wish I could get him to take an interest in the plantation or something serious."

Poking his son in the ribs, Isaac prompted, "Daniel, tell Jim what you told me this morning. Tell him what you said you wanted to do. Talk about sons not taking an interest in their fathers' business. . . . Go, on, tell Jim."

"What's there to tell?" Daniel answered. "I just said I wanted to study medicine, that's all."

Isaac slapped his hands on the little table. "How do you like that?" he said.

Jim patted Daniel on the back approvingly, wishing Antoine would express some kind of plans for his life —*any kind* at this point. "I think that's a fine idea," he said.

"Can you believe it, Jim?" Isaac continued. "Giving up the finest retailing business in New Orleans to go cut up people?"

"Raquel can take over the business," Daniel said. "She's got a better business head than I do."

"True," Isaac nodded in agreement. "A man should have a head for business like that daughter of mine."

Turning to Jim, Daniel went on about his proposed medical career. "I want to go into research. Take this yellow fever, for instance . . ."

"I don't want to hear about yellow fever," Isaac protested with a pained expression.

Ignoring his father, Daniel went on, "I'm not at all happy with what the doctors are advising to do about it. Firing those cannons and burning tar-pots on every street corner is like voodoo or witchcraft. There's nothing scientific behind it. It's all empirical, if you know what I mean. Scientists have got to get to the cause of the disease. That's the only way it can be successfully combated."

"Listen to him," Isaac chided. "Not even in medical school yet, and already he's talking like a doctor."

"I do know there's a right way and a wrong way to do things," Daniel asserted.

"Enough," Isaac commanded. Then, turning to Jim and changing the subject, he asked, "So, how's the shipping business coming along?"

"Fine," Jim assured him.

"See? What did I tell you?" Isaac said proudly.

"The trouble is I need more cotton than I can produce to meet the demands of my brother-in-law's French mills."

"They still have the boll weevil there?" Isaac asked.

"No, that's been under control," Jim replied. "Florestal, under Oberdorfer's supervision, is producing more cotton than ever—nine hundred to a thousand bales of cotton every season."

"A very good yield," Isaac agreed. "Is that crazy one—you know who I mean—giving you trouble?"

"Narciso?" Jim asked. "No. He stays out of things completely."

"Then what's the problem?" Isaac asked.

"I need more cotton—much more," Jim answered.

"So, get more," Isaac said. "Go to the other growers. Make them a good deal. Pay them more for their cotton than they can get from anybody else and they'll all sell. Get them to sign contracts in advance before planting, so you have it all sewed up when the crop is ready."

"That's going to take a lot more time and effort than I can spare," Jim objected.

"Who's talking about *you?*" Isaac said.

"Who can I get to travel up the river and talk the

cotton planters into doing business with me?" Jim
asked.

"What about your boy?" Isaac suggested.

"Antoine?" Jim said as he mentally pictured his son
the way he had just seen him that morning before
leaving Mandragore, sprawled naked across his bed in
the *garçonnière* reeking of alcohol, tobacco, and cheap
whores' perfume.

"Who else?"

"You mean, put Antoine to work for me?"

"Why not?" Isaac shrugged.

"Sure," Daniel echoed, mocking his father, "why
not?"

It was mid-afternoon by the time Jim returned to
Mandragore, thoughts of Antoine and the wild, pur-
poseless life his son was leading occupied his thoughts
most of the way.

Odile met him on the gallery and informed him that
Henri and Victorine Pilette and their two daughters,
Felicité and Angeline, were invited to dinner as well
as Nestor and Haydee Gaudet, distant cousins of hers
who owned a large cotton plantation north of Florestal
and who had been visiting locally.

"Good," Jim remarked, especially pleased that the
Gaudets were coming. He hoped that during the course
of the evening he might have a chance to approach
Nestor about buying his cotton crop or at least a portion of it.

Outside, in the *garçonnière*, Antoine's door was
closed. Annoyed that his son was still sleeping, Jim
rapped on the door.

"Who is it?" Antoine called out sleepily from inside.

"Get up," Jim ordered.

"What time is it?"

"Time for any self-respecting human being to be
up."

Surprisingly, Antoine padded across the floor of the
cottage and opened the door. "That new nigger wench
helping Lavinia makes too damned much noise for a
man to sleep," he complained, shaking his thick mass

of blue-black hair out of his eyes. "She was singing at the top of her lungs while she was beating the carpets earlier."

"Well, now isn't that just too bad," Jim said. "Your mother and I are expecting guests for dinner tonight and we want you to be present."

"I can't. I have to . . ." Antoine started to offer an excuse.

"I don't care what you have to do, you will be at the table. Is that clear?"

"Yes, sir."

"And you will not take off as soon as dinner is over, either."

"Yes, sir," Antoine repeated unenthusiastically. "Who are these guests?"

"The Pilettes and the Gaudets."

"I suppose the Pilettes are bringing their daughters with them?"

"I imagine they might be."

"Felicité isn't bad as long as I don't have to dance with her, but that Angeline is a whining ninny."

"Your mother and I expect you to be courteous to both of the young women."

" 'Women'? Angeline is no woman. She's a child, a baby."

"In any case, we expect you shaved, bathed, dressed and in the house at the sunset bell."

"Yes, sir," Antoine said and closed the door.

When the guests arrived, Antoine greeted them graciously, treating the female guests with the charm for which he was becoming celebrated throughout the parish. He even managed to feign interest when Henri Pilette cornered him after dinner and talked about his current cane crop. Antoine's impatiently tapping boot was the only betrayal of his boredom. Later, when the conversation turned to the season at the Metairie Race Course, Antoine entered into it with far greater enthusiasm.

"Some of the finest horses in the South are going to race on that track this season," he declared.

"You would certainly know if anyone does," Felicité said, batting her long eyelashes at him flirtatiously.

"Such a connoisseur of horseflesh, Monsieur Mac-Kay!" Haydee Gaudet exclaimed, impressed by Antoine's thorough knowledge of the equestrian scene.

Inevitably, the conversation turned to politics, as it did whenever planters got together, which was not surprising since they comprised the major political as well as social and cultural force in the state.

"I can't believe those Republicans will really nominate that Lincoln fellow in Chicago next spring," Nestor Gaudet said.

"It would be suicide for the party," Henri Pilette speculated.

"Please, if you gentlemen don't mind," Odile pleaded, "don't mention that crude and ill-mannered barbarian's name in my presence."

"He *is* disgusting," Victorine Pilette agreed.

"And to think that Mary Todd was from one of the finest families in Kentucky," Haydee Gaudet added. "I cannot fathom how she ever lowered herself to marry such a wretch."

"They say she's a little—shall we be kind and say —balmy," Victorine suggested.

"She would have to be," Odile asserted.

Getting away from gossip and back to serious politics, Henri Pilette said, "If they do nominate him, the Republican party is finished in the South."

"I should hope so," Victorine said, opening her fan with a loud snap.

"They say he's aiming for us to give up all our slaves," Nestor Gaudet related in an incredulous tone.

"They ought to string up every damned one of those Yankee abolitionists," Henri Pilette declared. "They've got no business meddling in our affairs down here. Let them tend to matters that concern Boston and Philadelphia and Cincinnati and let the South alone."

"Let's drink to that," Nestor Gaudet suggested.

Seizing the decanter from the silver tray proffered by Romulus, Antoine filled everyone's glasses with bourbon. "Down with those damned Yankee abolitionists!" he toasted, clinking his glass against each glass in turn.

"If those Yankees think they can boss this whole country and try to take our slaves away from us, I think we should withdraw from the Union and form our own nation," Henri Pilette declared. "What the hell do we need them for anyway?"

"And if they try to stop us, we'll fight them," Nestor Gaudet agreed.

"Right!" Antoine affirmed enthusiastically.

"Would you go to war, Antoine?" Felicité Pilette asked, wide-eyed.

"Damned right I would," he affirmed.

"Would you be in the cavalry?" she continued.

"Of course," he answered.

"An officer?"

"A gentleman would never consider anything less," he assured her.

Later, the four men smoked cigars outside on the gallery while in the parlor the women exclaimed over the delicate horsehair flowers Odile had made.

Inwardly disturbed by the political talk, especially that of possible war, Jim was relieved when the conversation finally returned to planting.

"Nestor, I'd like to talk to you sometime about the possibility of buying some of your cotton," he began. "You see, my brother-in-law's textile mills in France need more cotton than I've been able to supply."

"But Florestal is a big plantation," Gaudet said.

"Yes, but the demand for American cotton is great in Europe, especially in England and France," Jim said. "If possible I'd like to send my agent up to talk to you—perhaps to discuss prices and terms and other particulars."

"Your agent?" Gaudet repeated.

"You mean that German fellow?" Henri Pilette questioned.

"No. Oberdorfer doesn't handle any transactions," Jim replied. "He merely brings in the crops. That's his job."

"Then who, may I ask, is your agent?" Gaudet persisted.

Putting his hand on his son's shoulder and distracting his attention from the two Pilette sisters who at that moment were crossing the lawn toward the garden, Jim said, "My son."

❧ 41

Throughout the next few weeks it seemed as if Jim and Antoine were involved in one continuous row, the boy resenting his father's forcing him into the role of agent in lining up possible cotton contracts with up-river cotton planters. Their constant disputes were disturbing to Odile, following her even when she sought refuge behind the thick oak doors of the plantation chapel.

"You deliberately embarrassed me in front of our friends to force me into this cotton business, sir," Antoine complained. "Especially when you know I don't know the first thing about it or give a damn, either."

"Well, it's high time you did both," Jim retorted.

Muttering angrily under his breath, Antoine stomped off toward the stables, the one place on the whole plantation he felt at home.

Jim truly believed that he had done his best to be a conscientious, loving father, although he was forced to admit, regrettably, that the major portion of his time and energy was spent managing the plantation. It wasn't until the boy reached adolescence that the two seemed to drift apart, and Jim realized he had failed. Antoine seemed interested in nothing except horses and pleasure-seeking. Antoine, in turn, accused Jim of caring only for the plantation, obsessed with making it the most prosperous and successful in the state. Because of their contrasting temperaments and ever more disparate interests, the two males grew further estranged, at odds with one another most of the time.

The father-son conflict was a source of dismay to Odile who found it difficult to maintain harmony at home.

"What am I going to do with them?" she asked Verbena in despair one day. "They're constantly battling."

The old slave shook her head. "I declare," she said. "I don't think I ever seen two menfolks more different in my life than Marse Jim and Mister Antoine."

Odile knew that the maid was, of course, correct. Antoine and Jim could not have been more different in every respect, but to her it wasn't nearly so strange since she alone knew they were not father and son, as everyone assumed. At times, the differences between them were so marked and jarring, she was almost tempted to tell Jim the truth about the boy's paternity, if for no other reason than to alleviate his anguish. Naturally, she realized such a revelation would seriously jeopardize their marriage, to say nothing of Antoine's future. She had long ago reconciled her conscience to perpetuating the deception for the boy's sake as well as her own, deciding Jim must never suspect the boy might not be his issue. Often, she regretted her many miscarriages, feeling that if only she could present Jim with a child of his own, it would partially assuage her guilt, but what was not to be, was not to be.

Lately, her trips to town usually included a visit with Eugénie at the convent. She loved the atmosphere of peace and serenity within its cloistered walls and at times almost longed to take the veil herself so she could devote more of her time to prayer and contemplation and less to worldly concerns. When she was younger, she felt sorry for Eugénie, removed as she was from the world, and now, with the passage of time, she almost envied her.

As they strolled arm-in-arm around the convent herb garden, fragrant with the aroma of spices, Odile casually remarked, "I received a letter from Aunt Carlota in Havana last week."

Eugénie stopped and stared at her. "Why didn't you tell me before this?" she demanded.

"It must have slipped my mind," Odile replied innocently. Whenever their Cuban aunt's name was mentioned it never failed to spark her sister's interest.

"What news did she have?" Eugénie asked.

"Nothing really important," Odile answered. "She merely wrote to inquire if I might consider having little Ysabel stay at Mandragore as my ward for a while."

"Little Ysabel?" the nun questioned.

"You know, Aunt Carlota's granddaughter—the daughter of our cousin Beatriz."

"The daughter of Beatriz?" Eugénie repeated. "Then, she must be just a child."

"Ysabel is almost fifteen," Odile informed her. "Aunt Carlota wants her to perfect her English and learn American customs."

"What will your answer be?"

Odile smiled. "I think it would be quite delightful to be the mother of a daughter—even if it is only for a year or two. I've always wanted a girl, you know. I'm sure little Ysabel is a very sweet child. I can't wait to welcome her to Mandragore. Besides, I think that having a young lady in the house might be good for Antoine. I haven't been happy with his deportment lately. He's been rude to his father and me and using bad language. With a refined young lady present he'll be forced to mend his ways. Young men need the company of girls, if for no other reason than to civilize them."

Eugénie chuckled. "Suppose they should fall in love?"

"Antoine?" Odile scoffed. "His head is full of nothing except horses and carousing or politics and that cavalry unit he proposes to join. He has no interest in any of the local girls."

"Ysabel is not a local girl," Eugénie reminded her.

"If he falls in love with her, I will consider it a *lagniappe*—a bonus, something extra," Odile replied. "In any case, I shall answer Aunt Carlota tomorrow and tell her Ysabel is most certainly welcome."

Determined to be accepted into the cavalry unit of the state militia, Antoine spent almost all his time drilling Pegasus, his favorite horse, in complex military maneuvers. He was joined in this by several of his friends—Jacob Anspacher, the Chardonnier brothers, Auguste and Joachim, and the fiery Léopold Seguin. The five, and occasionally more, young men drilled in the fields and pastures of their various plantations, imagining them as battlegrounds. As a result of this passion for the military, Antoine was away from home a great deal, much to Jim's distress.

"What the hell does he think he's doing off cavorting about with that horse of his every day?" Jim demanded of Odile one evening when he returned from a particularly grueling day in the fields.

"Well, it's better that he's involved with cavalry exercises than off in town at some of those terrible places he and the other boys frequent," she commented.

"I'm not so sure I agree," Jim said, dropping down into a rocking chair on the main gallery, and allowing one of the young black house slaves to wrestle with removing his mud-caked boots. "He completely ignored the fact that I asked him to see Nestor Gaudet about his cotton. I'll tell you one thing," he said, wagging his finger sternly at Odile, "that boy is going to start taking an interest in this plantation or else."

"Come now, Jim, he's still young," she said.

"When I was his age I worked from sunup to sundown and had a lot of responsibilities as well."

"But that was a long time ago, back in the Ohio wilderness. Things are entirely different here."

"I'll be damned if I'm going to have him turn out to be some kind of dilettante," Jim declared.

"Maybe when all this silly talk about the South breaking away from the Union is over, he'll settle down," she suggested. "You know how talk of war and such things inflames young boys."

"I'm beginning to doubt whether our son will ever settle down," Jim retorted.

"I wish that dreadful Lincoln would just stop picking on the South. You know as well as I do, the South can't live without slaves. It's a fact of life. There's nothing wrong with slavery if the slaves are treated humanely and decently. After all, they're poor unfortunate creatures without a lick of sense who could never fend for themselves in this world. God intended for us to look after them and make them good Christians. In return, they repay us with their labor. It's only fitting. Besides, they're all happy—at least here at Mandragore. I never hear any of our Negroes complain, do you?"

"Of course they don't complain to our faces," Jim replied. "They're too clever for that. Sometimes I'd like to hear what they say behind those closed doors in the slave cabins. I suspect even our most loyal slaves despise us."

Scowling at him, Odile said, "You know, Jim, I know you don't mean to, but sometimes you sound a whole lot like those horrid Northern abolitionists and I don't much care for it."

"I'm just telling you the truth, that's all. The trouble is you Southerners can't face up to it."

Refusing to let him anger her, Odile rose from her chair and laid her hand on his shoulder. "I think you're tired. Go upstairs and tell Romulus to fix you a nice hot bath," she said. "You'll feel better."

Taking her advice, Jim soaked in the enormous copper tub that required four slaves to carry it into the bedroom, and contemplated the way Antoine had been swept up by the general climate of discontent and unrest currently pervading the entire South. Talk of possible secession was bad enough, but some had been so bold as to mention outright war as well. War —with one group of Americans fighting another— was preposterous! Certainly some peaceful settlement would be reached in the whole slavery question, and not at the expense of the Union. Jim fervently hoped

all the commotion would blow over and things settle
down. Perhaps then Antoine would take a serious
interest in the plantation. After all, someday it would
be his. It was time he learned how to run it.

A few nights later as Jim was going over Odile's
household expenditures in the study, he came across a
series of bills for several pairs of frightfully expensive
boots from a prominent bootery in the city made out
to Antoine M. MacKay.

Later that same evening, he heard Antoine arrive
and turn his horse over to a groom as he prepared to
retire to his room in the *garçonnière* for the night.
Because of the early morning cavalry drills the boy
had been turning in much earlier than usual. Going
to the window, Jim called to him and requested that
he come to the study.

Settled in the horsehair fauteuil opposite the great
rosewood desk, sullenly prepared for one of his father's
lectures, Antoine automatically reached for the brandy
decanter, but Jim intervened, taking the bottle away
from him.

"Why can't I have a drink?" he asked indignantly.

"Because from the smell of your breath, you've had
enough to drink tonight," Jim said.

"I just had a short one at Jake Anspacher's."

"You've been drinking too much lately. Both your
mother and I are quite concerned."

"Too much?" Antoine protested. "I've hardly been
drinking at all."

"In any case, I didn't call you in here to talk about
your drinking," Jim said, shoving the bills for the boots
at him. "What do you know about these?"

"They're the bills for my new boots," Antoine answered impatiently.

"These are very expensive boots," Jim pointed out.

"Well, I need them. What difference does it make,
sir, what they cost?"

"*I* have no boots as expensive as these," Jim said.

"You're not going to be an officer in the cavalry,"
Antoine retorted.

"What has that got to do with it?"

"An officer's got to have good boots, sir. He can't very well command the respect of his troops in shabby, second-rate ones," Antoine answered.

"I would think that an officer commands respect by his knowledge and ability," Jim said, "rather than by his boots. In any case, how do you expect to pay for them?"

"Pay for them?" Antoine repeated, astounded by such a question. "I've never paid for a pair of boots *before.*"

"From now on, you're going to be responsible for the costs of your own clothing," Jim declared. "No more giving the bills over to your mother to pay."

"How can I pay for boots like these? I have no money—no *real* money—except for that measly little allowance you give me each month."

"To say nothing of what your mother slips to you on the sly," Jim added.

"That's because she knows it isn't fitting for me to go around without money, like white trash."

"In any event, I refuse to pay for these boots. There's no reason on earth why I should subsidize the Louisiana cavalry. I pay my taxes, that's enough."

Antoine curled his lip contemptuously. "I knew I could expect something like that from you."

The boy was being deliberately provocative and Jim decided the best policy would be to ignore him, and stick to the matter at hand. "Of course, I am willing to pay you a salary—the same as I do Hans Oberdorfer —if you would just get involved in the running of this plantation."

"I'm no overseer," Antoine protested.

"No, but you will be master of Mandragore some-day," Jim reminded him. "Don't you think you'd better learn how things are run around here?"

"There's time for that later."

About to lose his temper, Jim grabbed the boy by the shoulders. "Listen, young man, in a couple of months you will be twenty-one years old. I think it's high time you took a little interest in this place."

Antoine sighed wearily. He had to have the boots. "All right, just what do you want me to do?"

Inwardly Jim smiled. At last he was making some headway. "Tomorrow, instead of saddling up Pegasus and going off somewhere, you can come down to the mill with me and begin learning its operation. That's as good a place as any to start."

"You know, sir, I marvel at you," Antoine said with a contemptuous scowl.

"How so?"

"Our whole way of life is being threatened by Yankees and all you can think about is your damned sugar mill," he exploded. Then, adding in a calmer tone, "Excuse me, sir, but I had to say it."

"I'm not ignorant about the political climate of the nation at this moment, if that's what you're implying," Jim replied.

"I'm not sure you realize just how serious things really are," Antoine said. "Some state legislatures are actually talking secession."

"Politicians are always talking about lots of things —most of it nonsense. Right now, I'm concerned about Mandragore, our family—and you. I want to see you a respectable man with a sense of honor and duty, a man who understands an honest day's work and the value of a dollar. From this moment on, I refuse to support the extravagances of a no-account wastrel," Jim asserted.

"Who, sir, may I ask, is a no-account wastrel?" Antoine asked indignantly.

Ignoring the question, Jim went on, "And in case you think your mother is going to go against my wishes, you're wrong. She and I are in perfect agreement about your future."

Antoine rose from the chair. "Is that all, sir?"

"Not quite," Jim continued, ignoring his son's impatience to leave. "Tomorrow morning you will be up and dressed at seven o'clock and ready to go to the mill with me."

"Now may I go, sir?"

With a sigh and a casual wave of his hand, Jim said, "Yes, you may go."

❧ 42

At forty-six, Narciso Valdéz had outlived both parents and many of the Florestal slaves as well. Residing alone in the great house, he spent most of his time in his book-cluttered bedroom, much as he always had, reading and rereading the many volumes he had accumulated over the years or playing the harpsichord. With regard to his health, he seemed, in middle age, neither better nor worse than in his youth. Many, including Dr. Zehner, were amazed that he had survived so long.

Probably the severest blow to Narciso, both physically and emotionally, had been Odile's marriage to Jim MacKay. Although he eventually recovered and was able to acknowledge the union to some extent, he could never completely quell his passion for his beautiful cousin and, though greatly suppressed, his desire for her remained as fervent as ever. After a few years, Odile tentatively renewed her friendship with Narciso, insisting it remain strictly on a platonic level. Occasionally things slipped out of control and she was forced to reproach him for his attempted advances, explaining tactfully but firmly, with a peculiar logic all her own, that any sort of capitulation on her part would be most unbecoming to a wife and mother. Eventually, Narciso accepted her terms, transferring much of his affection for her to the boy, Antoine. It was Narciso's adoration of the boy that provided her with an easy and completely acceptable excuse for visits to Florestal.

"You know how poor Narciso worships the boy," Odile would often say to Jim. "He has so little else. Please allow me to bring some happiness into the life

304

of an unfortunate invalid by taking Antoine on a visit to Florestal."

Now, alone in the great house, Narciso eagerly looked forward to Odile's visits, although in recent years Antoine rarely accompanied her, so absorbed was the youth with his own interests.

"I think the boy's outgrown both of us, dear cousin," Narciso lamented wistfully one day as he and Odile took tea on the second-floor gallery outside his bedroom.

Narciso anxiously anticipated her calls, not only to hear news of the boy but because Odile was one of his few contacts with the lively world of Creole society, a world largely denied him because of his physical infirmities.

"I want to hear everything," he said eagerly. "The more vicious the gossip, the better."

Unfortunately, because of the escalating turmoil throughout the country over slavery and states' rights and the increasing prominence of Abraham Lincoln on the American political scene, Southern social life had lost some of its carefree, abandoned gaiety.

"No one gossips any longer," Odile complained. "They're all too busy talking about secession or that awful Lincoln and boring topics like that. Even New Orleans isn't as gay as it once was before all this trouble started."

Currently, the actual day-to-day running of Florestal was in the hands of Munro Samples, the long-time overseer, with some occasional supervision by Hans Oberdorfer, who acted as Jim's special assistant and who was responsible to see that Florestal delivered the cotton for which Jim had contracted. Beyond that, Samples was in command. As long as Narciso was able to live comfortably, he was reticent to make an issue of Samples' blatant dishonesty. Alerted by both Oberdorfer and Jim, Narciso nevertheless chose to ignore the portion of the plantation's revenues the overseer diverted into his own pockets, as well as Samples' increasingly sadistic treatment of the slaves.

The only two slaves who seemed immune from

Samples' cruelty were Kitty and her adopted son, Achille. Because Narciso now lived alone in the great house and needed someone close at hand at night in case he became suddenly ill, he had moved Kitty out of the slave quarters over the warming kitchens, where house slaves had been traditionally kept, and into the room adjoining his. The awkward, angular woman seemed to have great skill with herbs and medicinal teas, learned from her African grandmother, as well as from catalogs and the *Farmers Almanac*—since she could marginally read, having been taught by Narciso. Many of the cures from the *Almanac* were for animals but Kitty made little distinction. In later years, Narciso came to count more on her for treatment than on Dr. Zehner. The preparation which gave him the greatest relief and on which he had come to depend more and more was a rather harmless-looking white powder made from special poppies she grew in the plantation greenhouse. Although it was somewhat constipating and caused his nose to run excessively, it made him feel better than anything else. Several times he had become severely ill and in seconds after his rapping on the wall, Kitty was at his side, ministering to him, saving his life—or so it appeared each time. Because of Kitty's close association and privileged position with the master of the plantation, it was inevitable that her son would enjoy the same benefits, spending considerable time with Narciso as well. Although teaching a slave to read and write was strictly forbidden by law and severely punished, Kitty pleaded with Narciso to instruct the boy in the fundamentals, as he had done for her years previously.

"I don't want my son to grow up ignorant like a field nigger," she said. "I also wants him to talk right—not no nigger talk, like his mama. I wants Achille to be like you, Marse Narciso."

"That's hardly possible, Kitty," Narciso chuckled, "when the boy is black."

"He ain't black, Marse. He's whiter than a lot of white folks," she insisted.

At Kitty's persistent urging, Narciso finally agreed

to teach the boy to read and write. Although active and inattentive at times, like most healthy children, Achille proved to be an extremely apt and intelligent pupil.

Whenever Achille failed to rise to her or Narciso's expectations, whatever the reason, Kitty whipped him severely. What she could never and would never reveal to Narciso was her desire for Achille eventually to escape up North to freedom where his fair skin and regular features would make it easy for him to pass as white, especially if he were literate and well-spoken, and become a leader of his people, a role impossible for a slave down South.

As a result of his education and polish acquired through daily association with Narciso, Achille became a thorn in Samples' side. He was a restless, rebellious young slave with notions of independence, but the overseer was powerless to suppress him as long as Narciso remained master of Florestal.

Aware of Samples' fear and hatred of Achille, Kitty knew the overseer would use the slightest provocation as an excuse to get rid of the boy. As a result she persuaded Narciso to make him his personal body servant, a role to which the defiant, independent youth was not particularly well-suited, and one at which he balked about assuming.

"I'd rather work in the fields with the others," Achille insisted.

"Are you crazy, boy?" Kitty rebuked.

"What good is all the learning I got inside my head if I can't pass it along to my own people who need it so bad?" he insisted.

"Samples would kill you just as quick as he'd swat a fly if he caught you preaching rebellion to his field niggers," Kitty warned.

"Not if I killed him first," the youth arrogantly replied, his blue eyes brimming with loathing.

On one of Odile's visits to Florestal, after she and Narciso had spent the entire afternoon playing duets on the harp and harpsichord, her cousin rang for

Achille and asked him to bring some mint juleps out to the main gallery.

When the boy left after serving the drinks in what Odile considered a curt and insolent manner, she commented, "Why do you keep him around the house? I'd send him straight to the fields."

Narciso smiled. "I suppose Achille is better suited to the fields than the house," he admitted. "I'm sure that's actually where he'd rather be—which is part of the problem. I only keep him here for Kitty's sake. She's afraid Samples would harm him if he came under his jurisdiction."

"Why?"

"For several reasons, one of them being that I, with my generous nature, taught him to read and write."

Odile was appalled. "You *what?*"

"It was rather foolish, I know, but Kitty begged so."

"Shame on you, Narciso, for giving in to her all the time," Odile reproached.

"Sometimes I truly believe she's all that stands between me and death."

"Nonsense," Odile chided. "There's nothing in those teas she gives you except alfalfa and a lot of other worthless weeds."

Narciso was reluctant to mention the wonderful white powder. "In any case, I am the one responsible for the boy's rebellious attitude. He's quite intelligent, you know. He reads Spanish and French as well as English and can do algebra and logic."

"If the authorities found out you were teaching your slaves to read and write you'd be in a great deal of trouble, Narciso Valdéz," Odile said. "Besides, educating blacks is bad for them. God created them as innocent savages. He had no intention for them to become educated. It makes them unhappy and discontent."

" 'Discontent,' " he echoed, raising the frosty glass to his lips. "I'm afraid that's precisely what's wrong with Achille. Truly, he's inept as a house slave—I'm well aware of that—but I don't know what else to do with him."

"Make him a coachman or groom," she suggested.

"He's not really fit to be *any* sort of servant," Narciso admitted.

"And it's all your fault, dear cousin," Odile said, wagging her gloved finger at him.

Catching her hand, he pressed it to his lips. Odile smiled, but gracefully drew her hand away.

"How is Antoine?" Narciso asked, after a moment of awkward quiet.

The question made Odile sigh wistfully. "As usual, he and Jim are at odds with one another," she replied. "Jim is vexed that Antoine takes such little interest in the affairs of the plantation. He thinks he has become a wastrel and profligate."

Narciso frowned. "Don't you think those terms are a little harsh for the boy?"

"Perhaps," she admitted. "To be perfectly honest with you, I wish he would settle into something—even one of the professions if he disdains being a planter. Right now, his head is full of ideas of becoming a cavalry officer. Antoine feels certain there is going to be a war. Can you imagine?"

Narciso considered a moment before he said, "Tell me, my dear, do you think he might be interested in law?"

"Antoine is interested in nothing of substance or seriousness of purpose."

"Perhaps if I could approach him about studying law . . ." Narciso contemplated.

"You are welcome to try."

"It's a good background for a gentleman no matter what he chooses to do in life—even if he chooses to do nothing. It is even desirable for a cavalry officer. My library contains a complete set of Blackstone which I have studied quite thoroughly. I should be most pleased to tutor him until he becomes proficient enough to pass the bar examination."

"I think that's a superb idea," she enthused.

"Thank you," Narciso smiled.

"I shall be most grateful to you for anything you can do with Antoine."

Leaning forward, he brought his face close to hers. "I live only to serve you and make you happy," he murmured, kissing her lips gently. "In whatever small, humble, woefully inadequate manner I can."

❧ 43

The clouds of concern which hovered over the South in early December 1859 only slightly dimmed the festive activities of the holiday season.

Shortly before Christmas, Ysabel finally arrived and Odile was pleased to discover that the girl was as pretty as she hoped she might be, although her complexion was just a shade darker and her hair a bit more coarse than she might have wished. But at fifteen, the girl was charming, intelligent, poised, and even managed to be reasonably witty on occasion, despite abominable English learned from Spanish-born nuns at the convent school she attended near Havana.

When Jim and Odile received news of her arrival they insisted Antoine accompany them to the boat to meet his Cuban relative, but at the last minute he refused, claiming he had to go off on maneuvers with his group of aspiring cavalry officers.

"Nonsense!" Odile snapped.

"But, Mama, you don't understand how important this is," he protested.

"I understand that it is important that you be at the boat to meet your cousin Ysabel," she argued.

"Here we are threatened by one of the worst situations this nation has ever faced, and you're worried about meeting some little brat from Cuba," he said.

"I don't know which I dislike more," she replied, "your constant talk of war or calling your cousin a 'brat.' Well, there will be no war and you *will* go with your father and me down to the harbor. Is that clear?"

"Yes, ma'am," he replied sullenly.

Looking lovely and self-assured, Ysabel accompanied Jim and Odile on their round of Christmas socializing, delighting their friends with her gracious manner and charming personality. At the Chardonniers' party she took along her guitar and sang Cuban songs in a sensuous voice that enchanted all who heard her.

Odile could not have been happier than she was with her new charge. Sharing many mutual interests—sewing, music, poetry, flowers, clothes, dancing—they seemed far more like mother and daughter than distant cousins. At times Odile could scarcely believe that Ysabel was not the daughter for whom she had always longed.

Jim, too, was pleased by the girl's presence in the house. He also would have liked to have had a daughter, although he repeatedly expressed a preference for a second son. With the prospect of Ysabel's accompanying them, he seemed more disposed than usual to attend many social functions he might not ordinarily have attended. When Odile called it to his attention, he explained, "If some of the more lecherous gentlemen of our acquaintance see me lurking in the background, they may be far less inclined to press their attentions on Ysabel."

"Somehow, I think Ysabel is quite capable of fending for herself, despite the fact that she's only fifteen," Odile speculated. "But if you prefer to think of yourself as her knightly champion and protector, go right ahead."

As the new feminine face in the parish, Ysabel soon became the center of interest among the young men of the families who owned plantations up and down the river, even though many of them, like Antoine, were caught up in the turmoil affecting the country. Several young men—Antoine's close friends, Léopold Seguin and Jacob Anspacher among them—approached Jim and Odile requesting the privilege of calling on the girl, but Odile discouraged them by saying that, at fifteen, Ysabel was too young to begin receiving gentlemen callers.

Jim disputed her decision. "I don't think she's too young at all," he argued. "Many girls scarcely older than Ysabel is now are married and have babies."

"They are *American* girls accustomed to this country and its ways. Ysabel is a foreigner. She must get used to America. I don't want her burdened with too much at once," Odile replied. "Besides, I want her and Antoine to get to know one another better before she becomes too involved with others."

Suspicious of her motives, Jim questioned, "You aren't trying to play matchmaker between those two, are you?"

"Of course not," she denied emphatically. "Shame on you for suggesting such a thing. I just think that, as cousins, they should get to know one another well, that's all."

"Like you and Narciso?" he suggested.

"Well . . . yes," she answered, uncertain of the inference of his question.

During Ysabel's first days at Mandragore, Antoine was away nearly all the time, pursuing one interest or another—usually his obsession with horses and the cavalry—so that it came as a great surprise to Jim and Odile when he announced that he intended to go to Florestal on an extended visit for some intensive tutoring in law by Narciso. Until then his enthusiasm for the subject had not been marked.

Astonished, Jim said, "Don't tell me that you are giving law precedence over cavalry drills?"

"Both are important," he replied with some conviction.

"But you just can't go running off to Florestal when your little cousin has so recently arrived all the way from Cuba," Odile protested. "You do have a certain obligation to her—just as we all do, and you've certainly not discharged it very well so far. When are you planning on leaving?"

"As soon as Romulus can pack my things," the boy replied.

Odile was aghast. "You mean—*today?*"

"Yes," Antoine affirmed.

"No," Odile declared. "You cannot leave today. I forbid it. I insist you have supper here and spend the evening with us. We've all been invited for punch at the Seguins' later on. If you must go to Florestal, tomorrow is soon enough."

"But, Mama . . ." he started to object.

"No 'buts' about it," Jim said. "You're staying here tonight, just as your mother says."

Antoine petulantly discharged his obligation to his cousin by sitting silently through dinner and later restlessly in the music room while, at Odile's insistence, Ysabel played Boccherini and Vivaldi on the piano.

"My, that was lovely," Odile applauded when the girl concluded.

Sensing Antoine's boredom with the musicale, Ysabel quickly left the piano and took up her guitar, playing and singing some spirited and dramatic Spanish and Cuban songs. Antoine had too much Hispanic blood in his veins not to respond and soon, much to everyone's amazement, he was smiling, clapping his hands and stomping his feet in rhythm with the lively music.

Later in the evening when it came time to depart for the Seguin plantation, Odile suddenly complained of a severe headache and requested that Antoine escort Ysabel to the party, asking him to convey apologies to Jules and Anais Seguin for Jim and herself.

Retiring to her room, Odile reclined on the daybed, a handkerchief dipped in eau de cologne tied to her throat, and had Verbena apply compresses of sedative water to her forehead.

Knocking and entering his mother's room, Antoine announced, "I'm not going to the Seguins'."

"Don't be silly," she said. "Of course you are."

"No. I must study, Mama. Narciso will expect me to be prepared when I arrive at Florestal tomorrow."

"I'm sure Narciso will forgive you if you arrive unprepared just this once," she countered. "Besides, it's much too close to Christmas to be so serious about something as dry as legal matters. There's plenty of time for law after the holidays."

"Who knows what will happen after the holidays?" he speculated. "The country could be at war."

"War! War! War!" Odile exploded, leaping off of the daybed. "I'm sick of all this constant talk about war and secession and that awful Lincoln. If people don't stop talking about it so much, there really will be a war."

"Getting so excited, Miss Odile, ain't no good for your headache," Verbena reminded her.

While they were talking, unnoticed by all, Ysabel approached the room and stood in the doorway dressed to go out in cape, bonnet, gloves, and muff.

"All this talk of war is ruining all the parties this season," Odile continued. "Every ball we attend ends in a political speech. I'm sick of it!"

Hoping to soothe her mistress, Verbena said to Antoine, "You go on and take Miss Ysabel to the Seguins'. It would please your mama and daddy."

"The Seguins are bores," Antoine snapped. "In fact, everybody around here is a bore. Up and down the river there are nothing but bores who sit and watch their cane or cotton grow and count their money. If Ysabel were smart—which she's not—she'd take the first boat back to Cuba."

Hearing his words, Ysabel burst into tears and fled from the doorway.

❧ 44

Although he knew he should hate Narciso in the same way he hated Munro Samples and all the other white overseers, landowners, and slave traders who brutalized, debased, and humiliated his people, Achille could not. This kindly, benevolent, and sensitive semi-invalid, who spent most of his time in bed endlessly reading, was far too ill and weak to take measures to prevent the outrageous abuses on the plantation of which he was nominally master. Despite the pale, sunken-eyed, blue-lipped Creole's infirmities, Achille nevertheless held him responsible for much of the fear and misery which afflicted the slaves at Florestal. After all, the path to Hell was paved with good intentions, was it not?

His people? he mused, staring at the piece of mirror hanging over the washstand in his room next to the taproom and atop the warming kitchens. Reflected was a face a shade lighter than the color of caramel with slender nostrils, blue eyes, and narrow lips. His hair, although it hugged his scalp in tight little curls, was fair, almost blond. But in spite of an appearance which strongly evidenced his white ancestry, Achille was as much a slave as the blackest field hand and perhaps more hated and feared because his obvious whiteness served as a living refutation of the chasm which supposedly existed between the races. How superficial and inconsequential these differences were, he thought, and how easily they blended under the cover of night, how readily they could be erased. His very existence challenged the entire concept of "race" itself, a word bandied about excessively in these times of political strife.

Fingering the only link with his past—the gold medallion with the cryptic inscription about his neck—Achille wondered about his parents: who they were, what they might have been. He knew virtually nothing about them except what little Kitty had reluctantly revealed.

"Your mama was a fine, beautiful lady who came to a bad end, poor girl. I did the best I could for that sweet child, but it wasn't enough," she said. "Your daddy was a white man. That's all I know about him."

Addressing his reflection, Achille asked, "Who the hell are you anyway?"

Ever since he was old enough to comprehend, Kitty had warned him, "You is mighty fine-looking and lots of white ladies are going to go after you in a lustful way, but don't you never touch none of them, hear? If a white lady starts talking to you in a way you know ain't fitting, you just get away as fast as you can. You is the kind of nigger they likes to string up because you is too much like they is, and they don't take to that."

Achille loved Kitty. This big, awkward, gruff-voiced woman was the only mother he had ever known, although she made it plain from the outset that he was not her child, that she had adopted him upon the death of his natural mother. Grateful for the devoted manner in which she raised and cared for him, Achille nevertheless resented her interference in his life, especially as he grew older. He knew it was she who had pleaded with Narciso to make him a house slave when he longed to cast his lot with the others in the fields. The overseer was furious when Narciso capitulated to her pleas.

"No white woman will be safe with a randy young nigger buck like that in the house," Samples warned, trying to sound ominous. "Better let me have him in the fields where I can lay into him with my whip when he steps out of line."

Although most of the field hands would gladly have traded places with Achille, he was discontent in the great house catering to Narciso, dressed in fancy livery complete with white gloves. He would have much preferred the fields in spite of the backbreaking work under the relentless sun and the threat of Samples' whip across his back. Working in the fields would strengthen his body and make him better prepared to confront his oppressors when the occasion arose. In the cotton fields he would be among his own people, free to spread the word that would someday set them free—the word that slavery wasn't the natural condition of the black man, that people in Washington and other parts of the country were fighting and struggling to change things, fighting to abolish slavery and make slaves free men. Because of his ability to read and the wealth of literature at Florestal, he had learned much, being especially impressed by newspaper accounts of the fiery abolitionist John Brown, and the daring exploits of the rebel slave, Nat Turner.

"If we could unite among ourselves and join with the white abolitionists, we could throw off this detested yoke of slavery in no time at all," he surmised.

"Don't let no white folks hear you talking like that —not even Marse Narciso," Kitty warned, although it was she who had imbued him with such ideals since childhood. But one had to be cautious. Many Negroes of her acquaintance had been severely punished and even killed for far less rebellious ideas.

Occasionally rumors of Achille's outspoken views filtered back to Samples who repeatedly warned Narciso to keep the young house slave with his radical notions away from the other blacks.

"You got yourself one bad nigger," the overseer said, scratching his pockmarked face. "If it was in my power, you know what I'd do with him, don't you?"

"I'm not sure I want to know, Mr. Samples," Narciso rebuffed.

Ignoring his answer, Samples continued, "I'd string him up by the heels and skin that hide off him with a dull knife—that's what the hell I'd do."

"He's young," Narciso said. "The young all have rebellious ideas."

"He sure can get the other niggers all fired up with his talk about rising up against the white man," Samples alleged. "Just like his mammy. When Kitty was young she was a mighty rebellious wench herself— one hellion I never could quite tame."

"I'm not worried about Achille," Narciso assured him.

"Maybe you should be," Samples insisted. "If we ain't careful, there's going to be a revolt around here if he keeps up that talk of his. Mark my words, these niggers are just ripe for something like that."

At first Kitty was proud of her son's literacy which went far beyond her meager abilities with the printed word, but as he grew older she feared that his outspoken advocacy of the ideas gleaned from reading might get him into serious trouble and prematurely spoil her plans for him.

Ever since Achille learned that Narciso was tutoring Odile's son-in-law, he, too, developed a desire to pursue such studies. Unhesitatingly, he approached Narciso about it one day when he brought the master his breakfast in bed.

"I'm afraid Mr. Antoine wouldn't much care to have you sit in on his 'classes,' " Narciso chuckled, admiring the boy's spunk and ambition, as he always had since Achille was just a toddler. "Besides, he'd be very upset to find out how intelligent you are and how much I've taught you already."

The young slave detested the mere mention of Antoine's name. Only a year or so his junior, the planter's son was insufferably arrogant and treated Achille with the utmost contempt, humiliating him at every opportunity whenever he came to Florestal.

Following Narciso's adamant refusal to allow him to study law, Achille began to develop an openly bitter and resentful attitude toward his master, a change which Kitty quickly perceived.

"It ain't good to feel that way about Marse Narciso," she said. "He's about as good to niggers as any white man is ever going to be—which ain't saying much, I know. I fear to think what's going to happen to us when he passes on. That's why I tries so hard to keep him alive."

"I don't want to have to depend on him or any other white man for my well-being," Achille retorted. "I want to make my own way in the world, be responsible for myself. I want to be free."

"We all wants to be free," Kitty assured him. "When I was young like you I was burning to be free. I was ready to fight the whole world—and I tried. It didn't get me nothing but trouble and sorrow. My greatest hope when you was a baby was that someday you'd lead us all to freedom. I don't reckon any more that it's ever going to happen, but it's still my hope."

During his stay at Florestal for tutoring by Narciso, Antoine's fancy was captured by a pretty teenaged house slave. After a raucous New Year's party at the nearby Broussard plantation, at which he imbibed far too much while watching the customary holiday bonfires burning along the levees up and down the river, he returned near dawn to his cousin's plantation and accosted the slave, whose name was Susie, in the cookhouse as she was preparing to start the fires for the day's cooking. Taking the frightened, trembling black girl in his arms, he laughed, amused by her fear.

"What you want with me, Mr. Antoine?" she asked.

"I'm not going to hurt you," he said soothingly.

"Please, Mr. Antoine, I ain't never been touched by no mens," she said, tears welling in her eyes.

"Never?" he challenged.

"Never, Mr. Antoine. I swears," she said, turning her face away to avoid his liquor-laden breath.

"Then, you're a virgin?"

"I is pure. I swears it."

"And none of these black bucks around here has laid a hand on you?"

"Not a one."

"Then you are indeed honored that I have decided to be the first to deflower you this day," he grinned, swaying a little as though about to lose his balance. "You and I, Susie, will start the new year right."

With that he seized her cotton dress and attempted to tear it off. Susie broke away from him and fled down the brick pathway leading to the honeysuckle-covered outhouse, a little heart-shaped window carved in the door. Once inside, she latched it for protection against him, but with a couple of thrusts from his shoulder, Antoine succeeded in smashing it in. Cowering in a corner of the toilet, Susie sobbed and pleaded with him not to harm her.

"Please, Mr. Antoine, don't hurt me none."

Knowing that he had her trapped, Antoine grabbed her and threw her across the bench-like toilet seat. He lifted her skirt high up over her hips, clamping her writhing body with his own as he rubbed her mound. "You be nice to me, Susie, and I'll give you a coin," he mumbled into her cleavage. "You just stop that kicking, hear?"

Antoine undid his belt, letting his trousers drop and allowing his jutting manhood to spring up. He interposed himself between her legs, separating them widely with his body.

Since kissing and otherwise preparing a slave woman for sex was considered improper and unnecessary, Antoine instantly rammed his quivering manhood between Susie's legs, plunging into her. She screamed with pain and fear and threw her head back, striking it hard against the wooden wall of the outhouse.

Thoroughly aroused before he entered her, Antoine finished in seconds and, withdrawing quickly, rested a moment, planning to repeat the act soon.

Still petrified, Susie took advantage of this respite to attempt to flee once again.

Hitching up his pants, Antoine jumped on the bench and attempted unsuccessfully to seize her as she fled past him and through the shattered door. Under the sudden impact of his weight the bench gave way, and Antoine went crashing through into the putrid collection below.

Cursing the girl all the way to the house, Antoine, filthy and reeking, was surprised to encounter Narciso, on the back gallery, fully dressed and apparently planning to ride, accompanied by Achille. Since Antoine's arrival his cousin's health had shown surprising improvement and he was participating in all sorts of activities, such as riding, which he hadn't done for a while. Both master and slave stared at him and, from the way they averted their noses, he knew it was obvious that he had fallen into the outhouse or some other equally stinking mess.

"My God, Antoine, where have you been?" Narciso asked. "What happened?"

Staring down at his boots, Antoine realized they were covered with a mixture of lime and decomposed feces.

"I had a little accident," he said sheepishly. "I fell through the outhouse."

Having seen Susie come flying into the house crying and screaming a few minutes earlier, seeking Kitty's protection, Achille was immediately suspicious that Antoine's mishap might well have been connected in some way with whatever had happened to cause the girl's hysterical state.

"Don't come in the house with those boots," Narciso admonished.

Turning immediately to Achille, Antoine commanded, "Take these boots off, nigger, and do it quick."

"Use the bootjack, Antoine," Narciso intervened.

Continuing to direct orders at Achille, Antoine said, "When I get them off, I want you to clean them, hear, boy?"

"One of the stableboys can clean them," Narciso said, and headed back into the house for something he had apparently forgotten, leaving the two young men alone. Achille waited patiently for Antoine to remove his dung-covered boots on the bootjack, his face screwed up in disgust from the stench.

When they were off, Antoine took the boots and, without warning, heaved them at Achille striking him across the chest with one and in the face with the other, splattering him with chalky white lime and brown feces. "Clean them, nigger. And fast!" he commanded.

Enraged, Achille threw the boots back at the wealthy young planter's son.

Stunned, Antoine leaped forward and attacked the slave with his riding crop, but Achille managed to wrest it from him and threw it across the lawn. Antoine then jumped on the slave and the two young men landed on the floor, locked in a desperate struggle.

The ruckus on the gallery brought Narciso out of the house once again. "What is going on? Stop it! Stop it this minute! I order both of you to stop!" he cried, his face taking on a purplish hue.

Ignoring his master's command, Achille seized Antoine by the hair and began pounding his head against the floor.

"Stop, I said!" Narciso shouted, pausing between each word to gasp for breath. In order to separate the two youths, he began beating them with his walking stick and shouted to the other slaves for help. It took Kitty's wiry but strong arms to break up the scuffle.

"Shame on you," she berated Achille as she jerked him away from Antoine and to his feet.

Clutching his chest in distress, his face blue and his breathing labored, Narciso shook his fist angrily in Achille's face. "I cannot and will not let such actions as this go unpunished," he declared. "I will not!"

For years Munro Samples had yearned for the chance to vent his hatred of Achille and it finally came, surprisingly at the direction of the master of Florestal himself, and in spite of Kitty's begging and pleading on her son's behalf. The pockmarked overseer could barely contain his glee.

Samples ordered the boy stripped naked and strung up by his heels to the whipping post that occupied a prominent place at the edge of the barnyard. Ordering the slaves to gather around and watch as an example of what would happen if they themselves tried to emulate Achille's attacking a white man, demonstrating that no slave enjoyed a privileged position at Florestal, Samples administered a series of searing lashes to the young slave's body with his gleaming black bullwhip. With each crack of the whip, another section of Achille's back was laid open, blood streaming over his inverted body, gathering in a pool directly beneath his head. The overseer made sure that Achille was gagged beforehand so that his agonized cries would not be heard by Narciso in the house who, out of pity, might have reneged and halted the whipping.

When he finally tired of brandishing the snarling whip, Samples ordered Achille cut down and left him lying unconscious in the barnyard.

Wiping the sweat from his forehead with his arm, tattooed with blue chains, Samples declared, "That'll teach that uppity nigger."

"It'd damned well better," Antoine, who had solemnly witnessed the beating, agreed. The sheer brutality of the punishment sickened him but he feared disclosure of such emotions might indicate a certain lack of masculinity to those around, feelings unbecoming to an aspiring cavalry officer.

When everyone had gone, Kitty crept into the barnyard and dragged the youth to the slave infirmary where she ministered to his wounds with a series of compresses imbued with healing herbs. As he lay on a crude cot, half-conscious, she was reminded sadly of his mother in the same infirmary a little over twenty years earlier.

For Narciso's sake Antoine struggled to keep his attention on the tutoring lesson in progress, but his mind was hardly on law. Inside his head, he could still hear the crack of Samples' whip as it tore Achille's flesh open.

As though he could read the boy's thoughts, Narciso said, "I hate to punish a slave so brutally. There must be a better way, but I honestly don't know what it is. Lately, Achille's become more difficult. On occasion, he's been outright insolent to me. I'd love to send him to the fields as he requests, but Kitty keeps talking me out of it. She's afraid that Samples will look for some excuse to kill the boy, he hates him so much. She's probably right. I wouldn't put it past Samples, especially after that beating he gave him today. It makes me shudder. Still, Achille's been creating a lot of unrest among the slaves and Samples fears a rebellion like they had in Virginia with that confounded Nat Turner." He stopped and sighed contemplatively "Of course, I suppose it's my fault. I educated him, exposed him to too much. I allowed him to fill his head with ideas which make even white men discontent. In essence, I've gone and created a kind of *bête noire*—no pun intended. I wish I knew what to do with him."

Looking up from the volume of Blackstone in his lap, Antoine's eyes brightened. "I have an idea," he suggested.

Narciso raised his eyebrows. "Really? What is it?"

"Let me have him."

Narciso was astounded. "What?!"

"Let me purchase him."

"Sell Achille to *you?*"

"That's right," Antoine affirmed. "I've always

wanted a body servant, but my father has never permitted it."

"What makes you think he'll permit it now?"

"If I buy him with my own money . . ."

"What makes you think you'll be able to manage him if *I* can't?" Narciso asked. "Look what happened this morning."

"I'll find a way. I look forward to the challenge, sir. Either I will succeed in breaking his spirit and making a good body servant out of him, or . . ." Antoine left the statement uncompleted, comparing Achille in his mind to horses he had broken.

"Easier said than done," Narciso said.

"What's your price for him?" Antoine demanded.

"Price?" Narciso repeated. "I will make you a gift of him."

Smiling, Antoine closed the law book. "I accept," he said.

Accosted by Samples and two of his drivers in the slave infirmary where he was recovering from the savage beating, Achille was manacled, hands behind him, and informed that because of his incorrigibility he had been sold to Antoine as a personal body servant. Slipping a coarse rope noose around his neck, Samples yanked the young slave to his feet and shoved him toward the door. Fearing Samples was lying and that he was about to be lynched, Achille panicked. But Samples and his henchmen dragged him across the barnyard to where Antoine's horse was hitched to a post.

"You're going to be taking a nice long walk, boy," Samples said with a grin as he tied the end of the rope to the saddle.

Eventually Antoine appeared from inside the house ready for the journey back to Mandragore, looking dapper in a well-tailored riding outfit. Displaying a bill of sale bearing Narciso's signature to Achille, he said, "You're *my* nigger now."

Achille spat on the paper, causing Samples to plant a hard kick on his buttocks.

"You behave yourself, boy," the overseer warned.

Achille glared at him with contempt and loathing, but made no reply.

Antoine climbed into the saddle, spurred his horse in the flanks making the animal bolt forward, yanking suddenly on the rope around Achille's neck and causing him to stumble forward, almost falling on his face. Along the River Road he was forced to run at a fast pace to keep up with the trotting horse. As they watched Achille struggle to maintain a running speed sufficient to prevent strangling himself at the end of the rope, Samples and the two drivers laughed heartily.

"Run, nigger, run!" Samples shouted after him.

Upstairs in his cluttered bedroom, Narciso lay sprawled across the bed, pillows piled over his head, unable to watch the boy's departure.

The news of the sale of Achille had been deliberately withheld from Kitty so that when she went to the slave infirmary to minister to his injuries, she was shocked to find him gone. Hearing about his departure from the other slaves, she became hysterical and ran up to Narciso's room, pounding on the bolted door.

"Oh, Marse Narciso, please get my boy back! Please bring him back here! Don't let them take him away from me. Please, Marse, please! I won't let him make no more trouble. I swear I won't! Please bring him back! Please!"

Behind the door, Narciso remained stubbornly firm in his resolve. "I'm sorry, Kitty, but a sale is a sale. Achille is gone now. There's no way I can bring him back. I'm sure he'll be fine at Mandragore. You have nothing to worry about. Mr. MacKay is a fine man and has a good reputation for treating his slaves kindly."

"It ain't Mr. MacKay I'm worried about," she said. "I know he has a good name. It's that son of his that's done gone and bought Achille. That Mr. Antoine ain't no good at all. He's got the demon in him. He ruined poor little Susie and she ain't but thirteen and wasn't never touched by no man before. He'll kill my boy. I know he will."

"No, he won't," Narciso insisted.

"I know Achille. He ain't never going to bow and scrape the way Mr. Antoine wants him to. He'll kill poor Achille, I swear he will!"

"Jim MacKay will never allow his son to mistreat a slave. You can count on that," Narciso assured her. "He's very strict about such things. There's no abuse at Mandragore."

"But if Mr. Antoine abuses my boy in secret, how's Mr. MacKay ever going to find out?"

"You needn't worry, I tell you," Narciso said, only half-believing his own words.

Kitty sniffed and wiped her tear-filled eyes on a corner of her apron. "Oh, please, Marse Narciso, if you has any pity at all for poor old Kitty who's been taking care of you since you was a baby, who's been nursing you every time you get sick, you'll bring my boy back. This here is a mother begging you. Please, Marse, please!"

"Achille is not a boy any longer," Narciso replied, finding it increasingly difficult to speak. "He's a man."

Later, when he was alone in the room amid the endless shelves crammed floor to ceiling with thousands of books, Narciso reconfirmed to himself that he was glad Achille was gone from Florestal. If the youth insisted on being a firebrand and stirring up trouble, let him do it elsewhere. Others were better able to deal with rebellious slaves than he.

Gazing wistfully out the window and across the lawns to the pastures and vast cotton acres beyond, he sighed, secretly doubting that even if he weren't afflicted with poor health he would have been able to deal more effectively with the slaves, especially one as defiant as Achille.

After they had gone a short distance down the River Road, Antoine looked back at Achille and saw that not only was he badly winded from trying to keep up with the trotting horse, but his feet were cut and bleeding and the rope tightening about his neck. Stopping beside a creek, Antoine allowed the animal to drink and offered Achille some water from a tin cup, obvious from the way he persistently licked his dry lips that the slave was thirsty. Because of his manacled hands, it was necessary for Antoine to hold the cup to his mouth in order for Achille to drink. At first the slave hesitated, glaring sullenly at his new master, but his thirst was so great that he suppressed his pride, and drank.

Observing his battered feet, Antoine offered, "I suppose you can get on the back of my horse if you like." It was going to be difficult enough for Jim to accept his having bought a slave without Achille's arriving at Mandragore in an injured and exhausted state.

"No," Achille refused proudly.

"It's a long way to Mandragore," Antoine warned. "I want you in good condition when we arrive."

"Then slow the horse."

"I don't want to spend all day on the road," Antoine complained.

"Nor do I," Achille agreed.

"Get on the horse," Antoine ordered sternly, dropping the guise of indifference.

"I'll walk," Achille insisted stubbornly.

"Get on the horse, damn it. There's nothing I hate worse than a slow ride. I'm tired of fooling with you. Climb up there in back of my saddle," Antoine commanded, prodding the slave with his riding crop. "Go on. Hurry!"

Reluctantly, Achille did as he was told.

When word eventually filtered to Jim that Antoine had arrived home with a newly purchased body servant, he was angry, but when he heard that the young man had been forced to walk, manacled, at the end of a noose much of the distance from Florestal to Mandragore, he was enraged.

Summoning Antoine to the study, he demanded, "What is this I hear about you and some slave you've supposedly bought?"

"What are you talking about, sir?" Antoine responded, feigning ignorance. He was fully aware of the speed with which news traveled between plantations. Slaves had few distractions from the drudgery of their everyday lives except for gossip and rumormongering.

"I understand that you have purchased a body servant at Florestal," Jim said, doing his best to remain calm in the face of his mounting indignation.

"Yes," Antoine admitted. "His name is Achille—a rather interesting name, don't you think? Classical."

Jim slammed his fist on the top of the great rosewood desk. "Listen, young man, I am the only one around here authorized to purchase slaves, if it ever becomes necessary," he asserted. "What on earth do you think gives *you* that right?"

"The right to what?" Antoine challenged. "To sully my lily-white hands with commerce in human flesh? That is, if you believe niggers are human. . . ."

Interrupting, Jim wagged his finger in his son's face. "You listen to me," he demanded. "I want that slave returned to Florestal first thing in the morning, is that clear? And you'll take him in one of the wagons. I don't care if you get your money back or not. You deserve to lose it."

"There is no money involved," Antoine casually announced. "Achille was a gift. Cousin Narciso is aware that I, as a cavalry officer, will be in need of a body servant to keep my boots shined and my uniforms in order, to prepare my meals and look after my horse," he enumerated. "This slave isn't a luxury as you mistakenly believe, sir. He's a necessity."

"Necessity, hell," Jim scoffed.

"If there's a war," Antoine began.

Jim cut him off. "There isn't going to be a war," he declared. "And if there is, I wouldn't think much of any army that would make a callow youth, who feels he can't survive without a personal slave, an officer."

Antoine bristled at his father's criticism. "For your information, sir, I have now been definitely promised a commission," he revealed.

"Enough of this foolishness," Jim declared. "You are going to pass the bar and become a lawyer, and that's that. Enough of all this talk of war and cavalry nonsense. The only reason I've allowed you to neglect your responsibilities here and spend so much time at Florestal is so that you could pursue your legal studies."

"No matter what else we might be—lawyers, doctors, planters, blacksmiths, storekeepers, carpenters, riverboatmen, or whatever—we're all going to be soldiers of the South someday soon," Antoine predicted.

❧ 45

It didn't take Achille long to realize that slaves at Mandragore were treated far more humanely than at Florestal. Although Oberdorfer, with his broken English and swaggering German beer-belly, expected the field hands to put in a long day of hard labor, just as he himself and the master, Jim MacKay, did, his treatment of them was free of the cruelty and sadism which characterized the treatment of slaves at the up-river plantation. Having been an indentured servant himself, Oberdorfer understood servitude and had no desire to perpetuate the abuses that could be so easily incorporated into the system.

Even in light of the more humane treatment, Achille still detested his slave status with every fiber of his being, assuring himself there was no way slavery—by its very definition—could be humane. He especially despised being the personal servant of a vain, arrogant, selfish, thoughtless, over-indulged fop such as Antoine Martinon MacKay, and would have much preferred cutting cane than attending to the wants and needs of his youthful master. He also hated his forced association with Verbena, Romulus, Lavinia and the other house slaves, all of whom he viewed with contempt for the way in which they fawned over the members of the family.

"There ain't no finer master in all Louisiana than Marse Jim," Verbena loyally extolled.

"Miss Odile is all right, too, when she don't get all riled up," Lavinia added.

"But that Mister Antoine," Romulus said, shaking his head. "He got a bad temper. He got a *real* bad temper. He gets it from his mama. Those Martinons is all hotheads."

Another far more important conclusion Achille drew after a couple of weeks at Mandragore was that this plantation offered one advantage that barely existed—if it existed at all—at Florestal and that was the possibility of escape.

For several years he had entertained the notion of escaping, ever since he had read about the Underground Railroad in Narciso's newspapers, but knew if he were caught and returned to Florestal, Samples would execute him as an example to the other slaves who entertained similar ideas. From all he could gather since arriving at Mandragore, the punishment for an escapee, if caught, would be far lighter, a conclusion which made the risk all the more enticing. From the time he was a child, Achille had heard tales from Kitty of slaves who had fled by way of the Underground Railroad or other means and landed in free territories such as Ohio or parts of Pennsylvania or Canada, and thus gained their freedom by virtue of their own daring with help from Quakers and other white abolitionist groups.

Achille was aware that he possessed certain attributes few other slaves had which could facilitate his escape. In addition to the ability to read and write—an invaluable asset for forging passes and other documents—he had light skin and generally white facial features which afforded him a far easier means of evading the dreaded slave patrols roaming the countryside. Now that he was away from Florestal, escape began to beckon as an ever more alluring possibility. It was merely a question of devising his strategy. A successful escape would have to be carefully thought out. For the time being he decided to grit his teeth, curb his tongue and try to tolerate the arrogance and unreasonable demands of his young master, adopting an obsequious air until he could formulate definite plans. Meanwhile, he would perform all the humiliating tasks Antoine demanded such as emptying his chamberpots, gathering his dirty clothing strewn about the room, accompanying him at night to saloons, casinos and brothels. One place, Xenia's brothel, he had to endure the taunts and teasing of the whores who enjoyed slipping their hands inside his trousers and speculating on his sexual prowess.

Although talk of war and possible secession continued, waxing and waning from day to day, Antoine persisted halfheartedly with his law studies, mostly at his father's behest, journeying to Florestal at least once a week for tutoring by Narciso. Naturally, whenever he went, whether by horseback or steamboat, Achille was expected to accompany him. Although such visits afforded him the opportunity of seeing Kitty, it was infuriating for him to have to suffer the taunts of his fellow slaves who observed contemptuously the way he kowtowed to his new young master.

"I thought you was a rebel," young Susie scoffed. Antoine's rape in the outhouse had made her bitter and sullen. "Hah!"

Since being acquired by Antoine, Achille's most humiliating experience occurred at a fashionable bawdyhouse on the edge of the French Quarter when he had been forced into fighting the body servant of Antoine's best friend, Léopold Seguin, a radical champion of the Southern cause.

Badly beaten by his powerful young black opponent, who fought savagely and with a spirit that reminded Achille how human beings invariably cling to the very chains that bind them, the light-skinned slave was jeered by the men and laughed at by the whores. Because Antoine had laid a huge wager on the fight and lost, he was furious at his body servant and publicly boxed his ears. The next day Achille resolved to escape immediately.

Going to the huge armoire in Antoine's room,

Achille selected an appropriate suit of travel clothes. Fortunately, the two young men were almost exactly the same size. From a corner of the bureau drawer, in what Antoine had assumed was his secret hiding place, Achille scraped together the pile of hoarded gold coins and stuck them in a leather pouch. Proceeding to the stable with the clothes and money in a traveling bag, he ordered one of the grooms to saddle up Pegasus, Antoine's favorite horse, explaining that the young master was going on a short trip. Leading the animal to the carriageway, Achille suddenly leaped into the saddle and took off as fast as he could, galloping through the plantation gate to the River Road. *Freedom* was the only word on his mind.

His escape was noted shortly thereafter when Antoine entered the stable and was shocked to find his favorite mount gone. When the grooms related Achille's story, he knew instantly what had transpired. Antoine then went to his room to check what might be missing and found both the gold coins and clothes gone.

"Achille has escaped," he announced breathlessly to Oberdorfer who was breakfasting with his Swedish wife and their four children in the overseer's cottage. "Not only that, but he's stolen Pegasus, the horse I've been planning to take to the army with me," he added.

Biting off the end of a sausage and stuffing a chunk of bread into his mouth behind it, the big-bellied German nodded, *"Ja,* I knew he was planning something like this. I can always tell when a slave has got running away on his mind."

"I want you to notify all the slave patrols in the parish at once," Antoine directed.

"Ja, ja," Oberdorfer agreed, wiping his mouth with the sleeve of his shirt.

Still smarting about the theft of his finest horse, which concerned him far more than anything else, Antoine angrily vowed, "When I do get that nigger back, I'm personally going to skin his hide."

"Ja," Oberdorfer nodded, washing the food down with a giant gulp of beer. "I think you will."

Astride Pegasus and attired now in his young master's smartly tailored clothes, pockets full of the stolen gold coins, Achille was faced with the immediate decision of whether to ride north to Baton Rouge and catch a steamer headed for free territories, or to go south to New Orleans and count on losing himself in the diversified crowds of the city. In any case, whatever decision he made had to be done fast. He was well aware that the moment Antoine learned his horse was gone, he would surmise exactly what had happened and notify the slave patrols that roamed the parish with their guns and bloodhounds in search of runaways. Undoubtedly, handbills with his description would soon be distributed throughout the South, offering a reward for his capture. There was no time to waste. Because he was better acquainted with New Orleans than Baton Rouge, Achille decided his chances for a successful escape were more favorable there. In addition, a greater number of boats sailed in and out of the Crescent City going to more varied destinations. The next problem facing Achille was by which route to get there. Obviously, he could continue along the River Road, the main thoroughfare connecting the city with the many plantations strung out along the river. On the other hand, several alternate roads and trails meandered through the marshes and bayous and offered comparative safety from chance encounters with those whose suspicions he might arouse, but he was not familiar with any of them. He considered lying low and traveling by night, concealing himself and the horse in the cypress swamps until dusk, but knowing he couldn't afford to lose time, decided to keep moving along the River Road, gambling on his ability to pass as a white gentleman with the combination of Antoine's clothes and horse and Narciso's manner of speaking to aid him.

Heading south, he rode openly with no attempt to conceal himself, acting the part of a planter's son, perhaps a visitor from another part of the state, and hoped that no one would challenge him nor be any the wiser.

Riding along cane fields, marshes and bayous, he

had several chances to test the effectiveness of his impersonation. Drivers herding gangs of slaves from one location to another, overseers, and gentlemen returning from business in the city scarcely took any notice of him, nor did the ladies who passed in their carriages accompanied by their maids and coachmen.

It was the poor whites, not the gentry, he feared most. Catching a runaway slave was a moneymaking opportunity for them. If, after advertising, an owner failed to claim an apprehended slave, the finder was permitted to sell him to the highest bidder. On the other hand, if the owner did claim the slave, the finder was usually given a generous reward. So far, no one, neither gentleman nor poor white, regarded him with the least suspicion, and as a result, Achille began to feel confident. Relaxing, he became more aware of the warm breeze which stirred the moss clinging to the branches of the cypresses, oaks, and sycamores lining the road, the strange cries of the laughing gulls and the dank odor from the surrounding swamps and bayous. His dream of escape and freedom seemed assured.

As he rounded a sharp bend in the road, a cypress swamp on the left, his horse suddenly raised its head, quivered its nostrils and whinnied. There, ahead of him appearing from among the trees were a group of horsemen—perhaps eight or ten—surrounded by a pack of yelping beagles and bloodhounds, unquestionably a slave patrol. Achille's hands froze on the reins. His first impulse was to direct the horse into the swamp and head for the bayou where he would abandon the animal and elude the men and dogs by swimming. As a rule, to prevent their escape, slaves were forbidden to learn to swim just as they were forbidden to learn to read and write, but Narciso, wishing for companionship when he bathed in the plantation pond, had taught Achille to swim when he was very young. Powerless when their quarry was immersed in water, on land the dogs of the patrol would attack a slave at their master's command and cling to him in the same way bulldogs clung to four-footed animals. But somehow managing to control his panic, Achille, realizing such an escape attempt could actually be more dangerous than facing the patrol and convincing them that he was a young Creole gentleman en route to the city, was confident that nothing in his speech, appearance or manner would betray him as a runaway slave. Narciso had been an excellent tutor. It would be a brazen alternative, but worth a try.

As he approached the group of men armed with pistols and shotguns in addition to the usual chains, manacles, leg-irons and ropes used to subdue errant slaves, he said politely, "Good day, gentlemen."

"Good day, sir," the leader replied, surveying him suspiciously as the others slowly spread themselves across the road in a solid line while the hounds barked and howled and nervously milled about his horse. The leader, a typical ne'er-do-well cracker with bloodshot eyes and a red, florid face, reminded Achille of Munro Samples and he found himself looking at the man's arms for the encircling blue tattoos. Although they were, of course, absent, he hated the man instantly, but knew he would have to control his emotions if his deception were to be successful. If he displayed any but the most casual attitude, all was lost. A true Creole aristocrat, he knew, would never reveal his deeper feelings when dealing with his white inferiors who were simply on earth to do his bidding and for no other reason. The fact that the leader had addressed him originally as "sir" gave him encouragement about the success of his masquerade.

"Sorry to inconvenience you, sir," the leader continued in a tone which was not at all sincerely apologetic, "but we just got a report that a young nigger buck escaped from Mandragore. The cheeky devil had the gall to steal the young master's best horse as well. Now, don't that just beat everything? That's one nigger who's going to be skinned alive when his master gets hold of him."

"I wouldn't give two cents for his life," one of the patrolmen declared.

"You ain't seen nobody suspicious, have you?" the leader asked.

"How do you mean?" Achille calmly asked.

"Like a nigger without a pass," he replied.

"Or one on a fine Arabian," the patrol leader's associate added.

Imitating Narciso's most arrogant, impatient tone, Achille said, "I can assure you, gentlemen, I've seen no one suspicious, now if you don't mind, I'm rather in a rush."

A third patrolman spoke up, "Just where are you coming from, mister?"

"I?" Achille replied. "I am Monsieur Paul Broussard, a native of Baton Rouge visiting my cousin, Robert Broussard, who has a plantation up-river. I am presently en route to New Orleans, and if you gentlemen don't mind . . ."

The leader cut him short by flipping open Achille's frockcoat with the tip of his shotgun and exposing the initials *A.M.M.* floridly embroidered on the silk lining. "Now what did you say your name was, mister?" he asked.

"My name?" Achille stalled ineffectively, as the patrol started to form a close circle around him. Why had he been so stupid? After aiding Antoine dress for weeks, he should have recalled that nearly every article of his clothing, including nightshirts and underwear, was monogrammed.

"That's right," the leader repeated, "your name?"

Realizing he was trapped, Achille, his heart pounding, decided to make a desperate break, hoping that the superb horse's speed would enable him to escape the patrol. With one quick jab in the animal's flanks, he spurred the horse forward, but instead of charging through the circle of patrolmen surrounding him, the horse, already skittish from the incessant yelping of the dogs, balked and reared, ejecting Achille from the saddle. Then, panicked, it galloped off, riderless, into the nearby cypress swamp.

At once the dogs set upon Achille as he lay in the dust, snarling, snapping, and tearing at his clothes and the flesh beneath. Almost in unison, the patrolmen dismounted and, kicking the hounds away, moved in and began beating Achille savagely with their clubs and gun butts. Outnumbered and overpowered, Achille attempted to fend them off, but it was impossible. The men quickly subdued him, placing him immediately in manacles and leg-irons.

"Okay, nigger, on your feet," the leader commanded, kicking him viciously in the small of the back.

When the slave patrol arrived at Mandragore with Achille in chains, Antoine, greatly agitated, met them at the gate, hoping to keep the news of the slave's return from his father. Earlier, Jim had learned of Achille's daring escape from Oberdorfer and had instructed his assistant to notify him as soon as the patrol caught up with Achille. For his part, Antoine had no desire for his father to learn of the patrol's capture of Achille until he himself had finished with him.

"Take him to the wagonshed," Antoine directed, casting a contemptuous glance at Achille. Then staring at the group of shabby horsemen, he anxiously asked, "Where's Pegasus? Where's my horse?"

"He done run off," the leader informed him.

Antoine was aghast. "Run off?" he repeated, dumbstruck. "Where?"

"Back into the swamps," one of the patrolmen answered. "Near Bayou Billetdoux."

After directing Dratt, one of the drivers, to organize a search party for the horse, admonishing them not to return without the animal, Antoine joined the patrol in the wagonshed.

"He's all yours, if you like," the patrol leader said, turning him over to Antoine.

He ordered Achille gagged, stripped, and hoisted over a pulley by his manacled wrists until his feet dangled a few inches off the ground. Since whipping was banned at Mandragore, no whips could be found, and Antoine was forced to use a wooden barrel-stave in beating the errant slave.

Circling Achille several times first, as a hunter might his quarry, Antoine laid the first blow from the barrel-stave on Achille's sweat-glistened back. Once the beating began, Antoine got quickly caught up in it, releasing his pent up fury by pounding the slave so hard and relentlessly that some of the patrol members flinched with vicarious pain as they watched the wooden paddle strike the slave's flesh time after time.

Antoine beat him so furiously that eventually Achille passed out and had to be revived by having a bucket of water doused over his head.

"If you don't mind me saying so, I think that's enough, Mr. MacKay," the patrol leader advised. "You don't want to kill or maim a perfectly good nigger."

As Antoine wiped the sweat from his brow, someone knocked on the door. "Who is it?" he called out.

"It's Dratt, Mr. Antoine," the driver called through the locked door. "We done found Pegasus."

Encouraged by the news, Antoine said, "So soon?"

"Yes, sir," Dratt assured him. "He was just lying there back in the swamps near Bayou Billetdoux—or what was left of him."

"What do you mean?" Antoine asked, apprehensive.

"He must have got hisself killed by a pack of mountain lions or something," the driver explained. "They had him half-ate by the time we found him."

Shocked, Antoine was on the verge of tears. "My beautiful horse, my Pegasus, gone!" he lamented. "Gone forever. I loved that horse. I was going to take him to the army with me."

"You still got yourself a whole stable of mighty fine horses—some of the finest in the parish," the patrol leader said, attempting to console him.

"But none like Pegasus," Antoine retorted. "There's not another horse in the whole world like him. I trained him myself when he was just a colt. And now, because of this worthless wretch of a nigger, he's gone—killed and eaten by a pack of mountain lions. My beautiful Pegasus . . ."

With that Antoine raised the bloody barrel-stave and resumed the beating, this time with greater fury and intensity than before.

So caught up in the beating was Antoine, that he failed to hear the insistent pounding on the barricaded wagonshed door until one of the patrolmen tapped him on the shoulder.

Short of breath, Antoine, assuming it was Dratt again, broke the rhythm of his blows and called out, "What is it this time?"

"What's going on in there?" Oberdorfer, not Dratt, shouted back through the door, rattling the latch.

"Nothing which concerns you, Oberdorfer," Antoine answered. "Go back to your cottage and stay there."

"Do I hear a beating?" the German overseer persisted. "You know, Mr. Antoine, how your father feels about beatings."

"What's going on in here is none of your affair, Oberdorfer," Antoine replied. "Go away."

Only when he heard the overseer's footsteps retreating did Antoine commence with the beating again.

He was still pounding on Achille's torn and bleeding flesh a few minutes later when an ax came crashing through the barricaded door, showering the floor of the wagonshed with wooden fragments.

As he sprang through the splintered door, Jim demanded, "What in God's name is going on here?"

Shocked by the spectacle of Achille hanging from the pulley, bleeding, battered, and only half-conscious, he turned, speechless, to his son for an explanation.

While the entire slave patrol focused their attention on him, Antoine nervously replied, "He killed my horse, my Pegasus, and now he's paying for it."

Glancing with horror at the bloody barrel-stave, Jim snatched it out of Antoine's hand. "What in the hell were you doing with that?" he asked, aghast.

"I'm doing what any good master would do to a runaway slave who stole his finest horse," the youth answered staunchly.

Turning to Oberdorfer who was standing behind him, Jim pointed to Achille and said, "Get him down and take him to the slave infirmary. My God, he looks half-dead. . . ."

"You can't beat a nigger to death," the patrol leader said, attempting to mollify Jim's anger and indignation, fearing it might spread from Antoine to them. The patrols were paid by the planters of the parish and he had no desire to alienate any of them.

"That's the only way you can learn a nigger," one of the patrolmen piped up.

Enraged, Jim shouted at the entire assembly of slave patrolers. "Get out of here! Get off my property right this minute! And don't let me catch you around here again!"

The leader and his men said nothing except a few mumbled "Yes, sirs" and petulantly filed out of the wagonshed, disappointed that their work had been so unappreciated.

When they were alone, Jim seized his son roughly by the front of his blood-spattered ruffled silk shirt. "I don't care how old you are or what a slave has done, I don't ever want to catch you beating a slave like this again. So help me, God, if I do, I'll kick you off this plantation for good without so much as a single cent to your name. Is that clear?"

"Yes, sir," Antoine replied weakly. It seemed incredible that only minutes ago one now so meek could have been murderously wielding a wooden paddle.

Referring to Achille who lay prostrate, face-down, on the straw-covered floor, Jim turned to Oberdorfer. "Help me get this boy to the infirmary," he said.

The overseer rolled the young slave over and was preparing simply to scoop him up in his powerful arms and carry him across the barnyard. Suddenly Jim stopped cold, staring at the gold medallion dangling from the boy's neck. Stunned, he read the engraved inscription, *"More than yesterday, less than tomorrow."*

In the infirmary Achille was attended by Oberdorfer's wife, Kerstin, who had had some rudimentary training as a nurse and midwife in her native Sweden. Because he was young, strong and resilient, his injuries healed quickly and he was soon ready to leave the facility. The question was, where would he go? Since Jim had decreed that his days as Antoine's body servant were definitely over, Oberdorfer assigned him to one of the slave cabins. On the morning he was to depart from the infirmary, he received an unexpected call from the master of Mandragore who requested that Kerstin leave the two of them alone for a few minutes.

"Yes, Mr. MacKay," she said and obediently withdrew from the building.

Achille regarded Jim warily, wondering what he wanted with him and why he had dismissed Kerstin.

"There's no need to be afraid," Jim said, sitting on the edge of Achille's cot, an unusual gesture since physical proximity between master and slave was generally avoided. "I have something I wish to discuss with you."

Ill at ease, Achille wondered what Jim wished to discuss. Undoubtedly, he had come to talk about his future. Was he about to tell him he would now be one of the field hands? Or was he going to inform him that he would be sold again—perhaps into a worse situation? Surely the bitterness and animosity his presence engendered between father and son would make his continued residence at Mandragore intolerable. Antoine was still nursing resentment over the way Jim had embarrassed him in front of the slave patrol and Oberdorfer and was deeply upset over the death of his favorite horse. Kerstin had informed Achille that immediately following the beating, Antoine had gone off to Florestal and remained there ever since, ostensibly resuming his law studies with Narciso.

"Discuss?" Achille repeated with a puzzled frown.

Without replying, Jim reached out and took the gold medallion around the boy's neck between his fingertips, studying it, a look of disbelief on his face.

"Why are you looking at my medal that way?" Achille asked apprehensively.

"Where did you get this?" Jim questioned.

"It belonged to my mother. She died giving birth to me and Kitty took it from around her neck and put it on me," he responded. "It's all I have of hers."

"Your own mother?" Jim questioned.

"Yes, sir."

Jim was surprised. From what Antoine and Odile said, he had always assumed that Achille was Kitty's natural son. The boy was light-skinned and spunky just as she was.

"Then Kitty isn't your mother?"

"No, sir."

"Did Kitty ever say where your natural mother got this medallion?"

Achille shook his head. "No, sir."

"What did she tell you about your own mother?"

"Not very much."

"I want you to tell me anything you can recall," Jim insisted.

"Why do you want to know? What do you care about some slave woman?"

Jim remained calm in the face of the youth's insistence. "Do you know her name?"

"Her name was Dolly."

Jim frowned as though disappointed by the answer. "Dolly?" he repeated.

"Yes, 'Dolly,' " Achille confirmed.

"That was her slave name, wasn't it?"

"Of course," Achille replied.

"Then she had another name?" Jim persisted.

"What do you want to know for?" Achille demanded.

"It's very important to me," Jim replied, unruffled by the boy's lack of cooperation. "And perhaps to you," he added as an afterthought.

Achille wondered what he meant by that. Pondering the strange situation, he decided there could be no harm in telling this white man his mother's real name. "Kitty said my mother insisted she was a Free Woman of Color who was sold into slavery by a jealous white man who wanted to punish her for something she did. None of the slaves at Florestal believed her story, but Kitty says it was true. She said my mother was very beautiful, as refined and elegant as any white lady."

"Her name—what was it?" Jim asked anxiously, seizing Achille by the shoulders.

"Delphine," he said simply.

Jim's eyes grew wide with shock and he gasped, repeating the name with the awe and reverence of a prayer. "Delphine?"

"Yes, Delphine," Achille confirmed, wondering why the name of a slave woman dead for over twenty years should have such a devastating effect on this prominent planter, seated on the edge of his cot.

"Delphine . . ." Jim repeated as though hypnotized by the sound of the name, his entire body trembling, his face white with astonishment and disbelief.

Inexplicably, he suddenly pulled Achille to him and hugged him in a bone-crushing embrace. "Delphine, Delphine," he muttered. "My God, I don't believe it! I don't believe it! It's not possible. After all these years . . . I don't believe that it's possible!"

Embarrassed and uncomfortable at such an unexpected display of emotion, especially from a man who had always seemed so controlled and unemotional in the few brief encounters Achille had had with him, the youthful slave tried gracefully to ease out of his suffocating bear hug.

Just as suddenly as he had grabbed him, Jim released Achille and, staring at him, his face suddenly ashen and contorted, clutched his chest. Gasping for air in a way Achille had often seen Narciso do during his spells, Jim rolled off the side of the cot and slumped to the floor unconscious.

❧ 46

The elderly Dr. Zehner diagnosed Jim's episode in the slave infirmary as a heart seizure and ordered him confined to bed at once. For ten days Jim lay in a semi-comatose state, barely moving, hardly eating or drinking anything, straining for each breath and complaining of a severe, constricting pain in his chest radiating down his left arm into his fingers. Because he was unable to breathe lying flat, he remained propped against a mound of pillows attended by Verbena, Kerstin Oberdorfer and Odile, all of whom did their best to make him as comfortable as possible, keeping the delicate porcelain veilleuse faithfully burning by his bedside, filling it with whale-oil whenever it was low.

On Zehner's orders, Odile moved into the adjoining guest room. Profoundly shocked by her husband's attack and the gravity of his illness—the physician would give no assurances that he would ever recover —Odile was unable to function effectively for several days following the initial occurrence. Often kneeling on the prie-dieu by his bedside, she clutched the carved wooden rosary which had been her mother's and fervently prayed not only for his recovery, but for his immediate conversion to Catholicism as well, since it was her firm belief that only those of that faith could receive eternal salvation. Unfortunately, Jim slept through Father Daubigny's first two visits to the plantation. Often, late at night, Verbena would enter the room to check on Jim and find Odile asleep, still kneeling in a prayerful attitude on the prie-dieu. The maid would raise her to her feet, escort her, unresisting, to the adjoining room and put her to bed. "Come, child," she would say soothingly, as she had for more than forty years.

About two weeks following the seizure Jim rallied and began showing improvement, raising everyone's hopes for his eventual recovery. Odile was particularly encouraged by his state. When she wasn't busy administering the myriad of different tonics and medicines Dr. Zehner had prescribed, she was at his side reading to him, feeding him, talking quietly about affairs of the plantation or simply sitting very still holding his hand reassuringly in hers.

With Jim's improvement, much of her praying and meditation was transferred to the chapel. As she prayed alone, the sunlight filtering through the single stained glass window, she contemplated her marriage and realized that, although it had never been based on overwhelming romantic inclinations, she and Jim had grown to love and respect one another during their more than twenty years together. They were two old friends bound together by the cement of parenthood, as well as by the trials and tribulations, joys and sorrows they had shared.

"Oh, Lord," she prayed aloud, "please help him get well. Don't punish him for my sins."

Antoine, summoned immediately from Florestal on the advent of Jim's heart attack, was profoundly shocked by the calamity of his father's illness, even though their relationship had been openly antagonistic of late. As a gesture of sympathy and good will, he attempted to curb some of the excesses of which he knew Jim disapproved, spending less time with the girls at Xenia's brothel, gambling, drinking, and cavalry drills, and more on his law books. From discussions with Dr. Zehner he had come to realize that his father's attack was serious and his disability would be of considerable duration—perhaps several years or more which meant that Jim could no longer run the plantation. For the present, Oberdorfer had taken charge and was capable of managing things for a while. Having been associated with Jim for more than two decades, the burly German was quite competent as far as his knowledge went, but a whole spectrum of activities and responsibilities had remained Jim's domain, such as the complicated record keeping, bank dealings, agreements with up-river cotton planters, the shipping interests, and Placide's mills in France. Well-versed in the raising of cane and cotton, operating the mills and management of slaves, Oberdorfer was totally ignorant of the business end of the plantation. Antoine wondered whether this responsibility might fall to him and, if it did, how he would manage.

In some ways, Antoine feared the awesome mantle of Master of Mandragore, although he loved the authority, prestige, and power which accompanied the title. Fully aware that such responsibility would severely curtail his favorite pastimes, notably his cavalry aspirations, he almost wished at times that someone else would bear the burden. At one time it had been difficult for him to understand how his Uncle Placide could have so easily relinquished the plantation to his father. Now, it was easy to comprehend.

As soon as Jim had regained enough strength to voice more than a few urgent requests in a hoarse whisper, he began repeatedly to ask to see Achille. At first, everyone ignored this disconcerting request, dismissing it as one more manifestation of the confused mental state he occasionally exhibited since the heart attack.

"He's working in the sugar mill," Odile informed him. It was true. At Oberdorfer's direction Achille had been assigned to the mill and, unknown to her, was now learning the workings of the complex operation from Roger Guillon himself and, from all reports, proving remarkably adept.

Because of the disruptions in the routine at Mandragore brought about by Jim's catastrophic illness, Ysabel found herself less the center of attention than she had been when she first arrived. Although by no means neglected, except by Antoine who barely tolerated her, regarding her a nuisance and an intrusion into the family's life, she frequently found herself on her own.

Like the other women in the house, Ysabel spent considerable time with Jim, reading to him in her rapidly improving English. It was she who was the first to take his desire to see Achille seriously.

"I think Cousin Jim's mind is very clear when he asks to see Achille," she said to Odile one evening as they were embroidering in the parlor together with Louise Chardonnier and Victorine Pilette.

"Nonsense," Odile scoffed, trying to make light of such a request. "What does Jim have to say to some rebellious runaway who's not only responsible for the loss of our son's horse but probably for his own illness as well. After all, he was the only one present when Jim suffered his attack."

"I really don't think it's fair to blame *that* on the slave," Louise Chardonnier said as she deftly poked her needle through the embroidery hoop.

"Just the same, I would love to know what transpired in the infirmary," Odile insisted. "I'm glad Oberdorfer assigned him to the mill. I certainly could not abide the sight of that blue-eyed devil nigger in this house."

Verbena, serving tea to the women, staunchly supported her mistress in the condemnation of the youthful slave. "I could tell the first time I laid eyes on that boy, he would bring nothing but trouble to this house," she said.

Finally, it was Ysabel, in defiance of her cousin, who went to the mill one day while Odile was in the city with Verbena and Antoine elsewhere, and brought Achille to see Jim in response to his repeated requests.

After escorting the young slave to the house, Ysabel tactfully withdrew. Jim reached out his hand to him and, at first, Achille was reluctant about clasping it, but when he did, Jim squeezed his fingers as hard as he could and whispered, "My son. . . ."

Looking puzzled, Achille wondered if the planter had lost his mind along with the heart attack.

"Son?" he repeated, attempting to draw his hand from Jim's grasp, but the older man held it with surprising strength.

"Yes," Jim repeated. *"You* are my son."

Achille shook his head in bewilderment. He was sure Jim was out of his mind. "I'm afraid, sir, I don't understand?"

"That medallion you wear around your neck—?" He paused to catch his breath.

"What about it?"

"I had it made and gave it to your mother."

Stunned, Achille listened in rapt silence as Jim recounted the entire story of his relationship with Delphine.

When he concluded, Achille was so moved, he told him once again all the details he could remember about the way his mother's lover retaliated for her infidelity by selling her to Florestal as a field hand.

Staring at Jim, Achille shook his head in disbelief. "My father?" he said. "How can it be? You, a white man?"

Dashing from the room and down the narrow spiral

stairs, he nearly collided with Ysabel who wondered what had transpired to upset the young slave so much.

With no fear of a chance encounter with one of the slave patrols, Achille rode north along the River Road to Florestal. This time in his possession were documents signed by Jim MacKay officially declaring him a free man, no longer a slave.

Riding proudly through the gate of the Valdéz cotton plantation, he proceeded around to the back of the main house on the carriageway seeking Kitty and found her supervising a group of slave girls with the laundry. Shouting orders while she stirred a steaming tub of dirty clothes with a long pole, beads of perspiration running down her freckled forehead, the black woman squinted, peering in his direction, a look of disbelief on her face. Could this really be the foster son she had raised since birth, astride a fine horse and looking so elegant in his obviously new clothes? Her last memory of Achille was his running barefoot behind Antoine's horse trying desperately to keep up and not be strangled by the rope around his neck, his hands manacled behind his back.

Abandoning the wash at once, Kitty ran to him and embraced him the moment he dismounted.

"Lord, boy, I can hardly believe my own eyes!" she cried.

Taking her by the hand, Achille led her to the shade of an elm tree, amid the curious stares of the other slaves, and the two of them sat on the grass while he related the events of the past month, but especially Jim's story of his relationship with Delphine. The other slaves would have loved to join them, but they knew Kitty well enough to stay away until she invited them.

"Is it true?" he asked anxiously.

Considering a moment, Kitty commented, "Your mama always told me her baby's daddy was a fine white gentleman with blond hair and blue eyes. That's Mr. Jim all right. If Mr. Jim says he's your daddy, I reckon he must be. I don't think no white man would fess up to being the daddy of no nigger child unless he was. Your mama would never tell nobody the name of her baby's daddy—not even me—but come to think of it, I remember she did want you to be called 'James.' That's Mr. Jim's Christian name. I didn't want you named for no white man, so I named you 'Achille' myself after a fine slave I knew when I was just a girl. He was such a rebel no master could tame him."

Achille reached out and broke off a long blade of grass and stuck it between his teeth. "MacKay wants to treat me like his real son," he said.

"No reason why he shouldn't," Kitty agreed. "He gave you your freedom, didn't he?"

"Yes," Achille nodded. "I mean, he wants me to live in the main house with him and his wife. And Antoine."

Kitty's eyes grew wide with shock. "Miss Odile would never stand for that! I know she wouldn't. That would kill Miss Odile—a nigger slave living in the same house! And as for Mr. Antoine—well, you know how *he* feels about you," she said. "I don't have to tell you. You have the scars to prove it."

"Mr. Jim—he wants me to call him *Dad,* but I just can't bring myself to go that far yet—has already announced his intentions to them."

Raising her eyebrows, Kitty said, "How did they take it?"

"I don't know," Achille admitted. "I decided to come here for a few days and let them get accustomed to the idea."

"What are you fixing to do when you go back?" Kitty asked. "That is, *if* you go back. . . ."

"I haven't made up my mind yet . . ." Achille replied. "I know I would never feel comfortable living in a house where I wasn't welcome—even if I've got a right to live there—if Mr. Jim is my daddy like he says he is. I know that Antoine loathes me more than ever now and so does Miss Odile, but that doesn't bother me. I'm used to being loathed. Still, now that I'm free, I've been thinking about moving on, going somewhere else, getting myself a trade or profession like Roarke, Mandragore's head sugar-maker, or Roger

Guillon, who's an engineer. His daddy was a white man, too. He saw to it that Roger got educated. I know Mr. Jim would help me get an education, if that was what I wanted."

"What *do* you want?" Kitty asked.

Bewildered, Achille shook his head. "I don't know," he admitted. "When I was a slave I used to dream every day about running away and being free, but now that I really am free, I don't want to go so bad. Funny, isn't it?"

"It ain't so funny," Kitty remarked. "It's good you can do what you want to without no white folks getting after you all the time. No sense in you running off if you don't feel like it. If Mr. Jim wants you to keep on staying at Mandragore with him, then you should, if that's what you have a mind to do. After all, as you said yourself, you got as much right as any other son of his and maybe more. Don't let nobody else tell you what to do. You do what you want. I raised you to be proud and to stand up for yourself. You always done that. I don't want you backing down now. Go on and let Mr. Jim give you your share of everything that's rightfully yours. Us black folks have a right to as much of these plantations as any of them do-nothing white folks. If it wasn't for our sweat and blood and us breaking our backs in the hot sun, none of them white folks would have nothing. When one of our people gets a chance to make something of hisself, he's got to take it—for the sake of all the rest of us. When one of us gets a chance to break free and throw off the yoke and make something of hisself, it helps all the rest of us." Taking his hand in her big, bony one she implored, "No, son, don't you go running off nowhere with your tail between your legs. You go on and stay right there at Mandragore and claim what's yours. And if you ever get to be master . . ."

Laughing, Achille interrupted, "Master? Come on now, Mama."

"You 'come on,'" she reproached. "It's possible you could be master of Mandragore someday. Why not?"

"That's ridiculous." Achille laughed.

"Don't you go laughing at your mama," she chided. "If you do get to be master, don't forget old Kitty who done raised you since you was a little sucker. Someday I hope you gets me my freedom so I knows what it's like to be free before I die."

Gazing at her strong, sharp-featured face, a face that could be as stern and demanding as it was loving, he saw years of frustration, humiliation and resentment in her flashing eyes. Though the hot, muggy day, aggravated by the tubs of steaming water all around them, made him uncomfortable, Achille was glad he had come to Florestal. He had found some answers here.

Jim's first step after acknowledging Achille as his son and giving him his freedom was to announce that the youth would be permitted to live in the house with the rest of the family if he so chose.

"I want him to be considered the same as any other member of this household," he said.

"Have you gone and lost your mind?" Odile said. Whether Jim was ill or not, she felt that such an outrageous suggestion was intolerable. "James Mac-Kay, how could you even mention such a thing?" she reproached. "The very idea of bringing that . . . that slave in here and expecting us to live under the same roof. Why, it's the most outlandish thing I've ever heard in my entire life! I must speak to Dr. Zehner when he comes to see you today. I think some of those tonics he's been giving you are too strong and affecting your sanity."

"There's nothing wrong with my mind, Odile," Jim replied.

"Any man who expects his wife and family to accept his pickaninny bastard as an equal has *got* to be crazy. That's all there is to it."

"Try to calm down," Jim pleaded.

"Calm down?!" she exploded, unable to contain herself any longer. "How can you expect me to be calm when you propose such an outrage as though it were nothing at all? Well, I will tell you one thing, Mr.

MacKay, I won't stand for it. I will never permit that nigger in this house—a house which has been in *my* family for over one hundred years. I will not allow him to violate my dwelling place. I simply will not. I don't care a whit that you set him free. That's your business. You run the slaves around here. You can set the whole bunch of them free if you want. Sometimes I'm surprised you haven't already. But as for this Achille, you tell him to take his freedom and go elsewhere. Let him go up North to those nigger-loving abolitionists. We don't need any uppity-free niggers around here."

"He happens to be my son," Jim reminded her.

"Hah!" she said, hands impudently on hips. "What proof have you got of *that?*"

"What proof have I got that *Antoine* is my son?" he retorted.

Odile gave a tiny inaudible gasp and blanched slightly at the question. *What proof did he have indeed?* Nevertheless, she decided to continue on the same tack. "He could have stolen that medallion. You know how light-fingered these niggers are. They'd steal the shoes right off a dead man's feet if they could."

"I happen to accept his story," Jim assured her. "I believe Achille *is* my son. That business about Delphine going off to Martinique with Bourrier and her and the boy dying there was all a fabrication. Even at the time, I never believed it. It was all a ruthless deception."

"None of that is important now anyway," she said. "The issue is that no matter whose son Achille is, he can't stay in this house. We can't all of a sudden take a nigger slave and make him one of the family. The very idea is not only mad, it's positively revolting!"

"Revolting or not, he *is* one of my family," Jim insisted. The stress of the argument was beginning to tire him.

"*Your* family," she reminded him, "but not mine."

"In any case, Odile . . ."

Suddenly bursting into hysterical sobs, Odile threw herself against him. "Oh, Jim, why are you doing this to me? Why do you wish to torture me this way? Have I really been such a terrible wife and mother all these years? Apart from that boy being a nigger, can't you see how humiliating it is to me, having to accept your bastard child? Have you no consideration for my feelings?"

"My God, Odile, I'm not trying to humiliate or torture anyone," he protested. "I'm only trying to do what's fair and just."

"Is that what you call it?"

Putting his arm around her, he said in as soothing a tone as possible, "Please, try to calm yourself."

Shaking his arm loose, she continued undaunted, "If you have no respect for me and my sensibilities, at least think of your son. How do you think Antoine will feel when he is suddenly informed that he is to share his home with his very own body servant whom he is suddenly supposed to treat as an equal—as a *brother*, for God's sake! Why can't I make you understand how insane it all is?"

"Antoine will simply have to get used to the idea and come to accept it," Jim replied, stubbornly determined that his will would prevail.

"You know he'll never do that," she countered. "You should know your son better than that by now."

"It won't be easy for him, I know, but that's the way it's going to be as long as I am the head of this house," Jim firmly decreed.

As he spoke, Jim was beginning to experience tiny twinges of pain within his chest and wished he hadn't allowed himself to get into such a heated dispute with Odile. He knew that accepting Achille would be difficult—almost impossible—for her with her lifelong, deeply ingrained prejudices, but acknowledging Achille as a son and treating him and Antoine equally seemed the only right thing to do.

Determined that Jim was not going to impose his will no matter what strategy she would have to employ or to what lengths she would have to go, Odile dried her eyes and tried to speak calmly and sound reasonable. "I'm sure Achille probably wouldn't want to stay where he knows he's not wanted. He seems like an intelligent boy, actually. If funds were put in trust so that he could obtain an education—perhaps at Yale or Harvard—or if he were to be established in a business or profession by a generous benefactor, he would have no desire to stay here. After all, there are plenty of opportunities elsewhere for Free Men of Color. Some of the finest tailors and shirtmakers and bakers and music teachers in New Orleans are our free colored people. As a charitable gesture, I would be happy to sponsor him in whatever new venture he elects for himself from my own personal resources."

Unfazed by her thinly veiled attempts at bribery, Jim replied, "Whatever Achille decides to do with his life is his own affair."

"But you *will* mention this to him?" she said.

"If you wish," he complied.

Grasping his face between her smooth hands, she tenderly kissed his lips. "Thank you," she said.

✿ 47

Hot, tired, and dusty from days of intensive drilling in a remote area with his cavalry unit astride Sirocco, a horse considerably less able than his beloved Pegasus, Antoine rode up the carriageway in a state of excitement. Because the Republican party had nominated Lincoln in Chicago in May, the legislatures of the states in the Deep South were convening to plan appropriate courses of action should the avowed abolitionist be elected president. Reports out of South Carolina alleged that this most rebellious of states would surely secede if Lincoln were to win the election. If South Carolina seceded, as its leaders threatened, it seemed certain that Florida, Georgia, and Alabama would immediately follow suit. Although there was considerable pro-Union sentiment in Louisiana, Antoine personally hoped that it could be overcome and the state cast its lot with its sisters of the Deep South. Like the leading planters in the lower part of the state, he wanted no part of Mr. Lincoln with his stand on slavery and tariffs and was more than willing to fight him and his Federal troops if it came to that. Each day of that summer and fall of 1860 further polarized the North and the South and made a war between the states seem inevitable. The vision of riding into battle against Yankees, heading his own cavalry unit, seemed irresistibly glamorous to the impulsive youth. One of the best horsemen in the state militia, Antoine had been granted a commission, conferring on him the rank of lieutenant, of which he was very proud. Now, he yearned to command his men in actual battle.

Intending to stay as usual in the *garçonnière,* he first circled the house on his horse and shouted for Romulus. Having been away at Florestal and then with the cavalry for weeks on end, he needed the old slave's help in bathing and dressing before paying his respects to his father and mother.

Obediently, Romulus shuffled into the familiar room in the cottage-like *garçonnière* and helped the young master out of his boots and uniform in his usual fashion.

"After you've hung my uniform up—carefully, mind you—I want you to prepare a bath for me—a nice hot one," Antoine directed.

"Yes, sir, Mr. Antoine," the old butler-valet replied. "But first I gots to go back to the main house and take care of something for your daddy."

"Damn!" Antoine swore aloud, venting his frustration at not being able to take an immediate bath. Cursing the fact that he no longer had a personal body-servant—not that Achille had been a very acceptable one, to say the least—Antoine had no choice except to wait for Romulus' return.

Naturally, while at Florestal he had received a carefully phrased letter from his mother informing him that his father had elevated Achille from slave to "son" overnight.

Even back at Mandragore, the situation still had no reality for Antoine who merely regarded it as ridiculous at best. Despite the absurdity of the whole thing, it nevertheless rankled and infuriated him—to say nothing of the grief, humiliation and outrage his mother felt. It had created a scandal and, understandably, was the talk of every plantation up and down the river. The major hope was that Achille, now granted his freedom, would be quickly gone so that they would be free of him forever.

Brother indeed! he said to himself in disgust. *The old man is truly mad.*

When it appeared as though Romulus were taking an inordinate amount of time in the main house, Antoine went looking for him and located the elderly house slave on the second floor where he was supervising two young male slaves who were attempting to carry a massive brass bed up the narrow, curving staircase to his former nursery.

"What on earth are you doing, Romulus?" he demanded. "I've been waiting more than half an hour for my bath. Now, you leave all this bed moving business and prepare my tub, do you hear?"

"I'm sorry, Mr. Antoine," the butler-valet apologized, "but Marse Jim told me to get this bed ready for Mr. Achille."

Antoine could not believe his ears. *"Mister Achille!"* he exploded.

"Yes, sir," Romulus nodded.

"Since when is a nigger addressed as 'mister'?" he asked.

"That's what your daddy told us to call him," Romulus explained.

"My father isn't planning on having him sleep in this house, I hope?" Antoine said.

"Yes, sir, he is," Romulus answered. "He's been up to Florestal visiting his mammy, but he comes back tonight."

Apparently Achille's arrival at the northern plantation coincided with Antoine's departure for the cavalry maneuvers and, fortunately, the paths of the two young men didn't cross there.

"And that bed's for him?" Antoine questioned.

"Yes, sir, it sure is," Romulus replied.

"Well, my order is to take that bed back wherever you got it."

"That's your old bed, Mr. Antoine," one of the two young slaves piped up.

"That nigger Achille is not sleeping in this house tonight or any other night," Antoine asserted. "Until he vacates this plantation, he can sleep in the slave cabins or the barn or the chicken coop where he belongs."

"You'll have to talk to your daddy about that, Mr. Antoine," Romulus said, indicating the closed door of Jim's room. "In the meantime, we gots to take this bed up to the attic like Marse Jim told us to."

Interposing himself between the stairs and the two slaves struggling with the heavy bed, Antoine said, "I don't have to talk to anyone. Achille is *not* sleeping in this house and that's final."

"Your daddy is going to be mighty riled at you if you stops us from moving that bed where he wants it," Romulus warned.

"That's right," a male voice said from the opposite end of the hall. Surprised, Antoine whirled around and saw Achille, elegantly attired, strolling casually down the hall toward him with an air of not only having lived in the house all his life, but rightfully *belonging* there as well. "I suggest that you allow them to get on with the moving of that bed," he said to Antoine.

Angrily clenching his fists, Antoine declared, "Not only do I intend to block their path, nigger, I intend to block yours as well."

Undaunted, Achille remarked, "Really?"

"If you don't get out of this house at once, I shall personally throw you out," Antoine threatened.

"You and who else—the whole slave patrol?" Achille taunted.

"Listen, nigger," Antoine said angrily, "I almost

killed you once and I might just be forced to try again."

"Let me remind you, white boy, that at that time I was bound and gagged and bodily restrained and you had the whole slave patrol to assist you," Achille replied. "This time I am ready for any challenge you might wish to make."

Provoked to flashpoint, Antoine exclaimed, "You arrogant nigger bastard!" He sprang at him with the rage and ferocity of a pit-bull. While Romulus and the two young slaves looked on in horror, Achille and Antoine went at each other with a flood of unleashed rage and resentment. Wrestling one another to the floor, each, weaponless, struggled to gain sheer physical advantage over the other. Fists pummeled heads, thumbs gouged eyes, knees pounded groins, elbows locked about necks only to be pried loose.

Alarmed by their unfettered hatred and violence, Romulus pleaded, "Please, Mr. Antoine. Mr. Achille, stop this! You are going to disturb your daddy and he's a sick man. You all got to stop this right now."

Hearing the ruckus and excited voices, Jim called out from behind the closed door of his room. "What's going on out there in the hall? Romulus! Verbena! Lavinia! Somebody come here and tell me what all the noise is about."

"See what you done?" Romulus scolded. "You done woke up your daddy." Turning to the two young slaves still holding the brass bed, he directed, "You all put that bed down and go get Miss Odile. She is out in the garden with Miss Ysabel. Maybe she can stop them before they kills each other and Marse Jim to boot." Giving them a shove toward the stairs, he admonished, "Now, you all go on and fetch her, hear?"

Achille and Antoine, locked together, rolled over and down the hall toward the spiral staircase, their feet leaving black bootprints on the wall and doors. As they landed against the banister, Antoine freed an arm and, reaching out, seized one of the balusters supporting the handrail. With a mighty tug, he ripped it loose. Wielding the hefty baluster as a club, he managed to gain momentary advantage over Achille and was about to strike him a powerful blow on the head when his arm froze in midair.

There, in the doorway of his room in his striped flannel nightshirt, stood Jim, gripping the doorjamb for support. "Stop!" he commanded, his face ashen and distressed. "For God's sake, stop, both of you!"

❧ 48

Although many planters socialized freely with their overseers and their families, Odile never encouraged familiarity with Hans Oberdorfer and his wife Kerstin nor welcomed their presence unduly in the great house. Uncomfortable with employees whom she considered only a few steps above the slaves, the mistress of Mandragore preferred to maintain a polite distance between them and tried, unsuccessfully, to get Jim to do the same. Since Jim's illness, however, both Hans and Kerstin were in the house far more than ever in the past, Hans conferring several times a day with Jim about plantation business and Kerstin playing a large role in his nursing care. Often they spent hours in the master bedroom and frequently, at his insistence, took meals with him.

"I wish you get well pretty soon," Oberdorfer said in his thick German accent. "This plantation is too much for me."

"Nonsense. You're doing a fine job, Hans," Jim said, giving him an encouraging slap on the back.

"I would like maybe some help, Mr. Jim. Is possible, *ja?*"

"Perhaps," Jim smiled noncommittally. "I have a few ideas."

No matter how much Odile minded the presence of

the Oberdorfers, it was something to which she could adjust and finally tolerate, but having Achille in the house, sleeping in the attic nursery, a room which had once been her son's and before that her own and Placide's, was another matter. *That* was intolerable. Not only was he a former slave, but a bastard to boot who would forever remind her of her husband's youthful indiscretions with a woman of a decidedly inferior race and morals as well. As for himself, she found Achille insufferably disrespectful and overbearing, and to Odile there was nothing worse than a Negro who didn't know his place.

She had hoped that through the combined efforts of Antoine and herself, they might somehow get him to leave Mandragore, but she now realized that if she were going to battle Achille it would have to be on her own. Her son was much too preoccupied with the current turmoil involving possible secession and war to care about such mundane matters. Almost as soon as Antoine had arrived home, he was gone again. Léopold Seguin rode over from Forest Point to inform him they must report to camp, this time for an indefinite period.

One day when Odile was railing against Achille, as she frequently did, Ysabel felt compelled to speak up in the youth's defense. "He's rather nice, I think," she remarked.

Begrudgingly, Odile had to admit to herself that he *was* literate, intelligent, and had acquired a certain polish through his association with Narciso.

"Yes, I suppose he is—to you. But it doesn't change the fact that he has no business in this house," Odile said. "The sooner he's gone and we're all rid of him, the better."

Repeatedly, she and Jim had confrontations about the boy's continued presence in the house, the strain of which had produced a considerable setback in Jim's recovery. At Dr. Zehner's admonition, she was forced to avoid the issue, at least temporarily, and accept Achille's residence in the house at least for the time being.

"I don't like a damned cheeky nigger like that

Achille living with fine white folks any more than you do, Odile, but if you keep picking at Jim about it, you're going to kill him," the white-haired physician warned.

It was not an easy concession.

With Antoine away and so heavily involved in his military activities, Achille was spending more and more time with Jim who instructed the boy in many aspects of plantation life. It was apparent to Odile that Achille was quickly encroaching on her own son's territory and she worried that he might usurp Antoine's place in Jim's life.

One evening as Jim and Odile were dining together on the gallery just beyond his room—Dr. Zehner had now permitted him to walk about the second floor though stairs were still forbidden—he remarked, "You know, Achille is really extraordinarily bright."

"Really?" she said disinterestedly. "I hadn't noticed."

"He comprehends quickly," he continued. "And, I'll tell you, he's a lot more interested in things around this plantation than Antoine ever was."

"Well, Antoine's been involved in other important matters—preparing for the defense of the South, for one thing," she said. "It's most unfair of you to criticize him this way, especially when he's not here to speak up for himself. I think you're showing this so-called 'other son' of yours much too much partiality, if you want my frank opinion."

One day while conferring with Oberdorfer, Jim casually announced that he had decided to let Achille play an important part in the running of the plantation.

Surprised, the German overseer said, "Him? Your wife said he was leaving Mandragore soon."

"That may be my wife's wish, but he's decided to stay," Jim corrected. "I've convinced him that his place is here. Naturally, he's had a difficult time reconciling himself to the idea that slavery is a fact of life. I don't like it any more than he does, but, as I explained to him, there's nothing we can do about it at

the moment. I favor a gradual freeing of the slaves—
by attrition—such as I've been doing at Mandragore
for years. They just can't be turned loose all at once
as Mr. Lincoln and the abolitionists advocate. They
must be educated first, taught skills and trades,
instructed in the rights and responsibilities of citizens.
Besides, there are the old slaves who must be looked
after. They'd be neglected and left to die if they were
suddenly set free. It's a complicated issue, you see, and
one which won't be solved by a war. I think I've successfully convinced Achille of this."

"I see," Oberdorfer nodded, anxiously waiting to
hear what more Jim had to say.

"Achille will be in charge until I'm up and about
more," Jim went on. "Naturally, any major decisions
he makes will be with my approval, but for all intents
and purposes, he has full authority. He will be my deputy, so to speak."

Surprised, Oberdorfer stared at Jim, wondering
how the other slaves would accept a former slave suddenly being in charge. "Full authority?" he questioned.

"Absolutely," Jim confirmed. "I have complete confidence in his abilities."

"And I'll get my orders from him, *ja?*" Oberdorfer
could scarcely believe his ears.

"Correct," Jim nodded.

"It will be difficult taking orders from a man who was
once a slave," he mused.

"Look at it this way," Jim said. "You won't be taking orders from an ex-slave, you'll be taking them from
my son."

One evening, because of mechanical difficulties at
the modernized old Mandragore sugar mill, Achille
was up nearly half the night working on the complex
machinery. He was finally able to get away a few hours
before dawn. Wearily he trod up the dozen or so front
steps to the main gallery of the great house. He would
have much preferred to reside in the nearby *garçonnière* but that was still considered Antoine's territory, even though he hadn't occupied it for months.
There, he could come and go as he pleased—just as

Antoine did when he was in residence at Mandragore —without disturbing anyone, especially Odile who claimed she hadn't had a decent night's sleep since he had occupied the attic, and had to be treated by Dr. Zehner with a sedative tonic.

Although his bones ached and his muscles were fatigued, he felt good about himself and his work. With Roger Guillon's help, they had located and repaired the source of the trouble, making the mill operational once again. In the morning the conveyor belt, cutting knives, rollers, and boilers would be going full blast as tons of stalwart, pithy cane were reduced to tiny sugar crystals to sweeten life for millions. Confident that at last he had earned the respect of the vast majority of the workers at Mandragore, both free and slave, Achille was beginning to feel comfortable with his newly acquired authority. Roger Guillon had been a tremendous source of encouragement.

"The way I look at it, we mixed bloods combine the best of both races," he said proudly. "We're as good as any man, white or black. When you have ability and can provide a needed service, no one cares what color you are. When a man's good at whatever he chooses to undertake, he's got a right to be proud and let others know that he's good. When they're aware of that, his race isn't an issue any longer."

Gradually, Achille began accommodating to the feeling of success and power, beginning to enjoy his right to assert himself when the occasion demanded without fear of punishment. He was no longer a groveling, bowing, scraping, boot-licking slave facing degradation and humiliation every day of his life. He was a free man, the acknowledged son of one of the parish's most successful planters, and he liked it. The one thing which continued to bother him, of course, was the slave labor which kept the plantation going. It made him feel guilty to realize that although he was free, thousands of his brothers and sisters were not.

"We're the beginning, the toe in the door," Roger assured him. "We're the ones who can make it easier for the others when freedom comes—and it will. Believe me, it will."

Inside the great house it was still dark. As yet the kitchen slaves had not arisen to light the fires in the cookhouse. Exhausted, Achille paused a moment at the top step, sat down on the edge of the gallery and yanked off his boots, deciding to save Lavinia some work by scraping the mud off before entering the hall. Sitting there in the darkness with only the sound of frogs and crickets breaking the stillness of the night, he began to perceive another presence, although he could see no one. Listening carefully, he thought for a moment he heard the sound of muffled weeping— a young girl's. Who could be outside crying at such an hour? Had Odile harshly scolded or punished one of the house slaves? She had been extremely cross and irritable lately, taking out her resentment and indignation at his presence on the slaves. Even Verbena and Romulus had not been exempt from her bursts of temper. Quietly, he rose and padded along the gallery in his stockinged feet, past the row of stately white columns, to investigate the source of the sound.

Just as he rounded the corner of the house, he caught sight of a woman's silhouette. She was leaning against the balustrade. Suddenly aware of his presence, she gasped aloud and attempted to conceal herself behind a column. It was then that he saw the woman was Ysabel.

"What are you doing out here?" he questioned.

Pulling her wrapper tightly around her nightgown, she pleaded, "Please, Achille, go away."

Ignoring her entreaty, Achille drew closer. "What are you crying about?" he asked.

She started to answer, but instead burst into tears, sobbing openly.

Gallantly he reached into his pocket and offered her his handkerchief. Accepting it hesitantly, she dabbed at her eyes and tear-streaked cheeks.

"Don't you want to tell me why you're crying?" he persisted.

"I'm not sure I know myself," she admitted.

"Is it because you miss your family in Cuba?" Achille offered.

"No. Although I do," Ysabel responded.

"Is it for some handsome young man you had to leave behind in Havana?"

"I was too young for that when I left," she replied.

"Is it because your cousin Odile has been cross with you, just as she has been with everyone else lately?"

"No. She treats me well."

"Then what is it that can make a lovely girl like you cry as though her very heart were breaking?"

Unable to restrain herself any longer, Ysabel blurted, "I'm crying because I'm so lonely here. All day I have no one to talk to except Odile and lately she is so preoccupied. . . ."

"Preoccupied with ridding Mandragore of me," he interrupted.

Without either agreeing or disagreeing, Ysabel continued, "And Jim is ill and absorbed with his slow recovery, as well as with the affairs of the plantation. He has little time for me. There are no parties for young people now because all the boys have gone off to the state militia, just as cousin Antoine has done. And you, Achille . . ." She stopped abruptly.

"Yes?" he urged. "What about me?"

"You are always too busy, also," she said sadly. "I never see you and when I do, Odile is always making trouble afterward. I want to have a friend, someone to whom I can speak my feelings."

"As you're doing now?" he smiled.

"Yes," she nodded, blowing her nose in his handkerchief. "I thought that with your kind face and your very nice eyes perhaps you could be that friend I need so much. But you, too, are always busy."

Slipping his arm around her shoulders, he said, "I hope I am never too busy for you."

"All the day you are either in the cane fields or at the mill," she complained.

Drawing her close to him, he inhaled the fresh scent of her smooth skin and hair. "I'm sorry. I didn't know how you felt. From now on, I shall never be too busy. I shall always have time for you—all the time you want," he assured her, kissing the dark lock which had tumbled over her creamy forehead.

Ysabel, slowly, put her arms around Achille's neck, pulling his head down for a passionate kiss. The tall youth moaned as he fought with impulses he had always been able to hold in check. Ever since reaching adulthood Achille had understood the attraction his fine features and handsome coloring held for the opposite sex, but the serious young man had always considered such pleasures less important than his goal of serving his people in their fight for freedom. Then, again, he had never met someone like Ysabel before. Achille kissed her eyes, to close them, and ran his hand down the curve of her back to cup the swell of her high, round buttocks. Gasping, the reckless young girl pressed herself against Achille, taunting him with the pressure of her firm nipples against his chest through the thin lace of her bodice.

"Ysabel, this is wrong," Achille sighed into her hair, "I love you, but our being together is something not allowed us here."

"It doesn't matter to me what's allowed," she answered. "What matters is that we're alone, and we want each other." She untied the lacy bow of her dress, exposing her shapely young breasts. "Please Achille," she murmured, "please kiss me here and here . . ."

The two slipped into the house and up to the tempestuous young woman's room. Quickly they undressed and fell into each other's arms, squealing like pups at the miracle of each other's loving touch.

"Achille, I want to belong to you," she said. "We can't ever be together in the real world, but here we can have each other, right now."

Throbbing with anticipation, Achille eased his manhood into the warm, moist cleft between her thighs. He thrust gently, fearful of hurting the inexperienced young girl. They hugged each other as Ysabel gave a small gasp of pain, and then began to rock back and forth until the uncontrollable spasms of their love overcame them both.

The young couple explored each other's bodies until

the early hours of the dawn, bringing each other to incredible explosions of passionate feeling. Somberly the two exchanged deep kisses and meaningful vows of love. As the sounds of the kitchen slaves at their chores reached their bedroom door, Achille checked the hallway, and then flew from her room.

๛ 49

Sparked by a series of provocative events—the election of Abraham Lincoln, the secession of South Carolina, Florida, Georgia, and Alabama, the formation of the Confederate States of America with Jefferson Davis as president—the War Between the States burst into full flame on April 12, 1861, with the firing on Fort Sumter. Most of the populace in both the North and the South believed the war would be over quickly, little more than a series of skirmishes. The Fort Sumter incident was treated as a popular amusement by the citizens of Charleston, South Carolina, who followed the action from carriages along the waterfront, on rooftops and other vantage points around the city, in much the same spirit as they would a spectator sport. Few persons on that fateful spring day envisioned, as they watched Confederate shells bursting inside the federal fort, that this event heralded the start of a civil war which would bring four long years of turmoil, bloodshed, and destruction, resulting in the near annihilation of the South.

Among the young men of Louisiana spirits ran high. For months they had been eagerly anticipating the war, drilling with their various military units, anxious to exercise their skills on the battlefield, tensely awaiting Lincoln's first move against the newly-formed Confederacy, and now it was suddenly a reality. By horseback, train, boat, and on foot volunteers streamed into New Orleans from the outlying parishes, joining up in record numbers, anxious to head north to Virginia where everyone was certain the real action would be. Naive and inexperienced, they had no true idea of the grim realities of war nor their own vulnerability.

Such serious concerns did not hasten Jim's recovery. Although still not permitted to climb stairs, Jim continued to walk about the second floor where he would sit on the gallery in the warm spring sun and gaze out over the endless fields of cane and the smoking chimneys of the sugar mills, wondering how and if the plantation would survive the war. As he contemplated the fate of all he had worked so hard to achieve, he felt angry, frustrated, and helpless, unable to understand why he had to be disabled at such a crucial time. Yet he was grateful that fate during this same period had brought him together with Achille. The boy was proving a godsend, doing an exemplary job as deputy. Having initially overcome tremendous obstacles, he displayed great tenacity and drive as well as interest in the operation of the plantation. How much more like himself was this bastard son, Jim often mused, than Antoine, but such were the ironies of life. He speculated, too, about the effects the war might have on the lives of the two boys, both so close in age, one already in the army and the other virtually running the plantation.

Although Achille and Ysabel were most circumspect in their behavior toward one another, their mutual interest and affection had not escaped the perceptive eyes of the house slaves who held varying attitudes about the relationship.

Curiously, however, the romance between Achille and Ysabel seemed totally and mysteriously to have escaped Odile's attention, although everyone else at Mandragore was quite aware of it.

"She must be blind," Lavinia muttered as she and Verbena were shucking corn one day in the warming kitchen.

"No, it's just that something like that happening don't ever cross Miss Odile's mind," Verbena said.

"You mean a colored boy with a white girl?" Lavinia questioned.

"That's right," Verbena replied, adding as a well-considered afterthought, "but if she knew some of the things I know, she might not be so surprised."

"What do you mean by that?" Lavinia questioned.

"Never you mind," Verbena snapped.

"I think it would kill Miss Odile if she ever found out about Achille and Miss Ysabel," Lavinia went on.

"I know one thing," Verbena said. "I ain't going to be the one to tell her."

If, indeed, Odile had observed the secret smiles, the covert glances, the subtle touching of hands between the young pair, she gave no indication of any such knowledge. Her relations with Ysabel remained loving, maternal, and cordial while continuing to treat Achille as though he didn't exist. Fortunately, although under the same roof, their paths rarely crossed and when they did, Odile refused to speak to him, sit at the same table, or be present in the same room. Knowing that it would be useless to invoke any sanctions against him with Ysabel, Odile permitted the girl to do as she pleased with respect to Achille, rarely reproaching her for her amicable attitude toward the youth.

Chronically weary and over-worked, Achille nevertheless forged ahead, goaded by the same compulsions that drove his father. Very often he worked sixteen to twenty hours a day, his only pleasure and relaxation being whatever few moments he was able to steal from his duties to be with Ysabel.

"You have no life at all except work and the plantation," she said wistfully as they rode together in the calèche to New Orleans. One of Jim's ships was expected with a load of fine French silks—luxury goods were becoming scarce—and he had promised her she could have the first selection from among the brightly colored bolts of fabric. "I hardly see you," she said with a slight pout. "Perhaps cousin Odile is right. Perhaps I should return to Cuba before there is a blockade and I am forced to stay for the duration of the war."

"Cousin Odile is never right about anything," he remarked.

"I'm not sure. . . ." Ysabel began.

Taking her hand in his, he looked imploringly into her dark eyes. "Would you really leave?"

"I have been thinking about it," she admitted. "My mother is afraid with the war. She wants me to return to Havana."

"But what about me? About us?" Achille pressed.

"You? Whenever I see you—and that's not often —you are exhausted and nearly falling asleep," she complained. "It is as though I am not with you at all."

"Is being with me important to you?" he asked.

"Why do you question it?"

"I must know," he murmured.

"Yes," she sighed. "Very important."

With that, he leaned over and kissed her passionately, eliciting the first smile from her he had seen in days.

One year from its inception, the War Between the States continued to rage with the bloody Battle of Shiloh commemorating its anniversary. At Shiloh, or Pittsburg Landing, Tennessee, the Union Army under Grant and the Confederate Army under Generals Johnston and Beauregard waged a ruinous and mutually destructive battle against one another. General Johnston was killed and the engagement ended indecisively.

A few weeks later, near the end of April 1862, exactly what Jim MacKay had been fearing all along finally occurred in New Orleans. David Farragut and a fleet of twenty-one schooners and seventeen warships sailed up the mouth of the mighty Mississippi and bombarded Forts Jackson and St. Philip with mortars. Although the barrage failed to defeat the valiant defenders of the forts, the Federal navy managed to cut the chain barrier across the river and get most of the fleet boldly past the defenses despite fierce resistance and retaliatory attacks on the Union ships by Confederate rams. Once past the forts, Farragut was able to sail the seventy-five miles up-river to the Crescent City, now virtually undefended.

News that Yankee ships had successfully overcome the defending forts was telegraphed ahead to the city where the frantic, terrified populace was awakened by the cacophonous tolling of nearly every bell in town. All shops and businesses were closed and transportation came to a standstill as everyone raced down to the levees. All along the river hysterical crowds burned bales of cotton and stocks of corn, sugar, and rice as well as ships to prevent their falling into enemy hands. On April 25, 1862, Farragut's fleet dropped anchor in New Orleans harbor, and he immediately dispatched emissaries to demand the city's surrender. With no means to combat such a formidable naval force, Lovell, the Confederate general in charge of the city's defense, evacuated his troops, and essentially delivered it into Union hands without a fight.

Although black smoke from the cotton and other commodities burning on the levees could be seen for miles up the river, details of the Federal navy's capture of New Orleans reached Mandragore slowly, in bits and pieces, most of the accounts exaggerated.

In recent months, Jim MacKay had made excellent progress with regard to his health. Dr. Zehner now permitted him to go about the plantation for several hours a day, usually in the company of Achille, and to once again take an active part in daily affairs.

One day while attempting to get information from Cecil who had just returned from the city on an errand, Jim and Achille were hailed by Nestor Gaudet, who had ridden down from LeRepose, his cotton plantation near Florestal.

"Have you heard the news?" Gaudet asked excitedly.

"I've heard rumors that Moore surrendered the city to the Yankees," Jim replied.

"That's correct," Gaudet said, dismounting and wiping his perspiring forehead with a handkerchief. "With those Yankees taking the city, we're going to be stuck with more cotton than anybody knows what to do with. There won't be a single ship allowed in or out of the harbor except Union gunboats."

"That's probably true," Jim nodded.

"What do you plan to do about the contract for my cotton which you and I negotiated earlier this year?" Gaudet asked.

"Plan to do about it?" Jim repeated with a puzzled frown.

"You've got to honor it, Jim, otherwise I'm going to be burdened with a lot of surplus cotton I can't dispose of. I don't want it falling into Yankee hands. And I don't want to burn it either. Then, there's the matter of the loans from the bank on this year's crop. They're going to be after me."

"I understand your concern," Jim said.

"That doesn't help me much unless you plan to do something about it," Gaudet replied. "What is the status of our contract?"

Not wishing Jim's health to suffer a setback because of undue stress that Gaudet might bring to bear, Achille decided to intervene on his father's behalf, although he was fully aware that planters such as Gaudet bitterly resented Jim's acknowledgment of him— a former slave—as his offspring. Usually he tried to remain as silent and as unobtrusive as possible, sticking close to the everyday workings of the plantation and leaving negotiations and dealings with the neighboring planters to Jim, but this was one occasion he could not. "You have nothing to worry about, Monsieur Gaudet," he declared. "The contract you hold will be honored. I promise you that you will not be burdened with worthless cotton. My father and I will assume all responsibility for it, just as agreed."

Considering Achille's words, Gaudet looked to Jim for a confirmation of what his son had just said.

Without having an idea of exactly what strategy Achille had in mind—especially in the light of recent events—Jim, trusting the boy's judgment and keen mind, replied, "Yes, Nestor, that's correct."

"But if our harbor is blockaded by Yankee gunboats how do you propose to ship the cotton?" Gaudet persisted.

For a second time Achille stepped in and came to Jim's rescue. "We have a certain plan for the cotton which the present political situation doesn't preclude," he said.

Looking surprised, Gaudet questioned, "And what is that?"

Although his inquiry was addressed directly to Jim, Achille once again replied, "I'm sorry, Monsieur Gaudet, but I am not permitted to reveal it at this time. I'm sure you understand."

Fully accepting such an evasive explanation, Gaudet agreed, "Yes. Yes, of course."

Without further ado, Gaudet bade them good-bye and was off in pursuit of more news of the Yankee invasion.

When they were alone, Jim turned to Achille. "Well, son, you certainly helped me get out of that one," he said. "But tell me, just what *are* we going to do with all that cotton? We certainly can't ship it anywhere, and if we store it here—and our storage facilities are severely limited—the Yankees will find it easily and confiscate it."

Smiling, Achille explained, "We will continue to purchase all the cotton we have contracted for, just as we have been doing, even though we can't ship it. What I propose is that we build huge, enormous sheds far back in the bayou, beyond the swamps—storage sheds out over the water supported on pilings driven into the ground. The Yankees would never search there for cotton. They know nothing of how to navigate our swamps and bayous. Besides, I suspect they would be frightened to penetrate them too deeply. They will undoubtedly search the plantation, but I'm certain they'll stop short of the swamps and the bayous."

His interest piqued, Jim urged, "Yes, go on, Achille. I want to hear more of this plan."

"When the war is over, France and England will have depleted whatever stores of cotton they now have and will be desperate for more. Since no one will have any because they haven't been able to plant during the war, cotton will be very scarce and the price for it very high. No one will have cotton for sale—

except Mandragore. We will have all the cotton we have been storing in our bayou sheds for one, two, three or however many years the war continues. I've already conferred with Roger Guillon. He and I have come up with a design for the sheds which is cheap and easy to construct, and yet will adequately protect the cotton while it's stored. Don't you see what a good plan this is? We will have cotton when no one else has it, and we'll get top prices for it as well."

Shortly after Farragut's siege and capture of New Orleans, General Benjamin Franklin Butler, commander of the Union forces, moved in with his troops and began the official occupation of the city. Because of his harsh treatment of the citizens, Butler soon earned the nickname of "The Beast" or "Beast Butler." Among the particularly offensive measures he instituted as part of the occupation were a series of punitive enactments which included special taxes levied against supporters of the Confederacy, freeing of slaves who disclosed information against their owners, and forcing all citizens over eighteen to take an oath of allegiance to the Union. In addition, Butler dispatched soldiers with orders to search all private homes in the area for arms. During the search, note was made of valuables at each house or plantation and plans made for future confiscation. In addition to earning a reputation for being particularly severe, Butler was purported to be a thief and economic opportunist as well, accused by some of the inhabitants of the city of appropriating their silver and other property. "The Beast" in some circles was also known as "Silver Spoons" Butler. Both he and his troops were thoroughly despised, women in particular being especially virulent in their hatred, often spitting in the faces of Union soldiers or striking them with their purses as they stood guarding important buildings or on street corners. The resistance on the part of the New Orleans females led to Butler's issuing the notorious "Women's Order," a proclamation which declared that any woman insulting or annoying a Union soldier would be treated as a common prostitute and punished accordingly.

Although not an official resident of New Orleans, Odile was infuriated by this order as well as by the Federal occupation of the city she knew and loved since childhood.

"Our beautiful city is daily being desecrated by these uncouth and barbarous Yankees," she complained bitterly.

Although Jim had asked her to avoid trouble by staying out of the city, not only because he feared for her safety but also because he didn't want the horse and carriage confiscated, Odile nevertheless decided to ignore his admonitions one day and go in the company of Ysabel. Ordering Cecil to park the carriage in front of the cathedral, figuring it would be safest there, she and Ysabel got out and decided to walk to one of the infamous blockade stores—shops which stocked scarce goods smuggled into the city in ships that had risked Union blockade.

Because of the exorbitantly high prices of the goods at the store, the great majority of the women who jammed it were from the wealthy, privileged classes, ready to fight viciously over a bolt of fine silk or a tiny bottle of French perfume smuggled in by the daring and intrepid blockade runners who were willing to risk their necks for the huge profits.

Successfully wresting a bolt of fine Italian velvet from an expensively dressed octoroon, obviously the mistress of a well-heeled planter, Odile declared to Ysabel, "I shall have Verbena fashion you a fine dress from this velvet."

"Why do I need a new dress?" Ysabel questioned. "Where would I wear it? There are no parties, no balls, nothing while the boys are all away fighting."

"True," Odile agreed. "But when our brave boys return, all the other girls will be wearing frumpy old rags of dresses. Material for new ones will be as scarce as hen's teeth after the war ends. But you, my dear, will be resplendent in a new dress. I want you to save it especially for Antoine's homecoming. Even if I have to pawn everything I own, I intend to have the most glorious and grandest celebration in the parish for my boy. Ah, I shall be so happy and relieved to have Antoine at Mandragore again! You don't know how awful it has been for me since he's been gone. I am sick with worry day and night." Then, suddenly clasping Ysabel's hand between her own, she smiled and spoke in a brighter tone. "Oh, wait until Antoine sees you and how downright lovely you've gotten since he's been gone! Will he be surprised! I'm sure he won't treat you like some pesky little sister any more. Oh, Ysabel, honey, do you know what my fondest desire in the whole world is? It's that one day you and Antoine . . ."

Uncomfortable with the trend of what her cousin was saying, Ysabel interrupted, "Oh, please, cousin Odile . . ."

Undaunted, Odile insisted on finishing her sentence. ". . . that one day you and Antoine will be married. Oh, I would be so pleased!"

When they left the blockade store, Ysabel persuaded Odile it was their moral obligation to pay a call on Eugénie at the Ursuline convent. Since the occupation of New Orleans by Union troops, Odile disliked calling on the nuns. The obvious deprivations the sisters were suffering made her feel guilty and ashamed of her own somewhat more comfortable life. As Cecil drove from the cathedral to the convent, Odile hid the bolt of velvet and the other articles they had purchased at the blockade store beneath the seat of the carriage. In her own way, she had tried to aid the sisters at the convent as best she could, but Mandragore itself was short of food. Because of the war, planting had been limited and, in addition, Federal troops periodically raided the plantation, confiscating much of their foodstuffs and livestock. Because rumors had reached the avaricious Butler that enormous stores of cotton were hidden there, Mandragore was searched more frequently and more thoroughly than most of the outlying plantations. Both Jim and Achille feared that one day the Federal soldiers might actually venture back beyond the swamps into the bayou and discover the concealed cotton, so they purposely encouraged tales of alligators, cottonmouths, bears, mountain lions, and rattlesnakes as well as supernatural occurrences often ascribed to such remote locales.

At the convent, Eugénie was delighted to see them, especially Ysabel whom she always regarded in a special way. Taking each by the hand, she led the two visitors to the former herb garden which the sisters had now transformed to a vegetable patch, growing okra, tomatoes, eggplant, onions, squash, and assorted melons. Beneath her worn and unstarched wimple, Eugénie appeared pale and drawn.

"And how are things at Mandragore?" she asked, sitting between them on the wrought iron bench.

"Somehow we are managing to survive," Odile sighed.

"And Jim?" Eugénie asked. "How is he getting along?"

"Much better. Dr. Zehner now permits him to go into the fields for a few hours a day," Odile replied.

"And Achille is still with you?" the nun questioned a bit cautiously.

Odile sighed again. "Unfortunately, yes."

Responding to an irresistible urge to defend the youth, Ysabel said, "Achille is a great help to cousin Jim. I don't think that the plantation could function without him."

"Nonsense!" Odile reproached. Then attempting to suppress the annoyance she felt at Ysabel's defense, she continued, "When Antoine returns from the war, there will be no further need of Achille at Mandragore —thank God."

"And my dear nephew?" Eugénie asked anxiously. "What news have you had of him?"

"The last letter I received was from Virginia," Odile revealed. "Antoine was fighting under General Lee. My, what a magnificent and brilliant general he is! The South can truly be proud of Robert E. Lee. You can be sure that if we had had him here in Louisiana, New Orleans would never have been made to suffer this terrible humiliation. We are a conquered people. Do you realize that, Eugénie?"

"Of course I do," Eugénie replied, smoothing the folds of her habit. Then turning to Ysabel, she caressed the girl's face with the tips of her fingers. "My, how lovely you are, child. If all our young men were not away at war, you would be turning many a head, the belle of every ball," she said.

"Ysabel is very clever as well as pretty," Odile quickly pointed out. "She has Valdéz blood in her veins."

"Naturally," Eugénie nodded. "After all, her grandmother, Carlota, and our mother were sisters."

"True," Odile murmured.

"How are your grandmother and Beatriz?" Eugénie inquired of Ysabel, referring to the girl's mother by her Christian name.

Fingering the miniature portrait of her attractive mother on a black velvet ribbon about her neck, Ysabel sadly replied, "There has been no mail from Cuba for more than a month."

Gazing curiously at the miniature, Eugénie asked, "Tell me, child, do you favor more your mother or father in looks?"

"Oh, Papa," Ysabel replied, laughing. "Mama is quite dark and her hair and features rather coarse."

"That's odd," Eugénie mused. "I wonder who Beatriz takes after. Neither Aunt Carlota nor Uncle Jorge are dark in the least and their features are rather fine."

"Yes, that's true," Ysabel admitted. "Mama used to tell me that when she was very young everyone was always teasing her and telling her she was a foundling left on my grandmother's doorstep. Grandmother never liked that sort of teasing."

"Indeed? A foundling?" Eugénie considered, more to herself than the other two women.

✣ 50

As the months of 1862 rolled by, the war seemed, for the most part, to be going quite favorably for the South. General Lee was now commanding the armies of eastern Virginia and North Carolina, sending the Union soldiers retreating at the end of the seven-day battle of Malvern Hill. In August, Stonewall Jackson defeated Union forces at Cedar Mountain, Virginia, and captured Harpers Ferry in September, together with a vast quantity of materiel and 12,500 men.

In spite of the fact that New Orleans was an occupied city, optimism ran high up and down the river. Everyone was sure that the Confederacy would soon win the war. Regardless of Southern gains on the battlefield, Jim still believed, as he had from the beginning, that the war was a disastrous folly which would eventually bring the entire South to its knees, despite the euphoria attending these victories and the clear superiority of the Confederate military leaders.

"We don't have the numbers of men, we don't have the factories and we can't get supplies with the blockade in effect," he pointed out to Henri Pilette, Nestor Gaudet, and Valentin Chardonnier one day when, seated on the gallery of Mandragore, they proposed a toast to the string of recent victories.

"Nevertheless we will win," Henri Pilette insisted. "We have the will to win and that is what's important."

"It takes more than the will," Jim reminded him. "Don't forget we have only one-third the total population of the United States. The North has two-thirds. We're outnumbered."

"No, no," Valentin Chardonnier disagreed. "A will is everything."

Fully recovered from his heart attack, but left permanently weakened by it, Jim hated the war and cursed all those Southern radicals who had foisted it upon the majority. Mandragore was in desperate straits—as was Laureldale, Palmetto Place and Le-Repose—despite his and Achille's exhaustive efforts to sustain it. The slaves were less unruly than on some of the surrounding plantations, but discipline, especially with Oberdorfer still nursing a grudge against Achille's ascendancy to a position of authority, was difficult, aggravated by the shortage of food and lack of work because of the curtailment in planting. Periodically, the Union forces raided the various plantations and drafted the very slaves they were supposedly fighting to free to work on the railroads, build roads, and repair levees. The slaves, Jim noted, no more enjoyed working for their Northern masters than they did for Southerners, although the Northerners paid them a token wage for their labors.

For her part, Odile witnessed with despair what was transpiring around her—the crumbling of her whole way of life, the total annihilation of the only society she had ever known. At first, she tried to deny the destruction and humiliation she saw, gallantly upholding the belief that all the things she valued would soon be reestablished. After a time, however, she was no longer able to display this courageous, confident attitude and began to retreat to a world of her own making, a world that encompassed little more than her bedroom and the chapel. Her sewing circles and quilting bees had become serious affairs where she and her peers, Louise Chardonnier, Anais Seguin, Victorine Pilette and Marianne Anspacher, stitched Confederate uniforms from cloth woven in their homes, just as it was on looms of nearly every house in the South.

On a more personal level, her anguish was severely aggravated by a lack of news from Antoine in recent weeks. His last letter informed them that he was in Virginia fighting under Lee and hinted that the esteemed commander might be planning to invade the

North. The youth had seemed excited by such a prospect. In the past, his letters had been sporadic at best and she probably would not have been so concerned if she hadn't had the persistent premonition that something was wrong.

One morning shortly after dawn, Jim awoke with alarm when he realized that Odile hadn't been to bed the entire night. The pillow on her side of the bed was smooth and uncreased. Calling for Verbena, he demanded, "Where is Miss Odile?"

"Last I seen her, Mister Jim, she was out in the chapel," the elderly maid answered.

"When was that?"

"Last evening."

Dressing hurriedly, Jim went to the chapel but saw no one as he opened the door. The building was dark except for a few scattered rays of morning sunlight filtering through the single stained glass window. Odile was nowhere in sight. Walking instinctively to the altar, he saw someone lying on the first pew.

"Odile?" he said.

Awakening with a startled gasp, she sat up and stared at him bewildered, as though unsure of the hour or exactly where she was.

"I'm sorry. I didn't mean to startle you," he apologized.

Reaching out her hand, she allowed him to take it and help her to her feet.

"You slept here all night, didn't you?" he asked.

"Yes, I suppose I did," she replied.

"You should never stay out here alone," he warned. "It's very dangerous with so many freed slaves and Union soldiers wandering around."

"I know I shouldn't," she agreed. "I came out to pray early in the evening. I must have gotten tired and laid down to rest a moment and fallen asleep."

"I should have come looking for you when you weren't in bed," Jim said. Since his heart attack he tired much more easily and had been advised by Dr. Zehner to retire early. Thus, it really wasn't so unusual for him to be in bed before his wife.

"I was all right," she assured him. "Antoine is the one we must be concerned about."

"There's little we can do," Jim said.

"I know," she conceded sadly. "I merely pray and ask our Lord to watch over him. Nevertheless, I'm so fearful, Jim."

"You mustn't be."

"But I am," she insisted as he led her out of the gloomy chapel into the morning sun. "So full of fear."

Sitting at the loom in the upstairs sewing room weaving the coarse cloth for Confederate uniforms, Ysabel was the first to spot the wagon carrying two Union soldiers as it headed through the gates of Mandragore.

"Some Yankee soldiers are coming up the carriageway," she called down the stairwell to Jim who was in his study.

Going to the window, Jim saw that the girl was indeed correct. Generally, in the past the soldiers had come on horseback, and he wondered—with some apprehension—why they were arriving this time with a wagon.

"My God, what's left for them to carry off?" Odile moaned as she joined him from the music room across the hall. "They've robbed us of everything we've got. What are these accursed Yankees trying to do—starve us to death? We wouldn't be so harassed if it wasn't for that cotton you've got hidden back in the bayou."

"We're not being singled out for any particular sort of harassment. The cotton has nothing to do with it," he assured her. "All the plantations around here are suffering the same kind of treatment we are from 'Beast' butler and his men. You heard Henri Pilette say the other day the trouble they've had at Palmetto Place. They're down to a single cow."

"Why don't you just go on and give Butler that cotton if that's what he wants," she urged, ignoring his arguments to the contrary. "Maybe then he'll leave us alone."

"That won't make him stop his searches and seizures," Jim said.

"It's all Achille's fault," she went on. "Hoarding all

that cotton was his idea. I don't care if he is your son, he's a devil and out to destroy us all."

"Whether you like it or not, Odile, Achille happens to be responsible for the fact that we've survived at all this past year," Jim asserted.

"Hah!" she scoffed.

"With me being so sick and Antoine away, this plantation would surely have gone under if it weren't for that boy," he said.

"Go on and defend him if you want to," she chided. "I say he's the very devil and will bring us all to ruin."

As the Union soldiers rumbled through the porte cochere, Jim was surprised to see that a third occupant lay on the floor of the wagon. Odile, too, saw him at the same instant.

"Antoine!" she cried, racing out of the house. "I just know it's Antoine! I know that's my son in that wagon! I've had a premonition for weeks he was coming home soon. Antoine! Antoine! At last you've come back to me!"

As the third man in the wagon sat up and peered curiously over the sideboard—he looked as though he had been sleeping—Jim observed that he was wearing the remains of a Confederate uniform. Startled, Jim realized that Odile was right. It was Antoine! Despite Dr. Zehner's repeated admonitions not to exert himself and to avoid excitement, Jim found himself dashing down to the porte cochere after his wife.

Hearing the commotion, Ysabel abandoned her loom and hurried downstairs. As she reached the back gallery she, too, was astonished to see Antoine sitting in the Union wagon. Wanting to rush forward and greet the returning soldier, she nevertheless restrained her impulse and hung back, allowing Jim and Odile to be the first. Strangely, at that moment, her thoughts were not of Antoine but of Achille who, that very morning, was somewhere around the plantation trying to scratch their survival out of the stubborn, neglected soil.

Poor Achille, she fretted. *I'm sure there's going to be trouble now.*

Although Jim loved Antoine dearly despite the many conflicts between them, he, too, found himself full of misgivings about his unexpected return, and hoped his presence would not mean new trouble—something Mandragore didn't need. They had already suffered enough privations and difficulties.

Jim's first thoughts were not to question why Antoine was suddenly home, escorted by two Union soldiers. Certainly, he wasn't on leave. It was also doubtful that they would return a prisoner to his home at this crucial point in the war. *Why, then, was he there?* Something was seriously amiss and Jim dreaded to think what it might be.

"Oh, Antoine! Darling! Dearest boy!" Odile cried. "Get out of that wagon and let me hold you! Let me put my arms around you! I've missed you so!"

In the cookhouse where she was supervising the boiling of butternuts from which the dye for the Confederate uniforms was extracted, Verbena heard the excitement and ran toward the house, closely followed by Romulus and Lavinia. "Mister Antoine! Mister Antoine!" they cried in unison.

Turning to Jim, one of the Union soldiers said, "He's going to need some help, sir."

Puzzled, Jim asked, "What do you mean?"

Remaining silent all the while, Antoine sullenly picked up a crude wooden crutch from the floor of the wagon. At the sight of it, a feeling of dread swept over the assembled group.

"Did you break your leg, dearest?" Odile asked anxiously. When Antoine didn't answer, she turned to the soldiers. "Did he break his leg?" she repeated.

"No, ma'am," one of them answered, averting her imploring gaze.

"Then what on earth is that crutch for?" she persisted.

Placing Antoine's arms across their shoulders, the Union soldiers hoisted him over the side of the wagon to the ground. Jim, Odile, Ysabel and the slaves looked on in horror as an empty trouser leg, folded over and pinned closed at the cuff, flapped loosely from his hip in the languid autumn breeze.

❧ 51

If Antoine had been willful, impulsive, and temperamental before going off to war, he was all those things and more since his return. Sullen, ill-tempered and hostile, he cursed and mistreated the slaves without provocation, found fault with everyone and everything, often refused to speak to anyone for days and in general proved to be a seriously disruptive presence in the household. No one seemed exempt from his abuse —not even his mother who adored him and empathized excruciatingly with his plight, perhaps suffering the tragedy of his amputated leg more than he himself did. At times, Jim found his patience getting short with the youth but in deference to the loss he suffered in the war, he refrained from reproaching him, even when his behavior became especially reprehensible.

"It's a terrible blow to him. If only he hadn't been such an active youth . . . if he were only more like Narciso," Odile lamented.

"I know what it's like to have one's activities suddenly curtailed," Jim reminded her, referring, of course, to his own heart attack.

"But you weren't in the prime of youth, like Antoine," she retorted. "It's much worse for him."

Achille, correctly surmising that if he remained in the main house he would be the principal target of Antoine's wrath and frustration, transferred his belongings to the empty *garçonnière*—the formal dining room was converted into a bedroom for Antoine so that he would not have to climb more stairs than necessary. His move was not prompted by fear or intimidation but because Achille wished to spare the others, especially Jim and Ysabel, any possibly distressing incidents

385

which might arise from his continued presence in the house.

Strangely enough, the only member of the household who seemed to escape most of Antoine's abuse was Ysabel. Prior to his going off to the army, he paid her scant attention, but now she seemed to be the one person whom he treated with a modicum of civility. Only in response to her gentle coaxing—instigated by Odile—would he accept clean clothes, eat meals regularly and allow the slaves to enter his new quarters to clean and dust and change the linens on his bed. Preferring silent, brooding solitude most of the time, Antoine occasionally asked Ysabel—in a rather oblique fashion—to join him in a game of dominoes or checkers, but she was the only one so invited, much to his mother's chagrin. Odile longed to be close to her son once again, to soothe and comfort him and sympathize with his loss.

Because of Ysabel's apparently privileged position, the girl eventually fell into the role of emissary for the rest of the family, serving as liaison between Antoine and the others.

One day as the two of them, Antoine and Ysabel, were playing euchre, he suddenly raised his eyes from the cards before them and asked, "Where's that cowardly half-nigger been hiding himself?"

Refusing to acknowledge that such a description could be Achille, Ysabel stared at him blankly. "Who are you referring to?" she asked.

"You know perfectly well—don't pretend you don't," he said.

Ysabel smiled innocently. "No, Antoine, I don't."

"Achille."

"He hasn't been hiding. He's here," she answered casually.

"Not in the house," he corrected.

"No. He's staying out in the *garçonnière* for a while."

"Why? Is he afraid of something?"

Responding to his question with another, she said, "What would he be afraid of?"

"Facing me," Antoine said, reaching for a cigar

from the humidor. Since his return he was smoking excessively and had ceased to ask women present for permission to do so.

"No, I don't think Achille is afraid of you," she said. "Why should he be? He's done nothing to harm you."

"Then why is he staying away from the house?"

"Maybe he doesn't want trouble," she speculated.

"If there's any trouble here, it's because of him," he asserted.

"For trouble, there must be two people," she said.

Antoine let the smoke escape slowly from his lips and narrowed his eyes suspiciously. "Why are you always taking his side?" he said.

"I take no one's side," she denied.

"You're sweet on him, aren't you?" he guessed correctly.

Ysabel hoped her complexion would successfully conceal the blush she felt creeping into her cheeks. "Achille is very kind. He works hard so that the plantation will survive the war and these terrible times. He's good to everyone."

Interrupting, he said, "Especially to you—correct?"

"To everyone," she repeated. "To your father, your mother, the slaves, everyone."

"But especially to you," he persisted.

"Yes, he's good to me," she admitted. "But no more than to anyone else. The times are very difficult for all of us. Achille tries to help us survive."

Antoine scowled. " 'Survive,' " he quoted. "What do you know about survival? What do you know about this war?"

"Well, I admit I am a foreigner," she conceded.

Waving the lighted cigar in her face, he said, "You know nothing. You know nothing about this war or anything else. Do you have any idea what it was like on those battlefields in Virginia and Tennessee and Maryland?"

"How could I, Antoine?" she replied helplessly.

"I'll tell you what it was like—it was hell. That's what it was. Sleeping in the mud, nothing to eat except salt pork and hardtack, everyone all around bleeding, wounded and dead, having your horse shot out from under you, burying all your best friends."

Laying her hand sympathetically over his, she said, "I'm sorry. Truly, I am."

Agitated rather than quieted by her sympathy, he blurted, "How would you like to be me? Shall I tell you about how they amputated my leg? Shall I?"

Growing uncomfortable, Ysabel attempted to divert his attention to the cards before them once more. "Shall we continue the game?" she suggested.

Grabbing her chin, he raised her head and forced her to look directly at him. "Shall I tell you what it feels like to lose a leg?" he persisted, his voice seething with anger and bitterness. "Shall I tell you about the way I was operated on in a filthy field hospital full of thousands of men dying of their wounds, dysentery, fever, pneumonia, and every other affliction known to man . . . operated on by a butcher if there ever was one. The only things they gave me before they sawed off my leg was some opium and a shot of whiskey. Thank God the men around me were screaming so loud that I couldn't hear my own screams. . . ."

Unable to bear any more of his story, Ysabel clasped her hands over her ears, pleading, "Please, Antoine, stop. I don't want to hear any more."

"Well, you're going to, whether you like it or not," he said, and with one quick move, jerked her hands away from her ears, overturning the card table at the same time and splashing the glass of port he was drinking all over the front of her dress. Jumping to her feet, Ysabel dabbed helplessly at the enormous red stain with her handkerchief, tears filling her eyes. Realizing the futility not only of attempting to remove the stain from the fabric, but in relating to someone as inwardly bitter and angry as he, Ysabel burst into sobs and ran from the room.

Grabbing his crutch, he hobbled after her, shouting down the hall, "Go! Go on! Go to that lily-livered half-nigger of yours. Go tell him to stop hiding and come in here and face me like a man. Go tell him I want to see him. Go on, you deceiving little bitch, tell him!"

Refusing to let either Antoine's presence or antics intimidate him, Achille entered the main house whenever necessary. Even though he sympathized with his half-brother's having lost a leg in the war, Achille felt Antoine was being indulged to too great an extent by the family and from all reports was more difficult and tyrannical than ever.

"That boy is turning the house into a living hell," Verbena declared one day as she swept his room in the *garçonnière*. "Miss Ysabel is the only one he's halfway decent to and sometimes he ain't even civil to her."

Although Achille disliked admitting it, it distressed him that Ysabel seemed to be the only one with whom Antoine was willing to deal on any kind of a rational basis.

"He's horrible to everyone else," Ysabel said one day as she and Achille stole a few moments together and sat on the velvet settee in the music room. Although Antoine's bedroom was next door, he shunned the music room, unabashedly proclaiming his hatred for music since losing his leg.

"I guess it's because he loved to dance so much," Ysabel said wistfully. "Cousin Odile and I must wait until he leaves his room and goes outside before we practice the piano or harp. Once, I dared to play when he was next door and he threatened to smash the piano. I think he would have if it had been cousin Odile instead of me."

"I think Antoine has been getting away with entirely too much nonsense—disability or not," Achille said.

"This morning cousin Jim and Dr. Zehner tried to convince him that he must go into the city and have a wooden leg made. He became so furious at their suggestion that he threw a full chamberpot at them. It seems he prefers to hobble about the house on that single crutch," she continued.

"Well, if that's what he prefers, let him hobble," Achille said indifferently, growing impatient with the way Antoine seemed to be dominating their conversation, as happened so frequently lately.

"He falls all the time," Ysabel went on, failing to sense Achille's displeasure with the fact that Antoine remained the topic of conversation. "Yesterday he fell three times and the last time when Romulus went to help him up, he struck the poor old man with the crutch."

"The slaves should stop fussing over him," Achille said.

"He refuses to get an artificial limb, even when I try to convince him. All the time he says, 'Let the world see what I gave for the cause of our glorious Confederacy.' I don't know what to do," she sighed.

"It's not your responsibility to do anything," Achille said. "Antoine is not a child who must be wheedled and coaxed into doing what's best for him. He's got to learn to live with his disability and take care of himself. There's been much in my life I've had to contend with. Why shouldn't he?"

"I know you're right," she admitted. "Yet, still I feel very bad. I feel so sorry for him."

Taking her hand in his, Achille pressed it to his lips. "Enough of Antoine," he said. "Let's talk about us. Ah, Ysabel, how I long to take you in my arms. It seems that lately it's so difficult for us to be together."

"Since Antoine came home," she added, snuggling closer to him.

Lulled by the balmy breezes wafting through the open French windows leading to the gallery, Ysabel rested her head on Achille's shoulder, and he put his arm protectively around her, kissing her face, her hair, her lips.

"Ysabel, Ysabel, how I long for you!" he declared.

"You mustn't talk like that," she cautioned. "It's not proper. Someone might hear."

"Who?"

"One never knows. . . ."

Just as she said it, the peculiar familiar clomping sound outside on the gallery announced Antoine was near.

"Antoine! . . ." she gasped, attempting to slide away from Achille, but he held her fast.

"Why should we hide our feeling for one another any longer?" he demanded.

Ysabel continued to struggle to free herself. "Please, Achille. . . ."

"He's got to find out what the situation between us is sometime. Let him find out now."

"No, Achille. . . ." she protested.

Entering through the window, Antoine was stunned to see the two of them together on the settee in what he regarded as a highly compromising situation. "You nigger bastard!" he shouted. "You filthy scum! Take your hands off that white woman at once before I kill you!"

Before Achille could reply or make a single move, Antoine threw his crutch aside and made a dive for him, clamped his hands around Achille's throat and knocked Ysabel to the floor.

Bracing his single foot against the leg of the nearby piano, Antoine forced Achille deep into the velvet upholstery of the delicate settee, closing his hands ever more tightly around his rival's throat.

Stunned by her fall and the rapid succession of events, Ysabel tried to figure out what was actually transpiring. When it was clear to her that Antoine was trying to strangle Achille, she cried, "For God's sake, Antoine, stop!"

Taken by surprise by the attack, Achille, pinned to the settee, found it difficult to defend himself because his opponent's strong hands were rapidly cutting off his windpipe.

With a desperate surge of strength, Achille arched his back and managed to move to one side just quickly enough to knock his assailant off balance. Together, the two of them rolled off the settee and onto the floor where Achille tried to break the viselike grip Antoine had managed to maintain on his throat despite the fall.

Realizing she herself could do little to stop the two young men from killing one another, Ysabel dashed out of the room, hoping to summon Jim or Romulus or someone to help break up the fight.

As Antoine's hands squeezed still tighter around his half-brother's neck, bright points of light began to scintillate before Achille's eyes obscuring his vision, warning him that he would have to resort to something desperate to save his life. Wrenching his knee upward, he planted it hard, squarely in Antoine's groin. With a shriek of pain, Antoine released his hands from about Achille's neck and, moaning, clutched his genitals.

Gasping for breath and rubbing his throat, Achille took advantage of his opponent's distress to get to his feet and dust himself off.

"I'll get you for this, you nigger swine!" Antoine threatened, shaking his fist at him. Reaching out for the settee, Antoine intended to use it as a support to pull himself to a standing position. Seeing what he was about to do, Achille kicked the delicate piece of furniture out of his grasp, sending it sliding across the floor and crashing into the wall. Suddenly looking pitiful, helpless, and bewildered, Antoine fell to the ground again, crawling toward his discarded crutch, the stump of his amputated thigh bumping rhythmically against the hardwood floor.

Anticipating this move, too, Achille picked up the crutch, threw it across his knee and, before Antoine's astonished eyes, snapped it in two.

Stunned by this action, Antoine stared at his rival open-mouthed, dumbfounded.

"If you plan on continuing to be a menace," Achille said, "you'd better get yourself something you can depend on to get you around." With that, he threw the two halves of the crutch at his half-brother and left the room.

After his music room comeuppance, Antoine became extremely withdrawn, refusing to leave his room, to eat or to talk with anyone, including Ysabel. Antoine's obvious depression and self-imposed exile from the rest of the family worried Jim greatly, not only because he loved this son and was concerned about his health, both mental and physical, but because of the devastating effect his behavior seemed to be having on Odile. It seemed to him that his wife, who had grown increasingly religious with the passage of years, had become obsessively so lately, spending hour after hour in the chapel.

"I pray for a miracle," she said.

"What sort of miracle?" Jim asked skeptically, never able to share his wife's spiritual preoccupations.

"That Antoine will return to the way he used to be before his tragedy," she answered sadly.

During the summer of 1864 the war ground achingly on. Shortages, hardship and deprivation were the norm. What little food Achille and the few remaining loyal slaves could scratch out of the soil without fertilizer, horses, or help, was often confiscated by Union troops, their own rations acutely short as well. Since Lincoln had issued his Emancipation Proclamation, what few slaves hadn't been tapped to aid the Northern forces behind the lines in support positions gradually drifted away from the plantations, aimlessly wandering about the cities and countryside, frequently drunk and bewildered, resorting to petty thievery and attacks on frightened whites—often goaded by Union soldiers—adding to the general unrest and confusion.

General Sherman had taken over much of the fighting for the Union, advocating a cruel and ruthless policy designed to bring the war home to the people, causing them to suffer as the men on the battlefields had been suffering. In that fashion he hoped to bring the South to its knees begging for Northern mercy. His rapacious troops cut a wide swath from the Mason-Dixon Line south to the Florida Peninsula, burning, pillaging, raping, destroying everything—homes, crops, livestock. The once thriving state of Georgia had been reduced to a smoking rubble, a victim of Sherman's "scorched earth" policy. Despite everything, the South held out tenaciously with Lee whipping Grant every time their respective armies clashed. Yet Grant stubbornly pressed forward, leaving battlefield after battlefield littered with thousands of Union dead. Despite the bloodshed, losses, destruction, pestilence and untold agonies, the war dragged on.

Will it never end? Jim asked himself, wondering how much longer such insanity could possibly prevail.

After weeks of virtual isolation in his room, Antoine

suddenly reversed himself following a visit from his close friend Léopold Seguin, also discharged from the army because of a head wound which resulted in occasional epileptic fits. He began participating once again in the life of the family, socializing and going out mostly in Léopold's company. Stubbornly hobbling around on his single crutch, Antoine frequently visited the stable, looking over the two or three remaining mounts.

"What pitiful specimens of horseflesh!" he exclaimed to Cecil as he looked over the animals.

With Cecil's help, he fashioned a kind of trapeze contraption which cleverly allowed him to hoist himself into the saddle despite his disability. Riding once more boosted his spirits considerably, although Odile feared for his safety.

"Suppose he falls or gets thrown?" she speculated. "What then?"

"That's something we can't help," Jim replied. "He's determined to ride again and there's nothing we can do to stop him."

As Antoine gradually reaccustomed himself to riding once again, he began taking off, sometimes leaving the plantation for hours at a time, often staying out all night, returning in the early hours of the morning.

"You've got to be careful riding around at night with all those trigger-happy Union soldiers everywhere," Jim tried to caution him.

"Even a Yankee wouldn't shoot a man with one leg," Antoine retorted.

One morning when he had been gone the entire night and failed to return the following day, Odile was frantic with worry. "Where on earth can he be? Where does he go? The city is so dangerous these days no one dares to set foot in it with all those Yankee soldiers and wild-eyed niggers everywhere," she fretted.

Shaking his head in equal dismay, Jim said, "I haven't got the slightest idea."

Later, when he and Achille were alone in the barn, he posed the same questions to him that Odile had asked earlier in the day.

"You know where I think he goes?" Achille ventured. "I think he's joined up with that group of rebel guerrillas."

Jim was stunned. "What?!"

"I know for a fact that Léopold Seguin is a leader of a band of rebel guerrillas that's been raising all kinds of hell," Achille said. "I think Antoine has joined them."

"How do you know?"

"I've heard," he said, unwilling to betray his sources.

Since the Federal occupation of New Orleans early in the war, the North controlled much of Louisiana one way or another, but many stubborn, determined Southerners refused to knuckle under to Northern rule and formed secret bands of armed guerrillas which perpetrated sudden surprise attacks on river shipping, blew up railroads and ambushed small units of Union troops. The fact that the Yankees retaliated harshly, destroying entire plantations and publicly hanging saboteurs didn't deter the rebels.

"How could he participate in guerrilla activities with only one leg?" Jim questioned.

"Every night Antoine's been gone, there's been a rebel attack somewhere—Yankee ships burned in the river, sentries shot, sections of railroad blown up. I've been keeping track," Achille revealed. "Last night, for example, there was a spectacular fire at the waterfront in which eight Federal ships valued at more than three hundred thousand dollars were destroyed. The rumor is that the Yankees caught the group responsible."

A sudden feeling of apprehension gripped Jim. "You don't think?" He could not bring himself to finish the speculation.

"That Antoine might have been among those captured?" Achille said. "I have no idea. It looks suspicious since he's failed to come home today. I do know, however, from some of the slaves at Forest Point that Léopold Seguin was caught."

Jim and Achille did not have to wait long for confirmation of their suspicions. Shortly after noon a pair of Union soldiers called at Mandragore and informed Jim that his son was indeed being held with a group of rebel guerrillas in the prison at Fort St. Philip, charged with sabotage.

At such news Odile turned white with shock and dread, but she did not faint, as she might have done before the war. Ignoring the presence of the soldiers, she said, "We must go there right away. I cannot allow my only son, my own flesh and blood, to rot in a filthy Yankee prison. What kind of barbarians would arrest a man with only one leg?"

As soon as the soldiers were gone, Jim went to the wagonshed and readied the carriage for their first trip to the city in months.

❧ 52

The Union officer in charge of the prisoners at Fort St. Philip finally agreed to release Antoine to the custody of his parents, not so much in response to Odile's near-hysterical demands, but because hanging a young man who had already suffered the loss of a limb would reflect badly on the Northern occupation forces. The alternative to hanging—retaining the prisoner in jail and forcing him to perform manual labor—was not practical because of his disability and the problems it would entail.

"Lieutenant MacKay is heretofore confined to the grounds of the plantation, Mandragore, indefinitely," the officer decreed as he signed the release order. "If he is caught outside the confines of the plantation, I can assure you, ma'am, that next time I will not be so lenient."

"Thank you, sir," Odile murmured, tears of gratitude and relief running down her face. "I knew that

I could depend on your sense of Christian charity to prevail."

As they started on the long journey back to the plantation, Odile turned to Antoine and angrily demanded, "Why on earth did you ever do such a thing—joining up with those rebel guerrillas? Haven't you suffered enough? Haven't we all suffered enough? Oh, poor Anais and Jules! How my heart bleeds for them. There's no way they're going to stop those damned Yankees from hanging Léopold—their only son!"

"I won't rest until I see every last Yankee and Yankee sympathizer dead," Antoine declared. "I'd like to personally strangle every one with my bare hands."

"Oh, dear Lord, the bitterness in this boy's heart!" Odile bemoaned.

"Gall and wormwood," Jim agreed, shaking his head in helpless dismay.

Instead of sequestering himself in his room or behaving in an irrational, alienated fashion, Antoine surprised everyone by suddenly displaying a reasonably pleasant facade, participating in the usual life of the family, sharing meals with them, engaging in their limited social activities and treating all with civility.

"I can't believe it!" Odile declared joyfully. "He's just like he used to be before this dreadful war."

"Better," Jim corrected.

Antoine even went so far as to inquire after Achille from Ysabel, who was still not totally convinced that the new face he was displaying was either sincere or lasting.

"Achille is fine," she replied coolly.

"Tell him he no longer has to confine himself to the *garçonnière* on my account," Antoine said. "I welcome him if he wishes to return to his old room in the house."

"I don't think he's uncomfortable in the *garçonnière*," Ysabel said.

"Nevertheless, tell him that I shall make no scenes if he wishes to move back in here," Antoine assured her. "That's a promise."

"I'll tell him," Ysabel said.

One day as Verbena was mending a dress of Ysabel's—she, too, suffered the deprivations and effects of the war, foreigner or not—the girl remarked on the sudden change in Antoine's attitude.

"Don't you be fooled, honey," the maid warned, threading the rusty needle—new needles were impossible to obtain. "A wolf is still a wolf even if he do put on sheep's clothes. If Achille is smart, he'll stay far away from this house as long as Mister Antoine is around."

When Ysabel relayed both Antoine's invitation and Verbena's warning to Achille late one afternoon when she secretly slipped into the *garçonnière*, Achille reacted much the way she expected.

"So 'Mister' Antoine has announced that his old body servant is welcome once again in the house, has he? Well, you tell him I'm quite comfortable out here in the *garçonnière* and I'll return to the house in my good old sweet time," he said. "Right now Roger Guillon and I are busy trying to work out a sharecrop system so that we can retain the slaves as free men to work the plantation after the war is over. We're trying to devise a system of apportioning the profits that is truly equitable to all parties. I know such a system is feasible. It's just a question of figuring the whole thing out. Unless we do, there's no way Mandragore can survive. It's going to be difficult enough as it is."

"All you do is work, work, work," Ysabel complained. "And worry about this place."

"I can't help it," he admitted. "Does it bother you?"

"Yes. When I don't get to see you," she pouted.

"And you miss me?" Achille continued.

"Of course I do, silly!" Ysabel answered.

With that he lifted her lithe, slender body in his strong arms and hoisted her above him in the air, as one would a small child.

"Achille! Put me down!" she giggled.

Slowly he lowered her and as they came face-to-face, she folded her arms around his neck and planted a sensuous kiss on his eager mouth.

Because they needed frequent advice from Jim on the new share-crop system he and Roger Guillon were devising, Achille eventually abandoned the *garçonnière* and returned to his old room in the attic-nursery to be closer to his father.

On his first night back, Antoine, smiling most amicably, walked into his room on the new prosthetic wooden leg he had finally been prevailed upon to accept, and invited Achille to share a bottle of champagne which had been carefully hidden from the Union troops who periodically plundered the plantation.

"At least they haven't burned us to the ground yet the way they did Forest Point after Léopold Seguin was captured," Jim said, referring to the vicious retaliations of the Federal occupation army for the raid during which Antoine had been captured. "You'd think it was enough just hanging the poor bastard."

Achille could hardly believe his eyes as he read the label on the dark green bottle. It was one of the finest French vintages.

"You will join me, won't you?" Antoine said, filling two glasses. "Let's bury the past, let bygones be bygones. We've had some unpleasant encounters, but that's all behind us now."

Wary of such a sudden and inexplicable change of heart in someone who had proved so murderously antagonistic in the past, Achille was hesitant to participate. "Tell me, Antoine, what accounts for this new attitude of yours?" he asked.

"Let's just say I've seen the error of my ways and have decided to repent," he replied matter-of-factly. "I've had a change of heart."

"I see," Achille nodded, not entirely satisfied with such an explanation. "And what prompted this?"

"Oh, many things," he replied, proffering the bubbling glass to Achille. "Come, drink up," he urged.

Feeling no harm could be done by taking a drink with him, Achille accepted the champagne, wishing to make his contribution toward healing the bitter, longstanding feud between them—willing to do anything to make life easier for everyone at the plantation in such difficult and trying times. "Thank you," he said.

Clinking his glass against Achille's, Antoine toasted, "Brothers!"

Perhaps because the whole spectrum of problems with which Mandragore was beset inevitably came to rest on Achille's shoulders, whirling about in his brain, he had a difficult time falling asleep after Antoine left his room in spite of the large quantity of champagne his half-brother had forced on him. When he did finally drift off, it was into a restless, dream-haunted repose.

Suddenly in the middle of the night, he was awakened by the feeling of someone in the room. Sitting up in bed he peered into the blackness of the attic chamber and felt around for a match with which to light the whale-oil lamp beside the bed.

"Don't move, you traitorous bastard," a familiar voice threatened from out of the dark.

Reaching for the pistol he kept under the mattress, he was showered by bits of glass which flew into his face when his visitor smashed the chimney of the bedside lamp.

"Reach for a gun and you're a dead man," the voice that was Antoine's said. As Achille's eyes accommodated to the darkness, he saw that he held a gun in his unsteady hand and had it aimed straight at his head.

More angry than alarmed, Achille was furious that he had allowed himself to be taken in by the overtures of friendship offered with the champagne earlier in the evening. "What is this?" he demanded. "What do you want?"

"You know, you nigger, you Yankee-loving traitor," he hissed. "Don't think I don't know it was you who turned us in to those Yankees."

Achille was astonished by such an accusation. "What in the hell are you talking about? Have you gone and lost your mind completely?"

"Well, the Yankees fooled you, didn't they?" Antoine persisted. "See? They didn't hang me after all. They turned me loose. You're disappointed, aren't you?"

"You're drunk," Achille accused. "Get out of here and put that pistol down before it goes off and hurts somebody."

"The person it's going to hurt is you," Antoine said. "I also know about all that cotton you've got hidden back in the bayou. Any loyal Southerner would have burned it by now. You know damned well it's going to fall into Yankee hands. How long do you think you can hide it from them?"

"We've been pretty successful so far," Achille replied.

"Maybe you *want* it to fall into Yankee hands, don't you?"

"Look, Antoine, I had absolutely nothing to do with the capture and arrest of you and your rebel friends," Achille assured him, not even wishing to get into the whole cotton question. "Nothing whatsoever."

Antoine cocked his head suspiciously. "I know you went following me at night when I left here—trailing me to see where I was going—spying on my activities. You wanted me to get caught and hanged by the Yankees so I'd be out of your way forever. I'll bet you're sorry that bullet only took my leg instead of killing me, aren't you?"

"You're crazy!" Achille said.

Undaunted, Antoine continued, "You want me out of the way, don't you?"

"I want no such thing. My God . . . !"

"Well, nigger, you're the one who's in *my* way."

Achille was incredulous. "*Your* way? What in God's name are you talking about?"

"You think that now that I've only got one leg, you can steal Mandragore away from me—rob me of my precious birthright—contaminate this plantation that has been in my mama's family for over two hundred years with your nigger blood!"

"You're drunk. You've been drinking too much again. Go back to bed," Achille said, trying to keep his voice as quiet and unemotional as possible. He had no wish to rile Antoine and have him accidentally fire the gun.

Stepping closer to the bed, Antoine waved the pistol

in Achille's face. "So you think I've been drinking too much, do you?"

"Yes, I do," Achille affirmed. "Lower that pistol and get out of here."

"Lower it?" Antoine repeated, shoving the weapon so close the end of the barrel brushed the tip of Achille's nose.

Knowing he must act swiftly, Achille grabbed Antoine's wrist and, hoping to take advantage of his liquor-slowed reflexes, attempted to wrest the gun out of his hand. Despite his inebriated state, the young Creole's reactions were still quick. Jumping backward, he freed himself from Achille's grip but lost his precarious balance on the new wooden leg and, in an attempt to regain it, discharged the weapon. The bullet struck Achille in the chest knocking him backward onto the bed and splattering the linens with blood.

The sound of the shot on the floor above and the overhead scuffle brought everyone scurrying from their rooms into the second-story hall. Thinking it was Yankee soldiers or an errant slave ransacking the house as in the past, Odile and Ysabel huddled protectively together in a corner, while Jim, wielding a pistol in one hand and a flickering lamp in the other, cautiously advanced toward the stairs.

"Be careful, Jim!" Odile whispered.

Warily, he climbed the winding steps to the attic. "Achille . . . ?" he called out at the landing. "Are you all right?"

Holding the lamp over his head, he surveyed the former nursery beneath the eaves and was stunned to discover Achille lying unconscious among the bloody sheets. "My God!" he gasped, feeling at the same moment a twinge of pain in his chest.

Rushing to his son's side, Jim was greatly relieved to discover that Achille still had a pulse in his wrist, albeit weak. "Who shot you?" he demanded, seeing no one about. Receiving no response, he yelled downstairs. "Send Romulus for Dr. Zehner at once!"

"What's wrong?" she anxiously shouted back up the spiral stairwell.

"It's Achille. He's been . . . shot."

At the news, Ysabel let out a scream and leaving Odile behind, flew up the stairs in her nightdress. Flinging herself across the youth's bloody body, she cried his name over and over.

Crossing the room to an open window where the curtains were flailing in the gulf wind, Jim peered through the night. By the light of the moon he observed a lone figure with a most peculiar gait hurrying across the lawn. Remembering that earlier in a half-awakened state he had heard scraping sounds against the side of the house and what sounded like footsteps outside on the gallery beyond the bedroom, Jim realized that Achille's assailant must have escaped by that route. At the same moment watching the dark figure hobble toward the stable, he knew, with a sickening feeling in the pit of his stomach, who the assailant was.

53

Digging his spurs into the horse's flank, Antoine forced the animal to gallop across the old cane fields, through a thicket and along the edge of the cypress swamp until they reached the bank of the bayou where the terrain became so soft that the animal could go no further. Dismounting—not without difficulty since he lacked the trapeze contraption he had rigged up in the stable—Antoine tied the horse to the trunk of a tree and, searching about in the moonlight, located a pirogue pulled up onto shore. The Indian log canoes were the chief means of transport through the narrow, winding, overgrown channels of the bayou and this one was undoubtedly used by Achille, Jim or Oberdorfer when they periodically checked on the hidden cotton stores.

What luck! he said to himself as he limped over to the small craft and managed to climb in without overturning it. Paddling swiftly and silently along the sluggish backwater, he was struck by the eerie stillness of the night, broken only by the occasional mournful hooting of an owl.

At various points in the narrow channel, the vegetation along the banks became so dense that passage, even for the slender dugout, seemed almost impossible and he thought at times he might have to hack his way through the thick elephant ears, cattails and reeds, but the boat always managed to squeeze through. Antoine could not help but wonder how the huge bales of cotton had been transported along this same waterway to the labyrinthine inner reaches of the bayou.

No wonder the damned Yankees have never found that cotton, he said to himself.

At times, he paused momentarily in his paddling, straining to listen whether or not he was being followed. Inevitably, once Achille's body was found, Jim would notify the sheriff and a posse would be sent in pursuit of him. A picture of Achille lying bloody and motionless in bed flashed into his mind and elicited an involuntary shudder. Although he had taken part in some of the bloodiest and most vicious battles of the war and been engulfed in mindless carnage and slaughter, none of the horrible memories haunted him in quite the same way as the mental picture of his dead or dying half-brother.

Attempting to rationalize his act, he told himself that Achille had it coming to him. *That nigger upstart was trying to rob me of my birthright—to say nothing of his carrying on with Ysabel.* He could not forget the day he had caught them in an embrace in the music room. Undoubtedly, the bastard had forced his attentions on her. There was no other answer. Surely, a white woman like Ysabel could not have encouraged him. Still, it did not appear as though she were resisting with the determination one would have expected. Antoine didn't want to think about it. His mind was too confused from drinking—he had finished off a bottle of cognac after leaving Achille's room the first time

—and the excitement of the shooting and the escape. *I only did what any self-respecting Southern gentleman would have done,* he said to himself.

Desperately, he tried to convince himself that his unrelenting hatred for Achille was the result of all the wrongs his scheming half-brother had perpetrated against him. He also indicted his father as well—the way Jim had shamed and humiliated him and his mother by declaring that conniving half-nigger mongrel his legal son and then—insult of insults—turning the running of the plantation—his mother's family's home for two hundred years—over to him. That was more than anyone should have to tolerate. No, he had no regrets about killing Achille. The bastard had it coming.

The narrow channel eventually widened into a kind of lagoon and there, Antoine saw outlined in the moonlight, the series of enormous cotton sheds designed by Achille and that other presumptuous mulatto bastard, Roger Guillon, who was always around, ingratiating himself with his father. Basically, the sheds or warehouses were merely wooden platforms with roofs, built on sturdy cypress pilings rising from the underlying mud. The platforms were several feet above the level of the water so that the air could circulate freely around the bales of cotton stored within to help prevent mildew and other harmful processes.

Paddling to the closest shed, Antoine drew up alongside it, tied the canoe to a piling and, with considerable difficulty, climbed a short ladder to the platform. Inside the warehouse, he hobbled up and down the narrow aisles between the cotton, stacked bale on bale, stunned by the vast amount which had been accumulated.

If those Yankees could see this! he exclaimed to himself.

Pausing in the center of the shed, he fished around in his pocket and produced a tin of wooden matches. Striking one against the heel of his boot, he lighted it and casually tossed it into the bales. Limping down the aisle he repeated the action—lighting a match and throwing it into the cotton—until all the matches were gone. Some of the strikes merely extinguished themselves, but others ignited the fluffy white fiber, smouldering at first and then eventually bursting into bright orange flames. Soon, everywhere around him bales were burning, eventually becoming a conflagration which spread from the first shed to the adjoining one and on down the line around the entire lagoon until all were on fire.

As the flames roared and crackled higher and higher, Antoine was so hypnotized by the daring of his act and the magnitude of the holocaust that he failed to realize at first that he was now situated on the opposite side of the warehouse from where the canoe—his only escape vessel—was moored. As the heat and smoke escalated, he suddenly knew that he was trapped unless he could reach the canoe. The only way would be to jump into the water and try to swim to the boat, either around the burning sheds or beneath them.

Although he had not been swimming since the loss of his leg, he was confident he would experience no difficulty. Swimming could be mainly done with one's arms and shoulders, with little assistance needed from one's feet and legs. Drawing in a deep breath, he jumped off the platform into the water just as flames from the burning cotton were licking at his back. Surfacing at once, he decided that the less time spent in bayou waters, with the ever-present danger of alligators and poisonous snakes, the better, and elected to swim beneath the shed—the most direct way to the canoe—rather than around it. Heading under the platform, he swam as fast as he could but found, disconcertingly, that his missing limb upset his equilibrium in the water and he kept rolling to the affected side, making slower headway than he hoped. In addition, he was surprised by the intensity of the heat from the fire overhead radiating through the wooden flooring. Above him he could hear the almost deafening roar of the flames, fanned by their own self-generated winds, as the row of wooden structures and their highly combustible contents were totally engulfed in the swirling conflagration.

This will teach those traitors a lesson, he declared to

himself as he swam. *Trying to hoard Southern cotton and speculate on it—cotton that's only going to fall into Yankee hands anyway and help them prolong this miserable war.* If he had done nothing else, Antoine resolved, he had taught those greedy opportunists a lesson they would never forget.

All of a sudden, as he was within fifty yards of the bobbing pirogue, he listened in cold terror as the timbers above him began to groan and crack. Fearing that a collapse was imminent, he tried to swim faster but with his disability progress through the water was slow and difficult. The groans and cracks of the floorboards soon escalated into a rumble which climaxed in a deafening roar as an avalanche of flaming cotton and timbers came crashing down on him. Antoine gave one single, abortive, terrified cry before he was buried beneath the burning mass.

Recovered by a team of searchers after the holocaust deep in the bayou had burned itself out, Antoine's body was interred simply and quietly without the traditional pomp and trappings which had characterized Creole funerals before the long and disastrous war.

After a brief mass recited by a now slender Father Daubigny, the casket, a simple cypress affair, was enclosed in one of the above-ground marble tombs in the family cemetery behind the plantation chapel, there joining his Martinon grandparents and the tiny tomb of his Aunt Eugénie's illegitimate offspring, among others. After the service, the mourners drifted quietly back to the great house to offer their condolences to the grieving family.

Much to everyone's surprise, especially Jim's, Odile, in the same now ragged and shabby black dress she had worn to her father's funeral and a thick veil which obscured her face, had remained amazingly stoic throughout the service, her only outburst occurring just as the casket was sliding into the marble vault. At that dramatic point, she sprang forward and pounded her fists against the lid, crying her beloved son's name.

Strangely, the one who seemed to take the youth's death the hardest, apart from his mother, was Narciso.

Looking pale and wan, he insisted on journeying from Florestal for the funeral against everyone's advice, having suffered a near fatal seizure when informed of the boy's demise. Throughout the services, he sobbed uncontrollably, collapsing completely when the tomb door was finally closed, and had to be revived by Kitty and Dr. Zehner.

"No one understands," he wept.

"I do, Marse Narciso," Kitty replied.

"No. No one does," Narciso insisted. "He was exactly like a son to me."

"He was a son to all of us," Dr. Zehner said, attempting to disguise the impatience he felt at Narciso's overly emotional behavior.

"Before this insane war, he would come to Florestal for weeks at a time. I would tutor him in law. His mind was one of the most brilliant I have ever known. He would have been the finest attorney in the state. He would have gone on to the legislature, the senate, anywhere he chose! What a loss! What a terrible loss to us all! Ah, my poor beloved cousin Odile—her only son—her only *child!* How can she survive this tragedy? How can any of us survive?"

"We all shall," Dr. Zehner assured him drily. "Somehow."

"What a waste!" Narciso continued. "What a waste of a beautiful life! Ah, it's too much. It's too much!"

"Hush now, Marse Narciso," Kitty admonished. "Calm yourself."

While the funeral arrangements for Antoine were in progress, Achille hovered close to death from the serious chest wound which had punctured one lung and narrowly missed his heart. Dr. Zehner attended him around the clock and when the physician was not present, Kitty ministered to her foster son with all sorts of secret African herbs and potions. On the day Antoine was enclosed in the marble tomb, Achille seemed to rally for the first time and the doctor felt optimistic that if nothing unforeseen occurred, the boy might recover in a few months. "Fortunately, this young man has a constitution like iron," the physician declared.

"He got a strong will to live," Kitty said.

Against Oberdorfer's advice, Jim had accompanied the search party into the bayou and, as luck would have it, it was he who first spotted his son's bloated body floating just beneath the surface of the murky waters, encased in a layer of charred cotton.

In the household, Ysabel was greatly affected by Odile's profound yet silent grief. Remaining at her cousin's side, the girl did her best to attempt to console her.

Dressed in whatever black garments they could muster, the house slaves wept and wailed in unison throughout the service. Their grief seemed genuine enough, considering that since his return from the war and even before, Antoine brought a certain amount of misery to the lives of Romulus, Verbena, and Lavinia. Still, slaves were accustomed to misery and forgave more readily than most.

Jim was no less stricken by his son's death than was his wife—or her cousin—but his feelings were well-concealed beneath his characteristic Scottish stoicism. Filled with confusing feelings of doubt and guilt, he feared he had rejected the boy for being the way he was—carefree, reckless, irresponsible, haughty, arrogant, impetuous—when he should have accepted him, if for no other reason than for the sheer joy he brought his mother who was ready and eager to forgive her offspring anything.

If only I had another chance, Jim lamented to himself. *I would make so many things up to him.* But Jim knew there would be no other chances. Antoine was gone forever.

✲❧ 54

The calamitous war finally ground to a halt on April 9, 1865, when Lee surrendered to Grant at Appomattox. For the Confederacy it was a tragic but not disgraceful defeat. Lacking manpower, munitions, railroads, factories, food, money, and practically everything else on which an army depends, Southern forces had put up a fierce, determined, and noble fight, compensating for their lack of materiel with superior military leaders, loyal homefront support and a passionate will to win. The Union had been forced to pay a bitter, bloody price for victory.

The results of the defeat were quickly experienced throughout the South. Few areas had escaped devastation. The major cities were reduced to rubble, towns annihilated, plantations destroyed. By the grace of God, Mandragore was still largely intact, saved from the vengeful destruction of most of the surrounding estates, but a whole new kind of threat would soon appear.

Within days of Lee's signing the surrender, avaricious Northern opportunists descended like the proverbial locusts on the South, many of them carrying all their worldly possessions in the notorious velvet, floral-patterned carpetbags. These carpetbaggers, as they were disdainfully called, joined forces with the local scavengers called scalawags, and together they conspired to feed off the defeated corpse of the South. Because supporters of the Confederacy—and all planters were automatically categorized as such—were disenfranchised and stripped of political power, local governments were quickly usurped by coalitions of Southern Republicans, scalawags—the two were often synonymous—carpetbaggers and newly emancipated

Negroes, the latter flocking to the cities in aimless, bewildered droves without the slightest notion of how they would live, but nevertheless anxious to exercise their new-found freedom. As might be expected, political and domestic chaos reigned.

Punishment of the planters by the acquisition of their wealth and property was the prime motivation of those newcomers who seized political power. One of their favorite methods was to impose astronomical taxes on the disenfranchised planters.

One of the most ruthless of this new class of political opportunists was none other than Hiram Davis, still smarting twenty years later over his expulsion from Mandragore. Recently appointed assistant tax collector by the new and thoroughly corrupt local government, his first objective was to seek revenge against Jim MacKay. Knowing that MacKay, like all the local parish planters, was in deep financial trouble, Davis hoped that by imposing an outrageous tax on Mandragore, he could thereby force Jim into bankruptcy and acquire the property for only a tiny fraction of its actual value at a sheriff's sale.

One day when Jim and Achille, now recovered from his serious chest wound, were away from the house, Davis arrived in a fancy new carriage accompanied by the elegantly attired Hilaire, a haughty mulatto who had long ago replaced Willie as the former overseer's constant companion, and insisted on presenting the tax bill to either Jim or Odile in person. Verbena attempted to put him off, but he was so insistent she finally capitulated and informed Odile of the caller.

Reluctantly, Odile received him in the parlor with Ysabel in attendance.

"What is it, Mr. Davis?" she asked brusquely.

Davis, accustomed to seeing her both beautiful and stylishly dressed in the past, was startled by her battered appearance. Apart from the shabby dress she wore and the gray of her hair, she sported fine worry lines on her usually flawless cheeks. "Well, it looks like the war's been mighty hard on you, Miss Odile," he said with a semi-smirk on his face.

"The war has been hard on all *loyal* Southerners, Mr. Davis," she replied, emphasizing the word loyal as she looked at him disdainfully in his new, expensive but vulgar outfit.

"But it looks like it's been especially hard on you in particular, Miss Odile," he persisted, a tiny droplet of tobacco juice running down his chin from the corner of his lip.

"If you refer to my present appearance, Mr. Davis, it's because I am still mourning my son who was killed in the service of our beloved Confederacy," she said. "But I am sure that's not what you are here to discuss today."

"I heard your boy's death had nothing to do with the war, but I wouldn't argue such a point with a grieving mother," he said slyly.

"That's very wise of you."

Extending an envelope to her, he said, "I came out here to bring you folks your tax bill. Since I'm the new assistant tax collector I sort of thought I might like to deliver it to you all in person."

"You needn't have," she said coldly, taking the envelope from him, removing the bill and staring at it. As she expected, it was a ridiculously high assessment and her first impulse was to protest angrily, but she knew it would be unwise to deal with white trash like Davis in such a way. A woman of her social status and background must not lower herself to a position of supplication with the lower classes, no matter how dire the circumstances. "There is obviously some error," she said, returning the bill to him imperiously.

"No, ma'am, there's no error," he assured her, grinning broadly and displaying the big gap between his tobacco-stained teeth.

"In any case, this is a matter for my husband," she decreed. "You must return when he is here."

"Actually, ma'am, it was you I was hoping to talk to. . . ."

Odile raised her eyebrows. "Me?"

"I reckon that with a tax bill like this you all will have to give up this place," he ventured.

"The bill is absurd. There's obviously a mistake," she insisted "As I just indicated."

"The bill is correct."

"Impossible!"

"And final," he asserted. "There'll be no changing it."

"Ridiculous!"

"As I was saying, ma'am, you all stand to lose Mandragore, and since it's been in your own family for over a hundred years, I thought I'd make you an offer and see how you like it before saying anything to your husband. You see, ma'am, what I'm prepared to pay is a whole lot more than you all will get at a sheriff's sale," Davis smiled.

The words struck Odile like a rapier through her heart. *Sheriff's sale!* "There will be no sheriff's sale here, Mr. Davis," she said, her narrow nostrils flaring angrily.

"I hate to contradict you, ma'am. . . ."

Leaping to her feet from the horsehair settee, she angrily wagged her finger inches from his face. "Sheriff's sale indeed! Get out of here! Get out of here this minute, you white trash scum! Get out of here before I personally have you thrown out!" she screamed.

Trying to soothe her, Ysabel said, "Please, cousin Odile, you must not get so excited. . . ."

Ignoring her admonitions, Odile repeated, "Get out of here at once, you scalawag!"

Nervously, Davis began backing toward the door. "I'm going, but you'll be sorry you didn't hear me out on my offer," he said.

"Get out and don't you ever come back!"

"Yell all you want to, but this place will be mine yet!" he shouted as he raced down the gallery steps.

"Never—" she shrieked out the open window, "—over my dead body will I ever let scum like you take over my house! Never—do you hear? Never!"

Back in her room, recovering from Davis' shocking news, Odile read the latest letter from Placide for the second time.

Dearest Sister,

I have just now received the tragic news of my dear nephew's death. My deepest regret is that because of circumstances, I was never permitted to know the boy whom I, nevertheless, loved from afar. You may be sure that my deepest sympathies and those of my wife go out to both you and Jim at this time of sorrow. I regret that such a great distance and the aforementioned unfortunate circumstances separate us at such a time, but it can't be helped.

Denise and I are relieved to know that the dreadful war is concluded, although we have heard how difficult life now is in the American South and what great hardships and deprivations you are forced to endure. As you know, our mills have been closed for some time, but it is our hope that things will not remain inactive for much longer. We eagerly look forward to receiving shipments of American cotton in the near future. Naturally, I am aware that with the emancipation of the slaves, labor problems will be inevitable. I am also aware that loans for planting and equipment will be quite difficult to obtain. In any event, despite all the current problems, I have complete faith that Mandragore will overcome all obstacles with which it is now beset.

As always, I hunger for news of you, dear sister, and the family. Once again, I regret that the last news was so devastating and I offer you our condolences. Know that you are always in our prayers.

> With deepest affection,
> your loving brother,
> Placide.

Still clutching the letter, Odile sat on the windowseat and gazed through the magnolias, jasmine, and oaks across the vast expanse of once green lawn, now brown and overgrown with weeds since the departure of many of the slaves. Those that remained were needed to work the fields and tend what livestock was left, leaving no one to do the routine gardening. Whenever she realized how the war had ravaged Mandragore and caused its steady deterioration, it filled her with overwhelming grief and bitterness which, when combined with the shock of Antoine's death, was almost more than she felt she could bear. The letter from Placide only pointed up how much she missed him, despite their vast differences and past clashes, and made her acutely aware of how he would have been able to comprehend her misery in a way in which Jim, sadly, was totally incapable.

As she looked out the window, her attention was suddenly captured by the sight of an approaching horseman galloping up the carriageway, and for a moment she thought it looked like Antoine. It was so hard to believe that her only child was gone forever and would never gallop across the plantation again. As the rider drew closer to the house she saw that it was Achille and reproached herself to think that in her grief-stricken mind she had confused him for her son. *Even with only one leg, Antoine rode better than that,* she said to herself. *He was the finest young horseman in the parish.*

As he approached the gallery, she saw Ysabel, who must have been watching for him, run across the lawn to meet him. Dismounting, Achille gathered her into his arms and the couple embraced fervently.

So disturbed was Odile by the scene she had just witnessed that when she rose from the windowseat, she accidentally knocked over a lamp. The noise of the shattering glass brought Verbena to the room.

"What happened, Miss Odile?" the maid inquired.

Pointing to the window, Odile replied, "See for yourself."

"Shucks," the black woman said casually as if the sight of their embrace were no great surprise. "That's just Miss Ysabel and Mr. Achille."

"How long has it been going on?" Odile asked.

"A long time."

"To think that I could have been so stupid," Odile said resentfully. "To think that I actually considher suitable for my Antoine . . . poor Antoine."

"Well, Miss Ysabel is a mighty lovely girl," Verbena said.

Odile scowled at her reproachfully. "She's nothing but a shameless hussy, allowing that . . . that mulatto to put his hands on her."

"They likes each other," Verbena shrugged.

Pacing the room in an agitated fashion, Odile ranted, "I know one thing, that girl's going right back to Cuba. The war is over so there's no longer any excuse for her to stay here. I refuse to be responsible to Aunt Carlota and Beatriz any longer. Aunt Carlota, would kill me if she knew her granddaughter was carrying on with a half-breed bastard ex-slave."

Verbena stared at her mistress thoughtfully a few moments, as though she were deliberating a difficult decision. "There's something I don't know if I ought to tell you or not, Miss Odile," she said.

Her curiosity piqued, Odile demanded, "What is it?"

"Well, you see," the maid began hesitantly, "Miss Ysabel—she has colored blood herself."

Odile was stunned. In the more than forty years she had known and loved the black woman, she had never known her to lie the way the other Negroes customarily did. "I don't believe you," she said.

"It's true, Miss Odile," the maid insisted. "I ain't never lied to you. For one thing, Miss Ysabel ain't Miss Carlota's granddaughter."

Odile could scarcely believe the black woman's words. "That's ridiculous. We all know she's cousin Beatriz's daughter," she insisted.

"Oh, she's Miss Beatriz's daughter all right," Verbena conceded. "It's just that Miss Beatriz ain't Miss Carlota's natural daughter."

"But that's impossible!" Odile protested, her head spinning from such shocking allegations.

"No it ain't," the maid assured her. "You see, Miss Carlota done took Miss Beatriz in when she was just a tiny baby and raised her like she was her own child."

"Then why did she hide the fact all these years— passing her off as her own daughter?"

"To make things easier for some folks," the maid replied ambiguously.

"What folks?" Odile demanded.

"For you all," Verbena answered. "For your mama and daddy—God rest their souls. For you. For Marse Placide. But most of all for Miss Eugénie."

"What has my sister got to do with all this?"

Verbena turned away and started to leave the room. "I ain't going to say no more. I done said too much already."

Odile seized her by the arm, preventing her leaving. "What about Eugénie? I insist you tell me."

"I don't think you'd want to hear," Verbena hedged.

"Tell me, damn it!" Odile stomped her foot, something she hadn't done for years.

Her eyes sheepishly downcast, Verbena sighed. "I guess for Miss Ysabel's sake, you might as well know the truth. You see, Miss Beatriz is Miss Eugénie's daughter and Miss Ysabel is her granddaughter."

"Ysabel is Eugénie's granddaughter! That's impossible!" Odile scoffed. "Eugénie's child died. Its tomb is near Antoine's."

"There ain't no body in that baby's tomb, Miss Odile," the maid revealed. "It's empty. That baby of Miss Eugénie's never died like folks was told. Right after it was born it was sent to Cuba with Annie, one of the slaves. She was its wet-nurse. When she got to Havana, Annie done give that baby to Miss Carlota to raise as her own and make up for the baby she lost herself a short time before. Miss Carlota and Mr. Jorge done named that baby *Beatriz*."

"But why?" Odile demanded, greatly agitated by the story. "Why was the baby spirited away to Cuba?"

"Because," Verbena said with great hesitation, "that baby's daddy was a black man."

Feeling she was going to faint, Odile reached out for the massive carved rosewood bedpost which supported the overhead tester. "That's a lie! How dare you say such a thing! You take back that lie this instant! Take it back or I'll whip you myself!"

"It ain't no lie," the maid said solemnly. "That's the truth. You ask your Aunt Carlota if you don't believe me. I never lied to you in my life, child, and I ain't going to start now. Beatriz's father wasn't no ordinary nigger. He was a handsome gentleman, well-educated, and cultured. He came here from Saint Dominique and was a free man of color. He made his living by going around and giving music lessons to all the high-born young ladies like your sister Eugénie. One day the daddy of one of his pupils caught him in a compromising situation and he had to get hisself out of here fast or he would have got hisself nutted or—more likely—hanged. They say he ran off to Haiti. I don't know. Anyway, after he left, no less than half a dozen white ladies gave birth to his black babies. Your sister Eugénie was one of them."

"Oh my God!" Odile cried and sat down on the bed to keep from fainting. "Oh my God!"

The convoluted story somehow answered many questions she had had over the years—why Eugénie always seemed so eager for news from Carlota in Cuba—why Carlota never spoke of Beatriz in the same way she did her two sons, Luis and Ernesto—why Eugénie had entered the convent so readily. . . .

"So you see, Miss Odile," Verbena said, "it's all right for Miss Ysabel to be with Mr. Achille. They is both of the same blood."

The following morning Odile slipped out of the house and headed for the chapel as she often did, but her mission this morning was more than just to pray. During the sleepless night before, Verbena's story kept repeating itself over and over in her mind, making her feel compelled to learn the truth. The whole thing was almost too upsetting, too outrageous, to contemplate—her sister Eugénie having conceived a child by a black man, a child falsely pronounced dead, given a bogus funeral and burial, while in reality still alive, and spirited away to Cuba to be adopted by her Aunt Carlota and passed off as the Latin woman's own child. It was all too much. Had Eugénie in reality been visiting with her *granddaughter* rather than her cousin when Ysabel called at the convent? Odile shuddered to think that she had actually considered this girl—

the descendant of her sister's illicit affair with a black man—as a possible bride for Antoine. It was almost more than she could bear.

A few yards behind the chapel was the family cemetery, a cluster of above-ground marble vaults, ornate tombs of the Martinons. The early settlers in the area at first had tried to bury their dead in the earth, but the watery terrain made traditional methods of burial unfeasible. After a heavy rain or flood the coffins came macabrely floating to the surface, bobbing about like wooden boats. Instead of entering the chapel, Odile headed for the cemetery and wandered back among the solemn tombs, stopping momentarily at Antoine's to offer a prayer in his behalf, until she came to a particularly tiny one adorned with the statue of a weeping angel. Beneath the angel was a baroque marble scroll decorated with a wreath of rococo stone flowers bearing the inscription:

MARIE MATHILDE MARTINON
Born January 25, 1826
Died January 25, 1826

Contemplating a few moments, her breath coming in short, nervous gasps, Odile looked all about to be sure no one could see what she was about to do. Then, with trembling hands, she took hold of the brass handle on the door of the tomb and pulled, but the ever-present Louisiana dampness had apparently corroded the marble, sealing it fast. The door refused to budge.

"Damn!" she swore, tugging, pounding and finally kicking the door in an attempt to loosen it, but her efforts were to no avail.

I must know, she said to herself. *I must!*

Abandoning the cemetery, she headed for the stable and had Cecil saddle a horse for her, saying she intended to take a ride. With a loan from Isaac, Jim had managed to purchase several decent horses to replenish the Yankee-depleted stable.

To avoid suspicion she did not immediately return to the cemetery, but instead rode first around the vast fields now planted with corn, oats, sorghum, beans, and melons replacing the usual cane. Eventually she ended up in the cemetery before the tiny tomb once again. This time, she fastened the horse's reins to the ring in the door and then, striking the animal suddenly and unexpectedly with the riding crop, forced the startled mount to rear backward and in so doing, tear the door off the tomb. Still attached to the horse's reins, it landed on the ground with a loud clunk. Odile, her heart pounding, murmured, "Oh, Lord, forgive me for disturbing the rest of the dead . . ." and peered into the dark vault.

Able to see almost nothing, she slid her gloved hand cautiously along the smooth interior, anxiously feeling for remains of a corpse—clothes, bones, skull, anything. Disappointed at feeling nothing, she stood on her tiptoes to check the most distant corners. Exhausted, Odile rested against the side of the tomb trying desperately to keep from fainting. With all of this, one thing was clear, however—the tomb was completely empty.

Still trembling badly from shock, Odile elected to ride along the River Road for a while until she could regain her composure. She knew that if she remained on the plantation she ran the risk of encountering Jim who, seeing her in such a shaken state, would undoubtedly demand an explanation.

As she rode along the top of the levee, gazing at the vast river which had always played such a large role in her life, and the thicket on the opposite side, she soon received a second major shock for the day. About every fifty yards or so, nailed to a tree, was a poster announcing the impending sheriff's sale of Mandragore, supposedly for delinquent taxes.

Appalled and enraged, she began ripping each poster down until she rounded the bend approaching the main gate of the plantation itself. There, on a ladder, was Elijah Doyle, a poor white dirt-farmer turned scalawag who had recently become a sheriff's deputy, nailing a poster to the gatepost. At the foot of the ladder steadying Doyle by holding his legs was none other than Hiram Davis.

Seeing her approach, Davis called out in a mock-courteous tone, "Good morning, Miss Odile. You sure are up and out riding early this fine day."

Refusing to acknowledge his amenities, she pointed to a poster with her riding crop and demanded, "What is the meaning of this?"

"Now, I told you, Miss Odile. . . ." Davis started to reply.

"How dare you nail anything to that gatepost!" she said, raising the riding crop in a threatening manner.

"It's the law, ma'am," Deputy Doyle answered.

"The law, my foot!" she exclaimed.

"If folks don't pay their taxes, they can't very well expect to hang on to their places, now can they?" Davis pointed out.

"Stop what you're doing immediately and get out of here," she ordered.

"My orders from the sheriff is to put up all these here signs," Doyle replied. "And that's just what I'm fixing to do."

"How dare the sheriff issue such an order!" she protested.

"That order came from Mr. Davis here," Doyle said. "You'll have to talk to him. He's the assistant tax collector now."

Riding perilously close to the ladder, Odile reached out, snatched the poster off the gatepost and began ripping it up.

"I wouldn't advise you to do that, Miss Odile," Doyle warned. "That's breaking the law."

"I don't care if it is!" she replied defiantly. "Nobody is going to put these signs on this property."

"Tearing the signs down ain't going to do one bit of good," Davis said. "It ain't going to stop the sale from taking place. It'll just mean that less folks will know about the auction and bid against me, and I'll get Mandragore at a lower price."

"You'll never get Mandragore," she said. "Never!"

"Oh, I think I will," Davis said confidently, aiming a stream of tobacco juice at a nearby hummingbird. "And when I do, nothing in this world will give me greater pleasure than running your uppity ass off this land."

Incensed, Odile cried, "How dare you talk to me like that, you scum! You rabble! You trash!"

"I'm going to be talking a lot worse than that when I kick you out of that nice big house you all are so high and mighty about."

"We will never leave Mandragore," she declared.

"You will or you'll find a load of buckshot in your fancy backside," Davis chuckled.

"Don't you dare threaten me!" she warned, and attempted to strike the former overseer with her riding crop, but he successfully blocked her blows with his arms.

"I order you to stop this assault, ma'am, or I'll arrest you right here and now," the deputy threatened.

"Go ahead and arrest me if you dare," she replied. Then, inciting the horse forward with a swift kick in the flanks, she drove the animal directly into the ladder, knocking it over and Doyle to the ground. Davis tried to snatch the reins out of her hands, but she struck at him viciously with the riding crop until he backed off.

"Get out of here, you scum!" she shrieked. "Go on, get!"

Covered with mud from the puddle he landed in, the deputy scrambled to his feet and shook his fist at her. "I'm coming back after you with a warrant," he threatened.

Laughing defiantly, Odile galloped up the carriage-way.

"I'll teach some humility to that arrogant bitch yet," Davis swore, rubbing his stinging face where it had caught the fury of her riding crop. "Mark my words, I will!"

When Odile returned to the house, Verbena informed her that Jim was in the study going over the account books. For days he had been desperately trying to figure out some scheme to meet the exorbitant tax bill.

Storming into the room, Odile demanded, "Do you have any idea what is going on around here while you pore over those ledgers?"

Seeing her highly agitated state, he replied in a calm, controlled manner, "Yes, I think I'm fairly well aware. . . ."

"Right now, Hiram Davis and that crooked sheriff's deputy, Elijah Doyle, were at our very gate with signs announcing this place up for auction at a sheriff's sale!" she informed him in an almost hysterical state.

"I was afraid that was going to happen," he said. "I've been doing everything I can to keep Mandragore out of Davis' greedy hands, believe me."

"Well, I'll tell you one thing, Jim MacKay, I don't know about you, but it'll be over my dead body that Davis or anyone else takes over this plantation. My daddy taught me how to use a gun and I'll shoot the first person who tries to set foot on this property without my permission. Mandragore is my home, my life, my blood. My great-great-granddaddy carved this place out of fever-ridden swamp and wilderness, fought the Indians and the British and everyone else for it. There is no way on God's earth that I am ever going to let one little bitty piece of it fall into the hands of tacky white trash the likes of Hiram Davis," she declared angrily, pacing back and forth across the room, her swirling skirts inadvertently brushing papers off the corner of the desk.

"Please, Odile, try and calm yourself," he advised quietly.

"Calm? How can I be calm at a time like this—when scum like Davis is threatening our very lives?" she retorted.

"No one's going to put us out, I promise you that," he assured her. "The tax collector has given me a few more weeks to come up with the money. He's none too fond of Davis, it seems, which is in our favor. By that time I hope that some of the pigs and cattle will be ready for market."

"Pigs and cattle!" she exclaimed. "This is a sugar plantation not a hog-farm. If only you would plant cane again instead of fooling with those silly pigs and cattle and livestock feed. I thought you aspired to being a planter, not a dirt farmer."

"How can I grow cane with only a handful of our former slaves left? Be reasonable, Odile. You know better than that. I've been having a difficult enough time just paying the workers the minimum wages the government demands. Besides, with inflation the way it is, it would take an investment of thousands of dollars to get the mills operational again and a whole new cane crop started once more. I can't get sufficient loans for that. If it wasn't for Isaac's help we wouldn't even be able to plant what we have. Those so-called 'silly' crops you're so ready to disparage are what I'm depending on to keep a roof over our heads."

"I have lived here all my life," she declared. "And I can tell you that this parish is cane country. When my daddy and my brother were running things, we prospered on cane."

"I don't know about your father, but when your brother was running things, Mandragore was in worse condition than it is now—and there hadn't been a war then."

"I still say any other crops except cane are sheer foolishness," Odile stubbornly asserted.

"I happen to believe otherwise," Jim insisted. "If we—and the rest of the South—are to overcome this defeat we have suffered and prosper once again, we will have to be flexible and resourceful in finding ways to clean up the shambles and put the pieces back together once more."

"Poppycock," she disparaged.

Ignoring her attempts to discredit his beliefs, Jim continued, "Food is scarce, as you well know. Our crops and livestock will bring premium prices on the open market. I'm confident that I can raise the money to meet the tax bill."

"That tax bill is outright thievery," she said.

"I'm aware of that," Jim conceded. "But if the scalawags insist on gouging us with taxes, I intend to gouge them on food prices. That way I'll have some leverage with which to get the taxes lowered to a reasonable figure. It's just a matter of holding out a few more weeks and having luck on our side so that we have a good harvest."

"And you expect to have good luck with that bastard son of yours running things?" she questioned skeptically.

Annoyed by her continuous deprecations, Jim reproached, "I'm tired of you talking about Achille that way. That boy has sweated blood for this place. He's worked harder in the plantation's behalf than anyone has a right to expect—considering how he's been treated by most of the people around here."

"Including me, no doubt?"

"Including you," Jim affirmed. "God forgive me for saying this, but Achille cares a lot more about this plantation than Antoine ever did."

Her dark eyes blazing angrily, Odile reproached, "How dare you malign Antoine when he's not alive to defend himself? Shame on you!"

"I'm not maligning anyone," Jim said. "I just want Achille to get a little credit once in a while for some of the things he's done, that's all."

"All he's done?" she repeated indignantly. "He's done nothing but bring trouble to this place since he came. He's a curse on us all."

"Let me remind you, my dear, that Achille didn't come here by his own free will."

"If it weren't for him, Antoine would still be alive," she asserted, suddenly choking back tears.

"Well, it wasn't Achille who shot Antoine and tore a big hole in his lung," Jim said.

"Antoine didn't mean to kill him," she insisted.

"If that wasn't an outright intention to kill somebody, I don't know what is," Jim scoffed.

"If it was—and I will never believe it was—Antoine was only trying to defend his birthright," Odile defended staunchly. "He recognized that half-breed for what he is. He's never been anything but an evil curse on Mandragore from the day he arrived."

In disgust, Jim slammed the ledger before him shut. "I refuse to listen to any more of your hysterical nonsense," he said.

"The sooner he's gone from here, the better," she continued.

"Achille has every right to be here," Jim asserted. "He's as much my son as Antoine was."

All of a sudden the anger in Odile's face was replaced by a sly, slightly amused smile. "Perhaps more," she ventured ambiguously.

Puzzled by her curious expression, Jim asked, "What do you mean by that?"

Almost matter-of-factly she answered, "Antoine was no more your son than Achille is mine."

Stunned by the implications of what she had just said, Jim said, "I'm not sure I follow you."

"It's very simple," she said flatly. "Antoine was not your son."

Contemplating her words a moment before he responded, Jim questioned, "Then, just whose son was he?"

"Narciso's," she answered, as she turned and walked out of the room.

55

By midnight Jim still hadn't come to bed, but Odile wasn't surprised. She knew that her shocking disclosure earlier had probably upset him too much to sleep—especially to share a bed with her. If he had gone to bed at all, it was probably on the divan in his study where he customarily slept whenever they had had a falling out. While she was undressing she had considered apologizing to Jim for her impulsive outburst, assuring him that it was a deliberate lie, that he really *was* the natural father of Antoine, but as she crawled beneath the covers, she decided against such a move, resolving not to compound years of deception with yet another lie.

Unable to sleep despite the unexpected relief she felt from having at last revealed the truth to Jim, Odile got out of bed and wandered into the hall. Peering down the stairwell she saw that the lamp was still burning in the study, and listening closely, recognized the voices of Jim and Achille discussing the problems of the plantation, attempting to figure out a way to hold onto it and keep it out of scalawag hands. As she listened she realized what a great closeness the two men shared—a closeness Antoine had never had with Jim. At times it was as though Achille had mesmerized Jim, so compliant was he with the youth's ideas and decisions.

Feeling anguished and resentful, she returned to bed and tried to sleep, but again could not, her mind being still too preoccupied with the enormous influence Achille seemed to have over Jim and the entire plantation. This ex-slave, this bastard, this child of shame and degradation was gradually dominating everyone —everyone but her, that was. Odile could not help but conclude that Achille's coming to Mandragore had initiated a whole string of disasters culminating in the greatest of all—Antoine's death. As she thrashed restlessly about there was no longer any doubt in her mind that what she had long suspected was indeed true—the youth was a demon, an agent of Satan. How else could he have survived her campaign of prayer against him, prayers which unceasingly pleaded for the removal of Achille and his evil influence from the plantation? Yet, still he remained and every day his power and influence seemed to increase. Her supplications had gone unheeded. Perhaps it was now time to try other means.

The next day Odile ordered Cecil to prepare the now shabby carriage for a trip into the city. Since the end of the war she had avoided going into town except when absolutely necessary. Besides being somewhat dangerous with the lawless hordes of drifters and opportunists, both white and black, it was depressing to see the once gay and elegant city in near ruin, a virtual shambles. Since the occupation, streets, sidewalks, public buildings and homes had been allowed to degenerate with little maintenance or repairs. In the South, President Johnson's "Reconstruction policy" was proving corrupt and ineffective.

"Where in town is we going, Miss Odile?" Cecil asked. "Ain't no stores that got nothing to buy these days."

"We're not going shopping," she replied.

"Then we going to the convent to see Sister Eugénie?" he persisted.

"We're going to see Nizilda Foucher," she said, ignoring his shocked reaction and extending her elbow so that the elderly coachman could help her into the rickety carriage.

When they reached the voodoo practitioner's dilapidated shack on the edge of the French Quarter, Odile was chagrined to learn that the old sorceress had been run out of town by her angry neighbors who accused her of bewitching them. No one would admit knowing her current whereabouts until Odile came upon a black newsboy who, after being plied with a few gold coins, finally admitted that Nizilda was now living somewhere back in Barataria Bayou.

"Will you take me there?" Odile anxiously asked him.

The boy shook his head. "My mama don't allow me to go back there where Old Nizilda's at," he said.

Finally, tempted with the prospect of more gold, the boy agreed to conduct Odile to Nizilda.

Much to Cecil's great consternation, the boy rode in the carriage with Odile to the wharf where the two of them left the coachman behind and took a small passenger steamer down the river, through one of the canals and into the vast and intricate network of waterways known as Barataria Bayou.

At one of the landings Odile and the boy left the boat, rented a pirogue from a Cajun crab-fisher and with the boy paddling, glided deep into the bayou through a series of channels nearly choked with the thick growth of water hyacinths. Eventually the boy pulled the canoe up to a ramshackle dock.

"This is where you gets out, ma'am, if you wants to see Old Nizilda," he said.

Odile looked around and saw only the dense tangle of palmettos, elephant-ears, and willows. "I don't see any houses," she said.

"You just follow that path and pretty soon you'll come to old Nizilda's shack," the boy replied, pointing to a narrow path through the vegetation.

Apprehensive, she asked, "Aren't you coming with me?"

"No, ma'am, I don't go near that old witch's house," he answered, his eyes wide with superstitious fear. "She got the devil hisself sitting right on her shoulder. You can see him grinning if you looks hard enough."

"But I can't go alone," she protested.

"I'm sorry, ma'am, but I don't go no further than this," he insisted stubbornly. "If you wants to go see Nizilda, you gots to go alone."

"Not even if I pay you more?"

He shook his head vigorously. "No, ma'am."

With an exasperated sigh, Odile climbed out of the pirogue, left the boy behind and started along the indicated path through the dense overgrowth. The Spanish moss hanging from the twisted branches of the cypress trees brushed her face and neck like ghostly fingers, making her shudder from time to time. It was already late afternoon and she was regretting their delayed start.

After proceeding about a quarter of a mile, Odile sighted a tiny cabin situated on the far side of a rickety bridge spanning a considerable expanse of water. Assuming that she had finally reached Nizilda's abode and anxious to consult the sorceress, she had little choice except to cross the insubstantial-looking footbridge. Under her footsteps it swayed and wobbled perilously and at one point she lost her footing and slipped, nearly falling into the murky water below.

Hesitant to approach the little cabin situated on wooden stilts high off the marshy ground unannounced, Odile called out Nizilda's name several times, her voice shattering the eerie stillness of the bayou. There was no response.

After a while, she mustered the courage to go up the shaky steps to the door and knock. Eventually in response to her pounding, the portal slowly opened a crack and a single eye peered at her.

"Nizilda?" Odile asked.

"What you want?" a screechy voice demanded.

Odile recognized the sorceress's voice at once. "Please, Nizilda, I must see you."

"I don't want to see nobody. I don't want nobody back here bothering me. Go on and get out of here. Who told you I was back here?" Nizilda said. "You ain't got no right to come pestering me like this."

"It's Odile MacKay. Surely you remember me? I consulted you years ago. Your help was wonderful then. Won't you let me come in?"

"I don't let nobody come in here," the old Negro woman said.

"You helped me before," Odile asserted. "I need your aid again. Please. . . ."

"I ain't helping nobody," she refused. "I ain't conjuring no more."

"But I'm desperate," Odile insisted. "I'll pay whatever you ask—in gold. I still have some the damned Yankees didn't get their grubby hands on."

Just as with the boy, the mention of gold brought about a sudden switch in the woman's resolve. Reluctantly the voodooienne opened the door. "All right, come in," she said.

Once admitted, Odile observed with surprise that Nizilda still looked the same as she had twenty-five years earlier—ancient, wizened and half-mad, the same shawl draped over her head. Odile lost no time in informing her all about Achille and the trouble he had brought to Mandragore. "I swear that boy has been sent by Satan himself to destroy us all," she concluded.

Instead of throwing back her head and laughing in her usual loud, blood-curdling cackle, Nizilda looked very grave. "Sounds to me like you all done got the very devil hisself in your house," she speculated. "It's going to be mighty hard to get him out. Mighty hard, indeed. He's a tough fellow to get rid of."

Odile was relieved by the sorceress's verification of her suspicions. She had been right all along. Achille *was* an incarnation of the Prince of Darkness. "I don't care what it takes," she declared, "I must be rid of him."

Nizilda shook her head discouragingly. "It's going to be mighty hard," she reiterated.

"If we don't get him out of our lives, and soon, the plantation and all of us will be destroyed. I just know we will. We're already in danger of losing Mandragore and if it's lost, everything is lost," Odile said. "You must help me."

After much deliberation and mumbling to herself in a semi-trance state, all the while stroking her scrawny three-legged cat, Nizilda leaned close to Odile, speaking in hollow, intimate tones. "Listen carefully, my child, and I'll tell you what you must do," she advised.

Eagerly Odile implored, "What? . . . What must I do? Tell me, oh, please tell me, Nizilda."

"To make this demon go away you must obtain a solid black candle, melt it completely and knead the wax like it was dough you was fixing to make bread with," the voodooienne began. "Then, write his name on a piece of paper, four times frontwards and five times backwards." Nizilda paused.

"Yes, yes . . . ?" Odile said, anxious for her to go on.

"Then, you roll the wax into a ball and you puts the paper inside. After that, you sticks nine pins in the ball. When you got that done, you gets a little boat and you puts this ball of wax in it and sets it to drifting down the river. When you is doing this, you snap your fingers and keep saying over and over, 'Saint Expédite, make him go quick! "Saint Expédite gets things done in a hurry. By the time that boat gets to the ocean, the person's done gone," Nizilda concluded.

It sounded much too simple. With a frown, Odile questioned, "Is that all there is?"

"Well, when he goes away," Nizilda continued, "you gots to take a piece of buttercake and go to Our

Lady of Guadalupe Church on North Rampart and leave it in front of Saint Expédite's statue in thanks."

"And that's *all?*" Odile tried to confirm.

"That's all," Nizilda assured her.

Anxious to leave, especially after she caught sight of the one-eyed snake coiled in a dark corner of the cabin, Odile paid Nizilda for her counsel and a black candle, resolved to do anything that would rid Mandragore of Achille.

"Thank you, Nizilda," she murmured, and left just as the snake began to crawl out of the corner toward her.

As she walked down the high steps from Nizilda's cabin, Odile realized that deep within the bayou the light was growing faint. Crossing the narrow, shaky footbridge she felt nervous and afraid and right in the middle dropped the precious black candle. Attempting to retrieve it, she slipped, lost her footing and tumbled into the water. Unable to swim—such an ability was looked upon with horror for aristocratic ladies—she thrashed about in the sluggish, murky water, hoping to reach either the bank or the bridge. Having dressed for a visit to the city, she wore layers of petticoats. These garments, quickly waterlogged, not only weighted her down but became tangled around the gnarled root of a cypress, holding her fast. Fighting desperately to keep her chin above water, Odile attempted at the same time to wrench the fabric loose from the tree root.

Suddenly on the opposite bank, she heard a sound of something lumbering through the tall grass and in the dusky twilight observed the surface of the bayou ripple as what looked like a great rough-hewn log slipped into the water and headed in her direction. Having a lifelong fear of the man-eating alligators which inhabited the swamps and bayous, Odile tried desperately to squirm free of her garments, but the more she struggled, the worse she became entangled.

All at once, she was able to make out two tiny nostrils at the end of what had looked like a log, and behind them a pair of unblinking, reptilian eyes staring

in her direction. They were the last thing she saw before she fainted into merciful oblivion.

It was the frightened black newsboy who finally led
the search party to Odile's body—or what was left of
it—in the bayou.

Just as they had been for Antoine, the funeral services for Odile were brief and simple and she was
buried in a marble tomb which adjoined her son's in the
plantation cemetery. At first Jim had not wanted her
buried there because of recent vandalism—a baby's
tomb had been opened, the door forcibly ripped off—
but he finally relented in response to Eugénie's pleas.

"I don't think my sister would tolerate being buried
anywhere else," the nun advised.

Ysabel, heartbroken at Odile's death, elected to
remain at Mandragore during the mourning period,
unobtrusively assuming her late cousin's duties about
the house and doing such an excellent job that she
earned the praises of Jim, the servants and, of course,
Achille. At the end of the year when she announced
that she would be returning to Cuba, everyone was
dismayed.

"My God, Verbena, what will I do without her?"
Achille despairingly asked the elderly Negro maid.

"We sure is going to miss Miss Ysabel," Verbena
replied, shaking her kerchiefed head sadly.

Pounding his fist in frustration against the butcher's
block in the warming kitchen, he said, "If only there
was some way I could convince her to stay—something I could do to fight this legislated prejudice against
us."

Feeling his anguish, Verbena finally volunteered,
"There *is* something you can do, Mr. Achille."

Surprised, he stared at her and asked, "What?"

Smiling, she answered, "You can marry that child
if you have a mind to."

"You know that's impossible under the Louisiana
law," he reminded her.

"No, it ain't," she insisted. "Not if you listen to
what I'm fixing to tell you." With that she related the
true story of Ysabel's background, just as she had

earlier informed Odile shortly before her death. When she concluded, Achille was stunned.

"You're not lying, are you?" he asked suspiciously.

Verbena rolled her eyes heavenward and raised her hand as though invoking an oath. "I swears, Achille, every word I done told you is true."

Overjoyed, he threw his arms around Verbena and began whirling her about the kitchen.

"Now you stop that, hear?" she protested, giggling with delight. "You is making me dizzy!"

Accompanied by Verbena, Achille and Ysabel went to the Ursuline convent to seek Eugénie's blessing on their upcoming wedding. When Verbena disclosed the Cuban girl's true identity, Eugénie broke through her serene reserve and wept, embracing Ysabel so hard her ribs ached.

"My granddaughter! My little granddaughter!" Eugénie cried. "My own baby's baby! In my heart, I knew all these years that my precious child hadn't died as they said she had. I knew that somewhere she was alive. And now after all these years of waiting and praying and hoping, God has finally seen fit to send me my very own granddaughter. At last the horrible agony of uncertainty is ended. My soul has truly found peace at last."

Later, as they strolled happily around the convent grounds, Achille informed Eugénie of their plans to marry and she gave them her wholehearted blessing.

Although initially Achille had insisted on only a small ceremony in the plantation chapel, both Jim and Ysabel—with some encouragement from Eugénie—persuaded him to agree to a wedding in the cathedral so that all those who had been excluded from Jim and Odile's wedding over a quarter of a century earlier could attend. They were aided in their cause by Kitty, who now resided in a lovely townhouse in the French Quarter that Achille had purchased for her as a gift and worked as a nurse in the clinic Isaac and his son Daniel had founded. Now that their business was thriving again, the DaCostas were formulating plans for a general hospital to be constructed in association with the clinic.

"I want to see you married right," the lanky black woman said, her light eyes flashing as they always did whenever she was excited. "I want the whole world to see you standing with your bride in front of that altar in the cathedral."

With the recovery of Mandragore, the wedding proved to be one of the brighter events in the bleak and chaotic Reconstruction and served to boost the morale of an otherwise demoralized New Orleans.

For a honeymoon-wedding trip Achille and his bride boarded a ship and sailed to Havana where he was introduced to her family, including Ysabel's mother, Eugénie's daughter Beatriz.

"At last the awful masquerade is over," Carlota sighed with relief as she hugged Ysabel. "Your mother may not have been my natural child, but I have loved her as if she were—and you, too, *mi querida.*"

Prior to the wedding, Achille had been reluctant to make plans for a honeymoon trip at all, not wishing to leave Jim, still grieving for Odile, with the responsibility of running the entire plantation single-handed, fearing it would be too much of a strain for him.

"You go on and go," Verbena encouraged. "Mr. Oberdorfer's still here. He and I'll look after your daddy. Maybe if you ain't around he'll stop feeling sorry for hisself and get back to his old ways again. It'll be good for him if you all are gone for a while. Don't you worry none about him."

As usual the old servant had been right. When Achille and Ysabel returned from Cuba they found that Jim had snapped out of much of his grief and was attending to things around Mandragore with his old vigor once again.

"You know what I've been thinking?" Jim asked Achille one day as they were walking through a field thick with ripening melons. "Now that you're married and about to settle down with this fine young lady, I ought to turn the whole place over to you."

Astounded by the suggestion, Achille wanted to

make certain he had heard correctly. "Turn Mandragore over to me?" he repeated incredulously.

"Well, why not?" Jim said. "You've been practically running it single-handed for the last few years anyway—with only an occasional assist from Oberdorfer and me. I've just been hanging around in the background occasionally giving advice—and not all of it good."

"Oh, sir. . . ." the youth started to protest.

"Besides," Jim went on, cutting him off, "I've been hankering to take a trip back up the old Mississippi to Ohio, now that the war's over. I've been away for nearly thirty years and I want to go back and see what the old place looks like. I figure I'd better go pretty soon—before I get too old and lame to make the trip."

"You've got a lot of life left in you yet," Achille said.

"Not as much as you think," Jim disputed. "In any case, thirty years or thereabouts of running this place is enough for any man. I'm about ready to turn the reins over to somebody. It might as well be my son. Oh, I'll stick around for a while—in case you might need help or advice from time to time—but for the most part, the place will be yours to run. And you know what? I think you'll do a damned good job."

Achille's face brightened with the prospect of becoming master of Mandragore. It was a challenge he welcomed. "Well, sir, I'd like to try," he said, smiling. "As a matter of fact, I had some thoughts about increasing our herd of cattle—getting a tougher breed that can stand up to the heat and the ticks better. There's a man who's talking about crossbreeding our local cattle with a strain from India to see if we can't get an animal that's sturdier and better able to take this climate."

"I'm all for it," Jim said, pleased to see his son's enthusiasm surface once again.

At the edge of the melon field, Achille stopped and, looking solemn, turned to Jim. "Sir, if I do take over Mandragore, there's just one thing I'm going to ask."

Curious, Jim said, "And what's that?"

"My mama—my real mama, Delphine—is buried in a slave plot at Florestal. I'd like to have her remains transferred here and interred in a nice marble tomb behind the chapel. I couldn't do anything about the fact that she died a slave, but I can at least see to it that she gets a decent resting place—the finest I can afford. That's important to me. As important as Ysabel or you or seeing Kitty a free woman set up in her own house."

"Delphine . . ." Jim mused, recalling his first love. "Bury Delphine here?"

"Is it all right?" Achille asked.

"Yes," Jim replied, already thinking of the white rose bush he would plant beside the grave. "It'll be your place. I reckon you can do whatever you want."

With that the two men embraced and it was the first time Achille had ever seen his father with tears in his eyes.

Dear Reader,
If you enjoyed this book, and
would like a complete list of
Ballantine's exciting romantic
fiction, we would be happy to put
you on our mailing list. Simply
print your name and address and
send to Ballantine Mail Sales;
Department LE/RF, 201 East 50th
Street, New York, New York 10022.

L-95